MisSpelled

TH LEATHERMAN

ACKNOWLEDGMENTS

There are so many people who helped me complete this book, it would be impossible to list them all here. That said, I'd like to thank my wife and boys. Your patience as I told you joke after joke and pun after pun was legendary. To my beta readers, your insight and suggestions made all the difference. To Rocky Mountain Fiction Writers, the best tribe of writers west of the Mississippi.

CONTENTS

CHAPTER 1: MY BROTHER'S KEEPER

I stepped around Chuck and put a hand on my brother's chest. "Hey big guy, let's take this down a notch. Middle of the morning, school in session, not the best time to get in a fight. I mean, you'll get blood stains all over your favorite ugly shirt."

Jerrod growled. "Step aside Evan, this is between Chuck an me."

"And if Coach Ballick saw you right now? Does the bench really need your big ass warming it this Friday?" I said.

That kind of worked. My brother stopped and looked over the heads of the other students. At six foot five, it wasn't hard. He glanced up and down the hall. I prayed for a teacher to emerge from a nearby classroom. No joy. The other students weren't any help. No one even pulled out their cellphones to catch it on vid. Jerrod was popular, and, well, Chuck wasn't. No one was going to snitch on the football star.

"Coach ain't here, but Chuckie the Chickie is. Stand aside, bro. He wants to tell me something. I can see it in his eyes." Jerrod grinned evilly.

Bringing mom into the argument wouldn't help. She was all about peace and love and the "find a way to get along with your brother" crap. I took a different tactic. I stepped next to Chuck and whispered into his ear. "He wants you to take the first swing. That way, no one can say he started it. Don't be this pansy's patsy."

"If I do nothing, he'll keep spilling my books and calling me stuff." Chuck glared at Jerrod. "I've had it. I'm going to end it."

Then he spoke to my idiot brother, "Between the buildings?"

Jerrod rolled his neck. "You got it, Chickie."

I closed my eyes and let out a slow breath.

Chuck kicked his spilled books out of the way and headed for the courtyard.

"Well, half-bro," Jerrod snarled at me. "Looks like today's the day. Chickie gets to prove how much of a fairy he really is."

Two of Jerrod's teammates, Will and Gary, appeared on either side of him. I studied their faces. This was going to be worse than last time. They beat up Noah last month. Poor Noah had gotten suspended for it.

Not this time.

I stood up straight and looked my brother right in the eye and sighed like I'd given up. "I get it. I understand what you're trying to teach here. First, it is impossible to underestimate you." Jerrod's head tilted in confusion as he tried to parse that, but I plowed on. "And when you have pea-sized balls, you have to beat up smaller guys to make yourself feel better."

The half-second of shock on Jerrod's face was worth it. I turned and ran.

Sprinting up the hall, I dodged fellow students. This had happened before. I was faster than Jerrod and Gary. Will was another story. When he grabbed my shoulder, I didn't need to look. I twisted out of Will's grip.

"Sorry, Rosy Palms," I taunted, "use less oil next time you play with yourself."

Will snarled and lunged. I side-stepped and left him grasping at air. Overextended, he went down. At the front doors, I slowed up a bit. By now, someone would have told a teacher something was up. Which would help me not at all. Can't punish the star player.

At that moment, being suspended for a couple of weeks didn't seem so bad, so I took a risk.

I hit the metal door. Instead of busting through the next set, I stopped and slammed the door shut.

Jerrod snaked an arm through. The heavy door caught his arm and part of his face. The combination thwack and crunch sound suggested something gave. It wasn't the door.

I shoved, but Jerrod kept his arm in the door. He spit blood and bits of tooth at me.

With Gary helping, Jerrod was getting the door open.

It was a losing battle. I bolted out the second set of steel doors. A wave of heavy and humid Texas air hit me like a gut punch. I sprinted through the parking lot. Heavy breaths. Too close. No need to look. I ran with all I had. If I made it to the woods across from the school, they wouldn't follow.

I ran into the street. The woods were so close. Freedom. Tires squealed, but nothing hit me. I jumped the ditch, took two steps and hurdled the fence, but the top wire caught my foot. My face slammed into the mud, but at least I was over the fence.

"Got you now, fart brain," growled Gary.

Dread ate at my gut. Will and Gary were climbing the fence. Jerrod was behind them. What the hell? They didn't follow. They never followed. I spit out the dirt and leaves and scrambled to my feet.

Okay, maybe taking the heat off Chuck wasn't the best idea. "Oh crap! Oh crap! Oh crap!"

My lungs burned, and my legs ached. Sweat trickled down my back. I needed to lose them.

"Son of an ass! I'm gonna kill you," threatened Will.

I believed him. They crashed through the underbrush.

There was a stream downhill. The morning mist shrouded the woods in an eerie half-light. My feet slipped on pine needles. I risked a glance. They were back there, but I'd gained some breathing room.

Something wet and prickly slapped my face. Pinetree. I put my arms up and ran. My arms took the worst of the assault. Water flew as the damp needles soaked my sleeves.

It was thick today. If I could get enough ahead of them, I could lose them in the fog. Why had Jerrod and the bumble twins followed me? They never had before. I was the target du jour. Today's menu: Stump Stomp.

Pain shot through my ankle and I plunged down the hill, struggling to stay upright.

I've got to get away. Anywhere is better than here. In the ravine, the mist was thicker. The creek sounded like breaking glass.

Agony shot through my ankle as I ran. On the hill, Jerrod and his friends were gaining on me.

Were they too close to lose them? What was I going to do at the bottom if I couldn't? Climbing the other side, they'd catch me for sure. Run along the streambed? The wet pine needles were treacherous, but rocks and mud in the stream would be worse.

I heard them panting. They were gaining on me. This was it. Any second now, one of them would grab my shirt and yank me off my feet.

I swallowed hard.

Almost there. Sucking in a breath, I angled for the creek. Maybe getting wet would deter them. Yeah, right. But slippery for me was slippery for them too.

Get away. Get away. I've got to get away.

I reached the bottom. The stream was six feet across. I jumped.

Pain exploded in the back of my head. In that instant, light outlined my body, like I was passing through a window without breaking it. A tingling sensation hit every nerve. Fingernails, toes, the tip of my nose. The world ceased to exist.

CHAPTER 2: STRANGE STRANGERS

I landed... somewhere else. Pain lanced up my ankle.

My ears popped like someone had used an icepick on them. The mist was gone. The sun was higher. Late afternoon? The smell of pine was stronger. Otherwise, it looked a lot like the stream bed I'd just left. And then there were the people. Yelling and fighting. Some people with pointy ears and fancy armor (elves?) swinging swords at a bunch of shorter green guys in leather (goblins, maybe?).

An unbelievable amount of pressure built in my stomach. It was unlike any burp I'd ever had. It started in my shoes, went through my gut, and out of my mouth like a cannon. "Buuurrrruuup!"

It echoed off the walls of the ravine. The force of it knocked one of the warty green guys down. I wasn't aiming for him or anything, he just happened to be fighting an elf in front of me.

All fighting stopped. All eyes turned to me.

"Uh, excuse me," I said.

The goblin I'd belched off his feet screamed and backpedaled. The other goblins shook in their boots. Liquid ran down their legs. Scrambling, the fallen goblin ran like a horde of rampaging monsters was after him. I checked. No monsters. But all the other goblins took off after him. They scurried up the other side of the ravine, leaving me and the elves to stare after them.

Despite the seriousness of the situation, I was a little offended. I sniffed at my armpits. Nope, anti-stinky stuff was still anti-stink.

Even more weird was that I could swear I saw a black cat at the top of the ravine, but I blinked and it was gone.

Two of the pointy-eared people (I tried unsuccessfully to stop thinking of them as elves) approached me. Their armor was a shiny blue-green color, except where it was marred with dirt or blood.

The two people nearest me removed their helmets. They had sharp features. The guy had long red hair. The woman had blond curls. They had slanted eyes with cat-like pupils. They didn't point their swords at me, but they didn't put them away either. As long as they didn't point them at me, being polite seemed like a good strategy.

The guy opened his mouth, and a weird bird warbling came out.

Birdcall? That couldn't be right. I shook my noggin to clear it, then tapped my ear to show I didn't understand.

The guy scowled and made the same bird sounds again.

I shook my head. Whoever these people were, they talked like a bunch of deranged robins.

The blonde woman eyed me oddly, then twisted her head sideways like she was looking over my shoulder. Or at the side of my head?

I touched the tops of my ears. They were all staring at them. "O-kay. Awkward."

The blonde woman looked like the head cheerleader from high school, short and athletic. I focused on keeping my gaze on those awesome leaf green peepers of hers. Getting caught staring elsewhere would not make a good impression. It was hard, though, because she was achingly beautiful. Just having her attention on me caused my heart to race. She closed her eyes and rubbed her temples for a moment, then refocused on me. "Hu-man?"

Human? Okay, this was getting weirder and weirder. Still, they had pointy ears and odd-looking eyes, so I nodded.

The elves glanced at each other, then spoke in their bird song language. And now it was an entire flock of deranged robins. Great.

They decided on something, and the woman approached me again. She pointed to her chest. "Thasina."

"Thasina," I repeated, pointing to her. I pointed to my chest. "Evan."

She smiled and pointed to her red-haired companion, who scowled at me. "Daricas."

I repeated his name as well.

Thasina swept her arm, indicating that I should follow them. Having no better options, I did as she asked. And my ankle chose that moment to remind me I'd recently been a klutz. I stumbled and groaned in pain.

The blonde elf held a palm up. I stopped. She knelt and put her hands on my shin. Warmth spread through my foot. She stood up, and I tested my ankle. The pain had vanished.

I blinked. "Wow. That's cool."

We climbed out of the ravine. Everything was subtly different. I knew the woods around my school pretty well. I enjoyed hiking, and it was faster to go through the woods than to take the roads around. Jerrod didn't like the woods, so it was a win-win as far as I was concerned. But my brain kept having hiccups. The pine needles were longer. Where there was supposed to be a large tree, there wasn't one. Sometimes there were large rocks where there shouldn't be.

Okay, not Texas, and maybe not Earth. Assuming the sun worked the same here, it was now late afternoon. There wasn't a trail that I could see. It didn't take long to go beyond the woods that I knew into terra incog-not-knownia. Nothing looked familiar, and I realized I might not find my way back. Yeah, Toto, we definitely ain't in Texas no more.

After about an hour, (I had to guess at this because my cellphone was doing a great job imitating a brick) the trees thinned out. Then we were on a dirt road to an honest-to-King Arthur medieval castle rising out of a grove of large trees. And when I say large trees, I mean redwood-sized monster trees. Which meant that the castle had to be frickin' huge! Moss and ivy climbed up the walls and the stone showed lines where rainwater had marked paths down the sides. When we got closer, I saw more elves. Instead of armor, the men wore loose-fitting silk shirts and tights. The women wore dresses with stays and bodices. They were standing beside some trees. With a start, I realized the trees had cleverly hidden doors in them. These people were living inside the trees? If that wasn't odd enough, people jostled each other to get a look as we passed. Everyone stared at my ears. Behind us, I heard murmurs in that strange birdsong they used as a language.

I couldn't help but stare in awe as we walked the well-worn road through this majestic forest village. Paths snaked away from the main road into the trees. At the castle, Daricas motioned to the soldiers to wait outside. While he did that, Thasina snagged a passing elf boy. He also stared at the amazing round-eared wonder until she snapped her fingers in his face. She chirped or tweeted something to him and he ran off.

Daricas led the way through some grand hallways filled with paintings of elves in fancy clothes, tapestries, and statues, to a set of huge ancient blue metal bound oak doors. The doors opened into a space bigger than the gymnasium at my high school. Stone columns carved to look like tree trunks that soared thirty feet into the air. Light shown through green leaf-shaped stained-glass windows in the ceiling. The floor was covered in some sort of sturdy moss that obviously didn't mind being stepped on. The room absorbed sound so that it was quieter than the school library during finals week.

We stopped about twenty feet from a regal blonde-haired elf woman sitting on a jewel-encrusted golden throne on a raised dais. She wore a green and gold dress with a fancy bodice and a simple gold circlet around her head. Thasina and Daricas bowed low, so I copied them. Whoever she was, she must be important.

A musical bird song issued from the older woman, and everyone stopped bowing.

She smiled and stood. The silk dress was distracting, and my neck warmed. I swallowed hard as she sashayed down the steps to the moss-covered floor. She performed a slow circle around us, but her eyes never left mine. The impression was that she wanted to know more about me than my name and favorite ice cream flavor. She wanted the whole cone with all the toppings.

The regal lady said a couple of things, which, of course, I didn't understand. Her voice was more like swallows than robins. That didn't keep me from wanting to do whatever she wanted, and more.

Finally, the woman licked her lips seductively and held her hand up, palm facing toward her. She slowly turned her palm around. Cupped there was a gorgeous red heart-shaped gemstone on a silver chain. She held it out to me.

I was drawn to the gem. The deep red stone glittered and glowed with an inner light. It was the most beautiful thing I'd ever seen. I reached for it.

"I wouldn't touch that if I were you, kid."

CHAPTER 3: THE OLD GEEZER

I yanked my fingers back from the gem like it was a bonfire. "What?" I spun, looking for the source of the voice.

A grizzled old man strode up the middle of the room. He had flowing blue robes, just like a fantasy wizard would wear, but two things destroyed that image. First, his hat looked like something out of a Civil War museum, wide brimmed with a gold braid. The second was his slippers, which looked like a pair of fuzzy trout. The trout squeaked as he walked.

Peep, peep, peep. "Thanks, Your Majesty," he said, his voice dripping with sarcasm, "but I'll take it from here."

The man (he was human, round ears and all) gripped my shoulders. The smell of body odor assaulted my nose.

"What's your name, kid?"

The man's breath put the BO to shame, and I recoiled as my eyes watered.

"Yeah, sorry about that," he said. "I was asleep. Someone woke me to say that a human was meeting Her Royal Pain-in-the-Ass here. I didn't want you doing something you'd regret for the next hundred years. I promise to clean up all pretty-like once we take care of the essentials."

I tried not to breathe through my nose. "Thanks, uh, sir."

"Johannes Sherman." The old man punched me in the arm. "Or Big Blue Jack to some. But don't call me that. Sounds all formal and crap. Call me Geezer. Back when I had human friends, that's

9

what they called me, even when I was younger. My hair turned all salt and peppered early."

"Hey... Geezer, I'm Evan."

"Of course, you are," he said with a toothy grin. He shook my hand vigorously. "And can I just say it's a mighty fine day to finally meet another from across the great divide."

"Divide?"

"Earth," said Geezer. "They call this world Stellaluna. This is elven country known as Shara and you're in the capital city, Lonathas. First things first. Never, ever, ever, accept a gift from a greater fae. There are always strings attached, and they ain't ever in your favor." The old man glanced around me. "Ain't that right, Queenie?"

I turned and saw an annoyed frown on the elven monarch's face, but she shrugged.

"Can she understand us?" I asked.

"Not a word," he said. "But she can make a good guess. Which brings us to the second thing you need to know. And let me just say, I'm sorry about this."

I turned back to Geezer. "Wha-"

The old man delivered a right cross with a glowing fist that sent me to the mossy ground.

I tasted blood. "What the hell, old man?" I yelled.

Thasina knelt next to me. "Are you okay?"

"Yeah, Mr. Tall, Dark, and Whiffy here just caught me off-" I stopped and stared at Thasina. "Wait, you speak English?"

"Nah," said Geezer, shaking his hand. "You speak Elvish now. Sorry about that, but I have to knock the spell clean into your noggin, or it won't take."

I tested it out in my head. It was like when I was in Spanish class. When I wanted to talk in Spanish, I thought in Spanish. Now, there appeared to be a third option in my head for Elvish.

"I'm afraid to ask, but is there anything else I need to know?" I made sure to speak in English.

"Yeah, a few things more," said Geezer. "What happened when you crossed into fairyland?"

I thought back to when I first arrived. "Um, my ears popped. Then I, uh, burped."

The old man chuckled. "I just bet you did. There's somethin' different about the air here. Our bodies have ta get rid of the old air. Which brings me to the next part. What did you last eat before you came over?"

"Bean breakfast burrito," I said.

"Excellent!" exclaimed Geezer, grabbing my shoulders. "Stand right here. No, a little to the left. Perfect. Now, pull my finger."

I knew this joke. My Grandpa had used it on me back before he'd passed on. "Uh, no."

"Suit yourself." The old man poked me hard in the stomach with a glowy finger.

Pain exploded in my bowels. Like before, it was too much pressure and there was no holding back. Burrrrappp. My butt vibrated like a jackhammer and my ass released a foul-smelling cloud... right at the elven queen. Relief and embarrassment flooded through me in equal measures. "Oh, uh, sorry." I said to the gathered elves.

Geezer chortled. "Serves the old Pain-in-the-Ass right."

Thasina and Daricas retreated, waving their hands. The elven lady covered her nose, and with a wave summoned a gust of wind to clear the air. "It's rude to speak Human tongue, when the rest of us do not," she admonished.

"Suck it up, you old bat," said Geezer, switching to Elvish. "It's more rude to trick a guest into fifty years of servitude. Which, as you recall, is what you were doing not five minutes ago."

An icy feeling settled into my gut. Fifty years? For a gem? I gaped at the queen and Geezer. I decided right then that, sucker punches and practical jokes aside, Geezer really was looking out for me. "How do I get back home?" I asked in Elvish.

"I don't know, kid," admitted Geezer. "The queen won't teach me, and none of the other elves know the spell."

"But I'll teach you, Evan," said the Monarch with a wink. "For a price."

"I can't do magic and I'm not giving you fifty years of my life," I growled.

She steepled her fingers in front of her. "Oh, but you can, dear boy, and the price for a young man like you would be much less. Say twenty years of service? I promise you'll enjoy every minute."

Was she going to hold me hostage here? I might never see my grandma again, or my brother. Well, my brother... I glared at the older elf. "What are you talking about?"

"Time and Magic," said Geezer. "You're human. Believe it or

not, that gives you a whole passel of advantages. You ain't from around here, so you can break some of the rules they all have to live by. One of them is magic. You can learn almost any spell. Using magic will make you tired, though. More magic equals more tired. Also, the clock here don't move the same as back home. In the time you've been sitting here chewin' bean curds, maybe not a second has passed in our world. The other possibility is that you've lost five years. There ain't no tellin' without takin' a look."

The queen gave a half shrug. "You've got no room to complain, Johannes. You would have died long ago in the mortal realm."

The old man deflated. "She's right, in a way. I came across the divide in 1883. I didn't age a day while I was working off my fifty years. The day she sent me back, I got these fine valleys and snowy whiskers." He indicated his laugh lines and gray beard. "I came right back. As long as I stay, I'll live, barring the odd spell or arrow sent my way. No one living here gets sick and they age real slow like."

"Send me back, now," I demanded.

The queen turned away, strode up the steps to her throne, and sat. "It doesn't work that way, little one. I am elf. I give nothing for free."

"What have you got in your pockets?" whispered Geezer in English.

"Wallet, cellphone, and a handful of chocolates," I answered.

"A cellphone? That one of them boxes the young'uns stare into all the time?"

Geezer must have a way to look into my world. "Yeah," I said.

"Probably worthless then," said Geezer. "Fancy doodads don't work here, and paper money is just pretty pictures to them. Chocolate is sweet. Lesser fae love sweet stuff. Food from across the divide might have some odd side effects, though. Hang onto it. Sugar won't work on the stuck-up witch in the big chair, though. Elves can't lie, but they can shade the truth six ways 'til Sunday, so don't believe everything they say. Offer to do her a favor."

The queen scowled at us. Probably because we were speaking English again.

"Won't that take too much time?" I asked.

"Maybe not," Geezer shrugged. "Near as I can figure, time between here and there works like a rubber band. It goes real slow mostly, but then it speeds way up before slowing down again. Over the long run it evens out, though."

I hoped time was going slowly right now. Standing taller, I approached the throne, switching to Elvish. "Your Majesty, is there some favor I can do for you in exchange for the spell to travel between our worlds?" It was odd hearing the strange bird warbling coming from my own mouth.

The Monarch blinked. Her gaze traveled to Geezer, then back to me. "What an intriguing idea. As it happens, the kingdom of Shara is under siege by the forces of the Darower elves. My soldiers are spread thin. Darower goblins, ogres, and dark elves have caused mischief at our borders, as Daricas says you've recently witnessed. There are several tasks that could use the attention of a human wizard. Someone seen as neutral, acting as a proxy for the kingdom of Shara, might succeed where my other agents could not. Complete five quests for me, and I'll teach you the spell."

Five quests. Long and complicated quests if she was willing to swap them for twenty years of service. "You are very generous, Your Majesty," I said, laying it on thick. "But I fear that five quests would keep me too long from my obligations in the mortal world. I suggest that two quests would be a more fair agreement."

"Three quests then?" she offered.

"I can agree to that," I hedged, "if you allow Geezer to be my guide and teach me magic while I visit your fair kingdom."

The queen smiled sadly. "I'm sorry, little one, but Johannes has duties to attend to here. I can loan you Thasina as a guide. She knows... some magic. I'm sure you can negotiate something with her for lessons."

I glanced back. Thasina's shoulders slumped as she sighed. Geezer shrugged and nodded.

Returning my attention to the queen. "I accept your terms, Your Majesty. I will complete three quests for you in exchange for the spell to get home."

CHAPTER 4: IT'S MAGIC, SORTA

The gem the queen had offered me was a powerful magic item, but one that only elves could use. It would have been worthless to me. Had I accepted the gift without terms, she could have dictated the price, and I'd have to accept whatever she said was fair. Greater Fae, it turned out, were big on service contracts.

That wasn't the end of the negotiations. There were a ton of details to haggle over. What happened if either of us didn't hold up our end of the bargain? What conditions had to be met? Time frames, resources, assistance, food, and lodging. Everything had to be spelled out. I relied heavily on Geezer. He had a hundred and forty years of experience with elvish bargaining, and the number of clauses and subclauses he insisted be part of the agreement were exhausting.

Night fell as we finalized everything. The stained glass turned dark, but the light level in the room didn't change. I couldn't tell where the light was coming from.

I read through the agreement. Once again, I mentally thanked Geezer for ringing my bell. The Elf Queen, I learned her name was Lycia, had tried to sneak in a couple of last-minute additions. I insisted they be removed before I signed.

When it was done, I was wrung out. At Geezer's direction, I pricked my thumb with his dagger and put my finger on the contract. Now, to be fair, I fully intended to keep my end of the bargain, but something odd happened when I signed the papers. A glow surrounded the queen and me. Whoa. Even the contracts are magical here.

But for me, it was three quests. Failure to complete any quest imposed a penalty of ten Stellaluna years of servitude. Servants could not be ordered to do anything risky, but Geezer told me there were a lot of immoral things they could order me to do that were not risky at all. Under servitude, spying on other elf nobles, lying, cheating, and stealing were all fair game.

Part of the deal was that I received quarters in the palace. Contract signed, the queen asked Thasina to show me to my rooms.

And what rooms they were. King size bed, silk sheets, fancy furniture, this room had it all. It even had a bathroom with gold fixtures and a marble tub and sink.

The only part that mattered to me at the moment was the bed. I threw myself on it and fell immediately to sleep. Do not pass go. Do not collect two hundred gold.

Let me tell you, the dreams in Stellaluna were wild. I was at a feast, but I wasn't a guest. No, I was the main course. My skin was a golden brown, and I had an apple in my mouth. The guests? They were a collection of goblins, trolls, and ogres. They kept trying to stick forks in me as I dodged about a large oaken table.

"I'm not done yet," I said, but they wouldn't listen.

The guests were all laughing, but there was some guy I couldn't see that laughed louder than all the monsters put together.

I awoke to someone yanking painfully on my ear. Fortunately, I was not dinner for orcs. Unfortunately, I was still in my room at the palace, so this wasn't some Shakespearian mid-spring night's dream. Crap.

"Hey round-ear, you're going to be late for your first day of work."

I groaned as I swatted at the offending pest. Then realized the pest was a five-inch-tall, winged ball of light.

Blinking, I focused on the tiny thing hovering over my bed. A closer examination proved that it was a small person. It kind of looked like a small naked winged elf, but without any parts identifying it as male or female. "What are you supposed to be?"

"Your wake-up call. Rise and shine morning breath."

I focused a bleary eye on the supped-up firefly. "Does my wake-up call have a name?"

The firefly put its hands on its hips. "Blueberry. And you better get your butt moving if you want to see the Old Fart before the queen summons you."

"I'm not the queen's servant. I agreed to do three quests. That's it."

Blueberry rolled its eyes. "So, you say, beck-and-call-boy."

I hauled my ass out of bed and went into the bathroom. With Blueberry's help, I was able to figure out how to use the bathtub. This comprised a series of commands said in elvish, like water on, water off, warmer, cooler, and so forth. Thankfully, my bathroom came fully stocked with flower-scented soap and magical mouthwash that made my teeth feel clean without brushing. Could take some with me when I made it back to San Antonio?

I gladly traded my clothes for a variation of the local garb. My original clothes stank from all the hiking yesterday. I refused to wear the tights, but there was a pants option. No pockets, so I tied a leather pouch to my waist. I put the cell phone and chocolate in a nightstand that had a sign that said it was enchanted so only the room occupant could open it.

Cleaned and dressed, I directed Blueberry to lead on.

Geezer's apartment turned out to be on the next floor up from mine. His suite was five times the size of mine. It included an office, workshop, and even a turn of the last century kitchen with an icebox and wood-burning stove.

"Thanks, Blueberry," said Geezer, handing the flying thing something and motioning to a plate of food on an oak table. "There's eggs and bacon. Eat while I talk. We got a little over an hour before her royal Pain-in-the-Ass gives you your marching orders. It ain't enough time to teach you a spell, but I can teach you the basics."

Geezer smelled much better today. "Great," I said, "but first, what's the deal with the elf shaped firefly?"

"It's a sprite," said Geezer. "Eventually I'll teach you how to summon one. Think of them as really smart dogs. You can train them to carry messages and perform simple chores. They can talk and hurl insults, but don't mistake that for smarts. Mostly, they're just parroting things they've heard others say. Don't expect much conversation unless you like blank looks. 'Fetch me that,' is fine, but counting any number higher than eight or performing any task that requires more than three actions will cause their little brains to freeze up.

"Watch." Geezer pointed at the sprite. "Blueberry, cook me up an egg."

The sprite tilted its head to the side. "Uh..."

"Forget it," Geezer waved. "Okay, Wax-for-Brains, get me an egg from the icebox in the kitchen."

"Oh! Right away, Old Fart." Blueberry flew to the cabinet in the kitchen, pulled out an egg, and returned with it.

At the stove, Geezer cracked the egg and dropped it into a pan. It sizzled.

I dug into breakfast, which wasn't too bad. The eggs were over easy-ish, and the bacon was just this side of burned. "Why won't the queen let you leave the palace?"

Geezer poked at his egg with a spatula while he talked. "You hear about the Darower elves up north a here? Let me tell you, they are a vicious bunch. Take, take, take. They'll kill you and eat your liver, just for saying hello. Assassinations an dirty tricks are the rule, not the exception. Queen Pain-in-the -Butt may seem like she's got her big girl bloomers on, but she's hangin' by a spider's web, and the web is filled with black widows. Me, I'm her insurance policy. Nobody says boo, while I'm around. I get a bunch of perks for protectin' her knickers, but she wants me close, just in case. So, I'm stuck in the big house."

"'Cause you're a Wizard?"

"'Cause I'm the rootinest tootinest slinger of magic and mischief you ever laid eyes on." He gave me a wink. "An they all know it. You will be too by the time I'm done with you."

"So, what's magic all about?" I asked.

"Okay, so unlike Earth, here in Stellaluna, magic is everywhere. You just have to know how to get it. Once you get it, you have to focus it properly to get it to do what you want. Some elves use words or gestures and newer magic users use pointy sticks to focus their will, but it ain't necessary if you have enough skill."

I munched on a strip of bacon and nodded, paying equal attention to my food and Geezer's words.

He pointed the spatula at me. "So, we'll start with a few words and hand motions and move on from there."

We finished eating and moved into the old man's workshop. It looked like some combination of a chemistry lab and wood carving studio. Vials and bowls with colored powders and liquids sat everywhere. There were wood blocks and metal tools I didn't recognize.

The tools gave me pause. "According to legend, elves can't use metal, but I've seen elves using weapons and armor with no problems."

"Metal's fine," said Geezer. "It's iron they have a problem with." The old man picked up something that looked like an awl. "Take this, for instance. It may look like steel, but it ain't. It's more like pewter. Mostly tin with some antimony and silver and crap. Their weapons and armor are an alloy using carbon, tin, and silver near as I can figure. They use magic ta make them instead of a proper forge, so hard to tell exactly."

I gave him a hairy eyeball. "Geezer, how does a man from around the civil war know about modern materials?"

He smiled. "Just cause I'm stuck in fairyland, don't mean I don't know what's goin' on back home. I got a crystal ball and everything. I can scry an see what's going on over there. It's kinda annoyin' trying to watch TV and movies with time being all weird, but paper books are fine. You just look at one page at a time like slicing bread." He made a slicing motion. "Speaking of which, take one of these." Geezer handed me a pocket watch.

"What, not digital?"

"Funny guy. A real clown." He tried to slap me behind the head, but I ducked. "Hang on to that," he said. "Time here is twenty-four hours a day, just like back home. That'll help you keep track. Or drive you nuts with worry. Time will tell."

Wait. Geezer said scrying. I could see how much time had passed. Maybe I could make a good guess about when I might get back. I eyed the crystal ball at the end of the worktable. "Can I see?"

"No time, kid," said Geezer. "Scrying takes a while to set up. Don't worry. I took a look last night. Right now, time over there is movin' like molasses in January."

I tried to keep the disappointment out of my voice. I would have liked to check on my grandma or my dad. Knowing it was possible lifted my spirits a little. "Okay, so what do I need to know?"

"Right now, we gotta get you pullin' energy so Thasina can show you a thing or two. She can't show you how to pull energy since she's been doin' it all her life. It would be like explaining to someone how to breathe."

I was a Class A idiot when it came to channeling magic energy. I lost track of the number of times Geezer said: "No." "Are you even trying?" and the confusing, "Are you wallpapered or what, kid?"

Finally, as I was sure our time was almost up, something clicked. I channeled energy and put it in my hands, which caused them to glow.

"Great, when it's dark, I'll be a one-man rave." I groused.

Geezer slapped me on the back, hard. "It don't matter. Ya got the hard part done. Although, I don't envy her teachin' your ignorant ass."

I ignored the jibe. "Any idea what I should offer her?"

Geezer stroked his chin thoughtfully. "Chocolate maybe, but you only got what you brought with ya. Save it for when ya need something big. You ever been camping?"

That brought back a flood of memories, both good and bad. "Yeah, my dad used to take me on hunting and fishing trips, back before Mom told me I couldn't see him anymore."

"What, he beat your ma or somethin'?"

I grimaced. "No, it's... complicated. I don't want to talk about it."

Geezer shrugged. "Sina's a bit lazy. Whatever the queen cooks up for you, it'll probably take a few days of camping in the woods to get there. Offer to do camping chores and she'll jump at the chance to teach ya somethin' in return."

"Sina, you mean Thasina?"

"Yeah, she prefers to go by Sina with her friends."

There was a knock on the door. "Come in," the old man called.

The elf boy from yesterday peaked in. "I'm sorry, Mr. Sherman, sir. The queen wants Mr. Evan."

"Well, then ya better take the kid to her, Flick," said Geezer. "Evan, this is Flick. Don't let his age fool ya, he keeps all the uppity lords and ladies around here from turning into a bunch a cats at a rockin' chair convention. Go see what the old Pain-in-the-Ass has planned for ya. And whatever ya do, don't let her walk all over ya."

Wrangling the butterflies in my stomach, I stuffed the watch in my pouch, stood, and offered my hand to the old man. "Thanks for all that. You're a mean crotchety bastard, but you've really helped me out and I can't thank you enough."

He took my hand and pulled me into a hug. "The queen will send Sina. Listen to her, and keep her safe," he whispered in my ear. "Show the queen just what us crafty humans are capable of. I'll see ya when you get back."

CHAPTER 5: YOU WANT ME TO DO WHAT?

Flick showed me to the throne room. As we walked through the ornate halls, I thought about the last thing Geezer had asked me to do: look after Sina. My impression of her was that she was a total badass with a sword and she could heal, which was handy. Why would she need looking after from the likes of me? Why was Geezer so concerned about her?

The queen was on her throne. Daricas and Sina stood off to the side.

"Evan," said the queen. "Thanks for coming so promptly. I have your first quest."

I approached the throne and bowed to the venerable monarch. "I await your request, Your Majesty."

"Arise, young human." She said with an amused smile. "On the northern border of our kingdom lies a deep chasm. Crossing this fissure is a sturdy bridge. The forces of the Darower kingdom cross it regularly to invade our lands. Your first quest is to parlay with the bridge's masters. Obtain their goodwill and convince them to stop allowing the northern kingdom's forces access to our lands. Failing that, destroy the bridge. The forces of Darower cannot be allowed to murder our subjects and plunder our towns and villages."

Wow. Okay, well, I knew she'd give me a difficult chore. Oh Frodo, Mordor isn't such a bad place. Just walk in and introduce yourself. "Of course, Your Majesty. Who are the bridge's masters and how are they defending the bridge?" Please don't be orcs. Please don't be orcs.

"Not who, but what," corrected the queen. "An outpost comprising fifty trolls defends the bridge."

I blinked. Well, it wasn't orcs. Maybe I'd get lucky and they'd have bright hair and sing songs. Since the queen had already sent emissaries and forces to the bridge, they were more likely the big, green, grumpy kind. I wasn't sure how well they had fared, or if they became elf pot pie. "Thank you, Your Majesty. What men and resources may I use to accomplish this?"

She nodded to the two soldiers standing nearby. "Thasina will accompany you. Daricas has volunteered to join you as well."

Two trained warriors and me against fifty trolls. Yeeeeeaaaaah. "And resources, Your Majesty?"

Her smile broadened just a touch. "Horses, and travel gear to speed you on your way."

"Nothing else?" I asked. Fifty marines? Fire-breathing dragon? I could guess the answer, but I was learning to take nothing for granted with the queen.

"Nothing else," she confirmed.

I groaned inwardly. "What can I offer to gain their cooperation? What can I use as a carrot or stick?"

"Carrot or stick?" asked Queen Lycia.

"A human phrase," I clarified, "it means reward and punishment. What can I give them to want to work with us and what should I claim are the consequences if they won't?"

She rubbed her chin in thought. "Let's say fifty gold a month, or anything that equates to that amount in resources. If they refuse, tell them I will bring the full might of the elven army down upon them. Tell them we'll send a dragon, or wizards with fireballs, or whatever gets them to do what we want." Queen Lycia looked down her nose at me. "You're a human. Lying comes naturally to your kind."

Geezer had told me that elves couldn't lie, but stretching the truth was fair game. Queen Lycia had said it as an insult, but it was also one reason she was so set on getting me to be her servant.

Based on what I'd seen, I didn't think fifty gold would go far. The 'sticks' she'd suggested were empty threats. The trolls likely knew this, and so they'd be worse than useless at the bargaining table.

I got an icy feeling in the pit of my stomach. She wants me to fail.

As if she'd read my thoughts, she licked her lips playfully. "You can always refuse. It's only ten years of life. It'll be over before you know it."

Ten years of bowing and begging for table scraps and playing fetch for your amusement. No, *thank you*. It might equate to only five years Earth time, but it could just as easily be fifteen. Remember Evan, smile and be polite. "I appreciate your generosity, Your Majesty, but it would be premature of me to give up without first having visited the bridge." After all, maybe they'd all left to perform a musical, or gotten sick and all died... Except no one got sick in Stellaluna. Crap.

Now that I had magical senses, I felt the contract like a blanket on my soul. I mentally tugged at the magic. Nope, still there, still bound to me.

I put on my poker face for the monarch. "Of course, Your Majesty. We'll leave as soon as we've gathered supplies for our journey."

"Oh, no need," she said. "We took care of that this morning before you were summoned. The saddlebags are packed, the horses saddled, and waiting for you in the stable."

Of course they were. "Thank you, Your Majesty."

CHAPTER 6: SINA

I followed Sina and Daricas to the palace stables. The stable hands had our horses saddled and ready to go. Like the contract, I would not leave my future to the whim of an elf. I checked out everything they'd packed for me.

The food consisted of dried meats and berries with three canteens of water. I had a tinderbox, a travel cloak, rope, bedroll, and the gear for taking care of the horses.

"I need a sword." I said.

"No," the elves objected in unison.

I rechecked the cinch on my saddle. "Listen, we're traveling through an area where we know Darower elves and goblins might ambush us. It'd be nice to defend myself with something more useful than rude language."

Not that sarcasm and insults didn't have their place, but I wasn't about bringing harsh words to a sword fight. My first encounter notwithstanding, I shouldn't count on scaring everyone with my impressive ability to belch. If Geezer was to be believed, that was a one-shot deal anyway.

"No," said Sina. "Without proper training, you'll be a danger to yourself and us in a fight."

I pointed at her. "If you don't give me a weapon, any fight we get into, you'll have to divide your attention. You'll have to protect me and fight opponents. Why not lighten your load?"

She scowled but returned with something someone might laughingly call a sword. It was blade heavy, slightly bent, and hadn't been sharpened since Clinton was President. I suspected it was a blade used to train recruits.

I thought about pointing out that I was on my high school fencing team, but thought better of it. I was getting the hang of negotiating with elves. Lesson one was that anything I knew that they didn't was currency.

"This will do nicely," I said with as much enthusiasm as I could muster. I waved the blade with a flourish. "Evildoers beware!" Strapping the sword to my hip, I mounted the horse. Horseback riding was another gift bestowed upon me by my father. What a cowboy saw in my hippy-dippy mom was anyone's guess. Whenever I'd asked him about it, his ears would turn red, he'd get a silly grin, and say that my ma was, "a special filly that was never meant to be tamed." There were some things I didn't want to know about my parents' life before me.

"What's the horse's name?" I asked Sina.

"Your horse's name is Nonam. It means docile."

"Are we riding through a desert?"

"No, the deserts are far to the east. Why would you think that?" she asked.

"No reason," I said as I hummed the tune.

We left the palace by the same road we'd used to enter it. This gave me another opportunity to examine the town outside the walls. The trees were about fifty feet in diameter and soared into the sky. Sina said they were called sufra trees. I'd never seen a redwood in real life, but I imagined they'd look similar to these, just without the secret doors.

Again, everyone stopped what they were doing to stare at my ears.

"Does anyone wear hats around here?" I asked my entourage.

"Not really," said Sina. "They wear woolen hats in the Darower lands where it's cooler. This close to the palace, it stays warm year-round, so no need."

"So, the Darower areas are actually colder?"

Sina nodded. "Yes. I've never been to the Darower Palace, but I hear it snows there all the time."

"I've seen it," said Daricas. "It doesn't snow there all the time, but it never gets warm enough for everything to thaw out. The peasants shovel the roads and walkways to keep them clear for travel."

Just how cold was it up there? "How long will it take us to reach the bridge?" I asked.

"About a week by horseback," said Daricas. "We could get there in a couple of days by griffin back, but the winged beasts are even more scarce than horses."

"Really? People ride griffins here?"

Daricas rolled his eyes. "Of course, they do. What do you think we are? Savages? Don't they have griffins on Earth?"

"Uh, no. We don't," I admitted.

Sina cocked her head and raised an eyebrow at me. "No one flies on Earth?"

"No. We do, but we use machines called airplanes."

"A machine. To fly," said Daricas. "And you trust them to work."

I shrugged. "Well, yeah. They work. Most of the time."

"What happens when they don't?" he asked.

"They crash." I chewed on my lip before adding. "And usually everyone riding it dies."

Sina shook her head. "Humans are weird."

If her only experience with humans was Geezer, I wouldn't be able to convince her otherwise. It had been a couple of hours since breakfast, so I dug out some dried meat from my saddlebag. I bit into it and twirled it with a flourish. "At least Earth has better food than berries and jerky."

Daricas sniffed. "So do we. The berries and jerky are in case we can't find game. I'll be hunting our food."

That brought me back to my conversation with Geezer earlier. I turned to Sina. "And I suppose you'll be the one cooking it."

She sighed. "Yes."

I grinned at her. "Tell you what. I'll do the cooking for our little trip if you teach me a spell."

"You know how to cook?" she asked doubtfully.

"I've been hunting and fishing with my dad since I was eight." I steepled my fingers together as best I could while holding the reins. "If you catch it and kill it, I'll cook it up for us. In return, you teach me a spell."

She grinned. "Deal, and I'll do you another. You tell me more about your life on Earth, and I'll teach you how to use that pig sticker strapped to your waist."

I found that I really liked her smile. It made the world seem brighter, like there was more sunlight and everything was going to be okay. It made me *feel* warm. I thought about that for a few moments. I already knew how to use a sword, but I was used to saber fencing. The longsword was an unfamiliar weapon. Some instruction in its use would be useful.

"Alright. You've got a deal."

We lapsed into silence for a while. Farmland turned into vast empty fields with the occasional copse of trees to break up the monotony of the plains.

Sina pointed to the horizon. "Daric, what do you make of those clouds?"

Daric, not Daricas. So, he had a shorter name as well. He squinted in the direction she'd indicated. I didn't see any clouds, but I suspected the elves had better eyesight than I did.

"Nothing to worry about," he said. "It'll be overcast in a couple of hours, but it won't rain."

"Do you mind if I call you Daric?" I asked.

He sighed. "If you must."

"I wanted to say thank you for coming with us. I know you didn't have to," I said.

The elf looked down his nose at me with an expression just short of a sneer. "I didn't come for *you*."

He didn't volunteer any more information, so I shot a questioning look at Sina.

She regarded Daric with an annoyed frown before explaining. "Daric is my fiancé."

CHAPTER 7: HOW DO YOU SPELL THAT

The clouds rolled in as expected. I didn't mind, as it gave us a break from the heat. With an hour of daylight left, Daric went to hunt game while Sina and I set up camp.

"You have bags that you sleep in?" asked Sina.

"Yes, sleeping bags," I explained. "They're great at night because crawly things can't get into them. During the day you can take a short rest in them, then they become a nap-sack," I said with a grin.

She gave me a blank look. Yeowch. Tough crowd.

Sina put two more rocks around the fire ring. "Aren't they hard to get out of if goblins attack in the middle of the night?"

I winced and continued to sharpen the hunting knife they gave me. "Uh, we don't have goblins on Earth. The worst we have to deal with are wild animals."

"Huh. Must be nice."

"What will we do about goblins?"

Sina stacked kindling and sticks the same way I would back home. "A couple of things. We'll set up a watch. You'll be responsible for a third of that. Daric also has an alarm spell that he'll cast before we bed down. It'll keep out the, what did you call them, crawlies, and alert us if anything tries to sneak up on us."

"Useful." I checked out the edge of the knife I was working on. It needed more work. "How do you know where to go? This looks more like a game path than a well-traveled trail."

"Well," she said, "I've been to the bridge a few times. I know the way. But even if I didn't, I have a map." Sina pulled out a rolled-up parchment and spread it out on the ground. She spoke the elvish word 'draw' and the parchment drew in the surrounding wilderness.

My mouth fell open. "That's neat."

"Thanks, but don't you have maps back on Earth?" she asked.

"Yeah, but yours is a lot cooler," I admitted.

"Tell me about your family," she prompted.

I sighed. Well, that had been part of the deal. "That's complicated," I began. "For starters, my family isn't like most human families. At home, it's me, my brother, my mom, and my grandma. My brother and I are twins but have different fathers. My mom is a bit of a free spirit."

"But you said that you travel the forest in your world with your father," Sina pressed.

"Yeah." I chewed on the inside of my lip. "After we were born, they did a paternity test. My dad was thrilled and wanted to be part of my life. It didn't matter to him that my mom didn't want to get married. My brother's dad left the state."

Sina looked thoughtful. "So, your brother's father lives in another kingdom? That must be stressful for him."

I laughed ruefully. "Yeah, that's an understatement. It seems like he does things, hurts people, just to see what they'll do. He'll punch me or steal my things if he thinks he can get away with it. It's almost like he blames me for his father being a jerk. Mom believes that my brother and I will find a way to get along if we try hard enough."

"And your mother and father don't discipline him?" Sina struck the flint with the back of her knife, sending sparks into the kindling.

"My mom? No," I said. "And my dad isn't around. I used to see him on the weekends until mom said I couldn't. Said he was a bad influence."

"And your grandma?"

I set down the knife and whetstone and smiled. "My grandma is different. She's, I don't know, weird and wise? It's hard to explain." I shrugged. "My brother avoids her. She doesn't put up with his 'shenanigans' as she puts it."

Sina nodded. "She disciplines him."

"If she catches him, yeah."

"Okay, the fire is started, we've set the camp," Sina glanced around, "and Daric isn't back yet. Time to see if you can learn magic." She pointed to a spot next to the fire. "Sit."

"Woof." I said as I sat cross-legged, and Sina sat across from me.

"You were with Geezer this morning. Show me what you can do."

I made the wavy motions with my hands and tried to pull energy from wherever it is I got it from. After ten minutes of effort, my hands glowed like I had a flashlight just under the skin.

Sina blew out a breath. "Okay, well, we all have to start somewhere. Take my hands."

I did, and there was something electric about her touch. It tingled like tiny static shocks. Her palms and fingers were calloused, but the back of her hands were soft and smooth. It was an odd combination of rough and silky. I rubbed her hands with my fingers for a couple of seconds before I stopped myself. Way to be creepy, Evan.

The blonde elf gave me a half smile, so perhaps it was okay with her.

Then, with a start, I realized she was okay with it. I could sense her. If I concentrated, I could feel her breathing, feel the warmth of the fire against her skin. It was like we shared the senses of each other's bodies.

She abruptly let go.

I rubbed my fingers together. "Wow. That was awesome."

She hesitated. "Yeah, that was... different. Give me just a moment. I need to... prepare myself."

Sina closed her eyes and frowned in concentration for a few minutes. "Okay, let's try that again."

We held hands. This time, the sensations I was getting from her were more muted. Not gone, but more like felt through a thick blanket.

"Better," she pronounced. "Okay, I'm going to teach you how to locate plants."

"Aww." I pouted. "Can't I learn something cool like fireball or flying?"

"I'm a Shara elf. Nature magic. If you want fire magic, go find an elemental or a fire salamander." She smirked playfully. "Perhaps you'll learn something before they burn you to cinders."

Burning to death sounded less than fun. "Right, plants it is."

"Okay, put one palm on the ground. Whichever is your dominant hand," she instructed.

Right hand on the ground. The grass tickled my fingers.

"Good," she said. Sina cleared an area of grass, picked up a stick and drew a symbol in the dirt. It looked like a leaf to me. She handed me the stick. "Draw that."

I cleared my section of dirt and repeated the symbol.

She sighed. "No, like this." She drew the symbol again. I didn't see any difference between her symbol and the one I made.

I dutifully repeated the symbol, making subtle changes to my technique at her suggestions. It took me two dozen tries to get the leaf to her satisfaction.

After that, she handed me an herb. "Do you know what this is?"

I recognized it from my mom's garden. Like so many other things, it was *almost* like the plants back on Earth. "It looks like rosemary."

"It is," she said. "Hold that image in your mind. Draw the symbol with the stick in your left hand and reach out with your mind into the ground to find another rosemary plant."

"Uh, what?"

"I said-"

"I heard what you said," I interrupted. "I don't understand what it means. Put my mind in the ground? Am I supposed to dig a hole and stick my head in it like an ostrich?"

"What's an ostrich?"

"Never mind," I sighed. "Geezer taught me energy. Where is it coming from? Where is it going to?"

"It's coming from the ground, into the symbol, through the wand," Sina picked up another stick and waved it around, "into your body and out through your other hand. You've taken the magic into yourself, so it's now part of your essence. You control it with your mind when you send it into the ground."

"That's a stick." I pointed out.

Sina frowned and held up her hands. "You know what, fine. I'll do the cooking. You can find your spells somewhere else." She stood.

"Wait. I'm sorry." I took a breath and let it out. "I apologize. This is all new to me and I'm getting frustrated. Please, I promise to be more patient and pay attention."

She scowled and raised an eyebrow at me. "No more interruptions?"

I mimed zipping my mouth shut, which elicited another confused look from Sina. I covered my mouth and patted the ground.

She eyed me suspiciously and sat back down. "In answer to your question, any piece of wood can be a wand. It is more effective if you spend time shaping and personalizing it, but anything will do in a pinch.

I wondered if she had a wand. I thought about asking and then dismissed the idea. While annoying cute girls seemed to be an unintentional hobby of mine, I resolved to control it as much as possible. My ass was skating on thin ice without a lifejacket. I had the feeling if I interrupted her again, nothing I said or did would help. She was willing to teach me and getting Daric to teach me a spell seemed as likely as swimming up a waterfall.

At her instruction, I practiced the spell over and over again. It was getting dark by the time she finally pronounced my efforts as sloppy but adequate.

Daric returned with two rabbits, and I cleaned and dressed them. I fashioned a spit and roasted them up just like my dad taught me. They weren't half bad, considering I only had one sprig of rosemary to spice it with.

We agreed on a watch schedule, which put me up for the shift before daybreak. I spent my shift going through the motions of the spell. I couldn't get it to work, but it felt like something was happening. Energy went somewhere, and my muscles ached.

I mentioned this to Sina over a breakfast of leftover rabbit and berries.

"Keep working at it," she said. "You'll get better with practice. Elf children often have trouble keeping all the steps going in their head."

Children? I guess that made sense. If elves lived with magic their whole lives, they probably learned to find plants in the elf equivalent of elementary school.

I thought about what she said. She was right. In my mind, I was doing everything in stages. Draw symbol. Pull energy into it. Think of plant. Bring energy into my body. Push it out into the ground. Maybe the right way to do it was to group the stages together.

That day, we rode through the forest. Daric led the way while Sina pointed out different flowers, herbs, and animals that grew and lived in the area.

As per our deal, I talked about my life on Earth. I thought Sina would be interested to hear about the gadgets and tools that made up modern human life. She found that interesting, but more in a 'humans are weird' kind of way. She was more interested in the stories about my family. Like the time my brother woke me up by farting in my face, or the time my mom made me give up my room to my brother for the unfinished closet in the basement. When I asked her why I had to move and why I couldn't have his old room, she laughed as she threw my things out into the hallway. I could be moved out in a few minutes, she pointed out, but it would take him a few days to move all his stuff. He never did move all his stuff out of his old room, and I stayed in the dusty, cobwebby basement.

I tried several times to get Sina to tell me about her family. She smiled enigmatically and told me that wasn't part of the deal. When I pressed, she relented a bit. And by a bit, I mean she said that she and her mother weren't very close either. And then she clammed up tighter than a mouse's ass at an owl convention. I realized if I wanted any more information about her family, I'd have to strike a deal for it. *Elves*, I sighed.

That evening, after we set up camp, Sina taught me how to fight with a longsword. I discovered that the parry positions were exactly the same as saber fencing, except that with the heavier blade, it was harder to get my sword in position fast enough to parry her blows. Attacks were a different story. My slashing attacks worked fine, but I had to learn a lot of pokey stabby moves.

After two hours, we were both winded. Sina had a fine sheen of sweat that glistened in the firelight, and I admired the way her muscles rippled under her skin. She called an end to our sword lessons. "You've used a sword before," she observed.

"Maybe," I hedged.

"Can you teach me what you know?"

"That wasn't part of the deal," I said with a wink.

She gave me a ghost of a smile and her eyes traveled up and down my body. "Okay, human, we'll revisit this conversation later. Now show me how you're coming with the Locate Plants spell."

I sat down and tried out the spell again. This time, as I tried to do the steps, Sina put her hands on my shoulders. I could feel her observing how the magical energy traveled through my body.

"You're doing good."

I rolled my eyes.

"No, really," she said. "You're doing much better. Here, let's switch places."

She sat, and I stood behind her.

"I can't feel your magic through your armor," I said.

"Gently, put your hand on my neck," she said as she tilted her head to one side. "Skin to skin contact is better, or so Geezer says."

Sina's skin was warm, which made sense since we'd been sparring moments before. Light from the campfire highlighted the curves of her face and the curls in her hair. For just a moment, I felt a tingle of excitement before she pulled the mental blanket over her thoughts.

It was just a moment, but it was all I needed to know that she liked me. My cheeks hurt because I was smiling so much. If I could feel her energy and feelings, then the reverse was probably also true. But I pushed those thoughts away as I concentrated on how she manipulated the spell energy. The mental blanket made it hard to see what was going on in her head, but I got the gist. Besides drawing the symbol on the ground, she also held the symbol in her mind. Sina went through the motions of casting the spell three times while I 'watched'.

We switched places. Sina put her cool fingers on my neck. I allowed myself to be momentarily distracted by the blonde elf caressing the nape of my neck before I caught myself and concentrated fully on the spell.

And... nothing.

I tried to cast the spell for half an hour before I gave up for the evening.

"You've almost got it," she said as she smiled encouragingly. "Another two or three days and you'll have it down. I'm sure of it."

Just then, Daric returned with three squirrels.

"Is that for me, Daric?" I asked. "Oh really, you shouldn't have."

The elven warrior frowned and wordlessly handed me the animals.

During dinner, Daric continued his impression of angry street mime with odd glances at me and Sina throughout the meal. The thought of him in face paint and black and white stripes tickled me so much, I had a hard time keeping a straight face as I ate. I didn't know what was up the arrogant bastard's butthole, but I hoped it hurt like hell and made him walk funny.

Sina was a sweetheart once you got past the elvish *let's make a deal* crap. How she ended up with the pointy-eared asshat was a mystery, but in my opinion, she deserved better.

We set up the watches the same as the previous night. Like the previous night, I spent my watch practicing my one spell. It was frustrating and tedious, but if elven kids could pull it off, then so would I. Like Geezer said, the more magic I used, the more tired I got. It felt odd try to catch my breath when I hadn't moved, but there must be some exercising going on. I tried it over and over. I tried doing it a few ways differently than Sina had taught me. Geezer had told me I wouldn't need words or a wand if I had enough skill. I tried drawing the leaf with my finger instead of the stick. I put my palm directly on it and felt a stronger connection to the energy in the ground. Encouraged, I experimented with this slightly different way of casting the spell. I was about to declare it a lost cause added to the long litany of spell failures I was racking up when I felt something. Just as the sun peeked over the horizon, I got it!

CHAPTER 8: PROGRESS

"Yes!" I yelled.

Sina and Daric threw off their blankets and stood with swords ready. They searched the surrounding woods.

"Where are they?" asked Sina.

I searched for a nearby rock to crawl under. "Oh, um, sorry. I got the spell to work, and I got carried away. I didn't mean to wake you." I smiled weakly at them.

Daric slumped to the ground and eyed me with disdain.

Sina rubbed the bridge of her nose. "That's... great Evan," she said tiredly.

"I'll just stoke the fire and make some breakfast tea," I offered. "You like willow and lemongrass, right?"

After breakfast, Sina asked me to show her what I'd done.

I sat and performed the spell. It was easier this time. "A rosemary bush is fifty feet that way."

We walked a short distance, and sure enough, there was a rosemary bush growing next to an oak tree.

She smiled at me. "Well done. And you didn't use a wand."

"Thanks." I grinned. "I figured out it was a problem of scale."

"Scale?" she prompted.

"Yeah, too much information. I had to narrow my focus so I could concentrate. I was trying to see the whole dog when all I needed was the flea."

"You say the strangest things."

I gave her a big, cheesy grin and waggled my eyebrows at her.

"Thanks!"

We broke camp and rode through more of the Shara wilderness. I marveled that we'd been traveling for days and hadn't seen a single village.

"Aren't there any settlements out this way?" I asked.

Daric sighed. "Yes, we're heading to one, remember?"

"No, I get that," I said, "but we're halfway there and we haven't seen another town or hamlet or anything. How big is this kingdom?"

"The Kingdom of Shara is about eight hundred miles east to west and seven hundred and twenty miles north to south," said Daric.

I did some rough math in my head. "Okay, a little smaller than the state of Texas. How many people is Queen Lycia responsible for?"

Daric smirked. "We're one of the larger kingdoms. There are just over a hundred thousand subjects."

"Oh, so that's why we haven't seen anyone. There just aren't that many to see."

Daric brought his horse to a stop. "What do you mean? Are you saying that there are more people in your kingdom, mortal?"

Sina turned her horse and eyed me.

I leaned on Nonam's neck and pondered that for a moment as I dredged up the facts from my civics class. "Let's see, for the state of Texas, that's about twenty-nine million people, give or take. For the United States as a whole, somewhere around three hundred and sixty million."

"You're lying," Daric said flatly.

I regarded him curiously. "Why would I lie about that?"

"There aren't twenty-nine million beings in all of Stellaluna," sneered Daric. "Are you seriously trying to tell me that in the entire world of the United States there are three hundred and thirty million? Don't make me laugh, human."

"No," I said.

Daric snorted in derision.

"The United States is a country," I said matter-of-factly. "The world I come from is Earth. Seven and a half billion humans live there."

Daric paled. Sina looked thoughtful. The silence stretched for longer than I was comfortable with.

Sina broke the awkward moment. "How old was your mother when you were born?"

"Um, nineteen," I shrugged. "A little young, but a lot of people have two or three kids by the time they turn thirty. Why, how old was your mother when she had you?"

Sina's gaze traveled to Daric, then back to me before she answered. "My mother was eight hundred and fifty-three years old when I was born. I was her first child. Most elves have their first child at about two or three hundred years old. It's rare for an elf to have more than two children."

"It's true. Humans breed like vermin," growled Daric.

"Hey! That was uncalled for," I said.

Rather than respond, or offer anything close to an apology, Daric turned his horse and rode north.

"What's his problem?" I asked.

Sina smiled sadly. "He's jealous. It's a big deal for elves to have children. A blessing and a great honor. I will not be Daric's first wife. He is five hundred years old and has had two wives before me. His first wife died in childbirth. The boy didn't survive. His second wife left him for a famous bard. He deeply fears that he will die without producing an heir."

"His first wife died in labor?"

Sina nodded.

That gave me pause. Sure, Daric was an arrogant jerk with a wand up his butt, but he never hit me or tried to steal my stuff like my brother often did. I could somewhat forgive him for being an ass, knowing that his life hadn't been a walk in the woods.

Sina and I followed Daric at a distance.

"So, no one ever gets old or sick here, and so birth rates are really low?" I asked.

"Yes," answered Sina.

"Is that true for all people who live here? Animals too?"

Sina waggled her head from side to side. "Elves, leprechauns, dryads, pookas, ogres, trolls, anything reasonably intelligent has a low birth rate. Animals are the exception to the rule. They can have young after a year. Goblins and pixies can produce young after twenty years, maybe because they aren't very smart."

An odd thought struck me. "Wait. Being human, is having kids one of those rules I can break?"

Sina didn't answer right away. When I glanced over at her and she stared down, lost in thought.

"Sina?"

"Yes," she finally answered. "I don't know if it's easier for two humans, since other than you, Geezer is the only one I've met. But human-elf partnerships can more easily produce children."

"So, Geezer has kids?" I asked.

Again, there was a long pause. Sina looked into my eyes, and it felt like her gaze pierced my soul. "Yes. He has a daughter."

Thunderstruck, I examined Sina's ears. I suddenly realized that they weren't as pointed as Daric's, or Flick's, or even the queen's ears. Her face was more rounded and less angular than the other elves I'd met.

I opened my mouth to speak, but Sina put a finger to her lips. She pointed to Daric.

He doesn't know? I mouthed the words.

She shook her head.

It fell into place then. Geezer had asked me to look after Sina. Look after *his daughter.*

CHAPTER 9: LITTLE GREEN OBSTACLES

When we made camp that night, I used my new spell several times. I discovered it used less energy to look at things nearby. Looking at stuff within a mile was easy peasy. Looking at things at roughly five miles out was a little draining, while using it to see twenty miles or so left me feeling like I'd just run sprints in PE class.

This was fine. I wasn't going to go far to gather herbs, anyway. I decided I could make our mid-day stops more productive by grabbing a few tasty plants along the way. Around the campsite I found more rosemary, but I also found oregano, wild onions, sage, and a few other herbs within a reasonable walking distance.

That night Daric returned with another pair of rabbits. This gave me an idea. A wild hare, if you will. I used the herbs I'd found and went all out in cooking the rabbits.

Ten minutes into cooking the rabbits, Sina returned from tending the horses, sniffing the air.

"What is that amazing smell?" she asked, licking her lips.

"Dinner," I said with a wink.

Daric appeared with an oil rag in his hands. He'd been obsessing over cleaning his armor. "Vermin can cook?"

I shook my head at the uptight elf. "Yes, apparently better than you can hunt. Two and a half hours to snare two rabbits? Did you stop and have tea with them first? Did you meet a mad hatter?"

He frowned at me. "Where do you come up with these odd ideas?"

In short order, I had the rabbits cooked. And just because it tickled me, I served them with a side of carrots.

We settled in around the campfire, and my companions dug in. All conversation stopped. I smiled inwardly as they both ate with gusto.

"Seriously, where did you learn to cook like this?" asked Sina around a mouthful of rabbit.

"I must admit," said Daric, "I'm a bit curious myself."

I shrugged. "My mom spends a lot of time with my brother. I thought that if I started cooking with her, we might develop a closer relationship. That worked for about two months, then cooking the family meals became my daily chore, along with the other things I was already doing: laundry, cleaning floors, dusting, and so forth. Unlike the other stuff, I actually like cooking. It's an art to mix flavors." I shrugged. "And food makes people happy."

Sina smiled and my ears warmed.

"You're a man of hidden talents," she said.

"Not bad for a human," said Daric begrudgingly.

The rest of the meal was fun. Sina shared stories about some of her instructors in magic and combat. Even Daric became almost civil.

Later, when Daric woke me for my watch, I continued to practice my spell. I experimented with my find plants spell. I found I could use it to get a decent mental map of the area by using it for common grasses and trees. I verified it was working by borrowing Sina's magic map. I was hoping to build up some endurance, maybe channel energy better, so I didn't get as tired. I didn't see results right away, but I figured it was like working out or fencing. Repetition and muscle memory would help me.

By the time we set out the following morning, I felt like I was getting the handle on this whole human wizard thing.

It was mid-morning when Sina stopped us. "Hold up, Daric." She dismounted.

Daric reined his horse to a stop and sighed dramatically.

Sina pulled her sword and waded into a patch of grass nearby. She used the point of her blade to uncover something. "Oh, crap."

I dismounted Nonam and joined her, but Daric walked his horse over to where we were.

"What is it?" I asked.

"Crap." She pointed with her blade. "Goblin poo and it's

fresh."

A shiver went down my spine with memories of my arrival. Daric and I both scanned the surrounding woods. Sina studied the ground around the barely covered fecal matter.

"I don't see or hear any nearby," said Daric.

Sina followed something, tracks I guess, but the signs were invisible to me. "The goblin came and went to the north."

"Where there's one, there's a dozen more." Daric chewed his lip. "The three of us can't handle a gaggle of goblins. We'll have to turn back."

Turn back? "Whoa, hang on now." I held my hands up. "I understand not taking on a superior force and all that, but failing this quest means ten years of step and fetching for me. You might be fine with the human vermin bowing and scraping for a decade, but it isn't your knees on the line. Can't we just go around them?"

Sina shook her head. "I understand, Evan, but goblins are tricky. They'll have set up an ambush and will have scouts to warn the rest if we avoid them."

"Ten years of your life isn't worth the rest of ours," said Daric, as if explaining it to a child.

I wasn't about to give up without a fight. "I get that, but presumably they haven't spotted us yet, right?"

Sina moved back over to the smelly pile and examined it. "A day old. It's better than fifty-fifty they haven't spotted us yet if we're at the outside edge of the patrol area."

"How far will they patrol around their camp?" I asked.

"Ten miles," replied Daric. "They won't want to travel farther than they can walk in half a day, but that doesn't matter. Unless we know exactly where they are, our best bet is to turn back. We can't risk being caught by a large patrol of goblins."

I wracked my brains to find an idea, any idea that would allow our quest to continue. Unfortunately, all I had was the one spell. My one... spell...

"We don't have to guess," I said with confidence. "I can tell you exactly where they are. We can go around them."

CHAPTER 10: A STICKY PROBLEM

Daric folded his arms over his chest. "You're not serious."

I grinned. "I am."

Sina raised an eyebrow at me. "What's your plan?"

"What do goblins eat?" I asked.

Daric scowled. "Whatever they can catch. Elves, gnomes, rabbits, and squirrels on a good day. Moss, lichen, and grubs otherwise."

"Excellent." I sat down to cast my Locate Plants spell.

"Stupid human," groaned Daric. "Finding some herbs within a hundred feet of us won't tell us where the goblins are. Stop wasting time and get back on your horse. It's a long ride back to the palace."

No way was I waiting ten years to see my dad and grandma again. Daric would have to drag me kicking and screaming.

"I'm not looking at plants around here," I told him, drawing the leaf symbol in the dirt. "I'm looking for all the moss and lichen for twenty miles in all directions."

Daric dismounted. "That's... that's not possible," he said, but without conviction.

He glanced at Sina, who shrugged.

I held the image of moss in my head. "Well, I can do it. So shut your nuts and berries hole so I can concentrate."

I cast the spell and my mind expanded into the land itself, searching for mosses and lichen. There was a lot of lichen clinging to trees and rocks in all directions. Moss was there too, but not as prevalent until it got closer to the river up ahead. I could tell it was a river buy the moss on the banks. The energy surged through me as I pushed my awareness farther and farther away from where I sat. My mind felt like I was in calculus class working on a complex equation, only the math problem was physically exhausting as well.

Pushing my mind to the limit, I could pick out individual mosses, individual lichens. The river was a long line of moss. There was a break in the middle with no moss or lichen.

I couldn't catch my breath. It was like there wasn't enough air. My muscles ached as if I'd just finished a marathon. My ears rang and my head spun as I let go of the spell and fell backward into the grass.

"Couldn't do it, huh?" sneered Daric.

"No," I panted, "I got it." I sucked in a big breath. "Just give me a minute," I said, waving a finger in the air.

A few minutes later, I sat up, still breathing hard. "Sina, can you pull out your magic map?"

Sina retrieved her map and spread it out on the ground. It magically drew in the surrounding wilderness. I studied the map. Sina and Daric stared at me as if I'd just covered my genitals with peanut butter and jelly and claimed to be a sandwich.

I had to admit, I was a little crazy, but it was a good kind of crazy.

I pointed at the upcoming river crossing. "The goblins are here. All the moss and lichen in this area has all been goblin-ed up."

"Eight miles," observed Sina. "We're at the outer edge of their patrol zone. And it makes sense. See this ridge next to the river? This gully is the only logical crossing spot for miles up or downstream. The little green bastards will have the high ground so they can rain arrows on anyone trying to cross."

"What? Surely you don't believe this nonsense," exclaimed Daric. "He just learned the spell two days ago. No one has enough power or control to see all the way to the river."

Something in me snapped. I got right up in his face. "Don't believe me? You use the Locate Plants spell and verify it."

I didn't realize it until that moment, but I had three inches of height on Daric. He glared at me as I stared down at him.

"I don't know the stupid plant spell," he ground out before turning and remounting his horse. "Come on, Sina. I'm done with this charlatan. We're heading back."

Sina didn't move. Her gaze traveled from Daric to me and back again. She chewed her lip in silence.

She took a sharp breath and let it out. "No. I'm sorry Daric, but I believe him. You can go back if you like. Watching after Evan is my duty, not yours."

Sina rolled up her map and remounted her horse. "Let's go, Evan. We'll need to backtrack a bit and head north. The next best crossing is half a day's ride."

I remounted Nonam, and we rode past a stunned Daric.

He followed us, but I could feel his glare boring into the back of my head. Until now, the ride had been with arrogant silent Daric punctuated with insults or a derisive snort. It was still quiet, but the quality of it had changed. We now had sulky, silent Daric with accompanying growls. An improvement in my book.

As if in response to Daric's mood, the trees along our route changed as well. Tall, straight pine trees became oaks, pecans, and hickory. The change created a dense canopy that made the forest dark and creepy. These trees also creaked and groaned in an unsettling way. The scent changed from piney to musty.

"Does this enchanting patch of timber have a name?" I asked.

Sina eyed the branches overhead with trepidation. "Yes, it's called The Webwood. Keep your eyes sharp. There's a reason we didn't come this way first."

"And that reason is because it's filled with playful nymphs and mischievous sprites, right? Things that might distract us from our true mission?"

Sina raised an eyebrow at me sidelong and didn't answer.

"A guy can hope." Then I asked, knowing I would hate the answer, "So, spiders?"

"Yes, big ones."

I suppressed a shudder. "How big?" My voice cracked.

"Some are big enough to take on a fox or wolf," Sina swept her gaze from side to side, up and down. "A few could eat our horses."

Great. Nightmare fuel. Just what I needed. My back itched thinking about icky eight-legged things dropping on me at any moment. I changed the subject.

Thinking of things I hated took me back to when I'd first arrived and met Daric. "Hey Sina, what was it about my arrival that spooked the goblins?"

Sina welcomed the conversational left turn with a chuckle. "They thought you were a dragon."

I looked down at myself. "A dragon?"

"Dragons are adept magic users," she explained. "It's widely known that they take on the form of elves or gnomes or other fae to blend in. They use it to help them locate treasure or food.

She grinned at me. "You appeared in our midst and released a, uh, breath weapon, knocking the lead goblin off his feet."

"So, they thought my burp was more than bad breath?"

"The two types of dragons found in Shara are green and red. Green dragons breathe a noxious cloud to kill their prey." She shrugged. "So yes, they thought you were a dragon descended from the heavens to wreak your vengeance upon all goblin kind."

I laughed. "Fear me, puny green men. I am Evan. Hear me roar. *Urrrrp!*"

Sina wrinkled her nose. "Ewwww." Then she burst into a fit of giggles, which changed into a nervous tittering as her gaze fixated on some webs in a nearby tree.

I liked it when she laughed.

As if dark woods and the smell of stagnant puddles weren't enough, soon the trees sported the kind of webbing usually reserved for old garden sheds and abandoned mansions. A few of the trees looked like they were homes for enormous colonies of tent worms. I decided to fool myself into believing they were those caterpillar colonies. I was thankful that Sina led us in wide arcs around those trees.

"Have I mentioned that I think this is a bad idea?" said Daric from a few paces behind us.

It was unusually quiet, and it took me a while to figure out why. No birds. I made the mistake of looking for them and shivered when I found bird-sized cocoons in the branches.

It was while I was looking up that something touched my face. I screamed and startled my horse.

Nonam bucked, and I impressed myself with my ability to stay in the saddle. Less so with the other results. I flew ahead, yelling at the top of my lungs as more webs clung to my hair, clothes, and got in my mouth. I whipped my hands in front of me and tried to pull the stuff from my head. It was then that I swallowed something and *completely* lost it.

Caught between trying to spit it out and screaming, I never saw what hit me.

Nonam continued forward, and I didn't. Pain blossomed across my chest, then my back as I hit the ground. I struggled to draw a breath. The forest spun.

Dazed, I rolled onto my stomach. And saw legs. Long and pointy.

"Ahhhhhh!" I scrambled backwards as a dog-sized spider lunged for me.

CHAPTER 11: THERE'S SPIDERS, THEN THERE'S SPIDERS

Thunk.

An arrow impaled the spider to a tree a foot from my head.

Sina performed a riding dismount and landed beside me. She nocked another arrow. "Are you okay?"

"Tree branch... Hurts... to breathe," I sputtered.

"Daric, gather the horses," she commanded. "I'll guard Evan."

Regaining some of my wits, I drew my sword. Leaning against the tree, I surveyed the surrounding woods. Then, with a start, I remembered to look up.

No spiders, thank dog. Well, no enormous spiders. My definition of big had recently been revised. "For the record," I said through clenched teeth, "I hate this place."

"Not going to build a summer cottage here? The trees are quite nice." Sina said as she glanced left and right.

"No," I laughed, then groaned as my ribs throbbed. "And I'm seriously rethinking getting a fire spell. Being crisped might be worth it."

We stood shoulder to shoulder until Daric returned. Nonam was wide-eyed and pulled from side to side, but the elf warrior had a firm grip on the reins. If her name really meant docile, someone had an awful sense of humor. Then again, there were spiders. That was enough to disturb anyone's calm.

53

Daric was almost to us when Sina fired another arrow.

A spider the size of a pony dropped from a tree fifty yards away. Leaves rustled as smaller shapes moved in the branches from where the monster had fallen.

And revising my definition of big, yet again. My mouth went dry. I clutched my sword tighter.

Nonam tried to bolt again, but Daric held her steady. "Good shot, Sina." Then he gazed upward. "It'll be getting dark soon."

"I am *not* camping here," I said emphatically.

"Oh, good," said Daric laconically. "You do use your head for more than screaming and attracting every spider within five miles."

I had a witty retort, but let it slide. In this case, Daric had an excellent point.

Sina put her bow away. "We'll need a torch. Evan, let me heal you, then we'll make one. We should walk from here, and it's about five hours to the crossing."

Torches. That was an idea I could get behind.

Sina touched my chest and warm energy spread through me.

Breathing was easier, but my muscles ached. "I really want to learn that spell."

Sina arched an eyebrow in my direction. "I seriously doubt you have anything valuable enough to trade for it."

I shrugged. "Give me time. I'll find something you want."

Sina gave me a smile and a wink before going a short distance into the trees. She returned with a tree limb. It took no time to cut it to size and wrap spider webs around it. Webbing made excellent kindling.

Daric held the torch. Sina kept her bow at the ready. I walked the horses.

It felt like a lot longer than five hours. The torch cast long shadows, and the darkness seemed infinite outside its light. I imagined beady little spider eyes peering at us from every half-fallen tree and moss-covered root. Skittering and chittering echoed from the unseen wooded depths. I remembered my mom mentioning that spiders hated mint and lavender. We rubbed the mint on ourselves and our horses after I used my spell to find it. I don't know whether or not it worked, but after four days of camping without a shower, the mint made us all smell nicer.

I was slapping myself to keep from nodding off by the time we reached the crossing. Moonlight glinted off rocks on the bank and eddies in the river as it gurgled along. This section was wider than the upstream and downstream parts, so it made sense that it was shallower here. Not that it wasn't deep.

"Do we just cross?" I asked.

Sina examined the far bank. "Mostly. I haven't been this way for a long time. I think the water is deeper than before."

"How deep was it last time?" I asked.

"Chest high," she said, chewing her lip.

I glanced at the dark, webby, spider-infested woods behind me and then at the noticeably friendlier trees across the way. Even in the moonlight, I could see farther into them. "Non—spidery trees versus icky infested death trap. Yep, this is me not caring about having to swim a bit."

"Daric, we should bag our armor," said Sina.

The broody elf scowled but nodded.

The elves removed their heavy gear and bundled it up. They attached ropes so they could drag their burdens across the riverbed. We didn't want to weigh down the horses if they had to swim too.

Sina went first, attaching her rope to the saddle pommel and leading her horse across. At the halfway point, she slipped underwater and but quickly bobbed back to the surface. The current carried her to the right as she swam. It carried the horse a little faster. They both found footing thirty feet downstream.

They made good progress until her horse was almost jerked off its hooves. The submerged bundle must have reached the swifter current. Sina was prepared for it. She had the horse angled upriver and so, between the two of them, they got the bundle across.

Daric was next. I let him get twenty feet ahead of me before I followed. Not having to deal with a heavy bundle, I entered the water a little farther down the riverbank. I had a little trouble getting Nonam to join me. It really was time to give her a new name.

Daric reached the mid-point and did a better job crossing the faster current there. However, when the armor bundle reached the same point, he wasn't as lucky.

Nonam and I had just found purchase on the far side of the fast current when his rope pulled taut. Daric's horse wasn't turned yet. It whinnied and fell with a splash. The horse recovered, but the rope fell off.

Something brushed my leg, and I did the stupidest thing ever. I reached down and grabbed it.

CHAPTER 12: EVAN'S WILD RIDE

Have you ever slid down a water slide, but you forgot to cross your legs? This was way worse. Think of every ride at a water park at ten times speed and at the same time. The river invaded my eyes and mouth. The rope snagged my arm and caused friction burns.

Despite this, I couldn't get it off. I tried swimming up. At least I hoped it was up. Up and down were fuzzy as I corkscrewed through the current.

I broke the surface gasping a lung full of air and muddy river. Then I was under again.

More certain of up now, I swam left. I managed two more dolphin impressions before finding the tree. Or maybe it found me. Either way, it hit me. The tree, that is. Then I finally did the first smart thing I'd done since entering the water. I wrapped myself around it.

The rope tried to yank my arm from my body, and I screamed in pain. Thankfully, my arm stayed attached. The tree bent and I got another mouthful of river. But the tree pulled me up and I spit it out.

For long minutes, I gratefully sucked air. What the hell was I thinking? Why did I even consider saving the armor of the one guy in all of Stellaluna that I didn't like? What was I doing hanging on to the dog darned thing?

I studied my partially submerged perch. The tree grew out of the bank and dipped down in the river before growing up again. It was my new best friend, and I kissed the rough bark repeatedly.

Regaining my strength, I dragged myself to shore. Since I had the armor anyway, I pulled it out with me. Mostly with my good arm. The tender muscles and abused shoulder joint of my right arm screamed at me to stop. I told it to suck it up. At least it was still attached and could tell me how it felt.

I hoped Nonam had survived. I'd let go of the reins when I was pulled under. The horse was obviously smarter than me, so it was likely fine, I told myself.

Studying the woods and water, I realized I didn't recognize any of it. Being a stranger in a strange land, it should surprise me if anything was recognizable. Still, if my friends hadn't written me off, they'd come looking for me, right?

Okay, Sina *might* convince Daric to come look for my body. Either way, they weren't likely to go back into spider central. I gazed across the river at the foreboding forest and gave it as many rude gestures as I could come up with.

It was the middle of the night. I'd lost all my gear, and I was beyond exhausted. I wasn't up for lugging the armor up the riverbank, so I stuffed it in a hollow and covered it with grass clumps, dead leaves, and a bush for good measure. I moved a dozen yards away and fell asleep in the grass.

I must have slept like the dead because the sun didn't wake me up. Nope. The sun was well above the horizon when someone yelled nearby. For once, they did not direct it at me.

"For the last time, the human is dead," said Daric. "The idiot drowned himself. The only thing that matters is finding my armor. It's been in my family for three generations."

"Evan might still be alive. You must admit that he's proven to be resourceful," said Sina. "Search the river. See if the rope is caught on a branch or rock. I'll search a bit more inland. I promise I won't move beyond your sight."

Daric sighed. "If, and it's a big if, the human pulled himself out of the river, he probably ended up on the Webwood side. By now he's spider food."

I stretched and groaned when my arm protested, then stood next to a tree. They were leading their horses and would walk between me and the water. Nonam wasn't with them. I waited. Whether because of their argument or because of Daric's insistence on searching the river, they were almost on top of me when I greeted them.

"Morning, guys," I yawned. "What a night, eh?"

"Evan!" Sina bounded over and wrapped me in a hug. "You

made it. You didn't die."

I would have enjoyed it more if the hug hadn't included my injured arm. "Ow, careful. That's tender. I missed you, too." I put my good arm around her.

Daric scowled, but otherwise didn't seem to care.

"You're hurt?" She held me at arm's length and examined me.

"Yeah, strained my arm trying to save Daric's armor." I pointed. "I have rope burns, too."

Daric's eyes grew wide. "You have it?" He rushed over and looked behind some bushes and trees, trying to find it.

It occurred to me then that I was dealing with an elf. "I said, I tried to save it."

His face reddened with barely contained fury. "Do you have the armor or not, human?"

I waited as Sina put her hands on my shoulder and healed my injuries. She panted as she channeled the spell energy.

"Thanks," I said to her, then spread my arms wide. "All I'm saying is that I might know where your armor is, Daric, and I might tell you for a price."

Daric started circling farther and farther from where I'd spent the night, but away from the river. "It's got to be around here somewhere. You're not that clever."

"You're probably right," I shrugged, grateful that it *didn't* hurt now. "After all, I'm just a stupid human who nearly drowned or became spider food."

The angry elf stalked over to me. "Give it back, Evan."

I made a show of thinking about it and tapping my lips in thought. "Huh? Where might it be?"

"I'm warning you," he growled.

"You know the healing spell, right?" I raised an eyebrow at him.

"I'm not teaching you the spell for something I already own."

"Huh," I shook my head. "I risked my life to save it. I realize that has no value to *you*, but it has a lot of value to me. It would be such a shame if some goblin found the armor first. Didn't you say it's been in your family for three generations?"

"I'll kill you," Daric sneered.

"Uh oh. That'd be unfortunate, seeing as Sina, your fiancé, has to protect me. Correct me if I'm wrong, but you'd have to fight her, too."

Sina regarded me curiously.

Daric turned on his heels and continued to search. He passed by the armor's hiding spot several times. I hadn't realized it, but I'd covered it up pretty well. The grass and bush I'd planted on top of them blended in with the surroundings perfectly.

Sina gave me a half-smile. "Are you sure you're not part elf?"

"Pure human, through and through," I said with a wink. "Did you find Nonam?"

She shook her head. "No, sorry. When you went under, she bolted into the Webwood. We looked, but we couldn't find her."

It made me sad. I hadn't known the horse that well, but she didn't deserve to be spider food.

After half an hour, Daric stomped up to me. "Fine," he growled through clenched teeth. "If you return my armor, I'll teach you the healing spell."

"Excellent," I held out my hand. "It's a pleasure doing business with you."

He eyed my palm like it was a maggot-filled dead rat. Finally, he gave it one hard shake.

I felt like rubbing the arrogant elf's nose with it for a bit, but decided against it. I really didn't want to have to fight someone with literally centuries more experience than me.

Instead, I sauntered over to the grass and bushes and cleared them away. "Tada."

CHAPTER 13: TROLL CALL

Daric was as good as his word. He taught me the healing spell, but I'd be hard-pressed to find a more surly and openly antagonistic instructor. Well, there was my eighth-grade English teacher...

He smacked me on the back of the head. "No. Do round ears make you deaf? You have to start the spell in the right frame of mind, or it won't work."

I rubbed my sore noggin. "And hitting me is supposed to get me in a generous and loving mood? Who taught you this spell, your drill sergeant?"

"Yes," said Daric, "and a more spiteful and evil elf you'll never meet, but he was right about this. If you can learn to cast spells under pressure, you'll never freeze up when your men need you. When your friend is lying beside you with a dozen arrows in his chest and a sword in his gut, and you're the difference between his life and death, you don't have the luxury of waiting until you get your head on straight. Now try it again."

To be fair, if my friend had a dozen arrows in him, he was probably well beyond any help I could provide. That didn't seem like a productive argument, so I kept my opinion to myself.

This spell was a lot more difficult than the find plants spell. Besides pulling the magical energy into your body, you then had to transform it using your essence. Having the right frame of mind meant five symbols and three ancient elvish words that were the modern equivalent of empower, restore, and regrow. And yes, like the plant spell, you had to keep it all in your head *at the same time.*

In the three days it took us to reach the bridge, I'd made

absolutely no progress in getting the magic to work. What was worse was that to use the spell, you actually had to have something to heal. I sported a half dozen minor cuts. It felt masochistic, but I wasn't going to injure someone so I could practice on them. Hmmm, could I slice Daric by 'accident?'

We entered a mountain range and spent more time climbing higher. The temperature dropped, and more rock outcroppings meant I had to watch my footing. I could easily twist an ankle. There were plenty of pine trees and the mountains cast long purple shadows.

We saw a lot of wild goats. Just like the Earthbound variety, they ate everything. No tree or bush was safe. Bare patches of ground with no grass, bark stripped from trunks, and de-leafed bushes punctuated the landscape.

We topped a rise about midday, and I got my first view of the troll outpost. It looked like the pictures of the early American settlers' forts. Upright pointed logs bound together with four interspersed guard towers perched atop the wall. The gate was a slightly smaller version of the walls, with some wicked-looking spikes pointing outward. There appeared to be some reinforcing stonework, but it was sloppy.

Given the medieval level of technology around here, I'd expected a rope bridge or maybe a larger version of a stone arch bridge. When Queen Lycia had described it as a sturdy bridge, she hadn't been kidding. The bridge resembled a modern railroad trellis. Stone pillars rose hundreds of feet above a raging river, supporting a sturdy roadbed of heavy wood beams sealed with mortar. The dichotomy between the slap-dash fort and the engineering marvel of the bridge could not be missed.

I pointed this out to my companions.

"The trolls didn't build the bridge. Dwarves did," said Daric.

"What happened to the dwarves?" I asked.

Sina shrugged. "The trolls ate them."

"Wait, really?"

Sina and Daric nodded in unison.

I swallowed hard as I surveyed the fort. I was going to have to go down there and negotiate with these monsters.

"Any suggestions on how I can avoid being eaten myself?"

"Don't go," offered Sina. "Run. Trolls aren't fast."

Daric frowned in thought.

"Daric?" I pressed.

He shook his head. "Um, no. It's probably a bad idea."

I sighed. "Any ideas would be helpful right now. Even the bad ones."

Daric rolled his eyes. "Fine. Aleric, the last envoy to come this way, told me that trolls hate the smell of rosemary. Perhaps if you rubbed it on yourself, like we did with the mint for the spiders, you'd at least get to talk with them before they ate you."

They'd told me earlier that none of the envoys had returned, but I asked anyway. "What happened to Aleric?"

Daric smiled, "Presumably, he was eaten."

I rubbed my face in frustration. "Okay, are either of you willing to go down there with me?"

"No," said Sina.

Daric snorted. "No way in Oskora."

"What's Oskora?"

"It's the fae version of hell," he explained. "You spend eternity being prey for wild beasts."

"This is *your* quest." Sina shrugged apologetically. "In this, we're here for moral support. We aren't allowed to interfere." She stepped up and hugged me. "But I'm starting to think you're not a bad guy, so be careful."

The hug was quick but appreciated. Even if it was for pity, I'd take what I could get.

The queen wasn't making it easy on me. I stood on the hill and studied the outpost. Right now, I can turn back. I'd lose ten years of my life, but I'd be alive. At least high school would be over when I got back. Jerrod would have moved on to tormenting a wife and kids. My mom? Mom would miss having me cook and clean for her. Dad would be sad, so would my grandma, but I'd see them again. Maybe.

Grandma was pretty old. Would she even be alive when I returned? That thought sent an icy shiver down my back. No, I needed to give this a go. Maybe if I stayed outside the gate and didn't enter the fort, I could increase my chances of escaping.

The quest was to get them to join the Shara or destroy the bridge. There was no way the bridge was coming down short of explosives.

"Do either of you know a spell that makes stuff go boom?"

"No," they answered in unison.

Well, worth an ask. "Okay Daniel, let's go meet the lions." Then to my companions, "Keep an eye on me. If I don't come back, tell Geezer I went to meet my Maker, but I'm not sure my Maker was ready to meet me."

They nodded solemnly, completely missing the joke. Well, it wasn't a good one, anyway. Sorry, Winston Churchill.

I started down the hill, leaving the elves in the clearing. I paused several times to observe the trolls inside the compound. To outward appearances, they seemed to be living their lives like any normal beings. Big and green, but otherwise regular people. They were the same color as goblins, but that's where the similarity ended. Goblins were short with long noses and ears. They had yellow eyes and sharp features. Trolls were tall, wide, and lumpy. They looked like a three-year-old had molded clay into a person. They had lots of cooking fires and carried spears. They didn't wear any armor, just simple brown and tan homespun clothes.

I was stalling with all the observation stops, but since I was likely walking to my death, I didn't begrudge myself a few breathers to smell the rosemary. I used my spell to find some on the hillside. Shrugging, I rubbed some on myself. It wouldn't hurt and might help. And it had been a few days since I'd been dunked in the river. An envoy should smell nice, I reasoned.

Stopping at the tree line, I took one last look at the fort and surrounding woods. *I'm not going to die*, I told myself. *I'm going to walk up to the fort and talk. If things go from bad to crusty nuggets, I can run away. Trolls are big, but not fast.*

I took a deep breath to steel my resolve and crossed the field. As hikes go, it was sunny with a light breeze, and not too hot and not too cold. I resolved to enjoy it as if it were my last. I swallowed hard. As I got close to the fort the smell of burning meat and something like dead skunk assaulted my nose. Ugh.

Of course, they saw me coming. The guards in the towers eyed me warily as I approached. They didn't ready their spears though, so that was a bonus in my book.

I stopped twenty feet from the gate. "Hail to the fort," I called.

The guard in the left tower answered. "If you want to cross the bridge, you have to pay the troll."

I blinked. Was that a pun? How clever were these trolls? "I'm not here to cross the bridge. I'm here to negotiate on behalf of Queen Lycia of Shara."

The guards exchanged a few words with someone inside the fort. A few minutes later, an awful grinding noise accompanied the gate being forced open across the packed earth and gravel.

A large troll emerged with two guards. And I found the source of the dead skunk smell. This pungent bouquet was accented with the subtle aroma of week-old jockstrap. I held my breath.

He planted his spear in the ground. "You're not an elf."

I nodded. "I'm a human. I represent the Shara in this negotiation."

The big troll sniffed the air. The trolls on either side licked their lips.

Uh oh. Note to self, no more rosemary. Did Daric set me up? He couldn't lie, but would he shade the truth?

"He smells really good," said one guard. "Not as good as elf, but good. Can we eat him now?"

The big troll waved him down. "Not yet. Let's hear what the queen has to say first. Then we can eat him."

I put a hand on my knee to steady my quivering legs and a tiny squeak escaped my throat.

The troll chieftain held out a hand.

If he wanted to, the troll could reach out and grab me. Next stop, Evan stew. Sweat glued my shirt to my skin. I shoved the thought aside and put my hand in his.

We shook, sort of. His hand was four times the size of mine, so the handshake was a little odd.

"I'm Bogore," he said. "Come inside and we'll see what the queen has to offer the people of the Troll Bridge."

I avoided thinking of him as 'Booger.' Being in mortal peril helped. "Begging the great troll's pardon, but several of the previous envoys have entered your fort never to return. If it's all the same to you, I'd prefer to conduct the negotiations *here*."

His eyes twinkled a bit and a half-smile formed on thin lips. "I understand that you feel safer out here. It isn't true. Trust me when I say that we control the lands for miles in all directions. If you ran, you wouldn't get far. So, by all means, let's discuss things in front of the gate." Bogore snapped his fingers and they brought crude chairs from inside the gate. Enough for the chief and his guards. No chair for me.

Fine, sitting would get in the way of running for my life.

"Honored and powerful troll warriors," I began, "the great

queen of the elves wishes to stop the Darower raids into the Shara lands. She has authorized me to deal with your proud people on her behalf."

The big troll's eyes widened. He looked over my shoulder in the direction I'd come from. "And what does the ruler of the tastiest people in the land offer in return?"

I'd decided that opening negotiations with what I could offer was a bad move. If I wanted a deal to stick, I needed to offer what the troll chief *wanted*.

"Great Chief Bogore," I smiled broadly, "It isn't what she offers, so much as what you need. What most pleases the formidable trolls?"

He chuckled. "What always pleases the trolls: food. We are a simple people, with simple wants and needs."

It couldn't be that easy. "That's what the Darower gives you to cross into our lands? Food?"

The chief nodded. "Oh yes, every time they cross, they pay the troll. We have no favorites. All who cross pay the price."

"And they don't get Rick-trolled. You're on the honor troll."

"What?" He asked.

"Never mind. What food do the Darower offer?"

"Goblins," he answered nonchalantly. "Dark elves taste better, but they never offer us any. More's the pity."

My stomach rebelled. I remembered the goblins we'd avoided on the way here. Had they sacrificed one or two of their number to cross the bridge?

This just kept getting worse. "You only eat other intelligent races? That's your preferred food?"

He grinned. "No, but Shara elves are delicious. I've never heard of a human, but I am excited to see what you taste like."

Yeah, let's navigate away from Evan kabobs. "So, trolls like food other than people?"

Bogore sighed theatrically. "Yes, we really like goats and sheep."

And my brain went snick. "There are a lot of wild goats in the forest around here."

Bogore crossed his massive arms over his chest. "There used to be. It's why we moved here. But our hunters can't find them anymore. The Shara, with their nature magic, convinced them to go away."

More likely, the goats learned to avoid the area near the bridge.

Moreover, trolls were slow and smelly. I bet the goats scented them a mile away and avoided them. "If I can bring you goats, and get the queen to give you a steady supply of them, will you close the bridge to the Darower?"

Bogore laughed heartily. "You will catch goats where my hunters cannot?"

"Yes," I said confidently.

Bogore motioned to someone behind me, and I whipped my head around. No one should *be* behind me. A male and female troll warrior strode toward us. The male carried Sina trussed up like a Christmas turkey over his shoulder.

My stomach turned to lead as I watched with horror. The female hunter stopped behind me, as the other carried Sina to the troll chief. Sina's eyes were wide with fear. She screamed into a gag.

Bogore pointed. "We caught an elf spy. She's obviously here to scare off the goats. Bring us goats by sundown, or she's our next meal."

Oh, crap. How'd they catch her? Where was Daric?

The troll behind me took a deep sniff, then licked the side of my face like a dog, leaving it wet and slimy. "Bring us goats, or we'll eat you, too."

CHAPTER 14: PAYING THE TROLL

I looked deep into Sina's eyes and tried to convey to her that she wasn't alone. That I would save her.

She gave me a barely perceptible nod, which told me she understood. She was scared, but knew I needed to leave so that I could rescue her.

It tugged at every heartstring I had, but I turned to Bogore. "How many goats will you need as a show of good faith?"

"Three," he pronounced. "If you can produce three goats, then we will know that the word of a human is good."

"And if I produce three goats by morning," I hedged for more time, "you'll let the elf go unharmed, stop letting Darower forces use the bridge, and stop eating the Shara."

"Sundown," he insisted. "We will agree for twelve goats a week."

I studied the big troll. Elves might not lie, but I bet the same didn't hold true for trolls. I didn't sense any deception, but that didn't mean it wasn't there.

Sticking my hand out, Bogore took it in his own.

"Deal," we said together.

I walked back to the tree line. I wanted to run. I was on the clock, but that would show fear. Looking at my magic pocket watch, I saw I had three, maybe four, hours until sundown. I was fairly certain that all the talk about eating other beings was for show, but I wasn't going to bet Sina's life on that. I hadn't been able to get a close look at the cook fires from the hillside, but I didn't imagine enough intelligent fae came this way to make a staple for the troll's diet.

At least I hoped I was right. Daric and Sina were convinced that the goblins preferred elves and gnomes, so maybe it wasn't.

As soon as I was in the trees and out of sight of the fort, I sprinted up the hillside. Daric might not give a sparrow's ass about me, but he loved Sina. How they had captured her but not him was a mystery, but I could certainly count on his help to free her.

Breathless, I reached the campsite. "Daric, Daric, they have Sina.

It wasn't until he moved that I saw him. He shimmied down a nearby tree. He was so well camouflaged that I wouldn't have found him otherwise. "I know. They approached from upwind, using some sort of magic to cloak themselves. By the time we smelled them, it was too late. Sina never had a chance."

"And you did nothing?"

I never saw it coming. One minute I was standing in the clearing, then next I was on the ground five feet away. My jaw and neck ached.

"She wouldn't even be here if it wasn't for you, human," he snarled. "This is all your fault."

"And I wouldn't be here if it wasn't for your queen making me wander around this wilderness like an idiot," I sprang to my feet and got in his face. "I don't want to be here. I want to be home, back in San Antonio. So, if you want to pass some blame around, make sure you put a little where it's deserved." I stuck a finger in his chest plate. "Lycia could have used the spell at any time to send me home, but no. I'm stranded here in this death trap of a land, doing crap jobs, losing dog knows how many years of my life for her amusement."

The fire didn't leave his gaze. His jaw muscles clenched and unclenched several times. "Trolls are very tough. Cut them up, they'll heal. I could fire every arrow in my quiver into one, and he'd shrug it off and keep coming."

"You're going to help me get Sina back, *right*?" I stuck my chin out, daring him to defy me.

Daric rolled his eyes. "*You* can get her back?"

"Yes, I've worked out a deal, but I need your help to pull it off. You're a better hunter than I am." I hoped appealing to his vanity would yield results.

"Hunting?" Daric cocked his head to the side. "What are we trading for her?"

"Three goats."

He cocked his head. "This forest is full of wild goats."

I shrugged. "And they can't catch them."

His gaze traveled around the clearing in thought. "The troll's scent. Goats have a keen sense of smell. Using spears, I bet they can't get close enough."

"And there you have it." I spread my arms wide. "Trolls prefer goat even over you magically delicious elves. Twelve goats a week, and they'll join the Shara."

"They can't be serious."

"The trolls might be lying to me, but I doubt it," I admitted.

"I'll have three goats here in about an hour." He turned to go.

"Great, I'll gather herbs and get a fire going."

He stopped. "What? Cooking them was part of the deal?"

"No," I sat crossed-legged and prepared to cast my Locate Plants spell. "But if we exceed expectations on our first date, it'll make every agreement from now on easier."

He looked at me askance. "Assuming you mean date metaphorically, why would you do that? It's not part of the deal."

"Spoken like a true elf," I said and drew the leaf symbol.

***

Daric returned an hour and a half later with three goats. Apparently, the goats around here were crafty. Together we cleaned and dressed them, then I cooked them up with the rosemary, garlic, and onion I'd found. I was willing to bet that the reason I smelled delicious to the trolls was *because* of the rosemary. With a bit of salt from our provisions, I was almost sad the food wasn't for us. The mixture of subtle and strong spices had my mouth watering, and I took a bite to make sure it met my standards.

Met and exceeded. Something about the game in Stellaluna made everything taste just a tiny bit better than Earth food.

"They're going to betray you," said Daric.

"Maybe," I said. I had also considered that possibility. "Besides, what choice do we have? Either we deal straight, and they deal straight, or they don't. If they don't, then Sina's as good as dead. But look on the bright side."

"There's a bright side?"

"If it's a double-cross, they'll eat me, too."

The joke fell flat as Daric nodded like the idea had merit.

We loaded the goats on a pair of poles, and I dragged them down to the fort. Daric, of course, wouldn't go near the encampment.

The sun was just above the horizon when I reached the gates and called out. "Hail to the fort."

The female hunter from earlier leaned out of a tower. "Go away, we haven't had time to eat the elf yet," she said in a high squeaky voice, very much at odds with her large stature. It reminded me of the pep squad back at school.

I decided to assume they were messing with me. "Kinda the point. Tell Bogore I have his goats."

She threw up her hands like it was a hassle, "What-*ever*," and disappeared inside the fort.

Minutes later, the gate opened and Booger, no *Bogore*, emerged with a guard and the female hunter. "You're early," he said.

"You have my friend," I explained. "I was motivated to uphold my end of the bargain."

He took a big sniff. "The goats smell... off."

"Off how?" I asked.

"Not burned," he elaborated.

Perhaps my efforts were in vain. "You prefer your meat burned?"

He waved the comment away with a dinner plate sized hand. "No, but it happens during cooking. I eat around it."

From inside the fort, I heard Sina cry out. "Run, Evan. They're going to kill you."

I raised an eyebrow at Bogore. "Troll of the dead?"

The big troll shrugged with his palms out. A dozen trolls appeared on the wall with spears raised.

My heart leapt to my throat. I forced myself to remain outwardly calm as sweat trickled down the back of my leg. At least, I hoped it was sweat... "Negotiating in bad faith, Bogore?" I asked.

"On the contrary, my men are here to take revenge after you poison us. We know how elves work."

"I'm not an elf," I pointed out.

"True enough, emissary of the Shara," he motioned to the female hunter. "Gemma, you're up. Try their food."

"Me, my chief?" she squeaked, turning a lighter shade of

green.

"You," he confirmed.

Reluctantly, Gemma stepped forward and yanked a haunch from my burden. She shot me a venomous look and another one at Bogore, then took a tentative bite.

She chewed thoughtfully for a few moments before her face lit up with surprise. After taking another less cautious bite, she threw caution to the wind and chowed down with abandon.

"Gemma?" said Bogore cautiously.

"It's amazing," she said through a mouth full of goat. "You gotta try it!"

The troll chieftain frowned. "The food is bewitched."

"No," I chuckled. "It's just cooked really well. No magic was involved, I promise."

The guards atop the wall glanced at each other in confusion.

Bogore came forward and sniffed at the roast goat.

"It's not poisoned," I assured him. "Try some."

Gemma reached for another haunch, but Bogore slapped her hand away. He took the leg for himself and nibbled.

"It's... good?" I watched in satisfaction as he rolled the food around in his mouth. "And not poisoned."

"Excellent," I indicated the slightly open gate behind him. "Now can you retrieve my elf friend?"

Bogore stared at me with hard, intelligent eyes. I could almost see the gears turning in that cunning troll mind of his. "New deal-" he started, but I cut him off.

"No," I made a chopping motion. "You uphold our existing deal, or you break it and eat me and the elf. No changing the terms after I delivered."

"I wasn't breaking our deal," he insisted. "I wanted to make a new arrangement. Why would you think I wouldn't uphold our bargain?"

"You're in con-troll." I pointed next to me. "No elf." I waved toward the trolls on the wall. "Your men prepared to turn me into Evan kabobs."

He huffed and motioned at the wall. "Return to your duties. Gemma, retrieve the elf girl."

The trolls on the wall disappeared. Gemma glanced at the goats, Bogore, and the gate. She snatched a hunk of meat and held it close to her chest, as if daring the chieftain to slap her hand again. Then she spun on her heel and went into the fort.

"As I was saying," Bogore bit into his goat, chewing as he talked. "I want to make a new deal. I can smell campfire on you. You cooked these goats yourself, didn't you?"

"Yes," I admitted.

"What is it you want?" he asked.

"For what?"

"To teach one of my people to prepare food like you do."

That rocked me back on my heels. "Teaching someone how to cook could take a while. What I really want is to return to my homeland, Texas."

Bogore glanced down in thought. "I don't know where Texas is."

"I need a spell to get there. It's why I'm running errands for the queen. She promised to teach it to me, for a price."

"Elves," he sighed.

"Tell me about it," I agreed.

"Nothing else I can trade you?" He ticked a few items off on his fingers. "Gold, goblin meat, information on Darower troop movements, magic?"

Gemma returned with Sina over her shoulder.

"Magic," I answered. "Supposedly, being human, I can learn any type of magic."

Bogore reached into his pants and scratched himself. I resolved to never shake hands with him again. "Even magic of the earth?" he asked.

Gemma set Sina down and cut her free.

"That's the theory," I said. "I've only been able to learn nature magic so far."

Bogore nodded. "Okay, you teach Gemma to cook, and she'll teach you magic of the earth?"

"What?" Sina and Gemma exclaimed at the same time.

I glanced from Gemma to Bogore as Sina massaged feeling back into her wrists. "How many spells does she know?"

"Three?" Bogore asked Gemma.

"Three," she answered cautiously. "What Wild Hunt are you roping me into, oh great Bogore the Flatulent?"

"Evan has to perform some chores for Queen Lycia. I want you to accompany him, keep him safe from elf treachery, and teach him your spells. In return, he'll teach you to cook. When you've learned everything he has to teach, come back, and share what you've learned with us." The big troll raised an eyebrow at me to see if I agreed.

Gemma jumped up and down and quivered like a schoolgirl, which was quite the image, since the troll was a head taller than me and twice as wide. "I get to learn to make food like this? Awesome! That means I get to eat a lot of it, right?"

I considered it. I'd learn three new spells and gain a powerful new protector. Daric claimed trolls were incredibly hard to kill. Downsides, she smelled like a sewer and might try to eat me. A waft of troll musk invaded my nose. Could I convince her to take a bath?

Deciding the good outweighed the bad, I stuck my hand out. "You have a deal."

It was only after we shook that I remembered where Bogore's hand had just been. With some effort, I plastered a smile on my face. "Great," I croaked.

CHAPTER 15: STRANGE COMPANY

We walked back to the tree line with me in the lead and Sina and Gemma behind me.

Gemma enthusiastically peppered me with questions. "Can I learn how to cook goats right away or are we going to work up to it? Do we start with squirrels? Because they aren't very big, and you can't make a meal out of them." Her high-pitched voice and the fact that she seemed to talk non-stop without taking a breath was impressive.

Sina glared at the troll, sparing the occasional raised eyebrow for me.

We crossed into the forest, and I shook my head. "Gemma, I'll cook dinner every night while we're traveling. What we cook will depend on what Daric catches. I'll take you through each step. How hot I'm making the fire, what spices I'll be using, which steps are important, and why. When we get back to the palace, I'll see what I can do about using their kitchen."

"Who's Daric?" she asked.

An arrow struck the ground inches from Gemma's foot.

"Elf treachery," she yelled and jumped in front of me with her spear at the ready. "Get behind me, Evan."

I sighed, then gagged as a wave of Gemma's stench hit me. "Don't hurt her, Daric," I called out. "She's coming back with us."

His voice echoed about the trees, making it hard to pinpoint his location. "Are you sunstruck? Why in all Stellaluna would we do that?"

"I learn earth magic. She learns to cook."

"Sina?" Daric's voice was somewhere closer now.

She rolled her eyes. "I think it's crazy, too, but the trolls liked his cooking. Can you blame them?"

"And the attacks?"

I jumped as Daric spoke in my ear. He'd somehow appeared behind me and had his sword pointed at the troll.

Gemma jolted and turned around. She eyed the sword, then Daric. "A sword? Really? You know that's, like, *half* a second of annoyance, right?"

"It'll still hurt," he insisted.

Gemma flipped her spear and stuck it in the ground. Crossing her arms over her chest, she frowned at the elf. "Is this going to take long? I mean, cause, the sun's going down and I'm still hungry."

The tense silence stretched out for a few minutes before Daric wrinkled his nose and lowered his sword. "Titania, help us. Can you at least convince it to take a bath?"

Gemma sniffed at her armpit. "Whadaya mean? I smell awesome."

***

We made it back to camp and Daric left to hunt for dinner. I began the lessons with Gemma by asking her to restart the campfire. Her solution was to go to the nearest sapling, uproot it, and make it into smaller chunks by breaking it over her knee before throwing it all in the firepit, starting with the root ball. This could have depressed me, but I treated it as a learning experience. Everyone has to start somewhere.

"You're wasting your time, Evan," said Sina. Apparently, it didn't matter to her that Gemma was there. "She's a troll. She'll never learn the finer nuances of cooking."

Gemma shook her head and blew on coals at the base of the kindling. The pile of sticks caught fire, and she squealed like a hamster on helium. "I did it."

"The trolls moved here to get better food, took over the bridge, fortified it, held it, and turned it into a profitable business," I pointed out. "Being tough and strong may have gotten them the bridge, but it takes smarts to keep it. If Gemma has even half the wits of Booger, I mean *Bogore*, she can learn to cook."

That earned me a dubious look from Sina.

It was dark by the time Daric returned with, you guessed it, another goat.

"If you're not going to use them, can I have the entrails?" asked Gemma.

"Ew!" exclaimed Sina.

Daric also had a look of disgust.

"Why do you want the innards?" I went a short way into the woods and buried the goat parts we weren't using. "We're making plenty of food."

"Because it's *food*," she said, like it was the most obvious thing in the world. Gemma gazed disappointedly at the spot where I buried the parts, but shrugged.

We cooked the goat and ate dinner together. Long after the elves and I had finished, Gemma was still eating. And still eating. And continued to eat.

I stared in awe as she kept going, stuffing more and more into her mouth. A quarter of the goat was in her stomach before Gemma slowed down.

"How much more are you going to have?" asked Sina.

Gemma patted her belly. "Oh, I'm done. I apologize. It's all your fault. For a scrawny human, Evan, you can really cook."

"How often do you eat, and how much do you need?" I asked. "I need to know for meal planning," I added, hoping she wouldn't take offense.

She scratched her armpit as she stared off in thought. "Um, let me think. About four times as much as you ate."

Wow. Talk about a healthy appetite.

***

Heading back was slower than the trip out. The horses couldn't carry a troll and we were short a horse, anyway. That said, the hike was pleasant, as long as Gemma was downwind. The temperature was just right and the terrain, while rocky, wasn't difficult to navigate. Then there was the crossing guarded by goblins.

"We're not going around," insisted Gemma.

"The crossing is guarded by at least dozen goblins," said Daric. "Probably more. Not a problem for you, but a big problem for us."

Gemma smiled. "For your information, there are ten goblins, and they won't be a problem."

"How do you know there are ten?" I asked.

She shrugged. "'Cause there were twelve when they crossed the bridge. They gave us two to cover the toll."

Sina gagged. "That's disgusting."

"Tell me about it," the troll stuck out her tongue. "I bet even Evan's skill couldn't make them taste good. No matter what you do, they still taste like moldy dirt. Yech."

Daric and Sina blanched.

"So, the goblins won't be a problem?" I prompted.

"Nope," she said cheerily, "I'll take care of them."

When we reached the crossing, the elves and I hid in the trees while Gemma crossed the river. This crossing was easier than the one we took. Gemma swam part of the way, but I think it was by choice. I was pretty sure the water never got above her shoulders. She reinforced this idea by standing occasionally.

When she reached the other side, she planted her spear in the ground. "Hello gobbos, it's time again to pay the troll."

"We already paid you," whined a voice from the top of the embankment. "Go away."

Gemma tsked. "Now, now, you paid us to cross the bridge. I'm talking about rent for occupying the crossing."

"What?" complained the goblin. "There's no rent for the crossing. We've been here for three weeks. Why is this the first we've heard about it?"

"We're expanding," said Gemma. "These days it's all about incorporation and acquisition. Bridges were only the beginning. The bridge trolls are branching out. Exploring new business opportunities like river crossings, mountain passes, and tunnels. If you want to build a successful business, you can't stay idle."

A goblin trotted down the hill. "That's not fair," he cried in dismay at the troll that was four times his size. "We already gave you Snot and Canker. You can't change the rules on us."

Gemma shrugged. "I'm not the chief. I'm not in charge. Bogore just sent me here to collect the fee. Send three goblins down. I'm hungry."

He gaped. "Three! That's more than the bridge toll."

She winked at the goblin. "New business venture. We've got startup costs."

"Startup costs?" His yellow eyes bulged.

"You could always refuse." Gemma smacked her lips loudly.

"You know, never mind. I can see we're not going to reach an understanding. I'm just going to eat *you*."

"Wait," he screamed as he backed up with his hands out. "We'll move to a new ambush point."

"Uh, I don't know." She shook her head. "Bogore was pretty clear. He said you have to pay, *or* you have to pay." She slammed her fist into her palm for emphasis.

He swallowed hard. "Food! Tell Bogore we weren't here. You can have all the rabbits and squirrels we've caught today."

Gemma squinted at the green-skinned runt. "*How many* rabbits and squirrels?" she asked conspiratorially.

"Five rabbits. Three squirrels."

She stepped forward. "Forget it."

"Eight rabbits. Six squirrels," he amended quickly.

Gemma cocked her head and motioned that she needed more.

"And five fish," he added weakly.

"What's your name, goblin?" she asked.

"Slimemold."

Gemma stepped up and patted the goblin none too gently. "Slimy, I can tell you're going to go far in this life. You're a real smooth operator. I like you so much, I'll let you in on a little secret."

Slimemold didn't speak so much as squeaked as Gemma's hand engulfed his head.

"The Shara elves came and visited us a few days ago. Tried to talk us out of letting you fine people into their kingdom. Can you believe that?"

"Eep!"

She shrugged. "Anyway, they avoided your little ambush by taking the crossing north of here. A smart goblin such as yourself could catch the next group that comes through, doncha think?"

The fear in Slimemold's frown was replaced by a bloodthirsty grin of greed. He smiled, showing a mouth full of brown stained teeth, and his yellow eyes almost glowed in anticipation. "Yes, oh yes. Thank you, great troll warrior. You are most generous." He ran up the hill, cackling.

After Slimemold delivered the food, Gemma waited a few minutes, then came back across the river. "See, no problem."

"How can you be sure they'll leave?" asked Sina.

The troll nodded. "I can smell them. Goblins stink. The leader called them all back and sent two runners out. Probably to gather the scouts."

I eyed her critically. "Wait, you can't find goats, but you can smell goblins at two hundred yards?"

Gemma scowled. "Trolls hunt mostly by smell. Gobbos are easy. No personal hygiene. I can't smell goats until I'm right on top of them."

Gemma's stink smelled similar to goats, but much worse.

Daric huffed. "Seriously? Can you smell anything over your own stench?"

Gemma cocked her head. "Stench? You've been complaining about my scent for days. What are you talking about?"

The elves shook their heads.

"Well, you don't smell at the moment because you just took a swim," I pointed out. "But most of the time, you're more than a little whiffy."

The troll turned serious. "Whiffy. Can you describe it?"

I thought about how best to describe the smell for a couple of moments. "It's sour, acidic, and musky all at the same time."

Gemma blushed. "You mean my perfume? You can smell that? I've been going easy on it since we left the troll bridge. You don't like it?"

Sina's mouth dropped open. "P- P- Perfume?"

The troll bit her lower lip. "Uh, yeah. You know boys. They're attracted to the smell of hard work. Girls rub herbs and aged meat on our bodies to, uh, accent our natural body odor." She gave an embarrassed shrug. "Guy trolls do the same thing."

Daric's eyes fluttered, then he stared at her with incredulity. "That putrid pungent stink we've been putting up with is... *perfume?*"

"You really don't like it?" She asked like she couldn't believe it.

I rubbed my hands over my face. "Sina, you've been using something vanilla as a deodorant, right?"

"She can't have my vanilla. It's expensive."

I sighed. "Fine. Gemma, do you like mint or rosemary?"

The troll's face screwed up in confusion. "Like to wear? Isn't that like weird or something?"

"To trolls maybe, but to humans and elves, you'll fit right in." I gave her a half smile. "When in Rome, right?"

"What?"

I pinched the bridge of my nose. "Uh, never mind."

CHAPTER 16: THE TROLL TRUTH AND NOTHING BUT THE TRUTH

After the perfume drama, Gemma chose mint as the *least weird* scent.

We waited an hour before we made the crossing. Gemma crossed first to verify that the goblins had indeed left. I felt bad that the little green monsters were about to become spider food. That was until I remembered they had intended to ambush and eat us. Then I felt okay about them joining the food chain. Which brought up another subject.

I stepped over a log and around a tree as I thought about how to phrase my question. We'd hiked for several hours, and I still couldn't think of a way to ask tactfully. In the end, I decided to just blurt it out. "Gemma, why do trolls eat other people?"

"Whadya mean?" she answered from behind me.

"I mean goblins and trolls eat other fae." I shrugged. "It seems odd."

"Humans don't eat other people?"

I glanced over my shoulder to gauge her reaction. She was frowning in confusion. "No," I said. "Elves don't eat other fae either."

She rolled her eyes. "That's not true. Darower elves will eat the hearts of their enemies. I've seen them do it."

"Okay, Shara elves don't. Is it a Darower thing?"

Gemma seemed to search the sky and leaves like the answer might be found up there. "*Maybe.* One thing's for sure, it's a lot easier to find food in the Shara Lands. You may have noticed that I eat a lot."

I nodded.

"Being a troll is awesome, but it has its downsides," she continued. "We're always hungry. In Darower, there's never enough to eat. That's why Bogore moved us to the bridge."

I mulled that over for a bit as I climbed over a rock and we started going uphill again. "Trolls regenerate really fast, don't they? Do you get hungrier when that happens?"

She nodded emphatically. "Oh, yes. Like, if a troll takes enough damage, the hunger takes over. You can't think. You lose all sense of who you are and what you're doing. It's like, the only thing that matters is eating. But it's not normally a problem. In a fight, you stop and eat your enemies. Problem solved. Unless, like, some clever dragon burns you to a crisp or someone poisons you. Some things are harder to bounce back from, ya know?"

I nodded. That made sense. Trolls must need a lot of calories to fuel their regeneration. If it was always cold in Darower, they probably had a short growing season. If food was scarce, you'd eat whatever you could.

Gemma walked next to me and lowered her voice. "Hey, Evan?"

"Yeah."

"So, like, I don't cast healing magic. Troll, you know, we just do it. But I've seen you working with Daric. It seems like you're struggling with the spell."

I grunted as I eyed Daric and Sina twenty yards ahead of us. Daric had been trying to teach healing magic to me for days, and I wasn't any better off than when I started.

"Well, you didn't hear it from me, but I think he totally skipped a step."

I thought about that. It would be just like Daric to teach me something, but do it badly. He'd adhere to the letter of the agreement, but not the spirit. But wouldn't Sina have said something? Maybe not, if she considered it a deal between me and Daric.

"What makes you say that?" I asked.

"You've got a good start on the Meld with Earth spell, the one I used to sneak up on Sina. The next spell is Stone Skin. It seems to me that this healing magic works kinda the same way. Like, Daric keeps telling you to pour energy into the wound. I don't think that's right. To me, it seems like you should totally cover the wound in layers."

"I don't get it. Energy layers?"

"It's like digging a hole, but like, the opposite. You've got dirt on top, mud halfway down, then rock under that. Except, in this case, you're digging the hole in reverse. Or filling it... But with the correct stuff..." She grimaced. "Okay, I'm totally explaining this badly."

I got where she was going. I decided the analogy that more favored my mind was a layer cake. You could fail spectacularly by just throwing all the ingredients in the oven. If you put it together in stages, you could make a delicious cake.

"Thanks, Gemma," I whispered. "I'll give that a try."

We entered the clearing we'd used as a campsite on the way out a little earlier than expected. We stopped for the day, anyway.

Daric went hunting while Sina and I sparred. Gemma shouted encouragement for me.

"You can do it, Evan! Split her head open," cried Gemma.

I kept my eye on Sina's hands and feet to better predict her movements. "You know she's won every bout this afternoon, right?"

"The winds are totally shifting in your favor. I can feel it," Gemma said with a grin.

"You're pretty good, Evan," Sina said through breaths. At least I was giving her a workout. "You're tricky when you feint at hitting my hand, then go for my shoulder."

"What can I say?" I gave her a wink. "I'm a cut above the rest."

I got my first touch when she groaned theatrically.

"Oh, so that's how it's going to be," she scolded.

"Got to get my point across any way I can." I gave her a cheesy grin.

She shook her blade at me. "Okay, you're done."

With a dramatic sweep of my arm, I sheathed my sword. "And with that I blade you goodnight."

Daric arrived with a quartet of rabbits. "I'm glad your cooking is better than your sense of humor."

During the hike today, I'd found some wild garlic, so dinner tonight what going to be something. Gemma paid rapt attention to everything I did.

Later, I finally healed my collection of nicks and cuts. The forced smile Daric gave me with his congratulations was worth a Golden Razzie award.

I had a dream about Sina that night. Except Sina was a dog. Daric and Dog-Sina were playing fetch, but he wouldn't throw it most of the time. He'd make the throwing motion but hide the stick behind his back and laughed. Dog-Sina went searching for the non-existent stick.

I don't know how long I watched, but eventually, I couldn't stand it. I grabbed the stick away from Daric and gave it to Sina. Daric didn't care and wandered off. Dog-Sina gave me a big doggie grin and played tug-o-war with me. She was stronger than any normal dog and easily pulled me down. I laughed as we rolled on the ground together. Dog-Sina pinned me down and licked me with her big sloppy tongue, getting my eyes, nose, and eating my hair.

So, imagine my surprise when I woke up to something *actually* eating my hair.

"Wha- didja- huh?" Startled, I flailed and tried to roll. But I hit a horse's leg. Horse leg?

The horse leaned in for another nibble.

"Ahhhh!" I scrambled backward and jumped to my feet.

Across the clearing, Daric, Sina, and Gemma burst into gales of laughter. Sina wiped away tears as Daric smirked. Gemma slapped her knee, eyes squeezed shut in mirth.

I stared in confusion at them, then at the horse... My horse. Nonam.

In my sleep-addled brain, something clicked.

"Nonam!" I rushed forward and wrapped my arms around her neck. My horse found her way back. "Good to see you, girl."

"About time you got up, human," needled Daric.

Sina came up beside me and rubbed Nonam's nose. "She walked right into camp and straight to you. You made a good impression on her."

I smiled at Sina as I replied. "She made a good impression on me, too."

Sina winked at me before retreating to her blankets to clean up.

"You see that Nonam," I whispered in my horse's ear, "I think I made a good impression on her, too."

***

We arrived back at the palace, and for once, I was not the center of attention. Apparently green-skinned giant beat round-eared wonder. Who knew?

Daric, Sina, Gemma, and I stabled the horses, then went around to the huge oak doors at the main palace entry. The elven guards ogled the troll.

Next task: get into the palace with Gemma. I expected the elves to regard trolls as monsters. I was horrified that they might make Gemma wait back in the stables or something equally degrading.

Daric tried to take charge, but I stepped in front of him. "Gentlemen, we've returned from our trip to the northern border. Please let the queen know of our arrival and that we'll deliver our report at her convenience."

Daric glared at me. I grinned back at him.

The guard on the right shuffled nervously. "Uh, the troll can't come into the palace."

I narrowed my eyes at him. "Are you telling me an ambassador from our newest allies in the fight against the Darower isn't allowed in the palace? Are you afraid she'll pee on the tapestries or something?"

"Allies?" The elf's eyes went from me, to Gemma, to Sina, and then to Daric. I got the feeling that's exactly what he thought might happen, but he wouldn't dare say so in front of the impressively built troll. Gemma towered over him with arms crossed over her chest.

Daric was about to speak up, but Sina stepped forward. "The negotiations were unconventional, but Evan did strike a deal with the trolls."

"Hence, the report I'm anxious to give the queen," I said.

Daric fumed.

"Can you... wait just a moment?" asked the sentry.

The other guard stared wide-eyed at his companion as if to say, *you're not leaving me here with a troll?!*

The lead guard disappeared inside.

"You're sure the queen sanctioned this mission?" asked Gemma.

"Oh, yes," I assured her. "I received the request from the queen herself, but she left the details up to me."

"What do you get out of it?" whispered Gemma.

"Three quests, and I get to go home." I gazed up at her. "Peace with the trolls was the first quest."

She frowned with concern. "What's the next quest? Stop the sun from setting? Conquer three kingdoms?"

I sighed. "Don't give her any ideas."

The guard returned. "The queen is busy, but she is eager to hear of your travels. She requests you and your entourage to wait in the solarium."

The guard led us inside. Daric and Sina strode ahead with confidence, but Gemma held back a bit. I hung back with her.

"What's wrong, Gemma?"

She swallowed nervously. "Nothing. It's just that I've never been in a building this big before. It's a little intimidating."

I laughed. "Gemma, I can't imagine anything intimidating you."

She smiled weakly. "I'm tough, sure, but I'm not invincible. There are *a lot* of elves here, and only one of me. They're sneaky."

I bumped her shoulder with mine. Well, more like her elbow with my shoulder. "You guard my body and let me deal with the politics. Between us, we can handle whatever they dish out."

"Okay."

I gave a friendly shrug. "And there's another human here. I'll introduce you."

The solarium turned out to be a waiting room with a mossy floor. It had a fancy wood table with surprisingly comfortable chairs. None of them were Gemma sized, so she leaned against a wall. Light came from a stained-glass window. Magic light, not sunlight, but a nice touch. I judged we were pretty close to the middle of the immense palace. They had laid a meat and cheese tray out for us. Gemma sniffed twice at it before pronouncing it safe, and dug in.

"Is this normal?" I asked.

"What, you think the queen of an entire nation is just waiting for you to waltz in, so she can drop everything and speak to *you?*" Daric sneered.

Sina rolled her eyes. "The queen usually sees her minsters around this time of day. I'm sure we caught her at the end of the meeting."

"And the lords in a little more than an hour," said Daric with an air of superiority. "I hope I'll have time to wash up."

An hour went by. I managed to get some of the food without

losing a finger to Gemma.

I noticed Daric and Sina looking at the door, so I turned to follow their gaze. Flick stood there, slack-jawed.

Walking over to him, I gave him a playful punch on the shoulder. "Hey Flick, how is the old lady?"

His mouth closed with a clack and his head whipped to me. "What?"

"The queen. Is she ready for us?"

He blinked. "Queen? Oh. Yes!" He returned his attention to Gemma and swallowed. "Uh. If you all will follow me."

Flick led us to the audience chamber. This time, six guardsmen flanked the throne. So, that's what took so long.

Queen Lycia leaned forward. "Evan, I'm surprised to see you... so... soon." Her tone suggested that she hadn't expected to see me at all. So much for having the crown's confidence.

I gave an exaggerated grin. "It turns out the problem wasn't as bad as I was led to believe. Let me give you the highlights."

I gave her a summary of events.

"Goats?" she asked.

"Goats. As long as your hunters provide twelve a week, the trolls will close the bridge to the Darower."

She frowned in confusion. "You made a deal for food? And they accepted it?"

"Everybody has to eat," I said. "It holds doubly true for trolls."

The queen's gaze traveled to Gemma. "And they sent an ambassador?"

"More like a bodyguard," I explained.

"The trolls have agreed to work with us, Your Majesty," said Sina, "but trust in the crown has not yet been earned. They sent a bodyguard for Evan. They do trust *him*."

The queen arched a regal eyebrow at me.

I shrugged happily. "It turns out the way to win hearts and minds of trolls is through the stomach."

Queen Lycia was silent for a long moment before speaking again. "We'll send hunters and a family of herders to the northern border. The deal you've struck on behalf of the crown is a good one, and we will honor it."

I bounced on my toes. "Excellent, Your Majesty. What is your next quest for me?"

"I'm afraid you're a victim of your own good fortune, young

human." The queen smiled playfully. "I don't have a new quest for you just yet."

My mind spun out of control as I agonized over this new wrinkle. The queen had to provide me with new quests, but there wasn't a time limit. I might never see my grandmother again. Never see my dad. The queen could keep me waiting indefinitely for the next quest.

The fact that she would even consider doing something like that triggered something. I'm not sure what came over me, but anger swelled up inside me like a wellspring of lava.

Daric looked smug. Sina gave me a small shake of her head.

My patience was gone. I clenched my teeth so hard it hurt. I'd had it and I was going to tell the monarch exactly what I thought of her. It was a good thing Daric and the guards were there, because I was seriously considering regicide.

CHAPTER 17: NOT MY DOG

My fingernails dug into my palms as I struggled to contain my rage.

"Just a moment." Queen Lycia addressed the room at large. "Clear the audience chamber. Evan and I need to have a private discussion."

The guardsmen moved immediately to obey. Sina and Daric gathered Gemma.

Sina spoke to the troll. "Come with me, Gemma. He isn't in danger. He's done very well in negotiations with the queen."

The troll hesitated.

"I'll show you the kitchens," offered Sina.

Gemma licked her lips and rubbed her hands together as she followed the elves out of the room.

I seethed, but waited until the big oak doors closed before I let my frustration loose.

"You think this is a game?" I yelled. "This is my life. I'm not an elf. I don't get an eternity to spend with the people I care about. Every minute I spend in this cursed place, my world ages. People I love might die before I ever get back."

The queen grew somber as she stepped off her dais and approached me. She took my hands in hers. "Evan, be reasonable."

I stared daggers at her. "Oh, I've been reasonable. More than. I've had just about enough of being reasonable."

She closed her eyes and nodded. "I'm sorry. I know I'm coming across as being callous, but I assure you, I have every intention of acting in good faith." She took a deep breath. "I made a grievous error in judgement with Geezer and ruined our friendship beyond repair. But I'd like to think that I don't repeat my mistakes. Humans are not elves. Neither of you considers yourselves my subjects, and you're both fiercely independent." She gently pulled my hand. "Come, I want to share something with you."

I didn't budge. A few kind words were not enough to shake my realization that she was a master manipulator and that she'd had centuries of practice.

She kept her eyes downcast. "I know you don't trust me, and I haven't given you much reason to. But please, come sit with me."

"I'm not your dog," I snarled.

"No, you're the man who saved many of my people from death at the hands of our adversaries. The least I can do is give you an explanation."

I let her lead me back to the dais. We sat on the steps together.

"Evan, the spell you'll earn has great potential to be abused. It is a tremendous gift."

I shook my head. "Then why offer it to me at all? You could send me back right now and be done with it."

"Because that wouldn't be the end of it, Evan," she explained. "No one brought you to Stellaluna. You brought yourself. If you did it once, you can do it again."

"I didn't do anything," I insisted. "It just happened."

She smiled. "Nothing like that just happens." Lycia shook her head. "Regardless, I believe you're a good person. I want us to be friends. That means trust, and it works both ways."

I squinted at her.

"So, these tasks, these quests, are a way of building that trust. It means I have to think very hard about them before I give them to you." She caught my eyes with hers. "I won't draw it out. I promise. Give me a couple of days to decide which of the problems that face my people are the right ones for you to solve. The ones that will prove that trust I'm giving you is not misplaced."

"A couple of days?" I asked skeptically.

"Three at most, and I promise to have the third quest ready by the time you get back."

I nodded and stood.

The queen continued to hold my hand. She gazed up at me. "Remember, the things that happen in this room are theater. I rule this kingdom, but that power comes with expectations. Whatever I might say in here, my goal is for us to be allies."

Which was not the same as saying that we had the *same* goals. "Two days."

"Or three," she added.

"Two days," I reiterated. I'd already lost two and a half weeks.

***

"Where are we going?" asked Gemma.

The paintings and tapestries in the hallway depicted battle scenes or momentous events. Gemma and I passed the third set of busts of aloof elves looking down on us as if we owed them something. I'm sure they were important, but I never asked. The shadows shifted, as if the light source couldn't decide on where it wanted to be.

"We're heading to my apartment." I was having trouble collecting my thoughts. My conversation with the queen had riled me up, and I was having trouble shaking it.

She cocked her head at me. "You live here?"

"For the moment." I stopped and imagined a waterfall washing all the anger and frustration out of me. That worked a little, and we continued.

Her gaze roamed over the carvings and intricate tapestries. "Where am I staying?"

I sighed. "With me. I tried to get you your own space, but the queen shot it down. My deal with her doesn't include companions. Since you're my bodyguard, that means you stay with me."

Gemma skipped and did a twirl with her arms outstretched, nearly knocking over a bust and forcing me to duck as her arm sailed over my head. "We're bunkmates! Don't worry, as you know, I don't snore, and I'll be fine as long as have some straw and a blanket."

"I'm hoping we can do a little better than that."

At my door, we found Flick leaning against the wall.

"Hey, Flick," I called, and he jolted to attention.

"Hello, Mr. Evan." The teenage elf glanced nervously at the troll before returning his attention to me. He cleared his throat. "Mr. Geezer would like the pleasure of your company as soon as you've settled in."

"Thanks, Flick. Hey, can you get us a cot or something for

Gemma? She'll be staying in my rooms, but I'd like to give her something other than the couch to sleep on."

He looked from her to me. "Uh, aren't you afraid she'll eat you, sir?"

I winked at Gemma. "Huh. You know, perhaps you can bring up some food. I can leave it outside my bedroom door in case she gets hungry in the middle of the night."

His eyes grew to the size of saucers, and I burst out laughing. I wiped away tears. "It'll be fine Flick. She won't bite, I promise."

Gemma licked the side of my face and Flick squealed.

"Ew." I rubbed the saliva from my cheek.

Gemma burst into chortles, and I joined her.

"You're really not going to eat Mr. Evan?"

"I've totally taken an oath to protect him. He's safe for the moment." Then she got a wild look in her eye, "But elves are still on the menu," and she snapped her teeth at Flick.

Flick jumped, but then grinned nervously as he realized we were playing with him. "Okay, I think I saw a large cot in the storeroom near the barracks."

We entered my rooms, and I watched as Gemma gaped at the space. "This is all yours?"

I smiled as she bounced on the couch and rubbed the velvet drapes between her fingers. "My home away from home," I said.

"This place is awesome."

That brought up memories of my house near San Antonio. "Yeah, but it's not Earth. I wish I could show it to you."

"Your home on Earth is even better than this?" she asked with incredulity.

Which reminded me of my cobwebby basement closet. "Uh, no. This is about a hundred times better. But it's home, you know?"

"Maybe, but this sure beats a drafty hut over a river gorge."

I shrugged. "Speaking of which, let me show you how to use the bathroom."

"Water? Indoors? No way! This place is way awesome." Her eyes swept around the room.

I took her over to the bathtub. "Okay, touch the spout and say 'water on'."

"Water on." She jumped as water spilled from the golden spigot into the tub. She put her hand under the running water. "That is so cool!"

I grinned at her excitement. "It is, so touch the spout again and say 'hotter' or 'colder'."

She did. "Hotter, hotter, hotter, colder. Hot, cold, hot, cold, hot, cold." She squealed in girlish delight.

"Alright, yell if you need anything."

"Thanks, Evan. You're the best." She wrapped me in a bear hug, then danced and gyrated next to the tub. "Oh, yeah. Hot water. Uh, huh."

I shut the door and left her to it.

Knowing that Geezer would ask how far I'd gotten with my magic studies, I took an inventory of everything I'd learned in the past three weeks. Locate Plants, Heal Wounds, and Meld with Stone.

The last one was really more like a camouflage spell. I became *one with the dirt,* which was more like convincing the ground that I belonged there. It took on a stretchy quality and covered me in a half-inch of whatever soil or rock was nearby. It gave me no protection from being stabbed, though, which I guess made sense since I could breathe and see through it.

I was still working on the Stone Skin spell but hadn't gotten it to work. I think that my main problem was how it felt. The sensation of the clay-like shell forming around my body tingled in a way that was hard to describe. It made it hard to concentrate.

A knock on the door interrupted my thoughts. I opened it to find Sina at which point all thinking stopped. Because Sina was in a *dress.* And by dress, I mean bare shoulders, plunging neckline, flowy skirt, and totally dog-darned distracting in every possible way dress. My breath left, and I had no assurances it would ever come back.

CHAPTER 18: UNEXPECTED GUESTS

Sina slipped gracefully past me, and my heart skipped several beats.

I mentally slapped myself. As attractive as she was, Sina was engaged to Daric.

"Am I interrupting anything?" she asked with a musical lilt.

"No. Please, come in." Well, she was already in, but it seemed like the thing to say.

"I never got the chance to thank you properly for saving my life at the bridge." Sina crossed the room and set a pair of boots next to a low table. She sat down on my couch, making herself at home.

"The boots are for me?"

She winked. "Yes, try them on."

Was she flirting with me?

I sat at the other end of the couch. As far away as possible and not appear rude. "Great. So, what do I need to do for the boots?"

Sina nudged the boots with her foot. "Nothing, they're a gift. No strings attached."

I arched an eyebrow.

Her cheeks reddened, and she turned away. "You know my secret. I'm not a full elf. I'm trying something different."

"Different?" I prompted.

She sighed. "Mom wants me to hide my human heritage. She believes other elves will look down on me for being part human, and she's right." Sina seemed determined to tie her fingers in knots. "There are a lot more people like Daric than not. People who believe elves are the most powerful race in all Stellaluna. That all other races should serve us."

99

That made sense to me. It must be something like being proud to be a Texan. "So, making peace with your human side means... boots?"

"You'll probably think it's silly, since you're not an elf." She gave me a half-smile. "But the thrust of it is giving you a gift and expecting nothing in return."

Because outside of family, elves are expected to trade things of equal value, I realized. "Thank you. I accept your gift."

I pulled off my sneakers and winced a little at the funky smell from the socks. They hadn't been cleaned since the river crossing. "Sorry. I'll clean them when I take a bath."

"You can ask the servants to clean them for you." She beamed at me. "You live in the palace. It's one of the perks."

"How do I ask them to do my laundry?" I asked.

"Same way you summon Flick, the little bell by the door." Sina pointed at a shelf next to the door. I knew the bell was there but hadn't figured out what it did. "It's magic. Ring it and someone will show up. Usually within five minutes or so."

"Good to know. Speaking of good things to know, while giving a gift in return is not required, we consider it polite." I thought about my meager possessions, which didn't amount to much. Then I realized I did have something to offer. "Hey, elves like sweet things, right?"

"Yes," she answered cautiously.

"Here." I reached around to the end table where I stored my Earth things. They had enchanted it so that only I could open it. I took out one piece of chocolate and put it in her hand.

"What is it? It feels like paper with something hard inside."

"It's chocolate. The stuff on the outside is a wrapper to protect it until you're ready to eat it."

Sina held it gingerly. "An artifact from across the great divide. I'll save it for a special occasion."

"Well, it's food," I laughed at her reverence. "So, don't save it too long. It'll eventually go bad."

Sina leaned in and kissed me. Our lips met and my head spun. The room was too hot. The kiss was sweet and tender, and I wanted it to go on forever. Even better, like when we did magic together, I could feel that she enjoyed it, too. It was longer than a friendly thank you kind of kiss.

I hadn't been this happy since I got here. It was like a whole new, wonderful kind of magic. Reluctantly, I separated my lips from hers and took a breath to steady myself. When I could trust myself with words, I said, "Wow. That was great, but... aren't you engaged?"

She smirked. "You've met Daric. Do you honestly think I'd be marrying him if I had a choice in the matter?"

"An arranged marriage?"

"Yes. His parents and my mom want to strengthen our families." She tilted her head. "Humans have arranged unions. Geezer told me so."

I blinked. "They do, but it's rare. No one I know has one."

"Geezer lied to me?"

"No. It happens, but mostly with rich or people in faraway countries." I shrugged. "Sounds like something the queen would do."

Sina glared at me. "What's that supposed to mean?"

I held up my hands. "Nothing, it's just that she's all about the deal. Anything to get what she wants." What had gotten her hackles up?

She squinted at me. "I can't expect you to understand, but everything she does, every deal she makes, is for the betterment of elves everywhere."

I probably should have let it drop, but I couldn't help myself. "Gnomes, felion, dryads, pooka? More people live within the kingdom's borders than just elves. Are her deals fair for Geezer? For me?"

"That's not the same thing," she slapped the chocolate down on the table. "She's the queen of the elves. Not the queen of the gnomes." Behind her, a sprite peeked over the edge of the couch. The glowing miniature fae had its eyes riveted on the sweet.

I ignored the winged pest and focused on Sina. "How is it different if they live in her lands?"

"Because there's a king of the gnomes, a king of the felion," she pointed out. "Their lands are to the east of here. They don't *have* to live here." I was reminded that elves viewed them as pests as the sprite creeped toward the table on the floor.

I nodded. "So, what happens when someone other than an elf runs afoul of the law?"

Sina waved in dismissal. "They get deported."

"And nobody cares what happens to a non-elf fae?" I shook my head. "The life they've built in this kingdom is ruined. They have to move their family to a new place and start over?" The sprite reached for the candy on the table. "You're about to lose your chocolate."

Sina jumped and slapped the table in front of the sprite. It squealed and flew off to a corner of the room.

She closed her eyes. "I'm sorry, Evan. I didn't come here to argue with you."

"Did you have a reason other than the boots?"

Sina stared at her hands and flexed her fingers a few times. "I wanted to get to know you better. And..."

I sighed. Not at Sina, but at the three sprites that appeared behind furniture about the room. The rumors that the palace had a sprite infestation were true.

Sina looked me in the face, probably misunderstanding the sigh. "I want to get to know you better. You're different from everyone else I know. In a good way. You've got these ideas about right and wrong that don't mesh with what I've been taught to believe. And... I'd like you to teach me magic."

"What?"

"Other magic. The stuff Gemma is teaching you." Sina begged for help with her eyes. "Listen, Dad can't teach me anything, because Mom won't let him. I wanted to ask you on the way back, but Daric was there, and he can't know. You're learning *different* magic, and I want to know if it's possible for me to learn it, too."

I chewed my lip. This was a new wrinkle. Teaching Sina magic would get me close to her, which would be awesome. And speaking of new wrinkles, what was up with all the sprites? They were sneaking up on the table again.

"This isn't a deal for the boots. You can say no, and I won't be offended or anything. I just..." she trailed off.

I pointed around the room and mouthed the word *sprites*.

Sina flushed and yelled at the winged pests. "Back off! This is my food, and you can't have it." She ripped the foil off and shoved the chocolate into her mouth.

She blinked in surprise. "Wow, chocolate is great!" Sina said as she chewed.

The sprites gaped at her.

Sina closed her eyes and savored every moment of the otherworldly sweet. After a long moment, she reluctantly swallowed. "That was amaze-wings. Can I do something to get more?"

I didn't have time to think of anything, as her expression changed from excitement to horror.

"Oh no, I'm going to-"

Brrrraaap!

A thick green fog erupted from under her dress. Being on the couch did nothing to slow it down. It filled the space around her for a dozen feet in every direction. And it stank. Really stank. Ten times worse than the port-a-potties at the state fair kind of stink. I struggled not to lose my lunch as I scrambled out of the foul-smelling cloud.

"Oh, sweet Titania. Make it stop." Sina exclaimed.

At that moment, Gemma stepped out of the bathroom, clutching a towel two sizes too small to her front. "Hey Evan, where do you keep the- Oh, wow. What's that amazing smell?"

Sina's mouth fell open. Eyes wide, she took in Gemma's nearly naked form. Her gaze shifted to me. Before I could say a word, she bolted from the room.

CHAPTER 19: GO SPRITE OR GO SPLEFT

I wanted to chase after Sina, but I stopped. Not only did I not know what to say, but I didn't know where to begin. How had everything spiraled out of control so fast? Was I obligated to turn her down because she was engaged to Daric? I mean, she was great and treated me nice from the beginning, but I was going back to Earth. She couldn't follow. But she was cute and strong, great with a bow and a sword, with those blonde curls and green eyes I could get lost in for days...

"Uh, hey. Do you have any more towels?" Water dripped from Gemma where she stood in the middle of the room. The arm covered more than the terrycloth. She stood tall and unashamed of her body.

Realizing I was staring, I shook my head to clear it and crossed to the closet. "I'm sorry, Gemma. I should have thought of that before you took a bath." I returned with three large towels, then faced the far wall.

"You totally can't trust her, you know."

"Because she's an elf?" I asked as I took a few steps to the left to stay out of the expanding green cloud. I kept my back to the washroom.

"Yeah. Like, they have that odd can't lie thing going on, but that only teaches them to be sneakier with words." Her voice took on an echo-like quality as she went into the bathroom. "Elves are born cheats and only get better at it with age. They don't know how to be any other way. You have to treat them like men. Show enough to keep them interested, but cover the important stuff."

I could easily see where trolls could justify that opinion. Which begged the question: was Sina more human or more elf? Not that I could bounce that off Gemma. "She's the only elf to ever be straight with me. I'd like to believe that she's better than the rest."

"That's going to make it harder to protect you. If you let that girl twist you in knots, you won't be able to cut yourself loose when she betrays you." She came up behind me and licked my face again.

I jumped. "Ew. Do you have to keep doing that?"

She grinned. "Because it annoys you, and you taste awesome. Like roast sheep with toe jam jelly."

I rolled my eyes and glared half-heartedly at her.

"Well, you do!" Gemma punched me lightly in the arm. "Go get washed up and let's go meet this Geezer I've heard so much about. While you do, I'll find the source of this amazing smell."

***

Gemma followed me to Geezer's apartment. I had my hand raised to knock when the door opened.

"Holy troll, they weren't kidding. Kid, I gotta hand it to you, you've got a solid brass pair for sure."

Remembering the rough lessons of a couple of weeks ago, I kept my eye on his hands and feet. "Yeah, let's not test that theory."

"Ha!" He swung. I moved to block and found Gemma's arm in the way... holding Geezer's wrist.

"No touchy the Evan," she said.

"But-" he protested.

"No touchy." The troll waved a finger back and forth.

"He's my-" he started.

"No... touchy..."

Geezer eyed her grip on his wrist, then gazed up at her. "Girly, I can burn you to the ground."

Gemma smiled brightly. "Not before I totally break your arms and legs and feast on your entrails."

"Ha, ha!" Geezer said something I didn't catch and slid his wrist from her grasp. "You did good, son." He turned, leaving the door open.

Gemma grimaced as slime dripped from her hand. "Grody, I just took a bath." She wiped her palms on her pant leg.

The old wizard ignored her. "Come in, boy. Show me what

you've got."

We sat on a couch as I demonstrated the three spells I knew. When I cast the find plants spell, I discovered Geezer kept his herbs in his lab instead of his kitchen.

"I'm not much for cookin'," he said. "I can make a few breakfasty things, but by and large, you'll be better off if anyone but me is makin' the food. I use a few herbs and spices for potions. Some are magic, others just make the god-awful things taste better."

"Potions?" I asked.

"Yeah, it's a hobby of mine." He ambled over to his lab table and popped open a drawer. He pulled out a vial of red liquid with glowy bits in it. He tossed it at me, then threw four more in quick succession.

I bobbled the first one, caught the second, the third, fourth, and fifth hit the ground. Thankfully, they bounced and rolled about but didn't break.

"Healing potions, speed potions, potions that make you strong, ones that make you weak. They're useful in a pinch, especially if you're knackered from casting other stuff."

I collected two of the vials from the floor.

Gemma held the third vial between two fingers. The glittery blue liquid swirled as if somehow alive. "Ooh. Pretty! How do you know which one does what?"

"There's a label on the side that tells you what they do," said Geezer. "Though they have some odd side effects."

Gemma handed me the potion. "Side effects?"

"Changing skin color, music from nowhere, briefly becoming a turnip, that sort of thing." Geezer's face lit with maniacal glee. "Nothing serious, but darn funny to watch."

I held up the red glowy vial. "Can I keep the healing potion?"

"Sure, son," said Geezer. "Can never have enough healin'."

I handed the rest of the potions back. "Speaking of funny to watch, I'll be here for a couple of days. Are there any spells I can learn in that time? You and Gemma can laugh your heads off as I try to get it to work."

Geezer chortled. "Yeah, there's one thing you can learn in a day or two. You may have noticed that the castle is infested with sprites. The little bastards are everywhere, eating your snacks and misplacing your stuff."

"Oh, yes." I remembered the sprites trying to steal Sina's chocolate.

"Anything you keep on your body is fine, but anti-pest enchanters make a killing around here. Really, sprites are more curious than mischievous. Kinda like untrained puppies or kittens. The enchanters use a spell to ward cabinets and nightstands and such." Geezer gave a wide grin, which caused his whiskers to stick out at crazy angles. "Yours truly, figured out a way to make 'em useful. Attract them and give 'em odd jobs. Not much, 'cause they can only lift a few ounces, and they have the attention span of a hummingbird. With the right incentive, you can get them to carry messages, small objects, and do this and that."

"And I can send you messages if I need to," I said, nodding.

"I wanna learn how to summon sprites." Gemma bounced on her toes.

"You're welcome to try, Darlin'," said the wizard, "but it's nature magic. Your earth magic won't power the spell."

"That's no fair," said Gemma. "How do you and Evan get to do everyone else's magic and we only get one type?"

Geezer tsked. "Ain't your fault, Darlin'. To hear the elves explain it, the gods Sume and Ugra created Stellaluna and gave all the beings their own magic. They gave humans the ability to learn it all so they could act as teachers and mediators. It was a disaster. Humans sucked at keeping the peace and created a whole passel of problems. Wars, famine, and worse. So, they asked the goddess Fifta to create a new world for the humans and send them there."

Gemma screwed up her face in disbelief. "The cat goddess? You believe that?"

"Naw, I think the magic power comes from ducks," he said.

"Ducks?" asked Gemma.

Geezer waddled in a circle, flapping his elbows. "Oh, yeah. Ducks. They fly north and south, east and west. They walk on land, fly through the air, and swim in the water. Magic power ebbs and flows with the seasons because ducks migrate. When they're around, more magic. When they're not around, magic drought."

Gemma's mouth dropped open.

"Aren't I right, Evan?" he asked.

I saw the twinkle in his eye and knew he was having her on.

"Honestly, I thought it was chickens," I said earnestly. "Eggs are powerful magic. But you might be right. Ducks make a bit more sense. They lay eggs, too."

"Eggs?" Gemma looked from me to Geezer and back again.

We held it together for half a second more, then burst out in snickers.

"You slimewads," she yelled and punched me in the shoulder.

I fell to the ground, rubbing my shoulder and howling with laughter.

Geezer was bent over, holding his stomach, tittering as he shook a finger at me. His shoulders jiggled.

Gemma put her hands on her hips and shook her head. "You totally got me with ducks. Unbelievable."

I slapped my knee a few times, then climbed to my feet. "Whew. Okay, let's learn to summon sprites."

Geezer went over the outline of the spell. Unlike the other magics I'd learned, this one required me to bait the sprite with a sugar cube. That took me back to the recent event in my apartment.

"Geezer," I said cautiously, "I gave Sina a piece of chocolate."

"Chocolate? From Earth?" He looked me in the eye. "Holy turd balls son, what happened?"

"Sprites tried to steal it."

He grunted. "Attracted to the sugar, no doubt. Sugar from across the divide must be like catnip. Go on."

"The sprites kept trying," I winced. "So, she ate it."

"Didn't I tell you Earth food has odd effects on the fae?"

"Yeah, well, I forgot. Sorry."

"What happened?" he asked.

"She, ah, farted."

He blew out a relieved breath. "Oh, is that all?"

"Oh, that's not all," said Gemma with a grin. "That dainty elf left a huge green cloud that smelled like outhouse and week dead goblin all rolled into one." She sighed. "Ambrosia."

Geezer blinked at Gemma, then turned to me.

I nodded.

"Evan, can you give me one of your chocolates? I wanna try somethin'."

"Sure." I handed him a square from my pouch.

Geezer cut it into quarters, drew a geometric pattern on the floor, and placed a small piece of chocolate in the center. He put a finger on the pattern and it glowed silver.

Immediately, three sprites converged on the circular pattern. The one with the shiny blue wing pattern I remembered from my second day in Stellaluna, got there first.

Blueberry held the piece of brown candy aloft and stuck its tongue out at the other two sprites. "Too slow, suckers. Okay, Old Fart, what do you want for this?"

Geezer rolled his hand a couple of times. "Call it a gift."

"Pffft. Whatever. Your loss." Blueberry waved the chocolate at the other sprites, then shoved it in its mouth. "Ooh! This is tasty! Thanks, Old Fart!"

Two seconds later, the sprite's eyes bugged out. "Uh, oh." The tiny androgynous fairy became a winged ball the size of a cantaloupe in the blink of an eye, then fired itself into the ceiling like a bottle rocket complete with light and sound effects leaving behind a three-foot diameter green cloud. *Feeeewiiip! Pop!*

"Oooohhh. I don't feel so good," Blueberry said weakly as it flew erratically and plopped on a nearby table. It lay breathing, but clearly dazed.

Gemma stepped up to the cloud and took a deep breath, sighing contentedly.

Geezer covered his nose and mouth and turned as green as the cloud. "I take it back. Way worse than turd balls." He moved to the table and nudged Blueberry with a finger. The sprite moaned but didn't seem like it was about to die. "Who's the crusty butt nugget now, Blueberry? You winged dickless bastard, serves you right for putting peanut butter and jelly in my favorite bunny slippers."

The sprite mumbled something I couldn't make out.

"What was that?" Geezer yelled, inches from the tiny fairy. "I couldn't quite hear you. Must be all that crow yer eatin'."

The spite's eyes squeezed shut. "I said screw you and the squirrel you rode in on, you shriveled up prune!" Blueberry shouted, before curling back into a moaning ball.

Geezer cackled and showed me the remaining chocolate. "I'm keepin' the rest of this, if you don't mind. A week from now, Blueberry will have forgotten all about this. I'll need somethin' to get him back for dumping a shaker of salt on my breakfast and puttin' tacks in my chair."

Gemma tilted her head. "But you just said you know the repel pests spell. Why not protect your things?"

"What'd be the fun in that?" asked Geezer. The wizard drew

the pattern on the ground again and put a sugar cube in it. The remaining two sprites edged up to the circle cautiously.

"Come on, Thistle," encouraged Geezer. "I need you to go ask Sina how she's doin'. Wait for her reply, then come back and tell me *exactly* what she said."

A sprite with green and purple tinted wings lowered its head and gazed up at the wizard.

"Simple message job. You've done it for me a hundred times before," assured the old man. "You've got nothing to worry about unless you're the one who put the orange dye in my soap."

Thistle grinned and made a rude gesture at the third sprite. It saluted and zipped toward the door.

Curious, I watched it go up to the door and poof out of existence in a shower of sparks.

I jerked my thumb. "Did it just...?"

"Yeah, it's the darnedest thing," he said. "The little bastards can pop short distances. Which is why sprite-swatters never caught on. A fly will stay put long enough to get clobbered. Even if you guess which way a sprite will pop, the little pests are tough. It takes several good whacks to put 'em down."

"Wouldn't that be like running over a cat or shooting a dog?" I asked.

"Son," he said, "do you think for a moment that would stop someone like Daric?"

I snorted. "How did Sina end up with Daric?"

He shrugged. "Arranged marriage. It was all her mom's doing. At that level, there ain't a lot of options."

"Not a lot of options?" I asked. "Her mom is someone important, then?"

Geezer squinted at me. "She didn't tell you?" Then he shrugged. "That figures. She keeps it secret so as not to attract attention." Geezer glanced at Gemma before continuing. "Yeah, I'm not allowed to tell you who, but her mom is important. You've met her."

But the only one I've... My insides turned to jelly. I'd seen a lot of men and women elves in the kingdom, but I'd only *met* one other female elf. *The queen.* Which made Sina, *The Princess.* Which meant that I really couldn't tell anyone who she really was for a whole lot of reasons.

I facepalmed hard and groaned. And I'd said a lot of not nice things about the queen earlier. Way to go, Evan. Way to make a good impression on a girl: insult her mom.

CHAPTER 20: NO PLACE LIKE HOME

"You gonna be alright, son?" asked Geezer. Gemma frowned at me with concern.

I took several breaths. If Sina was a princess, I really, really needed to watch my step. It also threw a huge anvil into her flirting with me. I didn't mind being friendly, but if Sina was destined to be the queen, and Daric the king, then that was a whole other crap sandwich with cow pie surprise center. That's the kind of thing that got people burned, strung up, then beheaded.

"Kid!" Geezer yelled.

What if the queen found out we kissed? What if there were rumors we were sleeping together? I knew my medieval history. I could die. Be tortured, then die. I really didn't want to die. My breath came faster and faster and I couldn't stop it. My ears rang, and the room darkened.

A bolt of freezing water hit my face. An icicle hung from my hair and my cheeks stung. I breathed out a small cloud of fog.

Geezer lowered his hands, and I stared into the worried looks of my friends.

I took one more slow breath. The frigid air stung my lungs. "Thanks. I let my head get away from me."

"Don't mention it," said Geezer. "I know the feelin'. You try to take things one day at a time, but every once in a while, several days gang up on ya."

"Ain't that the truth." I broke off the icicle. "Change of subject. *Any* subject."

"Do you want to check in on your family back on Earth?" asked Geezer.

"Yes!" My family was never far from my mind. Seeing if they were doing okay, and what they were doing to find me, was a priority. "Can I speak to them?"

The old man shook his head. "Sorry, son. The spell don't work that way. On the bright side, with all the newfangled gadgets they have nowadays, it'll be easy to check how much time has passed over there."

Gemma's face lit up. "We can look into another world?"

"Oh, yeah, Darlin'," said Geezer. "I only have enough stuff to make it work for about ten minutes, but you'll get to see Evan's home. If you've heard human-tales, let me tell you, none of them do the truth any justice at all. The stuff they got there will blow your warts off."

Gemma bounced up and down in a circle. "That is so *awesome*. I can't wait. A real live glimpse into a human-tale world. I totally bet it's full of like horseless carriages, impossibly tall castles, and heroic wizards."

Well, that was a pretty accurate description of San Antonio from a medieval point of view, except for the wizards. Cars would seem like magical carts. Skyscrapers would seem like castles instead of towering cube farms. Come to think of it, cell phones would seem like magic. Apps were like different spells added to a spell book.

With a shiver, I shook off the last of the anxiety. "Okay, let's do this."

"Come over here, boy. Let's see what's going on back home." Geezer went to his lab table and lit a fire under a large bowl of water. He added salt, something that looked like dried worms, then he lifted his robe and dug out some belly button lint and added that too.

Sooner than I thought possible, the water came to a boil and steam coalesced into a cloud over the bowl. The salt made it smell like the ocean. Geezer said something that sounded like the elvish word for sight, and the cloud glowed and parted. Through the fog, I saw... San Antonio. I didn't know what I was expecting, but it wasn't an aerial view of downtown. I could clearly see the Tower, the Riverwalk, and the Alamodome.

"This should be close to where you crossed over. Any of it look familiar?" asked Geezer.

"Uh, yeah. I live a few miles south of here." I pointed, and

Geezer moved cloud-o-vision where I asked. When we got to my neighborhood, we zoomed in on my house. Worn red brick with a gray roof, patchy grass in the front yard, and concrete steps to the front door canted a bit to the left. It wasn't much to look at, but it was home. It was the place I grew up, and it just felt right. Like your favorite pair of jeans with a hole in the knee. A patrol cruiser sat outside.

At first, I thought it was a still picture, but I realized it was a real-time image. A car drove past my house, but it crawled up the street. Geezer said the scry window was invisible to the people on Earth, but I wondered what we would look like from San Antonio.

Geezer swooped into my house through the door. It was like a super realistic first-person video game, where the walls were there for decoration, but offered no resistance to the player.

The living room looked much like it had the day I left, except Jerrod-sized dried muddy footprints led from the front door to the stairs. Same threadbare tan carpet. Same dirt brown couch.

"Huh, I expected your home to be a mansion," said Gemma.

"Sorry to disappoint," I said with a twinge of annoyance. "They're probably in the kitchen. Geezer, can you go through the door in the back of the room?"

"I didn't mean it was bad," said Gemma. "Your place is tons better than my hut at the bridge. It's just, like, you live in an elven palace, and the way you talk about your home, I expected velvet curtains and a fancy schmancy fireplace."

Cloud-o-vision cruised across the dining room table and through the door into the kitchen.

The living and dining areas were a bit dark, so it was a shock to zip into the brightly lit kitchen. They had piled the nice pots and pans I got last Christmas in the sink with dirty dishes.

Mom was next to the kitchen table talking to a police officer in super slow motion. Grandma leaned against the stove and scowled at mom. I knew that look. Whenever Grandma disapproved of something Mom did, she gave her that look. She never contradicted mom in front of anyone, but she'd give her an earful later. Just behind grandma sat her black cat, Fifi. The cat knew she wasn't supposed to be on the counter, but that'd never stopped her before. Oddly, the cat seemed to look through the scry window.

The police officer was tapping away on a tablet while mom talked. Geezer moved the scry window through the officer so we could see the police report as it was slowly being entered.

"Is that a magic piece of paper?" asked Gemma.

The date caught my eye.

"Kinda," I said. "Three days. That's how long I've been gone."

"But I was with you three days ago," said Gemma.

"Time moves differently there," I explained.

I'd never seen a police report before, but it wasn't what I expected. The police report was just my general description, and that I'd left school in the middle of the day three days earlier. My mother thought I'd gone to see my father. She hadn't called to check up on me. My heart sank.

Three days and my mom had just today called the police. Scratch that. Grandma's name was at the top of the report. She had called the police. That's why she was giving mom the stink eye.

Geezer looked around the screen and peered into the bowl. "We're running out of juice, kid. Anything else you want to see while we're here? Like, say, that amazing beauty next to the oven?"

That distracted me from the frustration and disappointment, and I chuckled. "I tell you what, old man. Let's check out my room in the basement, then if we have time, we can come back up here, and you can ogle my grandma."

"Hi ho, hi ho," said Geezer, "it's off to the cellar we go."

Geezer caused the scry window to sink through the floor. The unfinished basement came into view. The lights were on down here. Weird, since I was the only one who used it. The naked bulbs hung from ceiling joists. Marked and unmarked boxes sat in unorganized piles. Cobwebs and dust bunnies vied for control of the space.

"My room is back there," I said.

The image floated to the only corner without visible wall studs. On the other side of the hastily hung drywall was my room. We rounded the corner, and I jumped as a book appeared in mid-air in front of the scry window, slowly flipping through the air. Geezer brought the image around the book, and I saw the cause.

"Who's that?" asked Gemma.

"My brother," I said. He dug through the milk crate I used as a nightstand next to my bed. My books and papers were strewn about where he'd thrown them. My fencing gear scattered. Piled neatly beside him were my baseball cards. He'd offered to sell them for me several times, because some of them were worth a couple of hundred dollars. But my dad had given them to me, and that alone made them priceless.

Now Jerrod was stealing them.

By the time I got back, they'd be gone. Pawned halfway across town. I'd never see them again.

My gut wrenched painfully. "I've seen enough, Geezer. Take us back upstairs." I prided myself on the fact that I got it out without my voice cracking. Just barely.

I hoped we had enough time left to see my grandma. I needed one positive thing to keep me going until I returned. My vision blurred as I blinked away the tears. Dog darn it. Now I was crying in front of my friends.

I wiped my face and did my best to pull myself together.

Geezer put a hand on my shoulder. "Hey, son, cheer up. It's nothing to scry about."

Wait, did he just... I looked at him, and he gave me a cheesy grin.

I couldn't help it. I barked out a laugh.

We were back in the kitchen. Geezer had the scry window pulled in close on my grandma. Unnervingly, my grandma was gazing right at us. Apparently, it made Geezer feel weird too because he panned the image to the right...

And Grandma's eyes slowly followed it...

I sucked in a breath. "Geezer?"

"Uh, I don't know, kid. That shouldn't happen," said the wizard.

The cloud dissipated, and the image fell apart as the last of the water in the bowl boiled away. It left me with the memory of my grandma looking right at me, like I owed her an explanation.

CHAPTER 21: BELIEVE IN YOUR ELF

I rounded on Geezer. "You said no one could see the portals."

"No normal human can see the portals," he assured. "You have to have magic or fae blood to see 'em.

I whipped my arm at the space where the portal had been. "Then what was that? Grandma saw the portal."

Geezer grinned. "Oh, yeah, son. She sure as hell did."

Gemma's gaze shifted between us. "So, what does it mean if she saw it?"

The old wizard patted the troll on the arm. "That, my dear, is the thousand gold piece question, isn't it? Is Evan's grandma part elf, or does she have a touch of magic in her blood?" Geezer waggled his eyebrows. "Inquiring minds want to know. Hurry up and get that spell, Evan, so I can talk with that cute little filly."

"First of all, that's my grandma." I said, "Second of all, I'm not part elf, so my grandma isn't part elf. As far as her being cute, aren't you twice her age?"

"Son," said Geezer, "People don't age here. That means between adults, it don't matter a lick how old ya are."

I turned to Gemma for help.

She shrugged. "Don't look at me. I was, like, eighty years older than the last guy I dated." Gemma sighed. "I loved the way that big boy smelled, too. Arms like tree trunks." She shivered. "You elves and humans just aren't built right."

"Wait, how old are you?" I asked.

The old wizard interrupted. "Look, all I'm saying is that I like the way your grandma looks and carries herself. If the opportunity presents, I'd like an introduction. Ya get my meaning."

I shook my head to clear it. The scrying had left me with more questions than answers, and none of them were going to be solved any time soon. "Fine," I relented.

"Great, then I have a spell to teach ya."

It was just the distraction I needed to take my mind off Jerrod and my grandma. Geezer was right. The summon sprite spell was easy to learn. It was the ancient elvish version of saying, "Here spritey, spritey." The magic itself basically made the sugar irresistible to the winged fairies, while warning them the sugar had strings attached. They loved sugar so much that they rarely put up a fuss. Spend days delivering a message, versus sugar. Watch for people to show up, versus sugar. Waltz into near-certain death, versus a chance of sugar. The sprite would choose sugar every time.

The downside: like little street beggars, once you gave them a taste of sugar, the wizard was doomed to have a flock of the annoying pests following them around on the off chance there *might* be sugar.

Which made the reverse of the spell a necessity. Anything that was on your body was safe, but the moment it left your hands, fair game for all sorts of spritely shenanigans. Clothes and shiny objects could be stolen, items creatively misplaced, or even random objects showing up where you least expected them. "I left a turkey leg in your hat where you'd find it. It isn't my fault you didn't use the hat for two weeks."

The protection from sprites spell did the equivalent of spraying an area with the bitter apple stuff they use for dogs. It mostly worked, sometimes it didn't, and it told the critters that whatever was inside was yucky. Don't touch it or you'll get cooties.

I didn't get the chance to see Sina before the queen summoned me to her audience chamber. I had to give Queen Lycia kudos. The summons came exactly forty-eight hours from when I left her.

I arrived, Gemma in tow, to find Daric fidgeting with his weapons, and Sina seemed not to know what to do with her hands.

Queen Lycia lounged on her throne and smiled sadly. "Two days."

"I noticed, Your Majesty, and I appreciate your promptness," I said with a bow.

"You won't be thanking me when you hear your next quest," she said.

Uh, oh. Don't panic yet, I admonished myself. Just because Sina and Daric were nervous, doesn't mean you should be. Maybe I'm summoning an army of sprites to invade the Darower, or I'm feeding a hundred hungry feral gnomes. There's a big gulf between scary and downright terrifying.

"Flick, send in Master Ticset," commanded the queen.

I'd gotten used to elves being thin. It seemed like a racial thing, like brown skin or black hair. Ticset was the exception. He was shorter than the average elf, balding, and round. One could almost say portly.

He shuffled nervously up to the queen, looking downcast.

"Master Ticset, please tell the Wizard Evan what you told me," said the queen.

Wizard? When did I get an upgrade?

The man's eyes became sidetracked by my ears on the way to my face. Ticset didn't say anything as his head turned sideways and he reached out to touch them.

"No touchy," growled Gemma.

He yanked his hand back as he seemed to notice the troll for the first time. "Uh, I uh, troll? Troll! Don't eat me!"

Didn't see the troll. Didn't see the human. This guy wouldn't see an army of Vikings even if they were jumping up and down in pink tutus.

The queen rolled her eyes, and I took pity on the poor elf.

"Hi, Ticset. I'm Evan, and this is my companion, Gemma," I explained. "I promise not to hurt you, and Gemma won't eat you unless you try to hurt me."

He shivered like a naked mole rat at the north pole but nodded.

Gemma gave him a smile that was all teeth.

He swallowed. "I, uh, you see, we have a problem in my village. There's this dragon. He's accosting our people, stealing their valuables, and eating our sheep and cows."

Dragon? Oh, you have got to be fricking kidding me. The queen was sending me out to slay a doggone dragon? Hounds of hell. Not to mention, I was nowhere near capable of handling anything close to a dragon if even half the stories Gemma and Sina had told me were true.

I gazed up at the queen, who arched an eyebrow down at me.

My shoulders drooped and I let out an audible groan. Why me?

Hey, if memory served, there were two kinds of dragons in this kingdom. Maybe it was the slightly less deadly, poison-breathing kind of death with scales and wings.

I grimaced and balled my hands into fists. Please let it be green, please let it be green. "Master Ticset, what color is the dragon?"

"Red, Wizard Evan."

Dog, dog, dog dang it. As tough as Gemma was, fire-breathing death would definitely cook both our gooses, gizzards, and innards. Not that green was much better.

I scrubbed my face with my hands. "Tell me about every time the dragon showed up."

There had been seven encounters. Five of them played out much the same way. Villager with cows or sheep minding their own business. Dragon swoops in. Villager runs for their lives, and the dragon eats half the animal, then leaves. In two cases, the dragon appeared to travelers and demanded money. Since the village, Vimra, was poor, the peasants had only a few copper pieces. The irate dragon had roared and threatened the villagers, who had thrown down their purses and pouches and ran.

After I felt like I'd wrung every useful detail out of the hapless mayor, I turned to the queen. "Your Majesty, what do you want me to do?"

"Isn't it obvious? Slay or drive off the dragon. Do whatever it takes to keep the kingdom safe." Then she leaned back into her throne. "Or accept ten years of service. It's your choice."

Which was no choice. My gaze traveled to my companions. Sina gave me a small nod. She'd support the decision I made. Daric looked up to the ceiling as he shook his head with resignation. Gemma... Gemma bounced on her toes? An odd reaction, but it was nice to know I wouldn't be facing down a dragon on my own.

A wave of flower-scented perfume assaulted my nose as Ticset dabbed his bald head with a handkerchief. He was trying to put on a brave face, but the image was ruined because he shivered like an over-caffeinated chihuahua.

Then there was the queen. She seemed relaxed, but leaned forward when my attention shifted to her. A small smile played on her lips.

"What resources do I have for this quest?" I asked.

"No gold. Bribery never works with dragons." Queen Lycia shrugged. "They always want more. The crown will supply horses and provisions. As the troll is your responsibility, you'll need to handle her outfitting. The stable master should have supplies for you to buy."

"So, you'll save us from the dragon, Wizard Evan?" The village mayor looked up at me with hope.

I sighed. "Yes, I'll save you from the dragon." *Or more likely die trying*, I thought.

CHAPTER 22: OFF TO SEE THE LIZARD

"This is so awesome! We get to see a frickin' dragon." Gemma danced up the hallway, adding twirls and pumping her fists. "Awake dragon, drag-on. Asleep dragon, drag-off. Ooh. How cool would it be to sneak up on a *sleeping* dragon?"

I grinned at the excited troll. "Gemma, dragons are one of the few things that *can actually kill you*. You're excited to meet one face to face?"

"Duh. I mean, it's, like, *a dragon*." Gemma bared her teeth and made clawing motions with her hands. "You never see them, 'cause they're all pretending to be elves or pookas or whatever. And when you do see them, it's like," she mimed an explosion, "Oh my goddess, a frickin' dragon. Run for your lives!"

"Have you ever seen one?" I asked.

"No, and until Ticset, no one I'd ever met has ever seen one either. You hear stories about people who have met dragons and lived, but it's like seeing a unicorn or being visited by a god. You know they're out there, you know it happens, but it's always happening to someone else. It is possible to live twenty thousand years and never. Meet. One."

I blinked. "People talk to gods?"

"Yeah. It's called praying. Almost everyone talks to gods, but it's always a one-sided conversation, ya know. Every once in a great while, someone gets visited by Fifta or Titania, but it's always kings, heroes, or high priests." She waved it away like a fly. "But who cares about some stodgy old deity? We're going to meet a *living* dragon. Bogore is going to have *kittens* when I tell him."

Gemma sobered and her eyes narrowed as she looked over my

shoulder. I followed her gaze and found Sina coming up the hall.

"Gemma, could you give us a minute?" I asked.

"Yeah," said Gemma. "I'll be just up the passage. Yell if you need anything. I'll come running."

Gemma trotted up the hallway and Sina caught up to me but kept her eyes downcast. She must still be feeling embarrassed about the fart in my apartment.

"You're wearing the boots," she observed.

I shrugged. "Yeah. They're way cooler than my sneakers and I don't stand out as much."

We walked in silence for a bit before she spoke again. "Uh, about provisions, don't get them from the stable master. He charges four times the going rate. We'll swing by a shop I know on the way out of town."

"Four times?" I asked. "That's robbery."

She gave a one-shouldered shrug. "He calls it a convenience tax." Sina chewed on her lip for a couple of seconds, then huffed. "You're not going to ask, are you?"

"Ask what?"

"For money. You don't have any, right?"

I grinned. "Why, you wanted to ask me to do something in exchange for some?"

Her head popped up in surprise. "What? No!" She hung her head again and spoke to me, staring at the ground. "I just... wanted to do something nice for you." The last part came out as a whisper.

I chuckled. "Thanks, but your dad already gave me fifty gold."

Sina grabbed my shoulder to stop me. "He what?"

"Geezer gave me fifty gold," I moved my hand in a rolling motion, "for expenses. He said I'd need it for clothes, food, and camping stuff. Unless I'm mistaken, that's more than enough, right?"

The blonde elf gaped at me. "I can't get him to give me a few coppers for a new cloak, but he just hands you fifty gold."

"Why don't you ask your mom?"

She continued up the hallway. "*Pfft.* She's more tight-fisted than he is, and her deals are the worst. You don't know my mom."

"I do know your mom," I whispered.

She glared at me. "Who told?"

I didn't want to get Geezer in trouble. I held my hands up. "No one told me. I figured it out."

She scowled but didn't press me. "Don't tell anyone. Not Gemma. Not anyone. It would be very bad if people knew."

I couldn't argue with her there. "Want me to talk to your dad for you?"

"What'll it cost me?" she asked with a sidelong look.

I grinned at her. "The location of your provisions shop."

"I was going to tell you that, anyway."

I scratched my chin theatrically. "Huh, how about that."

***

The next morning, we collected the palace-provided provisions and walked the horses into town.

The main road in was fairly wide, and the sun beamed between the leafy canopies on either side. Sina led us off the thoroughfare between two ancient trees as big around as my house back on Earth. It wasn't a road, so much as a well-used path about five feet wide.

Sunlight dimmed as we entered a densely canopied section of the forest city. Moss grew on trunks and the air smelled like a greenhouse or nursery. We wove around roots that grew into the path as we dove deeper into the cool shade. Strange birdcalls floated down to us from far above. Doors into the residential trees became harder and harder to pick out.

The path led to a large clearing with a few elves wandering about. At first, I thought we would travel through, but Sina stopped us at the second tree on the right. It was then that I noticed that there was a branch just above head height with writing on it. Gazing around the clearing, I saw that every tree had a thick branch at the same height. The sign above us read Millow's Miscellany in elvish.

We tied up the horses and went inside. A tweet like excited sparrows announced our entry into a room with a bit of everything. Swords, shields, and bows lined a wood wall to my right. On my left were leather satchels, horse tack, and clothes of various sizes. Dried foods and camping gear stood proudly on some low shelves that ended in a rough-hewn counter at the back of the room.

Behind the counter was a dark-haired elf with shockingly blue eyes. "Sina! About time you dropped by for a visit. Is this the new human that's causing such a stir? And in the company of a troll,

127

will wonders never cease."

"Hey Millow," said Sina as we walked toward the back counter. "I'd like you to meet Evan and Gemma."

Millow's handshake was firm, and her eyes had a mischievous twinkle. "Evan, it's a pleasure. Considering all the good Geezer has brought to the kingdom, I hope we can expect great things from you, too."

Gemma's hand engulfed Millow's, but if it bothered the elf, she showed no signs of it. She eyed Gemma with a critical eye. "Honey, that burlap looks painful. Can I interest you in some new clothes? I've got some cotton, linen, and even some silk that would look and feel a heck of a lot nicer."

Gemma blinked. "Wha... uh. You have something in my size?"

"Not right off the rack, honey," Millow gave her a wink, "but I got a spell that will make quick work of any alterations."

Gemma's face fell. "I don't have any money."

I put my hand on the troll's shoulder. "Gemma, get three sets of clothes. My treat."

The big troll bit her lip. "Evan, I can't pay you back."

"Gemma, you pay me back every day. You keep me safe. The least I can do is make sure you have some good clothes. Do you want to meet a dragon in your old clothes?"

She smiled shyly. "Okay."

Gemma picked out some linen shirts and pants in various earth tones. Then she bought a frilly silk dress in the most eye-catching shade of pink I'd ever seen.

"Problem?" she asked with a challenge in her squeaky voice.

"Nope." If she wanted a pink dress, she could have a pink dress.

We picked up a few accessories, like belts and pouches, but no shoes. Gemma claimed they interfered with her connection with the ground. I also bought her a large backpack and a two-handed sword. Well, it was one-handed for her. We finished up with enough food to feed a small army... or one troll.

Then I got myself two more sets of clothes and a travel cloak. Enough elves wore them that I felt I could get by with wearing one and keeping the hood up while we were in the city. I could stop being the amazing round-eared wonder whenever we were near the palace. Who knew? Maybe it might help in the village as well. Unfortunately, nothing could hide the fact that Gemma was a troll.

She was just too big.

I was especially happy with one shirt that Millow had suggested. It was a poet's shirt in an amazing shade of forest green. With the lace-up front and billowy sleeves, I felt I could really get into the spirit of this world of magic and fairy creatures.

"What do ya think?" I asked Sina.

She nodded approvingly. "I like it. It suits you."

I put it on and spun around. "Gemma?"

"It looks good."

"It's to die for. Can we hit the road now?" grumped Daric.

"What do I owe you, Millow?" I asked.

"The total comes to six gold, two silver. Do you need credit? I can offer you a generous interest rate." The predatory smile that came with the offer would have put a hungry tiger to shame.

"No," I chuckled, "thank you, Millow."

She snapped her fingers. "You can't blame an elf for trying."

We left the store with a promise to drop by when we returned.

"Are we done wasting time now?" Daric huffed.

"I don't know," I said. "Anyone have any lollygagging to do? Maybe with a side of procrastination?"

Sina chuckled, but Daric sighed heavily.

"What's the matter Daric?" I wheedled. "Are you anxious to meet the dragon? Do the two of you have a hot date? Getting a little *tail?*"

Daric smiled at me, but it was all teeth. "The sooner we get there, the sooner the dragon can eat you and we can all go home."

It was at this point I remembered Daric might someday be king... so I checked *Sina's* reaction. She was slightly behind Daric with her hand over her mouth, to hide the fact that she was grinning at our exchange.

Well, as long as she was entertained...

"Aw," I said, "you do care. Do you think I'll taste better with garlic rosemary or lemon butter sauce?"

"I won't be sticking around to find out," he growled.

We exited the side path and reentered the main thoroughfare. Daric mounted his horse and trotted ahead.

"He's such a charmer," I said. "You're such a lucky girl, Sina."

"He can be sweet," she said defensively.

"How much honey does it take to overcome the sour?" asked Gemma.

"About as much mint as it takes to cover up the stink on a troll," Sina snapped.

The elf and troll glared at each other.

Okay, this is going to be a fun trip.

We were getting close to the edge of town, so I mounted Nonam. Sina saddled up as well.

The awkward silence continued.

Okay, time to break the tension. "Sorry that there aren't any horses big enough for you, Gemma."

She tore her gaze from the elf reluctantly and shrugged. "I enjoy walking and I don't know how to ride, anyway."

Sina sniffed, "Maybe if you-"

Gemma's hand shot in front of my face. *Twock!* Pain exploded across my cheek. Gemma pulled her hand away- with an arrow in it!

The troll slapped my horse with her uninjured hand. "Ride!" she yelled.

Nonam shot forward.

CHAPTER 23: MAKING A KILLING

Nonam charged up the tree-lined street as I held on for dear life. I wiped my right eye to clear it- and found my palm covered with blood.

I glanced up in time to see another arrow. I yanked Nonam to the left. The arrow sliced my arm. I used my knees to direct my horse right and left in a zig-zag pattern.

We left Sina behind. Gemma yanked the arrow out and ran after us.

A rain of arrows slammed into the ground all around me. I shot past Daric, who whipped his head around, looking everywhere but up.

The arrows stopped, but I didn't take any chances. I shot out the city gates and kept going. I brought Nonam to a halt five hundred yards away from the tall sufra trees of the elven city.

I dismounted and inspected Nonam. Thankfully, there were no extra holes in my horse. I gave her a huge hug.

Sina loped up to me, followed by Daric a short time later.

"Did you get a look at him?" I asked.

"No," said Sina. "Daric?"

He shook his head.

Sina dismounted with concern in her eyes. "Why haven't you healed yourself?"

I looked at my sticky and blood-covered hand as red drops fell from my face onto it. My shirt was plastered to me with dried blood. With Sina's help, we closed the hole in my cheek. Even though she was helping me heal, having her hands on me was distracting. I felt her genuine concern for me through the telepathic bond we shared through touch. Despite the situation, I couldn't get the image of the knockout dress she'd worn to my apartment out of my head. In that moment, I also realized that with Gemma's hand or no, if the arrow had been an inch higher, I'd have lost an eye.

Sina seemed about to say something but stopped herself. Instead, she touched my arm, helping me heal the gash there.

Gemma sprinted up, then bent over to catch her breath.

"Did you see who it was?" I asked.

She shook her head. "Perched sixty feet up," she wheezed, "in one of the huge trees. Couldn't make out a face or anything." She panted. "A bit stocky for an elf, though. Dwarf or gnome maybe?"

"Or troll?" Daric sneered.

Gemma rolled her eyes. "Seriously? Why would a troll climb a tree? If it were me, I'd ambush you half a day from the city. I'd wade in and slice you into pig food before you could do a thing about it."

I motioned to Gemma. "Let me see your hand?"

She shrugged and held it out to me. I couldn't tell where she'd been hurt. She'd healed completely. I turned her hand back and forth a couple of times to make sure.

"Amazing," I observed.

"Thanks," said the troll. "What about you? Also, do you have any food?"

"Tired. Healing spells takes a lot of energy." Then I glanced at my shirt. "Hey, what's brown and sticky?"

Daric and Sina shook their heads in exasperation. Gemma rolled her eyes.

"A stick," I said with a grin. "But also, me. Is there a stream or something nearby so I can wash up?"

"And can we stop for food there?" said Gemma. "I'm hungry."

***

If you're paranoid, just remember, you're not alone. I knew I was being paranoid, but can it be called paranoia if someone really is out to get you? At least my friends were looking over their shoulders too.

We were a bit jumpy. Gemma attacked a bush. Not sure why, the bush hadn't even rustled inappropriately. Sina shot a couple of birds and a squirrel. To be fair, the squirrel had it coming. Seriously, chasing us around and dropping nuts on our heads was totally uncalled for. To make matters worse, my two friends traded barbs about stuck-up elves and stupid trolls.

The only one who kept their head on straight was Daric. I guess if you're a badass elven warrior, nothing fazes you anymore. He was alert, unperturbed, and while still sarcastic, didn't allow himself to get drawn into arguments.

We found a nearby creek, but with all the blood my new shirt had soaked up, and had subsequently dried into it, I had to admit that it was a lost cause. Rather than clean it, I buried it and suffered the eye rolls and head shakes as I gave my poor shirt a eulogy.

"I feel like we barely knew each other," which was true since I'd bought the shirt this morning, "but I watched you grow and change... color during our brief friendship. You always had my back and shared in my pain, and, dear shirt, I'll never forget that. You became part of the very fabric of my life. From the earth you grew, were woven into life, and we now return you to the soil from whence you came. So, it is with the deepest regret that I lay you to rest in this grave. The shallow depth in no way relates to the depth of gratitude for your many minutes of service."

The respectful moment of silence was interrupted by Daric.

"Are you done?"

I considered the question. I had a lot of things on my mind, but this part, the shirt funeral service, was finished. "Yes, we can go now."

I mounted my horse and asked about the most pressing thing on my mind. "Why is someone trying to kill me?"

"Perhaps they've spoken to you," offered Daric. He, of course, was already on his horse.

"That can't be it. I'm a doggone delight," I cocked my head toward the surly elf, "unlike some other fae I know."

Sina joined us on horseback, and we began our trek west. "Darower maybe. They can't be happy about the trolls closing the bridge to them."

Gemma slung her pack over her shoulder and jogged to catch up. "No, that can't be it."

"Why not?" Sina frowned at the troll.

"Because they would have had to get to the bridge, discover they couldn't cross, then go all the way to the coast or the other way through the valley of World Tree," explained Gemma. "It'd take too long."

I thought about someone repelling into the gorge, crossing the raging river, then scaling up the far side. That didn't seem likely, either. "Griffin, maybe?"

Sina shook her head. "No, they would have to have a griffin at or near the bridge. Someone must have bribed their way across."

"No one bribed anyone," snapped Gemma.

"Why? Because trolls are so trustworthy?" Sina glared at the troll.

"We had a deal," said Gemma through clenched teeth. "Bogore won't break his word."

"Right, trolls don't do that."

"Because then we'd be as bad as elves."

"Elves don't lie."

"No, they just twist the deal into a pretzel to fit whatever they want."

Seeing my two best friends fighting was making me uncomfortable. "Guys?"

"What!?" they yelled at me at the same time.

"Uh... never mind," I mumbled.

It turns out the bickering was preferable to angry silence. I had no idea how awful the sound of nothing could be. It was so quiet I could have heard the p in pterodactyl.

When we made camp, setting the watches was done with as little talking as possible.

"Can you teach me the alarm spell?" I asked Daric.

"No."

"Please?"

Daric poured something that looked like fine dust around the perimeter of the camp. "No."

I followed him, paying attention to every motion and word he spoke. "What can I give you for the spell?"

"Tell the troll to go away."

"What! I can't do that."

He faced me and crossed his arms. "You absolutely can do that. Tell the green monster that you've taught her everything you can about cooking and send her back to the bridge."

"But I haven't taught her everything about cooking." I protested.

"You're a human. Lie. It's what you're good at." He turned his back to me to continue making the dust line.

Dog darn it. I followed him around as he cast the spell, but other than spreading dust and mumbling things I couldn't quite hear, I didn't pick up anything I could use. Which left me wondering if a spell was really cast at all.

That night, I got proof the spell was working in the worst possible way.

CHAPTER 24: THINGS THAT GO BUMP IN THE NIGHT

Screeeeee!

I went from fast asleep to wide awake in an instant. Have you ever heard a barn owl? It was like that, if the owl was ten feet tall, had found a squirrel in its nest, and had declared war on all squirreldom for the affront.

My ears rang and my head felt like it was going to split open right after my eyes bled out.

I threw off my blanket and jumped to my feet with my sword at the ready. Okay, well, that's what I tried to do. What I really did was jump to my feet, fumble my sword as the blanket wrapped around my ankles, causing me to fall, and almost impale myself on my own weapon. But the second attempt was flawless, trust me.

Nothing attacked right away. My companions and I gathered near the campfire, weapons out, back-to-back facing outward. The bird screech subsided.

"Did anyone see what set off the spell?" asked Gemma.

She received a chorus of noes.

I searched the woods for any movement. "Daric, does the spell tell you anything about direction or size?"

"No."

"I see something." Sina left our circle and crept forward.

The rest of us kept our eyes glued to the impenetrable darkness of the forest. The campfire was our lifeline. Our small chapel of hope, and I was preaching to the fire.

Unless someone fired an arrow into us...

Well, dog-doo. That would suck.

Sina inched forward without a sound. She seemed to be keeping a tree between her and something behind it. Time crawled as she made her way up to the tree and adjusted the grip on her sword.

She screamed her war cry and leaped.

"Arrrahhh-er-noooooo!"

The elf princess crossed her arms in front of her face, but it was too late. Yellowish fluid splashed up her front. A black and white animal darted into the night.

"Uh oh." Apparently, I have a gift for understatement.

Sina threw her sword. "Quick, get me water!"

The stench hit me like a wall as I ran to my pack. Skunk. I tossed her a waterskin, even though I doubted it would do any good. She used it to spray down her front. When it was empty, Daric handed her three more as he covered his mouth and nose with part of his tunic.

I didn't have a handkerchief, so I grabbed a clean sock from my pack and put it over my nose. "I don't suppose we have any baking soda?"

Daric moved from side to side, trying to find the best place not to be downwind. "What's baking soda?"

I winced. "I was afraid of that. It's something we use on Earth to bake with. It's also good for treating unpleasant smells." My eyes watered. "Gemma, what do you use for skunks?"

Gemma pinched her nose and waved her hand in front of her. "Nothing. We make them sleep in the woods for a week, sometimes two."

"You mean you don't use it as perfume?" asked Daric.

"Are you kidding?" she squeaked. "Who would want to smell like a skunk?"

"Nut oil. Nut paste." Sina sobbed. "Ugh, any plant oil. Oh Titania, why is this happening to me?"

Gemma was stifling a laugh, but she hid her mouth behind her hand. Easy since she was still pinching her nose.

I tried using my Locate Plants spell, but I couldn't concentrate. I had to move to the very edge of the camp to... uh... clear my head.

I thought peanut butter would be ideal. No peanuts. I couldn't locate any beans, in fact. Lima, fava, garbanzo, no dice. Nuts were also a bust. I thought being in a pine forest that pine nuts would be everywhere, but I guess it was the wrong season or something. What did I find? Olives.

Which led me to my next problem: how to get to them in the middle of the night? I sure as hounds wasn't going out into the dark alone. Solution: wake up a sprite.

I drew the magic circle on the ground and placed a sugar cube into it. I expected to have to wait, but a sprite zipped into the clearing like a supercharged firefly and hovered at the edge of the magic circle.

"Ew, what stinks?"

"Her," I pointed at Sina. Then I pointed at the sprite. "What's your name?"

"Call me Bramble," said the sprite with the spiky wings. "Okay, let's not mince words, Peach Fuzz. You have sugar. I want it. What do I have to do to get it?" The tiny fairy put its hands on its hips and tapped its foot like it was on the ground.

I pointed. "There's a grove of olive trees two hundred yards that way. For the next two hours, I want you to bring as many olives back here as you can. If I'm happy with the results, I'll give you two sugar cubes instead of just one."

The sprite disappeared in a shower of sparks. At first, I thought the poor thing had exploded, but it zipped into the clearing five minutes later with five olives.

I had to give Bramble kudos. The little sprite was industrious when properly motivated. In less time than I thought possible, we had a small mountain of olives.

I gave Bramble two sugar cubes, and it flew back into the woods.

Pressing the oil out of them ended up being easier than expected as well. Gemma's third spell? Stone shape. The magic somehow made stone moldable like clay before turning solid again. She used it to make arrowheads, but I could see tons of other uses for it.

By the time the sun was peaking over the horizon, we were using the olive oil on Sina's clothes and armor. I offered to help her rub the oil on her skin, but she said no.

Upside, I now had olive oil to cook with. The downside, Sina still stank. She buried her skunky clothes, but she continued to wear her armor and it was in her skin and hair. Her vanilla deodorant made her smell like skunk and vanilla. Not a fun combination.

We got a late start on the day, for obvious reasons. The rest of us kept our distance from Sina. Even when breaking camp, we made the blonde elf stay well away from everyone else.

By the time we got close to the village, five feet was enough distance. Close enough that we didn't have to yell to talk with her, and far away enough that we weren't gagging on eau-de-pew.

On a positive note, I finally got the Stone Skin spell to work. Unlike my other spells, it actually helped to distract myself a little. Setting the spell loose then keeping my eyes on a rock, bird, or chipmunk was just the thing to keep my mind off the creepy tingling as the rock formed over my skin.

Daric had Sina's magic map out. "If we get an early start tomorrow, we should be able to make the village before sundown."

Bramble plopped itself down in the middle of the map, studying it. Daric swatted him away.

"You just had to feed a sprite." He shook his head.

"How do you think I feel?" I reached into my pocket and pulled out a handful of olives. "Olives in my blanket, olives in my shoes, olives in my waterskin. It might be kinda neat if I could actually eat them, but these are raw, unmarinated olives, so they taste gross."

"If you lay with pigs, you get muddy." Daric waved it away. "Regardless, get to bed early tonight. Rest up. With a little luck, we'll make the village before nightfall and be able to sleep in the tavern instead of a campsite in the open. If someone is still trying to kill you, being indoors will help us keep you safe."

"I'm all for staying safe," I said with a cheesy grin. "Mr. Safe, that's me."

The elf warrior gave me a long-suffering sigh and handed me the map.

Rolling up the map, I put it back in its case. I wandered over to Sina. She was sitting on a fallen tree and caught it easily when I tossed the case to her from a safe distance.

I gave her a big smile. "Just another couple of days and you'll be as fresh as a daisy."

"I'll settle for any flower other than skunkweed. Can't *wait*." She gave me a resigned shrug.

Her eyes focused on something to my left, but as I turned to see what it was, I got a surprise. *Slurp!*

I wiped the slime from my face. "Gemma, why do you keep

licking me?"

She waggled her eyebrows at me. "You taste good."

"I don't taste *that* good."

"Yeah, you do. Prove me wrong. Daric totally got us a deer." She danced a little jig. "Show me how venison is *done*, Chef Evan."

So, we cooked and ate deer. I don't remember going to bed. The backstrap was awesome, and I probably ate more than I should have. Better, we'd have leftovers for a couple of days.

I do remember how I woke up, because at first, I thought I was having a nightmare.

It started out as a war between broccoli and cauliflower. The broccoli soldiers were armed with asparagus spears, and the cauliflower used potato slings. I was on the broccoli side, but cauliflower spies were everywhere. They'd dye themselves green and no one could tell the difference except me.

I was about to tell head broccoli general when a battle broke out. I was surrounded by cauliflower, but since I didn't look like broccoli, they didn't take me prisoner.

They escorted a broccoli into camp. When he saw me there free, not yet tied up, he broke free of his captors. He attacked me, accusing me of being a spy for the cauliflower.

The broccoli morphed into Daric, and he was kicking the crap out of me. He had ahold of my head and was pounding it into a sharp rock.

Then my eyes shot open. Something sharp really was stabbing my ear.

"Wake up, Peach Fuzz, he's going to eat you!"

"Bramble?" I swatted at the sprite, who countered with the thorn he was holding. "Ow! You little prick. I'm going to punt you into next week."

Bramble pointed past me. "Teeth!"

I rolled over... And saw teeth. "Holy dogs of hell!"

CHAPTER 25: SHARP AND POINTY TEETH

"Other way," I yelled as I spun in the opposite direction.

The teeth ate my pillow.

I searched frantically for my sword. It was on the far side of the clearing, in a pile of weapons. Teeth must have moved it.

The guy stood about four feet tall and built like a warty dark-skinned fire hydrant. It wore black leather armor and carried a sword and bow, but it had drawn neither. Its wide mouth split its face nearly in two and was filled with more teeth than I seemed possible. But its most disturbing feature was its shock of blood-red hair.

"Help! Gemma, Sina, Daric!"

Teeth gave an evil laugh. "Help, help, help." He said in a high pitch voice, then switched to a gravelly growl. "Yell all you want. They aren't getting up."

Then he charged mouth first.

I dodged left, and he hit a tree.

Scratch that, he took a huge bite out of the tree. And was chewing it! "I'm glad you're awake," he said through a mouth full of wood chips. "It's so much more fun when my prey can beg for their pitiful lives."

"Go away," screamed Bramble. "He's my sugar daddy, not yours."

Teeth backhanded the sprite, which disappeared in a shower of sparks right before he struck.

"Stay out of this sprite, or I'll eat you, too."

I searched for a weapon, any weapon. Nothing. All the pointy things were piled on the other side of the camp. Daric and Sina were asleep in their blankets. Daric was drooling. They were breathing, so not dead. A short distance away, Gemma was slumped over a rock.

Teeth charged again.

I faked left, then jumped right. Pain flared from my ribs.

Pulling my hand away, I saw bloody gashes in my side.

Teeth brought a claw to his mouth and licked it with an ugly purple tongue. "Mmm mmm." His eyes fluttered. "Human tastes *good*. Forget the appetizer. I want the main course!"

The thing stalked towards me.

I backpedaled and put a tree between us. I needed to heal! *Yeah, dummy, why don't you do that?* I put more distance between me and the tree. I held my side and was suddenly thankful that Daric had made me practice the spell under stress. Which led to my second epiphany.

You're a Wizard stupid, do Wizardy things.

Teeth bit through the foot-wide pine in one bite and stepped around the falling tree. "Healing? You're just delaying the inevitable, meat."

I found another tree to hide behind, but instead of putting more distance, I stayed next to the tree. Could Teeth bite through rock? I guess I'd find out. I cast Stone Skin. Stone? There were rocks all over the campsite. It had taken us half an hour to clear them for our bedrolls. I grabbed a rock and shaped it into a rough dagger.

A claw swiped on my left. I hopped back from the trunk. Teeth must have expected me to dodge right, because he chomped the air where I would have been.

"This is the end," Teeth sneered. "Nice gnawing you, meat."

Teeth bit through the tree.

And I stabbed him in the mouth mid-chew, right *between* the teeth. "Rock to the hand, because the meal ain't listening."

Teeth's eyes grew wide, then they rolled up into his head. My dagger stuck out the back of his neck. He slid to the ground, but as he did, his many incisors cut into my arm, making deep ruts right through the stone covering.

Well... dog-doo.

I canceled the Stone Skin spell and healed my arm and ribs. It made me tired and out of breath, but at least I was alive.

Back in camp, my spare clothes, which I had been using as a pillow, were gone. In their place was a huge divot in the ground next to my blanket.

Bramble popped into existence above my bedding. "Hey, Peach Fuzz, glad you're not dead. How about some appreciation?"

I pulled a sugar cube out of my pouch and tossed it to the sprite. "There you go, Bramble. You more than earned it."

"Yes!" The sprite flew in a circle. "I'm gonna find some fierce wild animals and lead them here. This is great!"

"Do that, and I'll never give you sugar again," I warned it.

"Awww!" It zipped off into the woods with its prize.

I knelt next to Sina. She still smelled a little of skunk, but I ignored it and put my fingers to her neck. She had a pulse. There was a small empty vial next to where she lay. I picked it up and sniffed. Whatever it was smelled both rotten and sweet.

Could I heal poison? Neither Daric nor Sina had said I could use the spell that way. No harm in trying, I supposed.

I put my hands on Sina and used the healing magic's energy to 'feel around' for what was wrong. And it said nothing was wrong, which I knew wasn't true.

Okay, maybe the spell wasn't supposed to work that way, but what if I could alter it a little so it did?

Well, elf biology wasn't too different from human. I used the layering aspect of the spell to feel down to the different parts of Sina's body. Heart, lung, kidneys, great, it's all there and totally not what I need to be looking at.

Or maybe it was.

The vial had liquid in it, what if Teeth had dripped it onto Sina's lips? I moved my hands up to her jaw.

Luscious full lips. *Distracting! Concentrate, Evan.*

Magic to the lips. Magic lips. I bet they are. *Concentrate.* Feeling about. Something's wrong. Okay, what's wrong? They're... darker than the rest of her.

Darker?

What's the quality of that darkness? There's something there with the lips. Something not lips. Now, we're getting some place.

And it was on the tongue, in the throat, and in the stomach. Good, how do I get it out? Could I make Sina throw up? What if I tickle...

Bleeesh!

Note to self: next time you make someone throw up, move out of the way first.

And now my lap is turning numb.

Quickly, I took off my pants, but when I went to grab my spare pants, I saw the divot in the ground. Double dog-doo, I no longer had any spare pants. *Awkward.*

Well, we'd be stinky together if I could ever get her to wake up.

How did you treat poison? If it was a snakebite, you could suck the venom through the wound. Can I do something similar here?

My eyes traveled to Daric, drooling on the other side of the campsite. Drooling...

No.

Well, maybe.

Worth a try. I knelt in front of Sina and positioned her head so that she drooled. Attractive. Then I used the healing magic to take the poison and move it to the glands around her mouth. I was pretty sure they were salivary glands, but Biology was never my best subject.

I positioned her shoulder on my legs and her head hung just next to my thigh. Drool dripped from her mouth onto the ground. It took something like forty minutes, but I finally got most of the dark stuff out of her system.

She stirred and groaned as her eyes fluttered open and settled on my underwear. "Not tonight Darith," she said sleepily, "I hathe a headache."

Oh yeah, half-naked in front of the elf I'm crushing on. Could we be in a more pervy position? Good move, Evan. I pushed her shoulder, so she was on her back, and no longer looking at my crotch.

"Sina, it's Evan. Wake up. I need you."

She blinked and was immediately more awake. "Where arthe your panths?"

"You threw up on them when I healed you." Not the whole truth, but...

"Health me?" She sat up, then grabbed her head. "Ooooo. Head hurths. Tongue ith numb."

"Yeah, the guy who tried to kill me poisoned you."

"Darith? Gemma?" Sina used healing magic on her head and I showed her the vial, which she sniffed and grimaced. We found a dart on the ground next to the troll and another vial next to Daric.

Sina sniffed at the vial. "I know this stuff. They'll be fine in a few hours," said Sina, "unless you want to donate another pair of pants. Where are your extra?"

I pointed at the hole in the ground. "Teeth ate them."

"Teeth?"

I led her over to the body.

She turned it over. "That's a redcap. Evan, these guys are seriously evil. They eat anything, and I do mean anything. Trees, rocks, fae, if it fits, they eat it." Sina glanced around the campground. "But it looks like you already figured that part out. The Darower use them as assassins. How did you kill him?"

Shrugging, I explained.

"And that worked?" She shook her head, then pulled me into a hug. "Obviously it worked. I'm glad you're okay." Sina searched the body and found a pouch. She opened it and sucked in a breath. "Evan, this is a fortune in gems." She handed it to me.

I emptied some into my palm. The rubies, sapphires, and diamonds sparkled in the dying embers of the fire. "Wow."

"Congratulations. You're rich."

"What?"

Sina spread her arms. "He attacked you. You killed him. Law of the Land is that anything he owned is now yours. The armor won't fit, but the short sword and bow are good quality."

I eyed the leather pants. Eh, no.

The village was nearby, so I'd only have to spend a day being stinky. Sina had put up with it for a week. Also, we'd probably cross a stream on the way there.

I set about un-poisoning Gemma and Daric.

"When did you learn to treat poison?" asked Sina. She was watching over my shoulder as I worked on Gemma.

Gemma's body was odd because her own healing ability kept fighting me. It was like arguing with a toddler that kept insisting that it knew what to do better than I did.

I panted as the spell sapped my energy. "No one taught me. I figured it out. I'm using the healing spell a little differently."

Sina cocked her head. "You altered the spell? I didn't think you could do that."

Gemma came to, but acted drunk as her own body took over the detox process.

I may have forgotten to turn Daric on his side, so he vomited down his front. Darn?

***

We rolled into town at dusk and dropped the horses off at a stable. Then we made a beeline for the tavern. Unlike the city, these trees weren't quite big enough to live in. There were a few structures on the ground, but a lot more treehouses with rope and wood bridges between them.

Gemma and I had our cloaks pulled low to hide our features. Because of Gemma's size, she attracted some hostile stares. Even with the cloak, it was hard to hide what she was. I heard a few muttered comments about stealing livestock and eating babies.

Gemma didn't say anything, but I could tell by the way she stooped and pulled at the hood of her cloak that it was affecting her.

From the outside, the tavern appeared to be a lively place. It was a solid-looking two-story structure built of large roughhewn timbers. Bright light spilled into the street from large windows and music and raucous laughter drifted from the door.

Then we stepped through the doorway. The lute screeched mid-note, and all conversations stopped. A dozen elves in dirty clothes and sun-kissed faces scowled at us.

Daric and Sina seemed unfazed as they strode to the bar. Gemma and I paused near the door.

"Don't worry. They're more afraid of us than we are of them," I whispered to Gemma.

"Scared people make stupid decisions," she whispered back.

I gave a big smile and waved, figuring as long as the tavern full of fae couldn't see my round ears, I'd be fine. I followed my companions across the room with Gemma a step behind.

"Two rooms," said Daric, "with a bath if you have one."

The elf waved a hand in front of his nose. "Good thing we do, 'cause you need it."

The barkeep looked over my shoulder and squinted. "Troll," he whispered.

"She's with us," said Sina. "Will that be a problem?"

"Of course, it's a problem," his eyes hardened as he leaned in and lowered his voice. "We can't have her in here eating our customers."

148

Gemma growled and leaned over me. I could tell she was on the verge of ripping his arms off. If she did, the tavern patrons would become a mob.

We'd be lynched by the very people we were trying to save.

CHAPTER 26: WELL, WELL, WELL, THAT'S A DEEP SUBJECT

Gemma clenched and unclenched her fists. "How about I just eat you, bartender?"

I decided this needed a human touch before it spiraled out of control. "Sir, what's your name?"

"Fikus."

"Fikus, it's hard to believe," I pushed Daric aside and leaned in conspiratorially, "but poor Gemma here is the victim of Darower elf sorcery. She was once an elf warrior known far and wide for her bravery and self-sacrifice."

"I've never heard of her," he remarked.

"And there's a reason for that," I continued. "You see, she was so revered and respected, Gemma inspired other elves to follow her example. As you can imagine, the Darower couldn't let that stand. They sent one of their most powerful sorcerers after Gemma. He caught her unawares and cursed her to live the rest of her life as a troll. The elves that had respected her, only saw the troll she became. They couldn't put aside what they knew versus how she now looked. As a result, they erased all her good deeds from the records."

"Truly?" the bartender asked.

"Oh yes, and I can prove it." I touched my nose. "What do you smell?"

"Skunk, and yesterday's meatloaf back for an unscheduled visit," he said, wrinkling his nose.

"And the troll?" I asked.

"Mint?"

"Exactly," I pointed at him. "Tell me, friend, have you ever heard of a troll that smells nice?"

"Uh, no." He grimaced. "They always smell like rotting garbage."

"That's right. It's because poor Gemma has been forced to live for the past two decades as a troll. But as a former elf, she knows the value of being clean. Certainly, you can see your way to renting a room to a hero who has given so much in the name of her queen and kingdom."

"Well, uh, yes," he sputtered. "When you put it that way, we'd be honored to have her here as a guest."

Fikus bowed deeply to Gemma. "My apologies, ma'am. Please accept the best room we have. Free of charge for a hero of the kingdom." He handed her a solid brass key.

Gemma held the key in her big hand, blinking bewilderingly at it. Daric and Sina openly gaped at me.

"Are we done?" I asked my friends. "I could really use a bath."

***

Daric paid for the other room, and we headed upstairs. There was a central sitting room with a low table, couch, and two chairs. The furniture was rustic, but serviceable. There were four bedrooms with two beds each. Each bedroom also had a large bathtub. Unlike at the palace, the spout didn't produce hot water, but there was a magic heating coil that could be put in the water and activated.

The bedroom Gemma and I shared was twice the size of all the other ones.

Daric insisted on taking his bath right away, which I thought was rude considering Sina was still stinky. I offered Gemma our tub first. That put Sina and me alone in the sitting room.

"You lied."

I leaned back on the couch and crossed my arms. "Yes. I did."

The elf glared at me. "Lying is wrong."

"So is tricking people, but elves do that all the time."

She waved it away. "That's different. That's the art of the deal. It's their own fault if there weren't smart enough to negotiate."

I sighed. "Okay, let's come at this differently. Your mom,

Queen of the Shara elves. She does things to make the lives of all elves better."

"Right. It's her job because she's the queen."

"What about you?" I shrugged. "You're her daughter. Is she required to work in your best interest?"

Sina rolled her eyes. "Of course."

"Daric?"

She slumped in the chair. "Technically, I'm supposed to support him. We are engaged to be married."

I pointed to myself. "What about me?"

"The queen assigned me to protect you. Of course, I work in your best interest."

"And..." I prompted.

She gave me a half-smile. "And I like you. You're my friend."

"Gemma?"

Sina snorted. "Let's just say I'm undecided."

"Fair enough." I laced my fingers together and leaned forward. "We're friends and family. We do things to help each other not because of a contract, but because we care about each other."

She nodded. "Yes."

"But your mom does things for other elves, just because they're elves."

Sina tilted her head in confusion. "I guess that's true."

I put a finger on the table and used my other hand to draw a circle around it. "As a human, my definition of friends and family is a little wider. If someone hasn't tried to hurt me, I might be inclined to help them."

"Daric would call you a fool."

I shrugged. "And he may be right."

She frowned. "What does this have to do with lying?"

"Fikus was about to turn Gemma away for being a troll. Gemma has done nothing to Fikus, so his basis for turning her away was his own prejudices. He was about to hurt her. The truth would have started a fight hurting even more people." I turned my palms up. "So, I lied."

"But lying is wrong."

"Which action served the greater good: my lie, or the truth?"

***

What a difference a night makes. A hot bath, a good night's sleep. It's enough to make you forget there are people out to kill you.

New day, new town. First order of business: find new clothes. After careful consideration, Gemma and I stuck to the ground-level shops. As fun as the rope bridges sounded, none of them looked like they'd support the troll's weight.

"Do you notice anything odd?" asked Gemma.

I glanced around at the elves moving about. "You mean how everyone's watching you, but no one looks pissed off about it?"

"Not just me, they're staring at us."

I studied the passing elves. "Nope, they're seeing me, sure, but their eyes are staying on you."

"Like, whatever, they're totally into you and your round ears."

I pulled my hood closer around my head.

We passed a shrine, and my brain did a little hiccup. For just a second, I thought I saw my grandma's cat. Fifi was all black and had one yellow and one blue eye. When I turned to look at the shrine, though, it had a bunch of wooden cat carvings but no actual cats.

I shook my head to clear it.

A few steps later, we were in front of a tailor's shop, and we stepped inside.

There wasn't nearly as much stuff here as in Millow's place back in Lonathas, but a wide range of clothes hung on the walls and display racks. A sandy-haired elf with pins in his mouth stood in front of a wireframe mannequin marking cloth with chalk.

He didn't notice we'd entered, so Gemma and I watched him work for a bit. Which lasted until he moved to the other side of the mannequin and saw us.

Pbbbt! He spit out the pins and they went everywhere. He seemed torn between picking up the pins or selling us something. He wiped his hands on his pants and stepped forward with his hand out. "Hi, I'm..." his eyes went wide. "Ow."

"Your name is Ow?" I asked.

He whimpered and put a finger up, in a wait a moment gesture, and knelt. I winced as he pulled two pins out of his foot and quickly grabbed most of the others on the floor. He deposited them in a nearby dish.

Returning to us, he held his hand out again. "Hi, I'm Ash."

"I'm Evan, and this is-"

"Gemma. I know." He smiled weakly.

"You do?" asked Gemma.

He shrugged. "Everyone knows."

"How does everyone know?" I asked.

Ash limped behind his sales counter and laced his fingers together. "There are just under five thousand people in our quaint little village. And that's if you include all the farmers within fifty miles, who will angrily deny it. Anyone new shows up, you automatically become the talk of the town. Add in that you're a hero cursed to be a troll." He spread his hands. "There might be a couple of people who haven't heard about you yet, but I doubt it."

"Can I heal your foot?" I pointed to where his foot would be behind the counter. "That looked painful."

He side-eyed me. "What do you want in return?"

I let my gaze wander about the store. "Give us a fair deal on any clothes we buy."

"I can do that."

He let me heal his foot, then we browsed the store. I picked out two pairs of pants in brown and black, in the wrap style that seemed popular with the locals. Then I picked three poet-style shirts in green, blue, and dark red. I also chose a travel cloak because it seemed like a good idea to have an extra. Gemma special ordered a dress after I offered to pay for it.

There wasn't a problem until I tried on the shirts... and I took off my cloak without thinking.

CHAPTER 27: I DON'T WEAR BOWS, I SHOOT THEM

In the middle of pulling off my shirt, I heard Ash suck in a breath. I froze. What was I thinking? Carefully, I let my arms down and peeked.

Sure enough, Ash was staring at me. There were several seconds of silence before he said, "You have round ears."

Gemma put a hand over her mouth to hide her chuckles.

"Yes?" I said.

"You're not an elf."

"No?"

I let my arms down as I watched a mixture of emotions play across his face. "A-a-are you a... human?"

I nodded. "Yes."

That spurred Ash into action as he rushed to the front of the store and closed the windows and doors. "That's why the noble warrior Gemma is traveling with you. You're a human wizard! Oh, you're looking for a way to change her back, aren't you? You have to tell me about Earth. Are there really impossibly tall castles and magic chariots everywhere? Are you on a secret mission for the queen?" Ash stopped and covered his mouth with both hands. "I thought you'd have white hair and a wrinkled face like in the stories."

"You've heard of human-tales?" I asked.

"Yes, they're my *favorite*." The tailor quivered in place as he went from shopkeeper to fanboy in three point two seconds. "Take the clothes. They're free. Just tell me a couple of stories about

157

Earth. Oh, Bunni is going to flip and be ten shades of jealous when she finds out I met a real live human!"

I glanced at Gemma, who was busy trying not to laugh. I smiled nervously at Ash. "Uh, okay. What the heck."

So, I told him about going to the water park with my dad as I tried on my clothes. As Ash took Gemma's measurements, I told him about the first time I tried to make tiramisu with my grandma, which ended up being tirami-soup. Ash hung on every word, asking for clarification when something didn't translate well.

"A whole park with rides made of water." Ash shook his head. "Your world sounds amazing."

"I'll say," said Gemma. "So, how do you make ladyfingers? Are they made from real ladies?"

I ignored Gemma's question in case she wasn't joking. "There are a lot of amazing things about my world, but you've got a lot of great things here, too. There are no trees that people live in and no magic at all."

Ash tilted his head. "If you don't have magic, then how do you build such fantastic things?"

I briefly explained how cars worked, but that led to a discussion of gasoline, which Gemma and Ash both declared alchemical magic.

"Listen, it isn't magic. We just do things differently," I explained.

Gemma shook her head. "If it looks like a sprite and talks like a sprite, then it's probably a sprite. I've had a glimpse into your world. A lot of human things look like magic to me. Books that rewrite themselves in front of your eyes, balls in the ceiling that glow when you ask them, too. If that isn't magic, I don't know what is."

At that point, I stopped arguing. Author C. Clark was right. Any sufficiently advanced technology is indistinguishable from magic.

Ash used magic to alter Gemma's dress. It was forest green with brown ribbons and bows. I don't know why it surprised me. Gemma liked practical clothes, but she enjoyed having cute stuff, too. She was a badass battle-hardened troll that also liked bunnies, flowers, and dresses. In many ways, Sina was a bigger tomboy than Gemma.

The troll stepped behind a screen to change.

I shrugged. "Ash, we're told that there's been a dragon

harassing the village. Do you know where it's been seen?"

His eyes lit up. "You *were* sent here by the queen. Yes!" Ash pumped his fists in the air. "North of here. That's where all the farms and ranches have been attacked. But all the travelers were waylaid east of here, coming to and from the capital."

"Has the dragon eaten anyone?" Gemma peaked over the screen with a gleam in her eye.

Ash gazed upward as if the answer might be found on the ceiling. "Huh. Now that you mention it, no. I mean, no one's said anything about being eaten, and no one has gone missing." He shrugged. "Everyone knows everyone else out here. If someone went missing, the well washer women or the alehouse pint pushers would know." He spread his hands. "Then everyone else would, too."

That made sense. It was a small community, and the most interesting things aside from dragons were everyone else's business. We now had a place to look for the dragon, even if it was a couple of hundred square miles. What would I do when I found it? How long would it take me to cover that much area for a dragon's lair? How much time was I losing in the real world?

Gemma stepped from behind the screen and did a twirl. "What do you think?"

If the dress were on someone a quarter her size, I would have called it cute. "Bows are a great look for you," I said.

She beamed. "Thanks, Evan."

I got dressed in my new clothes and bid Ash a good day. He opened the front of the shop to let us out, but I paused after I pulled my hood over my head. "Hey Ash, what's that?" I pointed to the collection of cat statues across from the shop.

"The shrine? It's to Fifta."

I regarded him over my shoulder. "Fifta is a cat?"

He grinned. "No, she's a goddess who sometimes takes the form of a cat. Imna, the elven goddess of fertility and magic is more popular around here. It's a farm community, after all. She's got a temple on the far side of town, but many people like Fifta, the cat goddess of protection and good health. Enough that we put up a shrine to honor her."

"Has she ever-" My question was interrupted by a scream.

The source was an elven woman pointing to the sky. I looked up and saw the silhouette of a dragon. It was flying over the village, heading north.

The elves scattered like football players at a kegger after the cops show up. Gemma and I didn't even have a tumbleweed to keep us company.

Ash was motioning for us to go back to his shop. "Come on, she'll see you!"

I waved at him. "Thanks, but this is what I'm here for. Come on Gemma."

We ran after the flying lizard. Gemma had an ear-to-ear grin. A hundred yards later, Daric and Sina joined us from the right.

"We'll never catch it," said Daric, huffing.

"We aren't going to catch it," I confirmed. "But if it's heading back to its den, we'll be able to narrow down the search area. Wherever we lose sight of it is where we search."

Sina gave the troll a quick up and down glance. "Bows?"

"Like them?" Gemma asked.

"I don't wear bows. I shoot them." After a couple of strides, Sina spoke to me. "What will you do if we find the den?"

"I haven't figured that part out yet," I admitted.

We jogged after the dragon. It stopped and circled several times before continuing north, which left me with the unsettling thought that it wanted us to catch up. What would happen if we did?

My muscles burned. I had just reached my limit and had dropped to walk when the dragon dove, disappearing into a wooded area.

I stopped and laced my fingers over my head as I tried to catch my breath. What was I going to do now? The dragon was on the ground about a quarter mile ahead. It dove, so it was probably hunting. If it held to the pattern, it would leave half its kill behind. Why? Was it a warning to the humans, or worse, to other dragons? The villagers hadn't said anything about two dragons, but really, had any of them gotten close enough to tell?

Get it together Evan. This is ten years of your life we're talking about here. Not to mention seeing Grandma and Dad again.

I took a deep breath and let it out. Turning around, I said, "I'm going to go over and say hello. None of you have to come with me."

Daric gave me a genuine smile. "You're a brave man. Go ahead. If you don't come back in a couple of hours," he clapped Sina on the shoulder, "we'll look for your remains."

Sina scowled at Daric. "Evan, don't do this. The dragon is hunting. If you interrupt his meal, you'll likely be dessert."

I turned to Gemma.

"As if!" She grinned at me. "I'm coming with."

I might be masticated, but at least I wouldn't die alone.

Giving the elves a salute, I trotted in the dragon's direction with Gemma on my heels.

We ran downhill, through a gully, and up the far side. I entered the trees but got a little turned around in the thick of the thicket. I couldn't see the sun.

"Gemma, I hate to admit this, but I'm a little lost."

She sniffed the air. "That way," she pointed.

I cocked my head. "You know what dragon smells like?"

"No," she waggled her eyebrows, "but I know what a lizard smells like, and the biggest one I ever smelled is that way."

Couldn't fault that logic, so we ran *that way*. Gemma used her meld with stone spell to hide.

It quickly became a non-issue. It was bright red and as big as a house. The head was the size of a Buick with a pair of gold horns just as long. Its claw held a deer on the ground with several large chunks taken out of it. Two golden eyes with slitted pupils watched me approach.

Its matronly voice echoed through the forest, seemingly coming from everywhere at once. "Don't you know it's impolite to interrupt someone when they're eating?"

It was in a clearing, so I stood at the very edge of it. I was one and a half dragon lengths away and didn't feel remotely safe. For as large as it was, it had a feline grace that reminded me of a mountain lion. One swipe would mean a quick death.

Bowing low, I smiled brightly, "Hi, I'm Evan."

She sighed. "Great. The villagers are sending me idiots for food. Come closer food. I promise your death will be quick."

I swallowed hard and my knees knocked together as I trembled before the towering beast. *Ten years, ten years, ten years.* "Ha. Good joke," I said, forcing a grin. "Queen Lycia of the Shara Elves bids you greetings, oh great dragon. She fears for the safety of her people and has sent me to negotiate on her behalf."

The dragon smiled and smoke curled past rows and rows of razor-sharp teeth. "Why should I care what some fancy titled elf wants?"

The echoed effect of her voice was a bit off-putting. It sounded like it was coming from in front of me and behind me at the same time.

"Because she is strong and powerful," I said, "and has many warriors and magic at her disposal."

The dragon waved a claw the size of a dining room table. "She can send as many morsels and as many spells as she likes. I don't mind teaching an uppity elf her place in the food chain."

"She's rich." I hedged. The queen had said that bribery didn't work with dragons, but if I could get her talking, perhaps I could find something she liked more before she ate me.

The dragon's eyes lit with interest. "Now you're talking my language. If food wishes to give me tribute to postpone their fate, I can be accommodating."

Except that the queen wouldn't give gold to the dragon. She'd told me as much.

"What else pleases your greatness?" *Please give me something other than gold to work with.*

She held up a claw. "Gems, jewelry, new and interesting elves to eat." She took a big sniff. "Wait. You're not an elf. What are you? Oh, and you can tell the troll to stop hiding. I know she's here."

She kept one claw possessively on the deer like she expected the dead animal to get up and walk away, or for me to somehow take it from her.

"Um, uh. Yeah. I'm a human." I took off my hood to reveal my ears.

The dragon's face lit up. "Ooh. The rarest of morsels. Can I eat an arm or a leg? I hear you taste delicious."

"Told ya," Gemma whispered in my ear from behind me.

"Not now," I whispered back.

"As interesting as having you eat me sounds," I said to the dragon, "I'll pass for now." I shook my head. The longer I talked to the dragon, the more something seemed off, but I couldn't put my finger on what.

The dragon's entire demeanor changed. In an instant, her posture became like a tiger ready to pounce, and she narrowed her eyes at me. "No? No?! No one says no to me. Let the uppity elf send another emissary. I'll eat you as a down payment."

MIS-SPELLED

CHAPTER 28: CRUNCHY AND GOOD WITH KETCHUP

The dragon lunged. It could have gotten me... if I had still been there. I was already sprinting full speed through the underbrush. I did not look back. Not once. I ran and continued running until I reached the edge of the woods.

At the tree line, I stopped. Not because I'd run out of steam, but because I was very aware that dragons fly. After getting nearly nibbled, I wasn't about to make it easy on her by skipping merrily across an open field.

I searched the skies and the surrounding woods but didn't see red. I did see green. Gemma ran toward me. She looked how I felt. With wide eyes and a paler shade of green than usual, it was clear she was just as scared of the big lizard as I was.

She stopped next to me, and we panted in unison for a few minutes as we searched the skies for pursuit.

Then she chuckled and slapped me on the back. "We did it. We totally saw a dragon and didn't die."

"Yeah." I smiled weakly. "Why didn't the dragon chase us?"

"Who cares! It didn't. We get to live."

"Yes... We get to live." I turned and stared into the pine forest. "Evan?"

The strange feeling that something wasn't right wouldn't go away.

"Evan?"

"Stay here, Gemma. I need to check something out." I waved her back as I marched into the woods.

"Oh, my *gods*. You aren't."

I ignored her and kept going.

She sighed heavily and hustled after me. "He is."

Gemma caught up and walked beside me for a few moments before she said anything. "So, you almost become dragon dinner and you're going back for more. Evan, are you insane?"

"That's what I'm trying to find out," I said as followed the trail Gemma and I had left in the underbrush. Thanks to Sina's instruction, the bent branches, disturbed pine needles, and fallen leaves led me right back to the clearing. When we got close, I took a page from Gemma's book and used the Meld with Stone spell to hide and Gemma followed suit.

The dragon was gone. The deer was half-eaten. The fresh kill hadn't even started to stink yet. It was at the edge of the clearing.

Scratching my head, I dropped the camouflage spell. I walked to where I had been standing. I was the right distance from the half a deer. Gross. The same distance I had been during our conversation earlier. I stepped to the middle of the clearing and measured it with my eyes. Was the space between the trees... smaller?

Gemma appeared beside me as she also dropped the Meld with Stone Spell. "What are you thinking?"

Spinning around slowly, I examined the area. "I'm wondering where the dragon went."

She sniffed and pointed north and east. "That way."

I looked in the direction she pointed. Then up at the sky. It was mid-afternoon. I could go haring off after the dragon again, but if I did, I'd forgo the comfort of the room we had at the inn. There was no guarantee I'd find her lair, and if I did, I probably wouldn't make it back to town before dark. Since we'd left town without our gear, that option didn't appeal to me.

"Let's go find Daric and Sina," I decided. I almost ran into a tree a couple of times because I was lost in thought, staring absently at the ground.

We found the elves pretty much where we left them.

As we came within speaking range, Daric frowned. "You didn't find the dragon?"

I shook my head. "No, we found her."

Sina ducked her head, trying to catch my eyes. "Her? It's a she dragon?"

Meeting her gaze briefly, I nodded, but I was too distracted to carry the conversation. The dragon was huge. Why did it eat only half the deer? What was north and east of here?

"Sina," I looked up, "can I borrow your map?"

She cautiously handed it to me.

"Thanks." I rolled it out on the ground and watched as it drew in the surrounding area.

"The dragon didn't eat you?" asked Daric with a curious expression.

"No." I studied the map but didn't elaborate.

So, Gemma filled in the details by regaling the elves with our close encounter with the dragon.

While she did that, I expanded the map to the north. There were only a few rocky areas suitable for caves. Thinking back on the encounter, the claws didn't strike me as being suited for building a structure. The dragon probably had a cave, or had dug out an area to nest in. I committed the map to memory and rolled it up, handing it back to Sina.

We walked back to town. I don't remember the trip, to be honest. The nagging sense that I was missing something important kept me thoroughly distracted.

When we reached the tavern, I ordered a meal and took it upstairs to the sitting room with me. I ate it while I ran the details of my encounter over and over in my head. I only remember eating a few bites of the hearty stew, but there was an empty bowl in front of me. On the other side of the table, Sina and Gemma watched me with concern.

Daric tapped me on the shoulder.

"Huh?" I gazed up at him. "Hey Daric, can I help you with something?"

"Are you going out tomorrow? To look for the dragon?" he asked hopefully.

I blinked. "Yes. Are you coming with me?"

"Not tomorrow," he smiled. "Truth be told, I probably shouldn't have been out there today, but I have a duty to report anything of note to the queen. We saw a real honest to Imna dragon. I think that more than counts as noteworthy."

I nodded and looked across the table at Sina and Gemma. "What about you two?"

Sina glanced up at Daric, who shook his head. "No. I'll wait for you in town. Are you planning on coming back tomorrow night?"

That was disappointing, but if the dragon ate me, at least she'd be safe. "I think so. Gemma?"

"As if." Gemma winked at me. "Try to keep me away, dragon charmer."

I cocked my head to the side in confusion. "Charmer?"

"*Yeah*," she said like it meant, *duh*. "You spoke to a dragon for ten whole minutes and lived to tell the tale. You must have a dozen rabbits' feet shoved up your butt."

Chuckling, I shook my head. "Thanks, Gemma. I'll search for the rabbit bits next time I head to the outhouse."

"Speaking of which, we need to see the tailor again. After today, I need a change of panties." She looked abashed.

"I did not need that image. Ew!"

"What?! I'm not still wearing them goblin brains," Gemma protested, then she grinned evilly. "I left them in Sina's pack."

Sina narrowed her eyes. "Oh, a prank duel? You are *so* going to regret that, green girl."

"Bring your best game, chipmunk breath," Gemma retorted.

***

I didn't sleep well. I was heading back out to talk to a beast that had already threatened to eat me. It was certainly very capable of doing so. But it hadn't. Ash had told me no one had been eaten. Or injured. Really, the only things missing were livestock or wild game.

I didn't for a moment think that made me safe. An intelligent creature as big as a two-story house had no reason to think of me as anything more than a nuisance. So why wasn't it crossing that line?

Gemma and I set off in the morning. We left late enough that the village shops had opened.

"What had you so bothered yesterday?" asked Gemma.

I struggled to put it into words. "Have you ever had an itch that you couldn't get to?"

She shrugged. "Yeah, you go find a tree and rub your back against it. Feels good."

I laughed. "It was like that, but I couldn't find the right tree and the itch wouldn't go away."

Gemma grinned at me. "Well, anytime you need something itched, just let me know. Crotch, armpit, butt, anything you need."

I looked at her askance. "Ew."

She licked me.

We made it to Ash's shop. True to her word, Gemma picked up underwear. I decided that carrying a fortune in gems in my pocket wasn't a good idea, so I asked Ash where the local magic shop was.

"You want Bunni's place," he said. "Tell her I sent you and that she owes me one. She's two trees east and three trees north. Her shop is one level up from the ground, but there's a sturdy ramp on her tree, so you shouldn't need to use one of the rope walkways. It'll hold Gemma's weight just fine."

We had no trouble finding the shop. Gemma had to stoop to get through the door. A mixture of smells hit me. I could pick out cinnamon, lavender, and frankincense. I took in the odd array of items occupying the wooden shelves on each wall. A blonde elf with straight hair and freckles on her nose was behind the counter, putting a label on a bottle with a purple-colored liquid inside. She looked up and went slack-jawed, dropping the bottle, which shattered, spilling the contents all over the countertop. An entire section of the counter disappeared, as if some giant had taken a bite out of it.

"Oh, fuzzballs!" She pulled out a rag, which she rubbed on the now invisible counter. The rag disappeared along with two fingers.

She groaned and threw the rag down with an audible but invisible splat. Stepping around the counter, she held out her hand. "Hi, I'm Bunni. How can I help you?"

She was a foot shorter than me and dressed in a simple green and red dress with pointy shoulder pads. I peered down at the half a hand she offered.

She had a nervous grin that was all teeth as she hid her hands behind her back. "Sorry." She blurted.

"Hi, I'm Evan and this is my friend Gemma. Ash said we should come to talk to you."

She plastered a fake smile on her face. "He did? Great," then, "he's trying to kill me with embarrassment now," through clenched teeth.

I pointed behind her. "Do you need help with that?"

"No, Wizard Evan. It'll be fine in an hour," Bunni bounced in place, "as I'm sure you know." She tittered nervously. "I'm Bunni, by the way."

"You mentioned that," said Gemma.

"I did? Oh, uh, what can I do to you?" Her eyes went wide. "For you! For you." She half-glanced behind herself. "Ah, hopefully not invisibility potions."

Her rapid-fire speech and slightly awkward manner was cute, and I warmed up to the young elf. Would invisibility potions be useful? Probably not for this quest, besides we had the Meld with Stone spell. "No. I'm carrying some heirlooms that I'm concerned about falling into the wrong hands." My chocolate sprang to mind even though I wasn't currently carrying that. "I'd like to protect things I'm carrying from being stolen."

Bunni winced. "You'd think that way out here, we wouldn't have to worry about such things, but kids will be kids. Shops on the outskirts of town have been robbed. While I can't keep someone from stealing your coin purse, I can make it so that it won't do them any good if they do."

"What do you mean?" I asked.

Bunni went behind her partially transparent counter and pulled out a lockbox. A quarter of it was also clear and there were silver and gold coins inside. "Fifta curse it," she muttered under her breath. Then, in a more normal voice, "Okay, invisibility aside, assume you wanted to get into this lockbox." She set it on the countertop. "Give it a go."

I reached forward and tried to open it, but my finger slipped right over the lock. I couldn't even feel it. "That's amazing."

Bunni reached forward and opened it up. "Tada. The person who blooded the spell is the only one who can open the box. Don't die or anything, because no one else can open it either. Damaging the box or pouch causes it to go poof."

"Poof?"

"It goes somewhere else at random. Maybe solid rock, or bottom of a lake, or anywhere."

I nodded. "Like my end table at the palace."

Gemma cracked her knuckles. "Can I try?"

Bunni grabbed her box and held it to her chest. "Don't hurt my lockbox."

"Do you have anything else?" I asked. "Carrying a large box around isn't very subtle."

Bunni snapped her fingers. "I can put it on pretty much anything." She put her lockbox away and pulled out a leather pouch the size of a paperback book. "Including this little cutie, which I think would be perfect for you."

It wasn't big enough for what I needed. "Do you have three?"

She grinned. "This is the only one you'll need." She turned over the bag and pulled out a blanket, a bottle of wine, two glasses, a small chest, two candlesticks with candles, cured meat, and a cheese wheel.

My eyes bugged out of my head as she pulled each item out. "Wow, that's amazing. Are you planning a picnic?"

Bunni blushed. "Slim pickings out here. A girl's gotta be ready to pounce when the opportunity presents itself." Her eyes flashed to me, then Gemma. She shook her head and muttered. "No. Down, girl."

I was sold. "Alright, what will that set me back?"

"One hundred gold. And I want to see your ears." She raised her eyebrows apologetically. "Please?"

Reluctantly, I removed my hood. Bunni bit her lip as she stood on her toes to study my round ears. Meanwhile, I dug a ruby out of my waist pouch. "I don't have that much coin on me. Can I trade one of these?"

The tiny elf sucked in a breath. "That rock could buy a quarter of the inventory in my shop." She peered up at me. "Are you single?"

"Sorry, chasing dragons." I dodged the question.

"Aren't they all," she said dejectedly.

It took Bunni ten minutes to key the pouch to me. Gemma asked for one as well. It ended up being her last holding pouch. While she could cast the locking spell, the bags themselves had to be enchanted by gnomes.

It turns out I was overpaying by *a lot*, so I asked for some healing potions, mana potions, one of those fancy magic maps, a leather-bound notebook, and instructions on how to cast the sealing enchantment. Having a magical biometric lock sounded very cool.

I expected it to work like the Repel Sprites enchantment. Nope, it was far trickier. I took notes in English so that after Gemma finished teaching me Stone Shape, I could work on this one.

After all of that, Bunni gave me an additional four hundred gold before she declared us even. At least I had walking around money now, and some place to put it.

We bid Bunni good day, and Gemma and I went back to the

tavern to grab our packs. On the way, we stopped by a butcher shop, and the troll filled her new pouch with an assortment of meats and sausages. It turned out the room-sized space inside the pouch was like a refrigerator. Food placed inside stayed fresher longer than in the open air. Gemma asked me what food I could prepare out of each of her purchases, which led to us visiting an herb and seasoning shop.

After that, we dropped by the stables. Nonam and the other horses begged for treats, and I gave them each a bit of carrot.

We arrived back at the inn to find Daric and Sina waiting with our packs.

"Here you go," said Daric cheerfully. "All packed and ready to go. Say hello to the dragon for me."

I squinted at Daric, then checked my pack. Everything I needed was there. "You're being very helpful suddenly. Why?"

The elf noble smiled. "You've got a job to do, and I want to help you do it."

Right. I'm dealing with an elf. "You expect me to be successful in convincing the dragon to leave the village alone?"

Daric shrugged but didn't answer. Which was all the answer I needed. He expected me to be eaten. Well, he may get his wish.

I turned and held my hand out for Sina to shake. She ignored the hand and wrapped her arms around me. Shocked, it took me a second to return the hug.

Sina whispered, "Be careful. Come back to me, okay?"

I tightened my hold on her. "I promise I'll be careful. This isn't the end."

It was a long hug, and I didn't want it to stop. It wasn't skin to skin, so I couldn't read her thoughts to tell if she was sincere. And really, I didn't need to. When it ended, Sina glared at Gemma. "You'll take care of him, right?"

"It'll be easier without you and the prissy elf lord around," replied the troll.

"I'm being serious."

"I am, too," said Gemma, turning on her heel. "Your armor makes a racket."

I chuckled. The armor clinked a bit as the elves walked, but nowhere near as much as the suits of metal armor I'd seen at the renaissance fair. With a wink and a wave, I joined Gemma as we strode out of town.

It was mid-morning and elves stopped and bowed as we passed. As we neared the edge of town, I noticed a few children were following us. When we reached the last tree of the sufra grove, there was a small crowd. Ash and Bunni were among them.

We waved, and they all started clapping. We left town to cheers and whoops.

***

Using my new magic map, we were able to make the first rocky bluff by early afternoon. We didn't find any caves. The second rocky hill was only a couple of hours further. The cave we found there was shallow and occupied by a bear. He wasn't interested in us, so we moved on with no trouble.

As we hiked toward the next hill, I resigned myself to the fact that we would not make it back to town tonight. It was sunny without a cloud in the sky though, so hiking across meadows and through stands of trees wasn't much of a hardship.

Well, other than someone might be still out to kill me. Or the dragon might change her mind and decide I was worth the hassle of chasing.

I scanned the skies. "Gemma, have you seen anything following us?"

She trotted up next to me. "You mean other than that family of foxes?"

I grinned at her. "Yeah, other than that. Those kits were really cute."

"If by cute you mean, like, delicious looking, I'll totally agree with you." The troll rubbed her belly. Then unslung her pack and pulled out a bag. "Fox for dinner?"

Stopping, I cocked my head in her direction. "You didn't."

She grinned. "No, but I wanted to." She put the bag back and grabbed a full water bottle. She took one gulp and then spewed liquid everywhere.

The smell of pickles assaulted my nose as Gemma coughed and gagged. It took all of two seconds to work out what happened, and I giggled.

"Rraaaahhh! I'm going to kill Sina next time I see her."

I winced. "She filled one of your water bottles with vinegar, huh?"

"Never trust an elf."

"Certainly not to pack your stuff," I agreed. "Always verify."

"Can I borrow..." Gemma accepted the water bottle I was already handing her. "Thanks."

She sniffed it before rinsing her mouth out, took several swallows, and handed it back. Gemma nodded at the hills. "Do you really think we'll find a cave big enough for a dragon?"

I shrugged. "I don't know. It's just a guess. Maybe they build nests like birds or sleep in magic clouds."

"Magic clouds?" She blinked. "Huh, I never thought of that. If we find her cave, what do you think the chances she'll be there are?"

"Pretty good, I expect."

"Why?"

"Because dragons usually hunt knights." I swung my fist like I held an imaginary sword.

Gemma rolled her eyes. "Maybe you'll scare her off with your bad humor."

It was twilight when we reached the rocky part of the hill and searched. We found a large cave. The entrance was behind a rockslide of enormous boulders. Studying the opening, I had a hard time imagining the house-sized dragon fitting through the entrance. Sunlight filtered through openings in the boulder pile but illuminated little beyond.

"Gemma, do you smell lizard?"

She sniffed the air, once, twice, then a third time with a long breath through the nose. "Uh. No... I don't smell anything."

"You mean nothing at all?"

She rubbed her nose vigorously, then sniffed again. "That is so weird. No. Nothing. It's like my nose is turned off."

That was odd. It could mean that there wasn't anything to smell, but wouldn't there be at least some bat poo or something?

I drew a circle on the ground and put a sugar cube in it. Bramble popped into existence beside the circle in a shower of sparks.

"Okay, Peach Fuzz, what do you want for the sugar?" The sprite flew in a spiral. "Hurry it up. There's a family of rabbits I'm teaching to play dead to get away from coyotes."

"I don't think that'll work."

Bramble flew up to hover in front of my nose. "Of course it

will work. The trick is to lure them in close so the rabbit can pee in its face."

"Um," I shook my head, "never mind. See that cave? Go in there, search the whole cave, then come back and tell me what you found."

Like a lightning bug on steroids, Bramble shot into the cave.

After a couple of seconds, Gemma asked, "What happens if there is a dragon in there?"

I glanced at her. She glanced at me. We sprinted for opposite sides of the cave entrance and flattened ourselves against the rocks.

Five seconds later, Bramble shot out of the cave entrance and stopped outside the summoning circle. It spun in place several times. "Peach Fuzz?"

I cautiously stepped from behind a boulder. "Bramble, what did you see?"

"Dirt, rocks, and an elf." The sprite reached for the sugar cube.

"No, no," I cautioned. "Tell me more about the elf."

The sprite huffed. "She was short, with red hair, and lying on the ground."

"Was she asleep?" I asked.

"No. Her eyes were open." Bramble jittered in place as its gaze bounced from me to the sugar cube.

"Then why was she on the ground?" asked Gemma.

"Because she was bound and gagged," the sprite screamed in frustration. "Please gimme the *sugar-ar-ar-ar.*"

CHAPTER 29: DRAGONS DON'T MAKE PLANS, THEY WING IT

Gemma and I ran inside the cave. Which wasn't the greatest idea because it was dark.

Outside, Bramble wailed.

"Bramble, get in here," I yelled. "I'll give you another sugar cube if you light our way."

The sobbing stopped as if a switch had been thrown. I was in a shower of sparks when the sprite popped into being over my head. The sound echoed off the walls of the cave. "Whatever you say, Boss."

Light from the sprite illuminated the large space. Yellow and brown rock walls gave way to lichen and moss-covered boulders set in the moist earthen floor.

Next to a rock, a young red-haired elf with green eyes lay tied up. She peered at us with hope as she tried awkwardly to sit up. Gemma and I dashed to her side and undid her bonds and gag.

"Thank you," she said. "I've been trapped here for days. I don't know what would have happened if you hadn't shown up."

Gemma knelt beside her. "We're here to take you home."

The child gazed up at the troll. "You're not going to eat me? The dragon threatened to eat me."

"She won't eat you. Gemma used to be an elf once." Better to stick with the lie since she probably came from the village. "What's your name?"

"Pi. My dad is a merchant in the village. The dragon said that he'd pay a lot of gold to get me back." The elf girl sniffled, then wrapped her arms around me. "I want to go home." She burst into tears.

"We'll take you home," Gemma patted her on the back. "Your family will be thrilled to hear how brave you've been."

"Pi, where is the dragon?" I asked.

She looked at the cave entrance. "I don't know. The dragon goes out a lot. Hunting I think." Then she regarded the sprite.

"Don't look at me flame brain," the six-inch fae groused. "I'm just here for the sugar."

We led Pi out of the cave. I gave Bramble his two sugar cubes, and he bolted for the trees.

"You can command the sprites to do your bidding?" said Pi. "You're like no elf I've ever met."

"He's not an elf, little one," Gemma motioned to me. "Take off your hood, Evan."

I pulled it back and Pi stared at my ears in awe. "What are you?"

"I'm a human wizard," I confessed. I was getting more used to calling myself that.

Gemma gazed at the horizon. "The sun is setting. We better get off this mountain before the dragon gets back."

***

We'd made camp for the evening. Since we were close to the dragon's cave, we didn't have a campfire. Instead of hunting, we ate dried meat and berries from our rations. It was amazing the amount of meat the little elf girl could pack away. I couldn't fathom where she was putting it all. My Dad often joked that I had a hollow leg. Maybe elves did the same when they went through a growth spurt.

The feeling that something was off had come back, though. I was missing something important.

The dragon?

No. Getting Pi back to town was more important. We knew where the dragon's lair was. I could come back and negotiate later.

Something about Pi?

Maybe. She was definitely a handful. For someone who had been kidnapped, it hadn't dampened her enthusiasm. She ran ahead of us to check out bugs, birds, and flowers, just like any other little girl might. She peppered us with odd questions. "Why do I have two

eyes if I only see one thing? Why do spiders run away when I fart?"
I wondered if Bunni or Ash knew her dad.

That's when it hit me like a ton of boulders. My stomach did flip-flops, and I broke out in a cold sweat. The answer had been dancing around me with flowers in her hair for the past two hours. According to Ash, no one from the village was missing.

CHAPTER 30: WHELP, WE'RE OFF TO A GOOD START

It was a struggle to keep it together. Thankfully, we bedded down early. I lent my sleeping blankets to Pi and propped myself up against a tree. After taking the first watch, I pretended to sleep. I was far too wired to do anything of the sort. I kept my eyes almost closed and waited.

It felt like four hours, but it was probably more like one. Pi got up and snuck over to our pile of gear stacked against a tree. She rummaged around until she found my pouch. She tried to open it, but of course, that didn't work. My pouch was spell sealed. Only I could open it.

She fiddled with it for fifteen minutes before she growled an un-elflike growl, then slammed it into the ground three times.

"It's spell sealed," I said conversationally, even though my heart pounded in my chest. With ten years of servitude on the line, I figured putting on a brave face was better than the alternative.

Pi's green eyes glowed bright, and she stalked toward me with my pouch. "Open it, human," she growled.

My heart pounded in my chest. In my head, I was running around in circles screaming *don't eat me*. Outwardly, I pretended I was as cool as chocolate-covered cricket-flavored ice cream. "No. And before you get any bright ideas, if you kill me, no one can open it."

Pi clenched my leather pouch in her fist. "Give me your treasures, human. I don't have to kill you. I just have to hurt you."

I stared up at the night sky and tapped my finger on my chin.

"Um... No. My answer is still no."

Her eyes glowed brighter. "I will *burn* you."

"Are you old enough to breathe fire yet?" I forced a smile at her in the moonlight.

She stopped. Pi's mouth worked silently for a moment, then her whole demeanor changed. "I can," she whined defensively.

"Prove it."

The green glow dimmed, and the elf girl slumped. "Okay, I can't yet." Then she raised her chin. "But my teeth and claws are very sharp. Mama says so. You'd better watch out."

I stood and stretched before crossing to the wannabe elf and kneeled. "And you are so good at illusions." I leaned in and winked at her. "You've been practicing, haven't you?"

Pi smiled shyly and dug her toe into the ground. "Mama says I'm really good at pictures. I can also make myself look like anyone, and I can even make pictures of mama."

"I saw," I said enthusiastically. "And can I let you in on a little secret? I was really scared."

Pi giggled. "You ran really fast."

I poked her in the belly, and her grin widened. "That's because you were so monstrous. Rawr." I made tickle motions at Pi and she laughed, retreating beyond my reach.

On the other side of the campsite, Gemma sat up and rubbed her eyes.

"Pi, is that your real name?" I asked.

"It's Pyra, but ma calls me Newt."

My Newt. Mama's little dragon, cute. "Well, I think Pyra is a very pretty name," I told her. "Where is your mom?"

Her face fell. "We had a fight. I want my own dragon horde, but mom wouldn't let me go get one. She says I'm too young."

I nodded. "I'm sure your mom just wants the best for you, but you want to know something. Moms and dads aren't always right. Sometimes they want to protect us, but we need to get out into the world to learn and grow."

Pi stamped her foot. "Right! I mean, I'm fifty years old. If I were an elf or a dwarf, I'd be an adult now. Being a dragon sucks."

That must have reached Gemma's sleep-addled brain, because her eyes bugged out.

Sitting, I patted the ground next to me. Pi obediently ambled over and plopped down.

I nudged her with my shoulder. "I think you being a dragon is really neat. I mean, you can fly, cast illusions, and eat whatever you want. You have claws and sharp teeth. Pretty cool stuff."

"Yeah, but to be a real dragon, I have to have treasure." Pi picked up a rock and threw it across the campsite. "I tried to threaten the farmers and steal from the town like mom taught me, but I've only collected, like, fifteen gold. I'm awful at being a dragon."

"Pi, do you have any brothers or sisters?"

"No. But I've always wanted one. I even asked mom for one, but she said no."

I sighed. "I've got a brother. And my mom is always telling me to be nice to him. But you know what? He's a real jerk. He's always mean to me and my friends."

Pi squinted at me. "So, maybe having a brother isn't a good thing?"

"No," I shrugged, "I know plenty of people who have brothers and sisters they like. I just got unlucky. And my mom doesn't understand that my brother will never be a good guy." I picked up a rock and threw it to join hers across the campsite.

Gemma watched us intently, but didn't interrupt.

I continued, "I guess what I'm saying is that maybe, just maybe, your mom has given you bad advice. Maybe if you try something different, you can succeed in being a dragon."

"How's that?"

I held my hand out and Pi put my pouch in it. I opened it up and pulled out a diamond. Even in the moonlight, it sparkled.

Pi sucked in a breath. "That's beautiful."

"You want it?" I asked.

Pi scowled. "You're not gonna just give it to me, are you?"

"No," I waggled my head from side to side, "but I could trade it to you."

She screwed up her face. "Trade it to me?"

"Yeah, teach me your spells, and it's all yours. Your very first treasure." I threw the gem up and caught it.

"But you can't learn mind and body magic. You're not a dragon," she protested.

I held up a finger. "Normally that would be true, but I'm a human. I can learn any magic."

"Mama says I shouldn't teach anyone who isn't family."

I shrugged. "So, make me family."

"What?"

"Friends are the family you choose." I held my palms up. "I'd like it if we were friends. I could be your big brother and look out for you, and you could be my little sister and look out for me."

Pi frowned at me. "Is that how that works?"

"It is if we say it is." I held up the diamond. "What do you say?"

Pi's green eyes glowed as she gazed into the diamond. Then she turned her attention to me. "You won't make me come in at sundown or practice spells five hours a day?"

"I'm not your mom," I shrugged, "but I could be your big brother. I think as long as you're home by midnight, that's fine. As for spells, practice as much or as little as you like. It's important to learn and be smart, but there's nothing that says learning can't be fun. We'll make a game out of it." I held the diamond between two fingers in front of her. "Deal?"

Pi cupped her hands under my fingers. "Deal."

I dropped the diamond into her waiting palms. "Congratulations. You're a real dragon now."

***

I managed to get Pi to go to bed shortly after. She let the shape-shift spell drop and her red hair seemed to melt into her body. She plumped up, her face grew long and thin as her skin and clothes turned into shiny scales. When she was done, the six-foot-long red dragon wrapped my blanket into a mini nest. She nodded at Gemma before curling up and falling asleep.

It was only then that Gemma quietly rose from her blankets and sat next to me. "How, in all of Stellaluna, did I not realize we'd 'rescued' a dragon?" she whispered.

I shook my head. "I think it's part of her shape change spell. Things kept not adding up, and yet my brain refused to put the pieces together. I'd get partway there, and my thoughts would hiccup."

"I should have smelled lizard, but I didn't." Gemma cupped her chin in her palm as she watched Pi sleep. "Now, I can smell her scent, clear as ice." She snorted. "What finally did it for you?"

"I think it was a combination of things." I chewed my lip. "She only ate half her kills because she's small. In the clearing, the image of her mom was bigger than the space we were in. She never moved the front claw because she was hiding in it. When we went back, the grass and trees weren't trampled enough for a house-sized dragon. My mind kept slipping away from the obvious signs. Then, when she told us she'd been kidnapped, it didn't line up with what Ash had told us. It was then I could finally shake my mind loose."

We sat in silence for a few moments before Gemma spoke again. "And now we have one of the most powerful creatures in all of Stellaluna, short of a god, following us around. What are you going to tell the town? What are you going to tell Daric and Sina?"

"The town? Easy. I'll tell them I convinced the dragon to move someplace else. Which is true since she'll be following us." I blew out a long breath. "Daric and Sina? I have *no* idea."

Dragon or no, there still was a very real possibility that someone was out to get me, so I finished the first watch while Gemma slept. We switched at about one in the morning, and I found a soft patch of ground to get some shuteye. It was a little cold without my blanket, but I wasn't about to wake the sleeping dragon to get it.

I'd like to point out that if you're tired enough, nothing will keep you from sleeping. Also, nothing is likely to wake you up either.

Case in point, when I woke up, I was so toasty and warm that I didn't want to move. The only thing spoiling my morning lie-in was that my blanket wasn't quite right. I pulled at it to get it more on my shoulder, but the leathery blanket wouldn't move that way.

Leather? My eyes shot open. The blanket was bright red. My pillow had scales. I gently lifted the wing I was using as a blanket and found a head underneath. Drooling on my chest. Pi was curled around me, and I was using a thick part of her tail as a pillow.

I sought Gemma and found her sitting on a log nearby with a huge grin.

"Help," I mouthed.

She made a show of looking us over before shaking her head no.

Well, doggone it, how was I going to get out of this mess? Realizing that there was nothing to do but try to untangle myself, I lifted Pi's head as gently as I could. I reasoned that leaving the wing over her head was best. The rising sun might wake her. I was only partially successful.

As soon as I lifted the dragon's head a couple of inches, Pi rolled over, freeing me from my draconic entrapment.

I scurried over to Gemma. "How in the holy dogs of hell did that happen?"

The troll shrugged. "Pi got up in the middle of the night and curled up next to you. About twenty minutes later, you rolled into her. From there, it kept getting more interesting as each of you tossed and turned, trying to get comfortable. At one point, I think you had your nose up her butt?"

"What?!"

"Kidding." Gemma put her hands up.

Pi was on her back, mouth slightly open, with just a bit of her tongue hanging out. I've never been fond of lizards or snakes as pets, but even I had to admit that she looked cute like that.

I ran a hand through my hair. "I have *got* to be out of my mind."

"Oh, yeah," agreed Gemma. "Have you thought about what you're going to do when mama comes looking for her baby? Or what will happen if the village or the elves in Lonathas find out you've brought a dragon into their midst? I mean, even being a young dragon, those scales will shrug off most blows and magic. You and I aren't so lucky."

I shrugged. "I'll burn that bridge when I come to it. For now, I'll just wing it."

Gemma blinked. "Was that a dragon pun?"

"Two of them."

"Jokes don't protect you from pitchforks."

Across the campsite, Pi yawned and blinked blearily. She jolted awake, popped off the ground, and flipped in mid-air. It would have been impressive, but she stumbled, landing on her stomach instead of her feet. "Oof."

"Good morning, Pi. Are you okay?" I asked.

The small dragon swung her head around in a complete circle, making a loop in her long neck, surveying the campsite. "Yeah, it's kinda weird not waking up in a cave." She shook her whole body and stretched, starting at her core, then spreading out to her head, tail, and wings.

"We were just about to have breakfast," said Gemma. "Evan is an amazing cook."

"Do you have any ham?" Pi twisted her neck one way, then the other, cracking her neck bones.

"No, I have some salted venison, though." I stood crossing to my pack.

Pi licked her chops. "I'm really in the mood for a pig. There's a farm near here. I'll go get one." Pi stood on her hind legs and flapped to take off.

"Whoa, whoa, whoa." I ran up to Pi, who stopped flapping her wings and twisted her head sideways, looking at me.

I made patting motions with my hands. "Remember what I said about doing things differently?"

"Yeah," she said cautiously.

"This is a perfect time for us to try something new."

CHAPTER 31: DRAGON STORIES? IT'S ALL IN THE TAIL

I convinced Pi to turn into an elf girl again and we walked in the farm's direction. "We're going to ask the farmer to feed us," I explained.

Pi's eyes shifted up to the right, then left, then right again. "But that's what I was going to do."

"How were you going to ask?"

"Use a picture of mama and tell them to give me a pig or I'll eat them instead." She shrugged. "It always works."

"A little help, Gemma?"

"Don't look at me," said the troll. "I like her idea." She sniffed the air and her head tilted in confusion. "Sina?"

I followed Gemma's gaze and saw Sina running towards us through the trees. The troll drew her sword and Pi stepped in front of me with her arms out.

Sina slid to a stop, panting. "I can't..." she huffed. "I can't let you do it alone."

"Evan, who is this?" asked Pi.

I put my hand on Gemma's sword arm and gently lowered it. "She's a friend," I said to Pi, then to the out-of-breath elf, "Sina, what are you doing here?"

Sina put her hands on her knees and gazed up at me. "Daric is wrong. We can't interfere in your quest, but there's no reason we can't accompany you. I won't let you face a dragon alone."

Pi lowered her arms and regarded me over her shoulder. "Is she serious?"

189

"You ran all the way out here to help me?" I asked. "When did you leave the village?"

Sina grimaced and looked everywhere but at me. "Around midnight. You didn't come back last night, and I couldn't stop thinking about what might have happened to you. You could have been eaten or burned alive, and I couldn't live with myself if I let you face that without me." Her shoulders slumped. "Since I knew your plan, I knew roughly where you'd be. So, I snuck out of my room and came to find you."

Gemma put her sword in its sheath. "Wait. Daric doesn't know you're out here?" Then the troll burst into giggles. "He is going to have kittens when he finds out."

Sina frowned at Gemma, then quickly returned her attention to me. "I know you're sleeping with Gemma, but I don't care. You're my friend. I shouldn't be jealous. I should be happy for you."

Wait. What? "Um, Sina, what makes you think that Gemma and I are sleeping with each other?"

The elf blew out a breath and threw her arm wide. "Evan, I was in your apartment when she came out of the bath."

Pi's eyebrows rose halfway up her forehead.

Gemma and I looked at each other.

"What?" demanded Sina.

"The queen wouldn't give Gemma her own apartment," I explained. "She slept on a cot in my living room."

The blonde elf's eyes traveled to the troll.

Gemma shrugged. "He's too scrawny for me. We're just friends."

Sina blinked twice with a lost rabbit look.

"Wait," said Gemma, "You mean you've been picking a fight with me for the past week because you thought I was sleeping with Evan?"

The elf's shoulders slumped, and her ears turned the same color as Pi's hair.

"What about your engagement?" I asked. "What about your mom and Daric?"

"Daric's a dung worm." Sina shook her head. "Mom doesn't like him either. With all the fighting among the nobility, she needed his family's support in the council of lords. Otherwise, she wouldn't get anything done, or worse, they might vote to remove her."

"Won't your mom get upset if you spend time with me?"

"Upset with you? Why?"

"Because I'm flirting with her daughter, who's engaged to someone else?"

Sina's face lit up. "You want to flirt with me?"

"Not if your mom is going to relocate my head from my shoulders."

Her mouth and nose scrunched up. "Because you're flirting with me? That'd be hypocritical. Daric doesn't care as long as I'm his wife and I don't have a bastard. Mom cares a little because she wants you for herself. Not enough to hurt you. She's upset you won't take an indenturement contract, but she's thinking long term. She feels that if she can convince you to stay, she'll have plenty of time to get you into her bed. Dad won't touch her anymore, and she wants another heir."

"Upset enough to cheat?" I asked.

"Elves can't lie," replied Sina.

Gemma snorted. I agreed with the troll. You could be completely honest and still swindle someone. But really, what choice did I have? Queen Lycia was the only person who knew the spell to travel between worlds. To get her to teach me, I had to do what she asked.

I felt a tugging on my leg and found Pi with the biggest pair of puppy eyes I ever recalled seeing.

"Big brother, you're not really going away, are you?"

My heart squeezed, and I welled up with tears. Doggone it, we'd just met yesterday. I couldn't be that taken with the miniature dragon so quickly, could I?

"I've still got a lot of things to do before I go back to the human world, Pi. I'll be around for a good while yet."

Pi sniffled and blinked at me. "A good while is like a hundred years, right?"

"I don't know yet, Pi. When I have a better idea, I promise I'll let you know."

"And humans always keep their promises, right?"

I knelt and pulled the little elf girl into a hug. "No, but big brothers do." She was warm and wrapped me in a fierce embrace. My brain knew I wasn't really holding a little girl, but my heart was just as sure that I was.

Sina's nose wrinkled. "Little sister?"

Pi released me and gazed up at the blonde elf. "Yes, little sister." Having experienced Pi's magic firsthand, I was getting better at sensing when it was working. I felt the mental suggestion envelop Sina.

The elf princess looked slightly dazed before saying, "Oh, right. Your little sister. How could I have forgotten that?"

***

The four of us were walking up a rutted dirt road to a farmhouse. Weedy fields of wheat and beans were on either side. The roof of the cottage bowed in the middle and some thatching was missing. No smoke came from the chimney that leaned into the house. That the stone hearth hadn't fallen on the house yet was probably more due to luck than anything else. Discarded rusty tools leaned against the walls of the small home.

Sina shook her head. "It looks abandoned."

"Like, are you sure someone is still here?" asked Gemma.

"Uh, huh," Pi nodded. "Can't you smell them?"

The troll stopped and put her hands on her hips. "I might if someone's magic wasn't messing with my nose."

The tiny elf smiled apologetically. "Oops. Sorry. Just a minute." Pi squeezed her eyes shut for a few seconds, then opened them again. "Okay, try it now."

Gemma sniffed the air. "Ah, much better. There are two elves in the house."

"Thanks." I raised my voice. "Hello?"

No one answered.

I shared a look with my companions before continuing. "Hey, we don't mean to bother you, but we're weary travelers on our way to Vimra and were wondering if we might trouble you for a bite to eat."

A panicked woman's voice issued from the hovel. "The troll will find nothing to eat here. My husband will be back soon. Move along strangers. We don't want any trouble. We have magic."

I lowered my voice. "Gemma, I know I'm not very good at the Stone Shape spell yet, but do you think the two of us working together could straighten that chimney?"

The troll shrugged. "Sure, let me do the hard parts. We could have it righted in an hour. You could definitely use the practice."

"You have magic?" I called to the house with a grin. "Excellent! I love seeing new magic. I'm a wizard and I'm always looking for new spells. If we can straighten your hearth, can you feed us breakfast and show me your magic? Gemma won't hurt you if you don't attack us."

"It's the human from town, ma," said a voice from inside. "He really is a wizard. Skit told me so." It sounded like a young boy. "And the troll hasn't eaten anyone. Skit also said she used to be an elf."

A little head peeked out a window.

"Are you really the wizard the queen sent to help us?" the woman asked.

"Yes, I really am that wizard," I assured her.

A larger head joined the smaller one in the window of the battered cottage. "And the dragon?"

"I'm negotiating with her to leave the area. She won't attack today. I promise." With some effort, I did not look at Pi. Instead, my gaze settled on Sina, whose brow was knitted in confusion. Should I tell the elf warrior who Pi really was?

The woman moved to the open doorway. "You *spoke* with the dragon?"

I nodded. "Yes. She's really nice once you get to know her."

She blinked rapidly. "Nice?"

"Well, she threatened to eat me and breathe fire on me," I shrugged, "but after that, we had a delightful conversation about our families."

The elf stared at me in slack-jawed. "Families?"

"Yeah, you don't think dragons just appear out of thin air, do you? They have families."

She tilted her head to the side. "You must be insane."

"Queen Lycia might agree with you. The great wizard Geezer is also pretty eccentric. But crazy people shouldn't scare you. At least they're committed."

The elf stood there. Her mouth moved, but no words came out. Then she threw her hands in the air. "Fine, by a strange coincidence, I have half a pig that the dragon didn't finish and a few eggs from what's left of my chickens. I don't have enough salt to preserve the pork, so it might as well feed someone. Do you like bacon?"

"Yes. What are your names?"

"I'm Winnue, and this is my son, Drin." She stepped inside, then stopped. "Um, can you fix the hearth before I stoke the coals for breakfast?"

Gemma and I had the chimney straightened in short order, while Pi and Drin played tag in the yard. Sina helped Winnue cook while I fixed the bent beams in the roof. I wasn't an engineer, but I could see where the wood supports had been pulled out of position by the leaning hearth. It didn't take much to stone shape some new grooves for the timbers to fit into. With Gemma's strength and my help, we reseated the beams.

Gemma was worn out and went to take a nap under a tree. I went inside.

"That will hold for a while," I said, wiping the mortar from my hands. "Your husband should have no trouble patching that hole now," I said, pointing at the sky through a hole in the thatched roof.

Winnue approached with a platter of bacon strips. She smiled, but the edges of her lips twitched nervously. "Yes. When he comes back. Soon." She said haltingly.

I glanced at Sina, who was a step behind her, and it was obvious we were thinking the same thing. I returned my attention to the elven farmer. "Winnue, how long has your husband been coming back soon?" I asked softly.

CHAPTER 32: GNOME ON THE RANGE

The smile fractured as Winnue dropped the platter. It hit the corner of the table and shattered, sending bacon and plate bits in all directions across the dirt floor. She burst into tears and hugged herself, her eyes pleading for forgiveness. "I'm sorry. I'm so sorry," she sniffled.

Sina and I rushed to her side. Winnue collapsed into us as we settled on the bench seat.

Just then, Drin and Pi burst in the front door, laughing, but the mirth died immediately.

"Come on," said Drin grabbing Pi's hand and pulling her back toward the yard, "we're not supposed to see my ma cry." Pi resisted for a moment, but I waved her on.

The farmer tried again to pull it together but failed. Like a dam had broken loose, she cried in great wracking sobs, her body convulsing as she dug her hands into my tunic.

I had had no experience with this sort of thing, so I just awkwardly patted her on the back. I'd seen it in a couple of TV shows, and it seemed like the right thing to do. Sina wrapped her arms around the elf and laid her head on her back.

We were like that for a while before the farm elf could pull herself back together.

"I'm sorry," she began, "Not many of the townsfolk come out this way. None since the dragon moved into the area. It was manageable when Runo, my husband, was here. Three months ago, he left to get help from our relatives in Lonathas. He said he'd be back soon. I haven't seen him since. I thought it was before the dragon showed up, but I guess he might have been eaten, but I have no way of knowing."

I shook my head. "The dragon hasn't eaten anyone. She told me that elves taste weird."

Winnue's brow creased in confusion. "You *talked* to the dragon?"

"Oh, yeah. You'd think dragons would be all fire and brimstone, and she is, but when you get past that, it turns out she's just a nice girl, just trying to make her way in the world." I shrugged. "What she really wants is gold and jewels. She's young and wants to build her own dragon hoard. Her mom told her that elves were rich. She didn't realize there's not a lot of gold rolling around farming villages."

Sina looked over Winnue's shoulder and mouthed the word, "Young?"

The farm elf sighed. "I wish I had a bit more gold. Fix this place up a bit. Buy some books for Drin."

"Your friends in town won't help you out?" asked Sina.

"Not with the dragon around. Perhaps I'm being too stubborn. The smart thing to do would be to write off the farm and move back to town. If the royal bank wants their money back, they can come out and deal with the dragon themselves."

"Don't abandon your dreams yet. I'm certain I can get the dragon to move on," I assured her. "Perhaps that'll be enough to get your friends in town to come out and help."

Winnue huffed, stood, and straightened out her dress. She regarded the scattered bacon and platter shards and slumped. "Do you mind sharing a plate? I seem to be running low on, well, everything."

"Hang on," I motioned with a finger. "I'm pretty sure I can take care of your platter. Not only can I serve it up, but I can dish it out."

My muscles were sore, and I was a little winded from fixing the chimney, but I gathered the pieces of platter, putting them together like a puzzle. I used the stone shape magic. It was tougher, but I reasoned that the earthenware was enough like rock, that it should work. After all, the cement holding the chimney together wasn't exactly rock. It was mostly sand, and to mold it, I was adjusting the sand.

It resisted my efforts. Apparently, pottery was different enough that I couldn't move it like sand. Wasn't clay just really fine sand? My magic kept saying it wasn't. I worked at it for a while and started to get out of breath. Finally, I found something in the earthenware that worked like the sand and used it to convince the platter to fuse back together.

Panting, I handed the platter back to Winnue. It wasn't like new. You could see gray lines where the pieces had been fitted together, but it should be fine for holding bacon.

The farm elf accepted it with a slightly bewildered expression. "Thanks."

"Evan," said Sina, "do you mind cleaning up while I help Winnue make more bacon?"

"No, of course not." I gathered up the pieces and went out the door... and found Pi and Drin using farm tools to rake rocks around, whistling loudly.

"You guys heard everything, huh?" I asked.

They looked at each other and winced.

I gave them a lopsided grin. "Drin, why don't you help your ma and Sina in the kitchen while Pi and I," I held up the soiled bacon, "feed the local wildlife."

Drin scampered inside while Pi followed me up the road. We waved at Gemma as we walked by her napping spot, but mostly we continued in silence.

"They're not rich," blurted Pi.

"Nope." I agreed. "They're not starving yet, but they might be in a couple of weeks."

"But elves help each other, right? Kinda like an ant colony?" The little girl gazed up at me.

"Do you really think elves are like ants?" I asked.

Pi frowned and kicked a rock on the road. "I guess not. Ants don't scream, 'help, help, please don't kill me,' when you almost step on them."

I cocked my head and raised an eyebrow.

She rolled her eyes. "Okay, when my *illusion* almost steps on someone."

We reached the edge of the fields, and I threw the bacon into the forest.

"What is that stuff?" asked Pi. "It smells kinda like pig, but a little different."

"It's bacon. Pig belly sliced up and fried," I explained. We turned around and ambled back toward the house.

"Oh," said Pi, "that's right, elves sometimes cook their food. It still tastes like pig, right?"

"Oh, no. It's much better."

By the time we got back to the house, Sina and Winnue had the platter and several plates piled high with bacon, eggs, and diced potatoes. Everyone else was seated, so we joined them.

The elf-sized table was straining under Gemma's weight, but it was sturdy construction, so I wasn't too worried. I thought nothing of it when Pi went to sit across from her.

Pi sat and the other end of the table came a foot and a half off the ground before she quickly stood back up. The table slammed back down, jostling the food and plates. Thankfully, the drinks hadn't been set out yet.

For three seconds, there was complete silence. Then I burst out laughing and everyone joined in.

Being in the shape of an elf didn't mean the dragon weighed the same as one. "Pi, how about you and I sit at the other end of the table," I suggested.

I wasn't sure what everyone else was thinking about the situation, but they took it in stride. Sure enough, having Pi and Gemma at opposite ends of the table balanced things out. The serving platter was passed around, and everyone loaded up their plates. Pi shoveled food onto her plate, which was fine since Winnue made a lot of food.

"Oh my, you must have quite the appetite, young lady," remarked Winnue with a grin.

"Uh huh," was Pi's only response. Though she was watching everyone around the table very closely.

I took the hint and picked up a strip of bacon and bit off half of it, demonstrating the expected eating etiquette. I repeated the process using a fork for the eggs.

Pi copied my movements with the bacon, and her eyes went wide. "Wow. This is amazing. Thank you, Winnue!" She then used the fork as an egg and potato shovel.

We were all finished as Pi started in on her third helping. I laughed as Drin's jaw dropped. He watched in fascination as bite after bite disappeared into Pi's mouth.

Winnue shook her head. "Young lady, I'm pretty sure you ate more than the troll."

"It's great. I love cooked food!" said Pi around a mouth full of potatoes.

"You poor dear," said the farm elf, "I bet you've been traveling for weeks."

A look of confusion passed over Sina's face.

***

We said goodbye and thanked Winnue for the meal. The farm elf couldn't say enough nice things about the repairs we'd made to her house.

"We'll send someone from town to check up on you. I don't think you'll have any more visits from the dragon," I said.

"I can't thank you enough, Wizard Evan. If you're ever out this way again, please drop by. We'd love to see you again," said Winnue.

"We'll do that," I assured her. Gemma, Sina, Pi, and I waved goodbye and started up the dirt road.

When we reached the tree line, Gemma sighed. "You know, Evan, it's kinda nice being friendly with the local elves. A girl could get used to this."

"I'll say," said Pi. "It's nice having friends to play with and elves do some amazing things with food."

"Pi," said Sina, "you say that like you've never had friends before."

"Well, yeah," the tiny elf shrugged. "I mean, when you grow up on the side of a volcano, you don't get many visitors. It's been just mom and me forever."

Sina stopped walking, and we followed suit. Her gaze traveled from Pi to me and back again.

"Yup, there it goes," said Pi.

I felt the suggestion spell snap.

Sina's mouth dropped open, and she staggered backward before landing on her butt. "D- D- dragon."

"Wow, nothing gets past her, huh?" Pi closed her eyes and morphed into her pony-sized dragon form, then shook out her wings and tail.

Sina sucked in a breath. The expression was equal parts shock and horror as she scrambled backward. Pi stalked towards her, and Sina froze as she realized running wouldn't do her any good. Pi reached out with a wicked, black-tipped claw... and flicked Sina's nose. "Boop."

The dragon turned around. "Come on, Sina. It's a long walk to town. It'd be *sooooo* much easier if we could fly. Hey, do you know any flying spells, big brother?"

"No," I admitted, turning to follow Pi, "but that'd be pretty cool. What races know that kind of magic?"

Gemma grinned and shrugged. "Djin, some demons, gargoyles..." then over her shoulder, "Come on, princess. It really is a long walk back to town."

"But gargoyles have wings," I pointed out. "They don't need magic to fly." Had Gemma figured out that Sina was a princess?

Gemma snorted, "What-*ever*. It's a rock. The wings are decoration. Trust me, they need magic to fly."

We'd traveled about forty feet when I turned around to see if Sina was following. She wasn't. "Hold up."

I jogged back to her and knelt. Sina was panting and her eyes were wide.

"Pi is a dragon," she whispered.

"Yeah. She is," I admitted.

"Evan, dragons eat people like you and me. She could snap your neck or burn you to a cinder if you look at her the wrong way. Even as a juvenile, there's nothing you could do to stop her."

I smiled, "And she's a kid, who's a long way from home, learning about the world, just trying to get by." I tapped my finger to my chin dramatically. "Hmmm, for some reason, I can relate to that."

Then she grabbed my shirt. "Evan, we're in real danger! She will kill us. I've seen what happens to villages that upset dragons. They kill everyone."

"Hey Pi," I yelled over my shoulder without taking my eyes from Sina, "are you planning on killing us and feasting on our bodies?"

The dragon chuckled. "No, like I told you, elves taste weird. I don't think humans or trolls would be any better. But cows and sheep are awesome and a lot easier to catch."

Sina rubbed her face with her hand. "Evan, you aren't *listening* to me."

"Sure, I am," I shrugged. "But everything out here is trying to kill me, so I have to choose who to trust. I'm going with my gut, and my insides tell me that Pi is okay."

Sina said nothing more, but her eyes pleaded for me to see reason. Her gaze was full of concern. It was clear she cared about me.

"Listen, I get it. I promise I'll keep an eye on the big hungry dragon." I took her fists from my shirt and wrapped them in my hands. Through her touch, I could tell she was sincere. "But I'd like you to do something for me, too."

Sina's gaze drifted to our hands, then back to my face.

"Give Pi a chance," I said. "I don't think she's the homicidal lizard you think she is."

The elf stared deep into my eyes and took several shaky breaths before she nodded.

Sina got to her feet, but her hands were shaking. She smoothed out her tunic and marched over to where Pi and Gemma waited for us. The petite elf stopped in front of dragon Pi and bowed deeply. "Please don't hurt my friend."

Pi cocked her scaly head to one side. Her head swiveled to me, then back to Sina. "Okay. What's it worth in gold to you?"

"Pi," I admonished.

"What? If she's willing to pay me not to eat you, why wouldn't I take advantage of that?"

"But you weren't going to eat me, anyway."

"Well, yeah, so it's a double win."

Throwing my hands in the air, I continued up the dirt road. Pi and Sina continued to argue over whether Pi would eat me. Pi seemed to do a good job of negotiating with Sina, by asking if nibbling on my arms and legs constituted actual eating.

I caught sight of a spiky winged sprite hiding up in a tree. Bramble was still following us, ever hopeful that sugar would materialize. I realized that I did have a chore for the winged pest.

Setting my pack down, I rummaged through it until I'd found paper and one of the magic writing quills that the elves favored. Pi's mom, Emberlee, was probably concerned about her daughter, so I wrote a note.

Dear Emberlee, I know you're probably worried sick, wondering if your precious Pyra is okay. Rest assured, she is fine, healthy, and in good spirits. I've convinced her to travel with me for the time being and I promise to look after her and do my best to keep her out of trouble. Please send a return message via this sprite. All the Best, Wizard Evan.

I rolled the scroll up with an extra slip of paper for the return message and sealed it with some wax and string I'd gotten in town. On the outside, I wrote instructions.

When Bramble appeared next to the circle, I was unsurprised. "Hey Peach Fuzz. Fancy meeting you out here. In the middle of nowhere. And you just happen to have my one true love. Hello sugar."

"Uh, huh, 'cause you're not following me or anything," I deadpanned.

The winged fairy placed a hand on its chest. "Me? Peach Fuzz, if I was following you, there'd be sap in your socks and sand in your underwear."

I waved a finger at Bramble. "And if you did that to me, you'd never get another pinch of sugar."

"Eep!" The sprite whined pitifully.

I held up a sugar cube. "One for carrying the message. Take this scroll," I held up the wax-sealed paper, "to the dragon Emberlee, living on the side of a volcano west of here. Wait for her to write a response, then bring her scroll back to me. Do that, and you get another sugar cube. If you forget, I wrote the instructions on the outside." Belatedly, I wondered if the sprite could read.

"Uh, dragon?" Bramble glanced nervously over to where the discussion between Sina and Pi was winding down.

"Uh, sugar?" I held the cube up between two fingers.

The sprite swallowed hard. "The things I do for love. Okay, you got it, Peach Fuzz." The sprite snatched the sugar and the scroll and popped away.

The discussion between Sina and Pi reached a conclusion and Sina was rummaging through her pack for something. "Hey, how did all this sand get into my clothes?"

CHAPTER 33: ARRIVAL

The dirt road met up with several others throughout the day. The more ruts that joined ours, the more worn the path became, and the less dried grass grew in between the gravel lanes.

We weren't in a rush to get back to town. As a result, we didn't make it back that night. We made camp, which led to a minor competition between Sina and Pi on who could hunt down the best game for our evening meal.

Sina returned with a trio of rabbits, while Pi came back with five ducks. I made both, choosing to stew the rabbits with carrots and potatoes, and roast the ducks with salt and rosemary. I didn't expect leftovers with Pi and Gemma's appetites and was proven right. They surprised me when all three declared me the winner even though I had only cooked the game, not killed it.

As she skewered and popped the rabbit in her mouth, I laughed and stabbed the last piece of rabbit from my plate.

"So, why didn't we see anyone on the road today?" I asked as I picked at something caught between two of my teeth.

"That's all thanks to our scaly friend here," said Gemma, waving a fork in Pi's direction.

"Me?" said Pi, crunching a duck bone. "But I've been in elf form all afternoon?"

"Now you're in elf form," said Sina, licking her fingers, "but you've been terrorizing the countryside for months now."

Pi swallowed a bite too big for an actual elf. "Terrorizing? As if. I mean, yeah, I swoop in and ask for food and money and stuff, but I haven't eaten anyone. Slime toads, I haven't even bitten or clawed anyone, yet."

"What do you think Drin would say?" I asked.

Pi opened her mouth, then closed it. She said nothing more, but frowned, deep in thought.

I took first watch. The clearing we'd camped in seemed to be a favored spot on the road into town. There were several flat areas for bedrolls. My shift passed uneventfully and soon I was waking up Sina to take my place. I choose a spot close to the dying embers of the fire, but not so close that a stray spark might catch my blanket on fire, and promptly fell asleep.

The next morning, I woke up with what felt like a wet rock on my stomach. Groggily, I opened an eye and found elf Pi using me as a pillow. Her drool had completely soaked through my blanket.

I searched the campground and found Gemma grinning at me from a nearby stump.

"Again?" I whispered.

"Congratulations. You're her new comfort blanket," said Gemma in a soft voice.

"Comfort blanket?" I asked.

"Yeah, don't little humans have a blanket or toy like troll children do? Something soft they sleep with."

"You're saying I'm Pi's Teddy Bear?"

"Teddy what?" asked Pi through a yawn. The tiny faux elf smacked her lips. "Oh, sorry, big brother. I didn't mean to drool on you."

"Do you have to sleep on me?"

Pi blinked. "Uh, yeah."

"Why?"

She yawned. "It's a dragon thing. We sleep on what's important to us."

"Really?"

"Yeah." Pi morphed back into a dragon and did her full body shiver from nose to tail before changing back into an elf. "Mom sleeps on her gold and stuff. She has this one book about a strong rich dragon that sweeps a younger female off her claws. I read it once. Seemed silly to me, but she loves it. She can't get comfortable when it isn't in her treasure pile. I slept on mom's tail until we had our fight."

I wasn't quite sure how to take that. "Um, ah, thanks."

Sina was still sleeping, so I stoked the fire and brewed up some of the willow tea she likes. I brought it over to where she was dozing and moved the cup back and forth under her nose.

She groaned appreciatively as she cracked an eye open. "Thanks, Evan," she said as she clasped the mug with both hands, trapping my hand in hers. She took a tentative sip, squeaked happily, then using my trapped fingers as leverage, she pulled me in and kissed me on the cheek.

And why was it suddenly warmer than it had been five minutes ago? "Thanks," I murmured.

Gemma shook her head and raised a cup in my direction with a grin.

We ate breakfast and hit the road. Unlike the hike to Vimra, Sina pointed out all the trees and plants along the way and what they could be used for. Some were edible, some could be used as medicine or potion ingredients, and some just smelled nice.

Admittedly, I was more interested in the edible plants than the rest, but I paid attention to every word. This was a different side of the elf maiden I hadn't seen before. She loved the forest and everything in it. She gushed about her people's connection to the trees and how the elves cared for the land.

Gemma peppered Pi with questions about dragons and vice versa, about trolls. In elf form, Pi was only as big as Gemma's leg. As shocking as the size difference was, it was fun listening to them carry on about dragon and troll culture.

However, the closer we got to town, the quieter and more reserved Sina became. Then she stopped talking altogether. Call me slow, but it took half an hour of silence to figure out why.

I took her hand in mine. She didn't object, and I felt her concern through our link. "You're worried about Daric, aren't you?"

Sina blew out a breath. "We'll be able to see town once we top this rise. By now, Daric has figured out where I went. He'll be waiting on the edge of town, ready to tell me how irresponsible I am."

He probably would be. Daric was all about telling people how wrong they were. I could picture him standing on the edge of town, arms crossed, with a smug scowl.

We crested the hill and saw a crowd of elves gathered at the edge of the village. As we got closer, I could pick out the individual faces of men, women, and children. Daric wasn't with them, but Ash and Bunni were there. I even saw Fikus scowling from the back. His disapproval was marred by an occasional look of hopeful curiosity.

When we got closer, I trotted ahead of our band and stopped in front of the villagers. "Hey guys, where's the party?"

"Right here, right now," said Ash, "if you can tell us you slew the dragon."

"I didn't slay the dragon," I admitted.

Ash's face fell. Fikus snorted and shook his head.

I grinned knowingly. "I convinced the dragon to move elsewhere. It wasn't a hard sell. She came here to get rich and was unsatisfied with the few coppers she'd acquired so far. She's off to find greener meadows."

Bunni's jaw dropped. "What? Really?" Sina and the others had caught up to me by then, and the elf shopkeeper rounded on the elf warrior. "Evan spoke with the dragon? The dragon is moving?"

Sina blinked. Her gaze traveled from me back to Bunni. "Yes," Sina squeaked, almost as a question.

The villagers cheered, danced, and waved their arms in the air. The children rushed forward and pulled Pi into a dancing chain that wove around the adults. The kids even danced around Gemma even though they gave her a wide berth.

Musicians struck up a tune. Bunni wrapped me in a fierce hug, followed by Ash, then several other elves I didn't know. Sina smiled nervously, Gemma laughed heartily, and Pi enjoyed the chaotic dancing with the elf children. Fikus produced a keg from seemingly out of thin air and distributed mugs of ale.

I clapped along with the tune for a few beats. Ash was standing off to one side, grinning like a madman. I took him by the elbow and pulled him aside. "You weren't kidding. Right here, right now."

He continued to slap his leg in time with the music. "Bunni said you were coming. Geezer had a reputation for getting things done, even if he never leaves the capital anymore."

"How'd Bunni know we were coming?" I asked.

"Oh! Birds. She has the speak with animals spell." Then he snickered. "But she claims it's the most annoying spell ever. Apparently, birds and squirrels think with their stomachs most of the time. It's almost impossible to get them to focus on anything else."

Briefly, I wondered if the sparrows had mentioned that Pi was the dragon, then dismissed it. We'd be having a completely different conversation if that was the case. "You guys were looking out for me?"

"Well, yeah. You were sent here to save Vimra from the dragon." Then he winked at me. "Besides, you seem like a guy with sparkle. Not like a lot of the other capital city elves. Most of them are like that guy at the inn, Daricas."

"Sparkle?"

"Yeah, you know, sparkle. Decent people who use their magic to help others. Sparkle."

I nodded to myself. Sparkle. A word to add to the elf slang dictionary. "Speaking of Daric, why isn't he here?"

Ash shrugged.

"Hey Ash, can you do me a favor?"

"Name it. I already owe you for the dragon."

"Do you know Winnue and Drin?" I pointed to the north. "They live out that way."

He nodded, "Of course. Drin sometimes comes to town to play with the local kids."

"Can you go check on them for me? We stopped by there on the way back, and their place looks pretty run down."

"Of course, Runo left for Lonathas, but we never heard from him again. It was before the dragon showed up, so he may have been killed by Darower raiders or something. The queen's army found a pack of goblins near here about that time."

Pi looked a little lost. I went over to her. "Hey, little sis, what's rattling around in that head of yours?"

Her eyes got big and watery as she gazed up at me. "They're happy I'm leaving."

"Yeah, I guess they are."

"Was I a bad person?" Her eyes pleaded with me to tell her it wasn't true.

I gently squeezed her shoulder. "A dragon showed up demanding their hard-earned money and taking their food. She took advantage of her size and threatened to hurt their families. These are not the things a nice person does. However, you didn't hurt anyone, even when it would have been easy for you to do so." I mussed up her hair. "Let's just say you're a good person who made some mistakes. If we can learn from our mistakes, then you can be a better person than you were yesterday."

Pi watched the celebration a bit before she nodded. "You're

younger than I am, big brother. How'd you get so smart?"

I sighed. "I'm not that smart. Sometimes I trust the wrong people." I thought of my brother, who enjoyed hurting people. I thought about my mom, who always chose my brother over me and did mean things to my dad. "But I've asked a lot of the same questions you have, and my grandma always gave me good advice. She's the smart one."

"Will I get to meet her one day?"

I thought back to when I'd scried my home. My grandma's eyes looked right into mine. "I hope so Pi. I hope so."

***

I found some wild carrots on the way back, so I stopped by the stables before going inside the inn. Nonam was excited to see me but shied away from Pi. I guess whatever magic mojo that allowed Pi to blend in with the elves didn't work as well on horses. Nonam didn't freak out like she did with the spiders, but it was clear that Pi was giving her a predator vibe.

Treats delivered, it was time to face the music. I did not expect it to go as well as the impromptu concert at the edge of the village. Whatever bug had crawled up Daric's butt didn't have a humorous leg to pull.

Inside the tavern, we found the barroom mostly empty. Fikus hadn't made his way back yet, so the counter was unmanned. That hadn't stopped Daric from helping himself to a bottle of spirits.

He didn't look up as we entered. He merely swirled his drink in a goblet. "You're still alive. Didn't find the dragon?"

I set my pack on the edge of the bar top. "No, we found her."

"You *killed* a dragon?"

"The queen didn't send me here to slay the dragon. The queen asked me to convince the dragon to leave." I shrugged. "Convincing usually requires conversation."

Daric's gaze shifted to Pi, and he sighed. "And I see you've picked up another stray. Wonderful."

"Pi meet Daric, Daric, this is-"

"I don't need to know the gutter trash's name!" The drunk elf warrior's fist held the goblet in a white-knuckled grip. A vein pulsed on his forehead, and he made a visible effort to calm himself. "Like the rest of this piss-hole of a town, she doesn't matter. None of it matters."

Sina stepped up beside me. "What does matter then?"

"You matter." Daric carefully set the goblet down next to the bottle and stood swaying. "You matter a great deal, *betrothed*. Three months. We'll be married in three months' time. After that happens, we can then dispense with all this quest nonsense."

"Our people are not trash. Helping them isn't-"

The elf noble swung his hand in an arc, shattering the bottle and flinging the pewter wine goblet into a corner. "They are property! They exist to serve *us*. You..." Daric pointed at Sina, "exist to serve *me*." His finger reversed and pointed at himself. "Property does not leave of its own accord. It does not get up in the middle of the night and hare off on some fool's errand."

That lit a fire in Sina's eyes, and she opened her mouth, but Daric held a finger in the air for silence.

"Yes. You are not mine to do with as I please, *yet*. But you would do well to remember that in short order, that will change." Daric smoothed back a misplaced strand of hair. "You cannot stop it. And when you are mine, I can put you in the highest tower or chain you to a wall in the deepest dungeon, and there isn't a thing you or anyone else can do about it."

Sina's gaze traveled to the floor. For a few moments, the only sound in the room was Sina's heavy breathing as she clenched and unclenched her fists. Finally, she spoke. "I'm sorry, Lord Daricas. It won't happen again."

"You're right, because if it does, there will be... consequences." The noble turned his glare on me. "You-"

Gemma and Pi interposed themselves between the elf and me. Daric sneered at Pi, but eyed the troll cautiously.

He returned his attention to me. "Are we done here?"

"Yes."

"Then we're leaving. Grab your stuff and meet me in the stables."

CHAPTER 34: SILENCE IS GOLDEN, BUT DUCT TAPE IS SILVER

Three days into the trip home, Daric still wasn't talking to anyone. No one minded. He'd given a good impression of a horse's rear at the tavern. Speaking of horses, we were walking them to give them a break from riding. Daric walked his horse ahead of the party in silence.

One downside was that Sina was standoffish again. Seeing her relaxed and excited had been fantastic. Away from Daric, she was a different elf. On one hand, I could see where her duty to her kingdom was that important. On the other, I just didn't get why she put up with Daric.

So, I did what any guy my age would do. I stewed on the problem and let it eat away at me. Had I pushed her toward Daric? Had I gone too far with the kiss? And doggone it, what the heck was I even thinking, being interested in someone engaged to another guy?

I let my fears run free like a pair of mutts chasing their tails in my head.

So, imagine my surprise when Sina took my hand in hers.

Can you hear me?

I concentrated on forming the words in my head. *Yes, is this normal? Can everyone here do this?*

No. At least no one I know of, she thought. *Dad can send me impressions, which is how I knew what to do with you. But what we have goes far beyond that. Elves have good hearing. I just realized we can talk like this without Daric listening.*

So why now? I squeezed her hand. *Not that I'm complaining. Actually, just to be clear, I'm as far from complaining as it's possible to get. The far side of the Darower Kingdom from complaining.*

I felt her amusement through our connection. *I like you, too. If I could do what I wanted, I'd like to see what we could become. But Daric is right about some things. You aren't staying. You have a life back in San Antonio. And where does that leave us?*

Where did that leave us? Dirty dogs, where did that leave me with Gemma and Pi? With effort, I pushed those thoughts aside. *I might not be staying, but that doesn't mean I don't care about you and your people.*

You let me worry about Daric. Sina adjusted our grip and laced her fingers with mine. *My mom is very smart, subtle, and a good queen. If she needs me to do this to cement her rule, it's the least I can do for our people. Plus, I've studied under the master. Letting Daric think he has me tamed, will give me a huge advantage when I slip through his fingers.*

I studied the back of Daric's head twenty yards ahead of us. *But what if something happens to the queen?*

Evan, she admonished, *you're thinking in human terms. Elves live forever.*

I shuddered at the thought of Sina spending forever with Daric. On the flip side, Sina spending forever with me sounded nice, though.

Sina must have heard the thought. *Daric has to catch me to imprison me. The kingdom is vast. I can live comfortably in a town at the edge of our domain. Daric is unlikely to stray far from the capital after we're married. He's a political animal. Being away from the court where he can scheme and plot against the other noble houses would be itchy clothes for him. He wouldn't be here if I wasn't here, which is why mom sent me to watch after you. You heard him. Until we're married, I'm his most valuable possession.*

I realized then, Daric was a lot like my brother. Jerrod was a bully. He loved lording his strength over others. My brother was much less dangerous without his friends. Will and Gary were followers. They didn't get in nearly as much trouble without my brother around. But Daric was a planner. He would surround himself with people who would carry out his schemes while he wasn't around. Who were Daric's friends? What were his friends doing while we were out here?

Bramble picked that moment to pop in front of me. He held out a scroll. "Okay Peach Fuzz, Here's your return message. Give me some sugar."

Bramble wanted a kiss? I shook my head to clear it. No, the sprite wanted a sugar cube.

Glancing around, I found Pi talking to Daric. Probably more accurately, talking at the elf warrior. Gemma was nearby, watching the one-sided discussion and holding the horses. "Sina, I need to read this message. Do you mind giving me a moment?"

"Yes, who's it from?"

We were still holding hands, so I send the reply silently. *Pi's mom.*

Her eyes went wide, and she moved ahead of me a couple of paces.

"Okay, Bramble. Here's your sugar." The sprite dropped the note in my hands. It wasn't on the paper I provided, but something that looked and felt like vellum. It was tied with a gold wire.

Carefully, I unwrapped it and read the flowy script.

Dearest Evan,

A letter. Delivered by a sprite of all things. What will you wizards think of next?

Thank you so much for contacting me. I already knew you met my daughter, of course, and I was so surprised when she accepted your invitation as a surrogate big brother. It's so hard on a mother when a young one leaves the nest, and even worse when they are as single-minded as my dear Pyra. Unfortunately, my daughter stopped listening to my excellent advice years ago. While I don't approve of all of your lessons, she could certainly do a lot worse than a fledgling wizard. Living among the lesser beings of this world will be very educational for a young dragon. I, therefore, agree with your temporary friendship. It will be a sad day when she eventually tires of you and feasts on your flesh, but such is the lot of you lesser beings.

Until then, feel free to discuss the mysteries of magic and creation with my exceptionally bright little girl. With a little luck, you might even glean as much as your primitively small mind can comprehend.

Much Love,

Emberlee Brightwing, Great and Powerful Master of the Flames, Exalted Wyrm of the Fire Ridge Mountains

P.S. – If any harm comes to my daughter, I will roast you alive and eat you while you watch.

I put the message away. Okay, note to self, don't piss off mom.

"Stop your incessant babbling, you disgusting cur."

I glanced up to find Daric yelling at Pi. "If I wanted annoying chatter, I'd throw an injured goblin into a rat-infested cell."

I ran up to them and made patting motions with my hands. "Easy now guys, we can talk this out."

"Talk? Talk!" ground out Daric. "That's all this street urchin ever does, spew forth gibberish."

"My big brother isn't vermin." Pi poked the haughty elf in his chest armor.

Daric staggered backward. There was a dent in his breastplate that hadn't been there before.

He drew his sword. "You dare talk back to me? I am an elf lord. I command more men and wealth than you'll ever see in your pitiful, meaningless life." Daric pointed at me. "And this son of a village idiot and desperate alley cat couldn't command a blind frog, much less his own magic."

Well, dog farts. Fine, Daric could dig himself out of this mess on his own. I was pretty sure Pi had enough restraint not to kill him. I shrugged and backed off.

Sina grimaced. "Uh, Daric, I really think you should-"

"No one cares what you think, cheap trinket," said the elf noble. "Get out of the way until you serve your purpose."

Sina's mouth fell open.

Pi smirked and looked the sword up and down.

Daric snorted with derision and waved his sword back and forth in front of Pi. "Still defiant. How about I bob those ears of yours? Let's see how smug you are after you can't go out in public ever again."

He swung.

Pi caught the blade in her tiny hand.

Daric's face twisted in confusion as he realized Pi was completely undamaged by the blade.

Pi shifted into dragon form, yanked the sword from Daric's grip, and snapped it in half.

The elf didn't move, stunned by the sudden appearance of the pony-sized dragon.

Dragon Pi grabbed the breastplate of Daric's armor and, using her claws, neatly sliced through the leather straps holding it in place and pulled it off him. The backplate clattered to the ground. Pi twisted the breastplate this way and that, looking at it critically. Then she gave a draconic shrug as she crushed it into a volleyball-sized hunk of metal, then tossed it over his right shoulder into the woods.

The elf noble sank to his knees and swallowed. "Dragon?"

Pi grinned, "Dragon."

"I... I... I'm terribly sorry," Daric stammered. "If I have caused offense. Please rest assured that such a terrible lapse in judgment will never happen again."

"What is your life worth to you, elf?"

"W- What?"

The dragon crossed her arms over her chest. "What will you pay me not to end your miserable life right now?"

***

The rest of the trip back to Lonathas was very different from the first half of the trip. Daric was polite and respectful to all the party members, and answered every question Pi put to him, even if the answer was, "I don't know."

The road between Lonathas and Vimra wasn't well-traveled, but we saw two or three other traveling parties a day. Compared to the trip out when we'd only seen people leaving Vimra, it was a pleasant change to see people traveling in both directions as word spread that the dragon threat was over.

The woods near Vimra had been a mixture of pine, oak, and hickory trees. I was getting a feel for the land, though. So, when the trees became more pine and less oak, I knew we were getting close to the capital city.

I should have anticipated the next problem, but I didn't.

"No," Daric told me in a matter-of-fact tone, "the dragon can't enter Lonathas."

"Why not?" I asked.

Daric put his hands together and spoke slowly, as if to a child. "Because she's a dragon."

Elf Pi twisted back and forth like the innocent little girl she pretended to be. Her light green skirt fluttered with each twirl. "What? Are you afraid of me?"

"Yes," he stated plainly. "If you went on a rampage inside the city limits, it would take a quarter of the army and all the city guard to stop you."

"She's just a kid," I protested.

Daric took a deep breath and let it out. "With deepest respect, she is not. While young, Pi is still a dragon. Dragons are forbidden inside the city limits by order of the queen."

I turned the other elf noble in our little party. "Sina?"

She bit her lip. "I'm sorry, Evan. Daric's right on this one. The queen will not budge. Eighty years ago, a black dragon entered the city as part of a diplomatic envoy. A hundred and thirteen people died."

Pi snorted. "Yeah, cause some elf lord insulted his mom. He said his mom was so fat when she sat around the cavern her butt covered the entire mountain."

Okay, next note to self. No "yo' mama" jokes with dragons.

I glanced from one elf to the other. "I'm not leaving Pi out here in the woods alone."

"Nothing can hurt her," said Daric forcefully.

Sina turned to Gemma, "Would you mind..."

The troll shook her head vehemently. "Like, no way in shiny slimy swamp toads. The last time we were here, someone tried to kill Evan. He's with me. End of Human-tale."

Sina frowned and paced back and forth a few times, muttering to herself. Then she stopped, moved her hands back and forth like she was debating something in her head. "Evan, do you still have some of that money left over from the assassin?"

"Uh, yeah. I still have most of it." Safely tucked away in my magic holding pouch. The ultimate money belt.

Sina waved her fingers back and forth. "I have an answer, but I'm not sure if it will work. Can you wait here for, say, half an hour while I get someone from inside the city?"

I looked to Pi and Gemma, who both shrugged. "Yeah, I guess."

"Great. I'll be right back." Sina took off at a jog.

"I'll come with you," said Daric. "Give me the horses. I'll make sure they get to the stables."

Reluctantly, I took my saddlebags and let Daric lead Nonam and the other horses away.

I regarded my remaining companions. "So... Parcheesi?"

CHAPTER 35: BENDING THE RULES

Sina returned about forty-five minutes later without Daric, but with her shopkeeper friend Millow. The elf merchant scanned us with her bright blue eyes and smile that promised she was up to no good. She crept up to Pi and knelt so they were at the same height. "Honey, I hear you have a problem with the locals."

Pi matched her grin with one of her own. "Not... yet."

"Oh, Honey. I can tell we're going to get along just fine." Millow stood and eyed me up and down speculatively. "I hear you need a safe space just out of bounds of the law around here?"

"Out of bounds?" I let that rattle around in the empty space where my brains should be. Slower than it should have, my gray noodle provided the answer. "City limits. You have a place for us to stay outside of the city limits."

"Honey, I might seem like a respectable businesswoman, but not long ago, I was anything but." She winked at me. "Just cause elves can't lie, doesn't mean we're all honest and upstanding folk. Sugar, I could tell you stories that would have you double-check your doors, triple-check your windows, and sleep with a sword under your pillow."

Gemma snorted.

"And let me guess," I suggested, "walking on the other side of a line in the dirt has some advantages."

Millow wrinkled her nose at me. "You bet your cute little round ears it does. Follow me and we'll take a walk on Lonathas' wild side."

We went toward town. When I thought we were in town, Millow stopped and pointed. "You see that line of yellow bricks

219

right there? The city guard will come right up to them, but won't cross. Over there, they keep the peace. Out here, the law is what you keep strapped to your hip." She patted a saber on her belt.

"Unless you're a goblin, winter elf, or banshee?" I probed.

"You getting involved in politics, Sugar?"

I shook my head ruefully. "Not if I can help it. But sometimes politics finds me."

She smiled. "Keep that attitude and you'll go far." Millow caressed a tree trunk we were standing beside. "If you could speak with plants, this old girl would tell you stories."

Sina, Gemma, Pi, and I stared up into the boughs of a majestic tree. It wasn't the tallest, widest, or most grand tree. It was average as tree homes in Lonathas went. Wide enough to provide about thirty feet across on the inside, if the other trees I'd visited were any sign.

Millow produced a key, inserted it into the side of the tree, and a concealed door opened. She lit a lamp with something that resembled a match. The inside of the tree was musty, dusty, and smelled of oil. Broken furniture sat in three piles on the floor. A set of stairs led up to the next level.

"I haven't been out here since I moved into town. I apologize for the mess." The shopkeeper ran a finger down one wall, then wiped it on her tunic. "Four floors. The top one is a hundred feet up with a balcony. If high places bother you, don't get close to the edge. There's no railing. The keyhole is hard to find if you don't know where to look."

"How much?" I asked.

"Oh, I love it when you talk money, Sugar. You're a friend of Sina's, a wizard, not to mention easy on the eyes. How does five hundred gold sound? I can extend credit at a generous rate."

I reached into my pouch and found a sapphire that matched the dark-haired elf's eyes. "What will this get me?"

Millow fanned herself dramatically. "Oh Honey, you know just what to do to make me all weak in the knees. Do you need furniture for three and an extra big and fluffy bed up top for you and a, uh..." Millow's gaze traveled to Sina briefly, "blonde companion?"

Sina's ears turned red to the tips. I struggled with words for a few seconds before I managed, "Uh, yes, furniture would be nice. Something appropriate for a living room and three bedrooms. A normal-sized bed will be fine."

Millow plucked the blue gem from my fingers. "Then this will just about cover it. Let me know your furniture preferences. And let me just say it is a genuine pleasure doing business with you."

***

Millow gave me a key and summoned an elf boy named Nip to take our furniture and house gear requests. I took the top room as my study/bedroom. The next level down was divided into two rooms, which Gemma and Pi each took one. The lower level would become the living room and kitchen. Knowing that the queen would summon me shortly, I stowed my things in the study and grabbed Nip. The wide eyed youth took my requests by frantically writing them down on a scroll. I ordered a few bookshelves, got enough food to fill a pantry, and I made sure I had the elf equivalents of kitchen gear. Sina made several suggestions for the living room and my study. Her suggestions were good ones, so I readily agreed. Pi and Gemma ordered sturdy four-poster beds and bedroom furniture.

We left the second floor alone for the moment. A lot of the broken things and stuff leftover from Millow's old shop went there for the time being.

Sina and I stood in the center of my space. She stayed with me while we decided about what was going to go where. Like before, Sina without Daric was all smiles and much more relaxed.

"You should put your bed over there and your desk next to the doors to the balcony."

I followed Sina's finger as it pointed next to the French-style doors. "What's your reasoning?"

"Glow stones are good for lighting up the inside of your tree, but nothing beats sunlight." She went over and waved her hand, presenting the view as if it were a painting. "If you're up here studying magic or whatever, it would be nice to look out at the leaf canopy occasionally."

I nodded in agreement. "You're right, that would be nice."

"And we'll put a couch over here with a low table, so I can stare at you while you work."

I grinned at her. "That'll get boring pretty quick."

She sauntered back over to me, bringing her face an inch from

221

my own. Her gaze traveled down at my mouth, then up at my eyes. "I don't think so."

Someone cleared their throat behind us.

I took a deep breath, then let it out. "Nip, this had better be important."

"Uh, yes Wizard Evan," the youthful elf said. "The Queen's Guard is downstairs."

Sina closed her eyes and whispered, "Daric, you fetid molding goblin sore."

"Thanks, Nip," I said, keeping my voice level. "Tell them we'll be right down."

"Yes, Wizard Evan," and I heard his steps retreat down the stairs.

Sina sighed and opened her mouth to say something.

I covered her mouth with mine and pulled her to me.

And lost my balance.

We fell toward her.

I shifted my weight and landed first. Which pulled her on top of me, banging our teeth together.

And she was still wearing her armor, so my crush crushed me.

"What was that noise?" asked Gemma from the stairs. "Oh, uh." The troll snorted as she tried unsuccessfully to control her giggles.

Pi appeared at her side. "Big brother, what are you doing?"

Sina buried her head into my shoulder as I answered. "Dying of embarrassment."

***

"What in all of Stellaluna were you thinking?" yelled the queen.

Since I'd done several dog fur-brained things recently, I played dumb. Which, admittedly, wasn't much of a stretch. "Can you be more specific?"

The monarch launched herself from her throne and stomped toward me. Daric and Sina flinched but didn't move from their usual place off to the side. "The dragon you brought back from Vimra," said the queen.

I thought about how to answer that. Really, I should have been thinking about this conversation the entire trip back. But I hadn't and so, yeah. Here we were, and me without a convincing excuse.

The queen held up her hands, clenched them into fists, and stalked away from me. She turned around after only a couple of paces. "I send you to take care of the trolls, and you come back with a troll." Lycia pointed at Gemma.

Gemma shrugged nonchalantly.

The queen threw her hands up dramatically. "And I think to myself, 'that's an unconventional solution.' Apparently, humans have that trait in common. If letting one troll wander around the capital keeps scores more from killing our people, it's a small price to pay. At least she doesn't smell like rotting meat."

The queen held up her hands, palms toward me. "But when I asked you to save Vimra from a dragon, I didn't think in a thousand years you would bring it home with you as well. Save the village from the threat, by bringing the threat to the capital? I thought only old humans suffered from dementia."

"It's a juvenile dragon," I protested. "Hardly a threat."

"Hardly a threat?" asked the queen. "So, do you think all the villagers the dragon robbed view it as a threat? And what happens when it does the same thing here? Do you have any idea what that will do to the kingdom's economy?"

"I'm teaching her a different way of doing things. She won't be threatening anyone." Wow, that sounded a lot better in my head, and totally unconvincing and lame out of my mouth.

"Oh, did the dragon give you her word on this?"

And another point for the queen. Stellaluna is a dog-eat-dog world, and here I am wearing rawhide undies.

"Have you even thought about what happens when mama dragon comes looking for her baby?" Lycia held her fingers up like she was holding a bit of string between them.

Finally, something I'd already thought to do. "Emberlee already knows she's with me and has approved me as her temporary guardian."

The queen's eyes went wide before she buried her face in her hands and let out a frustrated scream.

Several long seconds later, she pulled herself together and stared at me intently. "Emberlee, The Destroyer, Emberlee, Terror of the Skies, that Emberlee. The dragon you found is *her* daughter?"

"Uh," I said intelligently. "She introduced herself as Great and Powerful Master of the Flames, Exalted Wyrm of the Fire Ridge

Mountains."

The queen spun on her heel and walked stiffly to the throne before sitting down. "Daric, you're Evan's new guardian. Sina, you're confined to the palace until I see fit to release you. Wizard Evan, your next quest is to journey to the outpost of Azura. A giant has been smashing the fort there. No doubt the Darower have put the dumb brute up to it. Go there and kill it. Do not befriend it. Do not take it in like you would a lost puppy. Kill the monstrosity and return. Do this and you'll have the spell to cross between worlds. You will leave for Azura in two days, forty-eight hours from now, and you will take the dragon and the troll with you. Do I make myself clear?"

I glanced at Daric and Sina, who were both looking at the floor. As much as I wanted to protest, I knew better.

Instead, I bowed low. "Of course, Your Majesty."

CHAPTER 36: CARROTS CAN'T LEAVE THAT FIELD, THEY'RE GROUNDED

"I'm sorry you got grounded."

Sina regarded me oddly as we walked up the passage. "Planted in the dirt?"

I bit my lip. "Sorry, it doesn't translate well. In human terms, being grounded means your parents make you stay at home."

"It fits what's going on," said Gemma from behind us.

Sina let out a breath. "Even after going over everything in my head, I don't see what I could have done differently. Pi was going to accompany you, no matter what you or I said."

That was true. And while I could kind of see the queen's point of view, I didn't think Pi would go back to her old ways, and taking her with me had always been the plan. "Well," I grinned at her, "at least you'll be able to spend time with your dad."

Sina sighed.

"Ooh! Here we are!" Gemma raced past us and knocked on Geezer's door.

The door sprang open. The old wizard looked us over for a second, then stuck his head out in the hall, glancing left and right. "Where's the dragon?"

The elf snorted. "Good to see you too, dad."

"Good to see you, too, Sprout," said Geezer. "Where's the dragon?"

"They wouldn't let her enter the city," I explained.

"What? Because of that thing with Verde?" The Wizard cocked an eyebrow. "Daric's father started it. I should know. I was there."

He waved it away. "Besides, his mother, Emma, really is fat, even for a dragon. Too many goblins with buttercream frosting."

Gemma's mouth dropped open. "Oh, wow. I never would have thought of that. Like, I bet that would totally cover up the aftertaste. Evan, you need to teach me to make that."

Geezer nodded sagely. "Emma swears by it. The dairy farmers that live out near her leave it out as an offering."

All the talk of eating goblins was making me ill, so I changed the subject. "Lycia is mad at me because the dragon followed me home."

Geezer chuckled.

I continued, "And she grounded Sina."

"Planted her in a garden?" he asked.

"Mom confined me to the palace," Sina elaborated.

"What does that have to do with..." Geezer shook his head. "Never mind. She blames you for the dragon following Evan? What could you have done about it?"

Sina shrugged.

"Well, come in and sit. I've got some biscuits and fruit juice. Tell me all about it."

"Dad..." warned Sina.

"Don't give me that," grumped Geezer. "Your mom doesn't want us seen together because she doesn't want people puttin' two sheep and two sheep together and getting a cow. I'll check the hall before you leave. I haven't spoken to you directly in a coon's age. Come in and sit."

Sina glanced up and down the hall, bounced on her toes, ran in, and hugged the old wizard, giving him a peck on the cheek.

He had an ear-to-ear grin, and his blush made his whiskers look a lot whiter.

Gemma and I followed.

As soon as he laid the snacks out, the old wizard asked about our trip to Vimra. Sina and I took turns relating our adventures, with Gemma adding here and there if we missed something she considered important.

"A redcap assassin, you say?" Geezer rubbed his whiskers. "And he tried to kill you in Lonathas?"

"We don't know for sure, dad," said Sina, "But it seems likely."

The wizard gave a low whistle. "That must have cost a lot of coin. Those bloody-minded cretins don't come cheap."

"Gems," I corrected. "I'm pretty sure I got the upfront part of his payment."

"Well, now that you have your own place, I want to give you a tree warming present." Geezer went to a shelf and pulled two books off it. "I took the liberty of writing down a few spells you should be able to cast at your current skill level. I also want to give you your first spell book, so you can write your own stuff down." The old man leaned in close. "It's written in English, so it'll drive anyone who takes it from you nuts."

"Thanks," I thumbed through it quickly before adding it to my pouch.

Geezer stared at the bag at my waist. "Please, tell me you got the spell for that."

"Uh, the personalized lock, yes." I shrugged with my hands. "The larger on the inside spell, no."

Geezer sighed. "I need to convince Lycia to let me take a trip to see the gnomes." Then he grinned, "Now you'll have something for those bookshelves in your new place."

"Thanks, but I don't think I'll get a chance to use them." The room got quiet, and I felt everyone's eyes on me. "What? The giant is my last quest. I'll be going home."

No one spoke for a few uncomfortable seconds. Geezer finally broke the silence. "You're sure puttin' down a lot of roots for someone who's leaving in a few days."

He was right. I'd made friends. True friends. Furry fuzzy puppies, I'd even bought a tree. If I was being honest with myself, I was going to miss this world of magic, sprites, and dragons. But I had a life back in San Antonio. A grandma and dad who missed and loved me. They were important too. I took a deep breath and let it out. "I'm really going to miss you guys."

Geezer grimaced. "You gotta do, what ya gotta do, kid, but I for one will be sorry to see you go. I was savin' the bad news for last, but it's somethin' you'll wanna know." He huffed. "Time is speedin' up over there. In the two weeks or so that it'll take you to get to Azura and back, time will probably move at roughly the same speed here and there."

***

CRACK!

I went from sound asleep to wide awake in an instant. I panicked as I started sliding. Had someone chopped down my treehouse?

I stopped when I hit scales.

Sighing, I threw my sheets off.

"Oops! Sorry big brother."

Rubbing the sleep from my eyes and I stared up at the pony-sized dragon. Her weight completely crushed the legs of my poor bed. "Pi, you have your own bed. Heck, thanks to Daric, you have your own treasure to line your nest. What are you doing up here?"

"I couldn't sleep," she whined. "I've gotten used to curling up next to you. Can't I just sleep in here with you? Just for tonight?"

"Pi..."

"You're super comfy. Like my blankie, plushie ewe, and favorite claw warmers all rolled into one."

I groaned and fell back onto the remains of my bed.

"Just for one more night, I promise." She laced her claws together and squeezed her eyes shut. "Pleeeeease!"

It was like sharing a bed with the Great Dane from hell. But it was already ruined. I could pick up a new bed tomorrow. Was it worth it if I was only going to use the room for one more night?

"Fine. But don't steal my covers again. I don't want to wake up in the morning freezing my toes off."

"Cross my chest. You won't regret it."

"It's cross my... never mind."

***

My toes felt like icicles.

The dragon hadn't stolen *all the* covers last night, but my legs were sticking out. Pi was sleeping on top of my blanket, so my back, the part nearest to her, was roasting. Red dragons generated a lot of heat, but apparently not enough to thaw my toes.

Well, I knew a sure-fire way to warm them up.

"Yiiiii!" Pi leaped out of bed. "What did you do that for?" She complained, rubbing her back.

"You stole my blankets."

"Get more blankets."

"What happened to this being the last time?"

Pi opened her mouth to speak, then stopped. "Oh. Right."

Shaking my head, I went into the washroom. When I was presentable, I went downstairs. The aroma wafting up to me from the lower level had my mouth watering. Onions, bacon, and roasted potatoes. I found Gemma at the stove.

"You totally overslept. This morning, you eat *my* cooking, okay?"

I grinned at the troll. "Okay, show me what you've got."

What she had was the beginnings of some serious skill with a spatula. Over-easy eggs, crisp bacon, and a mound of hash browns that tasted as good as they smelled.

"Wow. Well done. Breakfast success," I proclaimed.

Pi agreed through a mouth full of food.

Gemma turned a darker shade of green as she smiled. "Aw, sweet berries and honey wine, you guys are too much. Told you I was paying attention." The troll sat down and joined us.

"I'm going to get some supplies together for our next trip." I pointed my fork at my companions. "What are you two going to do today?"

Gemma beamed. "Following you. You still have a lot to teach me about cooking, so, like, I'm not letting you out of my sight."

I expected as much. Someone had already tried to kill me once in this city. With Gemma watching my back, I felt pretty safe. "What about you, Pi?"

The dragon shoveled a fork full of hash browns into her mouth and swallowed. "Oh, Nip is going to stop by and show me how to pick pockets."

I blinked. "What?"

"I said-" she started.

Holding up a hand, I stopped her. "I heard what you said, I just didn't realize Nip was a thief or that you would risk going into town." I didn't bother to bring up the morality of stealing. I knew enough about Pi to know that was a lost cause.

Pi brightened, "Oh, yes. Nip and I talked yesterday. He says Millow taught him everything he knows about picking pockets and locks, picking marks, and running scams."

It was at that point I thought the queen might be right. Perhaps bringing the dragon here had been a bad idea. But, if we were leaving tomorrow, how much trouble could she get into? My twisted guts and frayed nerves provided the answer. A lot.

Perhaps I could decrease the likelihood of trouble. "You left time this afternoon to teach me more illusion magic, right?"

"Oh." The dragon looked disappointed. "You wanted to do that today?"

"Well, yeah," I pressed. "It's a lot easier than practicing while traveling."

"Okay, but we're coming back here after defeating the giant, right?" Pi held her head low and looked up at me with puppy dog eyes. For a big lizard, she was really good at that.

"Yes, we'll be coming right back." I relented, feeling bad about the fact that I wouldn't be around for much longer after that.

She nodded with satisfaction. "Good. I have so much to learn here and much more opportunity to get treasures!"

CHAPTER 37: SKILLS TO STEAL THE BILLS

After breakfast, I started toward Millow's Miscellany for many reasons. Mainly because I had a shopping list as long as my arm.

My trip to her shop was uneventful. Why, you might ask? Because while I wasn't very good at illusions yet, I still had a lot of work to do with Pi. I had learned enough to change skin tones and make my ears look long. I made Gemma look shorter and lighter-skinned, so wearing her cloak, she looked more like a tall dwarf than a troll. As a result, we garnered a few curious glances instead of the outright stares we usually received.

We entered the dark-haired elf's store to the chime of bird songs. She looked up from something she was reading and did a double-take. "Oh Sugar, that's a good look for you, but those ears..."

I winced. "I know. There's something not quite right."

"It's the tips," she explained. "They're a little too long and pointy. Round them off a bit and shorten them by half an inch, and I think you'll have it."

I made a mental note to do that and dismissed the illusion. It was hard to keep it going while walking and acting casual. It was also making me a little tired. What I wouldn't give for a cup of coffee.

I handed Millow my list. "So, Nip, he's one of yours?"

She studied it as she replied. "He is now. Poor boy, his parents died in a skirmish up north."

That was a new wrinkle. "I'm sorry to hear that. His relatives didn't take him in?"

"Oh Honey, a boy like him, no money, no education, and no magic ability to speak of, they wanted nothing to do with him."

"Ouch."

She raised her voice. "Eve, can you come here a moment?"

A young elf girl with curly white hair and dark eyes rushed from the back room. "Yes, Miss Millow?"

Millow handed her the list. "Some of these items are out back. Be a dear and bring them to the front, will you?"

The girl bounced and disappeared behind the door again.

I made an educated guess. "How many orphans do you look after?"

Her blue eyes twinkled. "Four. Nip, Eve, and a couple of others."

"How do they end up here? Are they all like Nip?"

"It varies. Eve's father is missing and presumed dead, and her mother just stopped coming home one day. I found her in Port Shaland occupying a stool at a sailor's bar to feed a fairy dust habit." Millow shrugged. "No reason to tell Eve the whole truth. She went far away will work until she's older."

I grinned at the shopkeeper. "And the picking pockets and locks? I thought you were respectable now."

She gave me an exaggerated wink. "Everyone needs a hobby, Sugar. Besides, the people who try to catch them are the same ones that'll be asking me to send them to do their dirty work. Honey, there're all sorts of things they'll pay for that they don't want anyone knowing about. I'm not about to turn down clean coin for dirty work."

That made sense. I could see the queen or one of the nobles quietly paying to have something stolen, planting evidence, or any number of misdirections. I'd discovered that elves were political creatures. Power games must become the norm when you lived forever.

Eve piled my purchases on the counter. Much of it was the stuff I didn't have yet, but I'd been making a list. The mound included things like more spices, better cooking gear, fishing line and hooks, a lightweight tent with stakes, and a grooming kit.

I grew little stubble, but what was there was uneven and patchy. I was feeling like a slob. Elves didn't have facial hair but sometimes did cool things with their head hair. I'd seen bald, a few mohawks, and even a few TikTok cuts in a variety of unnatural colors.

I regarded the gear critically. "Can you think of anything else I might need for my trip to Azura?"

Millow cocked an eyebrow. "Azura? Why the heck is she sending you way out there?"

"Giant," I answered.

She blinked. "Odd, the hill giants out that way are usually more concerned about filling their bellies than causing trouble." Millow tapped her lip thoughtfully. "Whatever you do, try not to antagonize the brute. If you have to fight it, take my advice and don't. Run away and use these." She pulled a bag from behind the counter and set it next to my stuff.

Curious, I opened the bag and peered inside. It was filled with a bunch of metal items that looked like jacks. All that was missing was a rubber ball. "You want me to play games with him?"

"Games?" Millow frowned. "Honey, those are caltrops. Hill giants don't wear shoes."

"Oh." Okay, that was new. I pulled out one of the spiky things and set it on the counter. I could tell no matter how it landed, at least two sharp points would stick upward. "They're like supped-up Legos. But if I throw them, they'll be gone, and I'll be Lego-less."

"What?"

"Legolas. Famous elf?"

"Never heard of him."

I waved it away. "Sometimes my mind goes to weird places."

***

We arrived back at my tree and I stood outside, staring into the branches as Gemma went inside to make lunch. "You need a name," I said to the tree. "I dub you Evan's Re-leaf."

"That's a funny name."

Glancing around, I searched for the source of the voice. "Pi?"

Her giggling came from somewhere nearby, but I couldn't pin down where. *Okay,* I thought to myself, *it's definitely Pi, but she's being playful.*

"Two can play at that," I said, then used my Meld with Stone spell and camouflaged myself.

"I can still smell you," said Pi in a sing-song voice.

But smell isn't the same as sight. I circled around, looking for

Pi's footprints in the nearby dirt and grass. I didn't find them, but I saw something odd. When I moved, the bark on a nearby tree didn't, like I was looking through a pane of glass with beveled edges.

Moving to the right, I went behind a nearby sufra tree. Sneaking around to the other side, I saw Nip and elf Pi snickering behind something that looked like a stiff curtain.

Quietly, I approached, until Pi went still and sniffed at the air. Then I dropped the spell and rushed them. "Rawr!"

They both shrieked and fell on their butts, the curtain evaporated, and we all burst out laughing.

"That was neat Pi," I said, helping them to their feet. "I've never seen you cast illusions like that before."

"Yeah, being a wizard, I knew you could handle the more advanced stuff. This is super easy."

"Not for me," said Nip. "I can't do any of it."

"But I'm having trouble with the advanced stuff," I pointed out. "My illusions are crap. I can't get the color right, I can't get the details right, and they're sight only. I haven't gotten the smell, feel, or sound to work at all. The suggestion part is still a long way off. It's like learning math or science. Show me the simple stuff first."

We walked toward my tree.

"What's science?" asked Pi.

"Like magic, but less cool." I wasn't about to go down that road. According to Geezer, the laws of nature were slightly different over here, anyway. I'd seen the proof that he was right. I really missed my cell phone.

"Okay, but I'm being serious," said Pi, "making an unmoving picture with no depth is super easy."

Approaching the tree, I grabbed the ridge of bark to open the concealed door. I was getting a lot better at noticing the cleverly concealed doors and windows amongst the tree homes of the elf city.

The door opened, and a wave of burnt meat smell assaulted my nose. Gemma was swearing at the magic oven. She pulled off her oven mitts and threw them at the misbehaving appliance. "I should become a vegetarian."

"That would be a huge missed-steak," I said.

The troll gave me a hairy eyeball. "I could always cook *you*."

"Then who would make lunch?" I asked with a grin.

"Ha!" she barked a laugh. "Lunch will be delayed as I try this again. I obviously need practice."

I gave her a salute. "And I will go practice illusions with Pi. Something I obviously need help with."

Pi and I turned the second level into a training area by pushing all the boxes stored there into a corner. The room looked as if it had been raining dust inside. I could have written my name in it, it was so thick. Which gave me an idea.

I drew the magic circle only to have Bramble appear beside it. Knowing that the sprite wouldn't be bound if I didn't complete the spell, I continued to draw. The sprite's eyes bounced between me and the circle and seemed to be on the verge of passing out from breathing too fast. "Come on, come on, finish the circle. I want sugar!"

Suppressing a grin, I finished the spell and powered it.

Bramble hopped inside and sat. "Okay Peach Fuzz. What must I do to get some of your sweet loving?"

Pi laughed as I sighed and shook my head. "Bramble, I need you to remove the dust from my tree. I don't care where it goes, as long as it isn't inside my house."

"*Anywhere?*" the sprite drew out the word as a question.

I eyed the androgynous winged being suspiciously. "I think by now, you've figured out that I enjoy a good joke as much as you do, but certain things are off-limits. Anywhere within reason."

"*Muhahahahaha!*" Bramble cackled maniacally and disappeared.

A little worrisome, but I didn't *think* the sprite would go too far. Pi and I started practicing while the sprite began cleaning using a brush and dustpan I didn't recall seeing before.

The dragon was right. The two-dimensional image was easier. Not as simple as she claimed, but in two hours I was able to keep the image from wavering, compared to the five days for the three-dimensional illusion was I still was having trouble with.

Lunch was served late, but the beef chili didn't taste half bad. Gemma had done well with the spices. It was easy to ignore the black bits where the beans had burned on the bottom of the pot. It's a good thing that the elves hadn't yet figured out magical smoke detectors. While getting better, Gemma's cooking was still a work in progress.

After dinner, it was more spell practice. After my success with the two-dimensional image, I was ready to try something a little different. Pi had been trying to get me to make large images like houses, trees, and dragons. Instead, I tried something small.

After three hours of flickering, stretched, rainbow zebra stripes, and even an image that looked disturbingly like it was inside out. I finally got it mostly right.

"A chicken?"

I admired my handiwork. "A chicken," I agreed with a firm nod.

Pi tilted her head as she peered down at it. "Not... bad."

I was mildly offended. "Not bad? It's a chicken. You recognized it as a chicken. You could pluck and cook it, this chicken illusion is so good."

Pi nodded slowly. "Are chickens in San Antonio shaped like watermelons?"

I examined my fowl creation with a critical eye. It wasn't melon-shaped, not really. Okay, well, maybe from a certain angle. I mean, chickens were kind of round anyway, right? Roundish with legs and wings tacked on...

Well, dog doo. I picked up my feathered basketball and held it aloft. "I dub thee melocken."

"What?"

"Chickelon?"

"Are you losing your mind?"

"No, I'm losing my rind." I raised an eyebrow at the dragon.

She rolled her eyes. "Hey, are you holding that picture?" asked Pi.

I held up the melocken. "Yes?"

The dragon poked at it with a claw. Because it amused me, I caused the melocken to squawk.

"It's solid," she pointed out.

"Yes. You told me to make the image as solid as possible. You said that if people could see through it, it would be bad."

"It shouldn't... but it..." Pi poked melocken again. "How come I can touch your pictures?"

I shrugged, "because?"

Pi called up an image of a sheep, then waved a claw through it. "See. Can't touch this. But I can touch yours. Just how solid is it?"

"I don't know. Hammer time?"

Pi stuck her claw into the Melocken. It popped like a balloon, covering me with feathers.

She giggled like a little girl.

I blew the feathers off my mouth and narrowed my eyes at the dragon. "Just so you know, this means war." I made a popping noise with my mouth.

Feathers exploded into being right in front of the dragon, covering her from head to scaly paw in downy white.

"Ah!" she squeaked. "Oh, you're gonna regret that. Mess with the dragon, get the feathers."

Poof! Poof! Poof! Three white explosions rained feathers in a ten-foot radius. They couldn't touch me, but that didn't matter, the gauntlet had been thrown.

It was on. I shot finger guns at Pi as she raced around the room, trying to avoid my feather bombs. The pony-sized dragon sent waves of feathers at me and even breathed a cloud of plumage at me when she got close.

"What's going on up here?" Gemma appeared in the doorway with a confused look and wearing an apron that said, "License to grill."

For several heartbeats, Pi and I froze. Tufts of down drifted lazily to the feather-covered ground.

"Ah," I held up a finger, then pointed it at the troll. *Pop!*

Gemma grabbed a handful of feathers and chased after me, and it was on again.

***

The War of the Chicken was declared a draw. Personally, I thought I'd won since my feathers stayed around and you could touch them, but Gemma and Pi argued that the sheer volume of chicken down Pi produced more than made up for the fact you couldn't actually touch it. At least clean up was a breeze. Just dismiss the feathers.

Exhausted, I climbed the stairs to my room at the top of the tree.

Oh right. That's what I forgot to do today. Get a new bed.

Only one of the wooden bedposts still stood upright, and it was at an odd angle. The rest lay with what remained of the splintered bed frame. I'd made a halfhearted effort to put the pieces next to the mattress. But the mattress was still in good shape and the blankets had weathered the night intact. I hadn't made the bed.

There didn't seem to be a point. There was an odd lump in the blankets. An extra pillow, maybe?

I was too tired to worry much about it. I sat on the mattress and took off my pants and socks, leaving my underwear and shirt on. I was living with two women, and even if they weren't human, I wanted to keep something on in case I had to get up in the middle of the night.

I pulled back the sheets on the lump I thought was an extra pillow and found... a sheep?

Not a live sheep, but it was some kind of stuffed animal with button eyes and stubby legs. It was dirty and tattered and was obviously well-loved by someone. I couldn't imagine how it had ended up in my bed, unless...

I shook my head, then rubbed my face with my hands. I grabbed the corner of the mattress and lifted it. Sure enough, there was a small pile of gems and coins that I was certain hadn't been there this morning.

"Pi..." I let out a long breath. Well, she wasn't here now, and I was too tired to argue with her about it. Placing the stuffed sheep in the corner of the mattress, I curled up under the covers. Just before I drifted off, I adjusted the blankets the way the dragon preferred in the vain hope I'd be able to keep my toes covered by morning.

CHAPTER 38: THE LONG GOODBYE

My toes didn't freeze that night.

We awoke early and headed for the palace. The castle gatehouse sent us around to the stables where Gemma and I found Daric. He was seated on his horse and Nonam was saddled and ready. I greeted her and gave her a piece of carrot from my pocket.

"Where's Sina?" I asked.

"My fiancé is confined to the palace." His tone said idiot without actually using the word.

"I know, but I thought she'd at least see us off."

He smiled down at me condescendingly. "Confined to the palace, in this case, means she is required to stay in her apartment."

Well, that sucked. "Oh, then I'll just pop up there and say goodbye before we head out."

"No," declared Daric.

"No?" asked Gemma.

"No," repeated the elf lord. "Since we have two party members who cannot ride, we will be hard-pressed to make the first campsite as it is. We have no time for such foolishness."

"You'll make time for me, you stuck-up peacock." Geezer crossed the stable yard in bright pink flamingo slippers that squawked with every step. "Come here Evan and give an old guy a hug." *Squeak, squeak, squeak.*

I grinned at the old rascal and hugged him. Daric scowled at us. He also stuffed something into my pocket, behind my back where the elf couldn't see.

We separated and Geezer winked at me.

"Any advice for the trip?" I asked.

"Yeah," he scratched his beard. "Hill giants are crazy strong and tougher than shoe leather dipped in ox piss, but not exactly the brightest candle in the room. They get fixated on things. Ever hear a catchy tune and find yourself singing it to yourself for the rest of the day? It's like that, but ten times worse."

I grimaced. "So, I should sing it to death?"

The old wizard rubbed his hands together thoughtfully. "Let me put it to you this way. I number of years ago, I ran across a giant harassing a village. Every time it got hungry, it would smash open a treehouse and grab all the food it found. Mind you, pretty much everything that moves is food to a hill giant. We fought. Spells, swords, arrows, it didn't matter what I threw at the beastie, nothing hurt it. It just got more angry and destroyed more village."

Geezer was easily twenty times the wizard I was. He'd lived here for over a hundred years and had scads of experience. If he couldn't hurt the giant, what chance did I have? "What did you do?" I asked.

He grinned. "During a lull in the fighting, I offered him some baked beans. I'm no cook, mind you, I can burn water with the best, but that didn't matter. The big oaf loved them. So, I showed him how to grow and cook beans. Then I told him that beans couldn't grow near villages," he cackled. "That beans were afraid of elves."

I laughed with him for almost a minute before we petered out. "The queen says I have to kill the giant."

"Like you were supposed to slay a dragon? Pbbbbt." He shook his head.

"I'm pretty sure she means it."

Geezer sighed. "You've got a troll and a dragon to help you out, but more importantly, you've got you. If something feels wrong, it probably is. Don't let some elf make you compromise your morals. You see, that's how they get you. They try to make their goals yours, and you end up doing something you'll regret for the rest of your life."

"Is that how they got you?" I asked.

The old wizard grew somber. "Yeah. That's exactly how they did it."

I wanted to ask more, but his expression told me it was a sensitive topic, so I let it go. "I wish Sina was coming with us."

Geezer put his hand on my shoulder. "She does, too."

Gemma punched me lightly on the arm. "What am I? Goblin leftovers? And Pi is meeting us at the edge of town."

I smiled up at her. "Your friendship is fit for royalty. Why you hang around with a guy like me boggles the mind."

She winked. "It's the food."

"If you're quite done," groused Daric, "every minute we sit here, we're losing travel time. At this rate, it will take ten days or more to reach the outpost."

We said the last of our goodbyes and left the stable yard. Thankfully, this trip through Lonathas was uneventful. No redcap assassins or arrows raining down on me from the trees.

Pi met us at the edge of town. It would have been nice if she could have ridden a horse, but that wouldn't work. The Change Shape spell she used to appear as a young elf didn't reduce her weight. She might look like a stiff breeze might blow her over, but try to lift her, no way. She weighed a ton.

The road to Azura was in pretty good shape. Daric said the reason was that the kingdom of Calabrain was the biggest trading partner with the kingdom of Shara.

"So, the lands to the east of Shara are scrub bush and desert," I clarified.

"Yes," said Daric.

"And the people that live there are mostly gnomes and cats."

He sighed dramatically. "Gnomes and felion. Fe-li-on."

"But the Fe-li-on look like cats."

The elf rubbed the bridge of his nose. "No. The felion look like felion."

I ticked the details off on my fingers. "Which are five feet tall, walk on two legs, furry, with short snouts, large canines, triangle-shaped pointed ears on their heads, and long tails."

"Correct."

"So, people-sized cats."

The elf lord groaned.

"Pi?" I asked.

The dragon was still in small elf form. She shrugged. "They taste gamey, and the fur gets stuck in my teeth. I don't recommend them."

"But are they like house cats?" I pressed.

"I don't know. I've never eaten a house cat."

Gemma nudged the tiny elf. "He means do they look like an elf-sized cat?"

Pi looked up at me. "Oh! Well, why didn't you ask that?"

"But, I..." I shook my head to clear it. "Do felion look like elf-sized house cats?"

"No," she shrugged. "They look more like cheetahs. You know, with the spots."

"Except for the ones with stripes," Gemma added.

"Or the ones with lots of head fur." Pi nodded in agreement.

Gemma waved a finger in the air. "But that's only the males."

"Really?" Pi twisted her face in confusion. "How can you tell? Have you seen many felion naked?"

Daric growled in frustration. "Stop with the inane chatter. We're not even going into Calabrain, just to Azura. The only felion we're likely to see will be traders traveling to Lonathas." With that, Daric spurred his horse into a trot and put fifty yards between us.

Glancing at Pi and Gemma, I saw they were fully engaged in the various fur styles they'd seen among the felion. I gently squeezed Nonam so that she sped up a little, so that I was a little ahead of the troll and dragon, but well back from the surly elf lord.

I reached into my back pocket and pulled out the note Geezer left for me. I grinned as I saw it was written in English.

Evan,

My daughter has always been a loyal hound when it comes to the people, and a rabid badger with a rotten tooth when it comes to following the rules. I don't know what it is about you that brings out the badger, but Titania help any that get in her way.

She showed up at my door, telling me she was leaving to follow you on your next quest. Honest to buckeyes, I think she expected me to talk her out of it. Ha, like I'd pass up the opportunity to bite my thumb at her ma.

So, my girl is on your trail. You probably won't see or hear her when Daric's around. The slug would see it as his duty to bring her back, if only to put her in her place. You might smell her, though. The scent of forbidden fruit is unmistakable at fifty yards.

I'm not sure what she expects to come of this, and I doubt she does either, but she's got a wild streak a mile wide. It reminds me of something I'd have done a hundred years ago in another life.

Good for her.

Look for stacked rocks. We used to mark trails that way back when we'd go hiking together. Back when her mom let me see her. Before that crown of hers choked off the air to her brain while her royal scepter got lodged halfway up her butt. I hope it's as uncomfortable as a crazy squirrel in her panties.

But I'm getting off-topic. I've included a spell with this letter: fireball. Don't get too excited. The ball is about the size of a grapefruit. It'll set stuff on fire, sure, or singe eyebrows, but don't expect it to turn a baseball field of enemies into goblin-kabobs. Being your first damage spell, do me a favor an don't let elf prissy pants know you've got it. Find a way to practice when his pointy ears and shifty eyes ain't around.

Take care of yourself, take care of my little badger, and above all, do what's right.

-Jack Sherman aka The Old Geezer

Smiling to myself, I folded the letter up and put it in my pouch. I perused the next three sheets of paper, which detailed how to "throw heat" as Geezer put it. It was a fairly complicated set of gestures and mental exercises, and I knew it would take me a long time to get it down.

I glanced up from the notes. Gemma and Pi were still deep in their conversation, and Daric was doing his best to ignore the rest of us. No one had even noticed my letter.

CHAPTER 39: ANGER MANAGEMENT, IT'S ALL THE RAGE

What did he notice? Stacked rocks. Daric would point at them and tell me it was my fault for calling sprites.

We'd made the campsite Daric wanted just as the sun was setting. A well-used ring of small stones sat in the center, with the remains of a recent fire. Not too recent, as there was no burnt wood smell. The space between the trees was already cleared, and some twigs and leaves were piled near some stacked rocks.

I pointed at the kindling. "It appears my use of sprites is producing some benefits."

He snorted and gave us our first introduction to drill sergeant Daric. "Evan, get our fire going. Gemma, hunt us some food. Pi, scout around the campsite to make sure we're alone."

Our response was probably not what he was expecting. We stood there staring at him for probably five full seconds.

I turned to Gemma. "Do you mind doing the hunting?"

The troll waggled her head from side to side. "No, I think I smell some rabbits over that way. Are you good with roast rabbit?"

I nodded and glanced at Pi.

The tiny elf shrugged. "Sure, maybe I'll find a snack before dinner."

"I am in charge here," yelled Daric, his face turning as red as his hair.

We all ignored him, but since our assigned tasks were what we wanted to do anyway, we did them. Did that make the haughty elf lord happy? Nooooo.

I started putting sticks together to get the fire going.

The elf warrior kicked over the stacked rocks and stomped over to me. "What game do you think you are playing?"

"It's no game." I shrugged. "It's my quest. My task to complete. *You* are our guide. You've made it clear that you won't help or do anything other than the bare minimum to get us from Lonathas to wherever the queen sends me."

He glared at me. "The queen put me in charge."

I smiled. "No, she asked you to accompany me. You're as much a leader of this group as a one-legged goblin with a leech infestation."

He ground his teeth together so hard I heard it. "Fine," he snarled. "You take first watch."

I gazed up into the trees and made a show of tapping my chin in thought. If Daric went to sleep early, he wouldn't be awake to see me practice spells or possibly meet Sina in the woods. Pi didn't have to stand watch. Daric wasn't about to inconvenience the dragon. Maybe I could get her help to watch the camp. "Yes, I'm okay with that."

Daric stalked over to the horses, muttering under his breath.

Gemma brought back three rabbits, they were large ones, so I guessed it would be enough for Pi and Gemma with their bigger appetites. I'd picked up some cooking wine and other supplies in Lonathas, so I was well prepared to roast rabbits and spice them up right with salt, pepper, garlic, and onions.

My mom would always ask if we liked our food, on the rare times she cooked. It was often half burnt, over-spiced, dry, or something. Me? I relied on reactions. People will lie and tell you they like your cooking, but the truth is found in how they eat. Gemma and Pi chowed down with gusto, and even Daric interrupted his scowl to chew with appreciative nods.

Gemma quizzed me on what spices I added when and why. Remembering her recent try at chili, I pointed out that temperature control was also a factor and showed her how I controlled the wood and coals to keep the temperature just right.

After dinner, Daric oiled his armor and weapons while I set up for first watch. Gemma would have second watch, and Daric would take the morning shift. We didn't require Pi to take a shift.

After Daric was situated and snoring softly, I pulled out Geezer's spell notes, but I had to put them back away as Gemma and Pi got up and crept over to where I was sitting.

I regarded them curiously as they sat in front of me.

"So," said Gemma in a low voice, "we've been talking, and Pi will stand your watch."

"What?" I whispered.

"You big dummy," said Pi as she hugged herself and made a kissy face. "Your girlfriend is hiding out there in the trees. Go touch lips or whatever you humans and elves do. Just make sure you get some spell practice in too. You need it. Your pictures aren't sharp enough to fool anyone who looks close enough."

"We'll keep an eye on Daric," said Gemma, "and cover for you if he gets up in the middle of the night."

"How did you know she was out there?" I asked. I hadn't told them about the stones or even mentioned Sina since we left the city.

Gemma rolled her eyes. "She's really good at not being seen, not so great at not being smelled. Every once in a while, I catch a whiff of the vanilla scent she wears. It's been making me hungry all afternoon."

I motioned with my fingers, pointing in several directions. The troll pointed in the direction Sina was in. I hugged my two friends and whispered in their ears. "Thank you."

I quietly picked my way through the woods in the direction Gemma had indicated. After about sixty yards, I came across a clearing with a ball of light hovering nearby. She was there, leaning against a tree with a huge grin. In the dim light, I could see that she was dressed a little differently. She wore a dark leather tunic over tight-fitting stiffened leather armor. The whole thing seemed designed for stealth, even more so than the black leather the Redcap had worn. It hugged her body in a way I'd wanted to since I met her.

"Wow," I breathed.

Sina wrinkled her nose. "A little less wow since we've been traveling all day."

I knew she meant from today's travels, but I didn't notice anything. I took a deep breath and gathered her in my arms. Our lips met, and it was amazing. No sprites interrupted us. No foul-smelling clouds appeared out of nowhere. There was the kiss, and it was pure, and it was beautiful.

Our lips separated, and Sina sucked in and breathed out. "Evan, never tell me where you learned to kiss like that."

That brought up memories of Heather and how she'd left me to date my brother and I sighed. "Deal."

Sina squinted at me. "Bad memory?"

"Yeah. Long ago in a galaxy far far away, though," I told her. "Thank you for coming."

She lowered her head and gazed up at me with those leaf-green eyes of hers. "You'd do it for me. And I don't get what my mom is thinking. Kill a giant? They're almost as tough as dragons."

"I'm thinking your mom gave me three impossible quests and I've done two of them," I said with a smile. "Are you going to get in trouble?"

"Yeah." She winced, "but it won't last more than a few months when..." she trailed off.

When she had to marry Daric. Okay, change of subject time. Let's leave that pachyderm safe and sound in the middle of the room.

"I, uh, used a sprite to clean a storage area." I grimaced even as I said it. Talk about lame.

"Smooth change of subject," she deadpanned.

"I'm a master of dis-merection, meri-diction, being sneaky," I said with a cheesy grin.

She did laugh then and hugged me close. We stayed like that for a while, not saying anything, but just enjoying being near each other.

Finally, Sina sighed. "What am I going to do?"

It was a statement, not a question, but I answered anyway. "Defeat a giant. After that, we'll see how things go and take advantage of any opportunities."

"Don't go."

"What?"

She snuggled into my arms. "Don't go back to San Antonio."

"I... I have a life back there." I protested, but even to me, it sounded halfhearted.

"You could have a life here, too."

I didn't answer her. Instead, I let everything about my life in San Antonio and my life in Stellaluna roll around in my head. This world had magic, trolls, dragons, and Sina. But San Antonio had my grandma and my dad. San Antonio had my brother and my mom. Here I had fairy assassins and conniving elves that wanted to use me for their own goals. Would my brother actually try to kill me?

"You don't have to answer right now," said Sina. "Actually, I don't think you should. Just... think about it."

"Well, there's this giant. And I think I should practice my spells if I'm going to help some poor elves just doing their jobs." Okay, still not smooth, but a little better than before.

Sina pulled her head back and raised an eyebrow at me. "You have a spell that can defeat a giant?"

"Yeah, no," I admitted. "But maybe there's a nearby beanstalk I can chop down."

Sina squinted and cocked her head to one side. "Beanstalk?"

"Sorry. Across the divide reference."

"You have giants across the divide?"

I sighed, "Only in stories. Geezer told me some stuff, but what do I need to know about real giants?"

"Rumor has it that this is a Hill Giant," said Sina, ending the hug and pacing around the clearing. "The descriptions of what it's done match typical behavior for them. Expect something that looks like an elf, but twenty-five feet tall. They're very strong. The outpost has dwarven masons. They've been repairing the stone walls the giant has been destroying. They're tough. Normal swords and arrows don't hurt them, and they're resistant to most magic. Also, they're stubborn. They get an idea in their head and nothing you say will convince them to do something else."

"Great," I groused, "super strong, super tough, and more single-minded than a dog rolling in dead possum. Got it. Do they have any weaknesses?"

"They're not smart."

"Not smart like, look over there, a purple sprite. Or not smart like, two plus three equals six?" I held up my hands as if weighing the two options.

Bramble appeared behind Sina. He'd turned himself purple and had a hopeful expression.

She made a rolling motion with her hands. "More the second, but distractible if it doesn't interfere with their current obsession."

"And our giant is obsessed with destroying an outpost. Great. Do we have a name to go with our towering elf squasher?"

"No. It comes in and destroys walls and buildings by using a tree as a club." Sina shrugged, "The soldiers there haven't exactly asked it to tea."

"Any suggestions on what spells I should work on?"

"What are you currently practicing?"

I gave her a list of the current spells I knew. "And the spells I'm working on, but don't really know yet, are 2D and 3D illusions."

"Two Dee? Three Dee?"

I winced. "Uh, flat images and whole images."

"I'm guessing flat is easier."

"Yes, but it only works if you're looking at it from the right angle."

Sina scratched her chin. "Work on the whole image, then. You can't count on the giant to stay in one place."

"Good point." I ran through the necessary energies and thought patterns in my head. "Oh, and Geezer gave me the fireball spell."

Sina stopped and her jaw dropped open. "He what?"

My brain hiccupped at her shock. "He, uh, sent me his notes on the fireball spell. He said it wasn't very impressive."

She put her hands up, palms out. "My father gave you an *offensive* spell?"

I didn't know what the big deal was, so I ran through what that might mean. The only thing I came up with was that he wanted me to defend myself with magic in addition to my sword skills. "Yes?"

Sina clenched her fists and took a deep breath. "You have to try to teach me."

"What?"

"I want to learn the spell. If there's even the slightest chance that I can learn fire magic, you have to teach me." There was an intensity I wasn't used to seeing in her eyes.

"Okay," I said. "Why is it so important to you?"

"My Dad never teaches that spell to anyone. Ever. If he's teaching it to you, he must think you are in danger. If you're in danger, I want to help."

"You're already awesome with a sword and bow. Why do you need a fire spell?"

Her green eyes practically glowed with excitement. "Because it's fire."

I chuckled, "Okay, let's learn how to cast fireball."

My watch was four hours. We spent three of them trying to get the fireball to work. No luck for either of us on that score. I spent the last hour trying to improve my 3D illusion. It was getting a little better. Less melon, more feathers. Practice makes for better rejects, right?

At the end of my shift, I left Sina to her little camp and went back to the clearing. Pi had taken my watch, so we woke Gemma for midwatch, and I set out my bedroll. I was too wired from practice that I couldn't fall off to sleep right away. So I was awake when a not-so stealthy dragon crept up to where I was laying and curled up next to me.

CHAPTER 40: OUTPOST REMOVED IN CASE IT CAUSED A FENCE

The trip to Azura took on a rhythm. Daric led the way. Sometimes he engaged us in conversation, but mostly he glowered or rolled his eyes. Pi, Gemma, and I joked, played I spy, and told stories to each other. Any tale about my life in San Antonio was a hit, but inevitably ended with me answering a ton of questions about culture, machines, or gadgets from my home.

Sina stayed out of sight, but left the occasional stack of rocks on the trail. Daric continued to blame Bramble. Since the sprite followed us and played the occasional prank, it reinforced the idea. Nettles in our clothes, sap in Daric's hair, and something that dyed all our teeth blue were just a few of the antics we put up with.

The tall pine forest near the castle gave way to smaller pines and then scrub oak as the landscape became more arid. Green grasses turned white and brown and patches of red and gray sand showed between clumps of vegetation.

Sina and I continued to practice spells when I snuck away from camp. My illusions got better. About halfway to Azura, I created my very first ball of fire. The day before we would arrive, I could throw the ball short distances.

"It's not fair!" Sina shouted in frustration.

"*Shhhhh*. You'll wake up Lord Prissy Pants." I tried to lighten the mood.

Her voice became a harsh whisper. "I'm half-human. I can't see or hear as well as other elves. My ears aren't as pointy. I've got to have something from my father."

"Maybe it's lying?" I offered.

She balled her hands into fists. "No. Whatever weird magic that won't let us lie also makes it really uncomfortable for me to try. It's hard to convince someone you're telling the truth when you're suffering cramps."

Sina snatched up the notes. "And this. What does this even mean?" She shook the paper at me. "Use the fire in your soul to power the spell."

"Near as I can figure it's passion or strong emotions," I said.

Sina wheeled on me. "I am passionate. See how passionate I am. I'm seething with passion." She held her hands up and threw them in every direction. "Nothing. Nothing. Nothing."

She stomped to the other side of the clearing.

"Maybe you aren't trying hard enough." The words had barely left my mouth, and I knew I was in trouble.

The blond elf glared at me with fury in her eyes. "I. Am. Trying!" She flicked her fingers to punctuate each word and my breath caught in my throat. Not because I was afraid of her, but each flick produced sparks from her fingertips.

"Sina, stop."

"No, I'm going to get this."

"You just did!" I said excitedly. "You created sparks. When you flicked your fingers. You're in heat." I stopped. "Uh, no. That came out bad."

Sina flicked her fingers, but nothing happened. "You're pulling my ears."

"I think you mean... No. Never mind. I'm not joking. You really did it."

Sina repeated the motion. Still no sparks. "It won't work."

"What was different?" I asked.

"I don't know."

"What was going on in your head?" I prompted.

"I was frustrated, but I've been frustrated for a week." She shook her hands. "Wait. No. I was angry."

"Well, get angry again."

She gave me a hairy eyeball. "And how do I do that?"

I smiled. "Daric wants to put you in a tower and throw away the key. To him, you're property. Something to possess."

Sina glared. It wasn't at me so much as towards me. She snarled silently and I saw her channel the energy into her hands. *Fwoump.*

Her hands caught fire. "Ah!" The fire went out.

I pounced and wrapped her in a tight hug. "You did it." Relief and joy flooded through our connection.

"I did it," she said, hugging me tightly. "I made fire. I'm a wizard."

***

Around midday, we reached the outpost. The land here was like west Texas. Mostly dried grass and scrub oaks. A warm wind blew from the east. Daric assured me that past this point, the land became even more dry and rocky with sandy soil. The very definition of a desert.

The outpost reminded me a bit of the Alamo. A rock and mortar building surrounded by the remains of a wall. Six elves and six dwarves worked tirelessly to repair what remained of the wall.

Daric rode ahead and shouted. "Who runs this outpost? We should have been challenged as soon as we were in sight of the walls. If we had been Darower elves, you'd all be dead."

The dwarves and elves stopped working and stared at the elf lord.

A stocky dwarf with a bushy black beard jerked a thumb at Daric. "Who da king carrot?"

I'd expected a Scottish or northern English accent based on movies and shows I'd watched. Not so. This dwarf's accent was more Danish or Swedish.

The sandy-haired elf he spoke to put down the trowel he'd been working with and wiped his hands on his pants before bowing. "Greetings, Lord Daricas. Did you have a pleasant journey?"

"Awful. The only thing that could have made it worse was if I'd had to spend it in the company of a troll." The elf lord looked back over his shoulder at Gemma, then gave the garrison captain a significant look.

We trudged up the last of the hill to stand beside them.

The captain tilted his head in confusion. "Uh. Okay. Yes, sir. Is that Gemma, the elf, cursed to be a troll?"

"W-w-what?" Daric stammered.

"The rumor going around is that the queen summoned another wizard from across the divide and that he's traveling in the company of a cursed elf." He pointed at the rest of us. "That's

255

them, isn't it? The queen has finally sent us some help, and a wizard, no less!"

"Wait, no. I mean, yes, but-" Daric protested.

I clapped the befuddled elf on the shoulder. "Thanks, Daricas. Your nobility and humility are truly boundless. You said it'd take ten days, and it only took seven. You are a wonder, and I'll be sure to tell the queen that."

The elf lord turned three different shades of red as he glared at me. I could hear Gemma and Pi snickering, even though I didn't look their way. Instead, I greeted the captain.

"I'm the Wizard Evan," I said, extending my hand.

"Captain Gabriel," he said, clasping it firmly. "I'm very happy to meet you, sir."

"Captain, I see that you're in the middle of repairs," I said, gesturing to his work crew, "But I wonder if you can spare a minute to tell me what I'm up against."

"It would be my pleasure, sir," then to his work crew, "carry on, men." The captain held out a hand, indicating I should walk with him. "Right this way, Wizard Evan."

The outpost was in shambles. A thirty-foot section of wall was nothing but rubble. The stone two-story building was missing most of a wall. Gray rock and ruined plaster lay in haphazard piles. Broken tables and chairs littered the courtyard where the giant had pulled them out. Other furnishings were strewn about as if a kid throwing a tantrum had tossed them.

"And you're sure it's a hill giant?" I asked.

"Very sure. Dumber than mud and twice as ugly." He pointed toward the field in front of the outpost. There were several large holes in the sandy ground. "It yanks out the biggest tree it can find and beats on everything. When the tree splinters, it uses its fists, all while yelling 'whack, whack, whack,' at the top of its lungs."

"By the dogs," I exclaimed. "How many men have you lost?"

"None yet, thank Titania," said Gabriel. "We have a below-ground bunker behind the barracks the dwarves helped us make. The giant isn't subtle. We have enough time to get everyone in before he wrecks the place. We have a potted bush we drag in front of the door. So far, he hasn't figured it out."

"And you know where he's coming from." I made that a statement instead of a question.

He made a scribbling motion, so I pulled some paper and a pen out of my pack. The captain drew a fairly credible map, freehand.

Some details struck me as odd. "He has a house with a garden?"

He shrugged. "More of a shack with some sorry-looking bushes out front."

"Do you know what kind of bushes?"

"No. We weren't willing to get that close."

I studied the map for a bit. I'd look at Sina's map later tonight to get a better lay of the land. "And you have no idea why the giant has it in for your outpost?"

"Maybe it disrupts his view of the sunset."

"And puts all of you in mortar peril."

He shook his head. "That'd be funny if the brute wasn't trying to kill us."

"It's still funny," I retorted, "you just have to lay it on brick."

He chuckled.

"Thanks for this." I indicated the map. "And don't let Daric get to you. He's a bit stiff, but he means well."

Gabriel rubbed the bridge of his nose. "Thankfully, we don't have to deal with the nobility much out here. I'll use small words he can understand."

I suppressed a laugh. "Where are your men staying?"

"In the bunker. The giant hasn't attacked at night yet, but no one wants to stay in the barracks. It's a minor miracle it's still standing."

I thanked him and trotted back to my team. "The men here have been staying in a hidden bunker. I don't think we should stay in the compound since it's a target. Suggestions?"

Pi shook her head. "I'd like a comfy cave, but this area isn't good for them. I doubt I'll find one."

Gemma pointed to an area a couple of hundred yards away. "There's a ravine over there. It's flat on the bottom. It'll be out of sight, and nice if it doesn't rain. I don't think it gets wet often around here."

Daric rolled his eyes. "You all do what you want. I'm taking over the captain's quarters. Tonight, I'm sleeping in a bed."

We all stared at him. He smirked at us.

"You realize that the barracks is missing a wall. It might collapse at any moment," said Gemma.

"The dwarves assure me it is sturdy enough," he said with confidence.

"What did the captain say?" I asked.

The elf arched a brow at me. "He'll say yes." He snorted. "He can't say no."

The rest of us looked at each other and shrugged.

It was early afternoon, so we set up camp in the ravine, then returned to help repair the walls. One dwarf had the stone shape spell, but when I offered to help, they readily agreed. I helped mold stone, Gemma helped carry blocks to where they needed to be, and Pi kept a lookout for the giant. Daric "supervised."

With the added help, we doubled the speed of the repairs. The dwarves sang as they worked. I didn't understand the words, but it sounded a lot like Irish folk music. By dusk, we had all but a ten-foot section of wall fixed. We'd have that completed by mid-morning tomorrow and could start on the barracks. Gabriel explained no one felt safe in the barracks since it seemed to be the giant's primary target. That put it lower on the repair priority.

Daric stood tall and surveyed our work. "Excellent job. When you all wash out of the army for incompetence, you'll easily find work as common laborers."

We ignored him as we all left to get dinner. I expected the dwarves and elves to eat together, but they didn't. The elves were at one large picnic table and the dwarves at another. Both asked us to eat with them. Rather than pick sides, we accepted both offers and ate a little of each of their dishes.

The dwarves had a hearty, creamy mushroom soup with tasty, spiced bread. The elves had a roasted vegetable with a sweet sauce and a small venison steak. They were both good, and I wrote the recipes down in one of my books. I included notes on what spices I would use to make it even better.

During dinner, there were a few new elves I hadn't seen before. They walked in, got dinner, then walked out of the compound.

After eating, Daric went into the barracks, through the missing wall. The elves and dwarves bade us goodnight as they went into the bunker. Gemma, Pi, and I left for the ravine.

I was unsurprised to find Sina in the middle of our camp, eating some of the dinner we'd just enjoyed.

Kissing her on the cheek, I sat down next to her. "Glad to see you're not starving out here."

"Yes. Jasmine and Apna," Sina waved vaguely in the road's direction, "have the watch for this area. Apna got some extra food for me when she went in to eat."

Pi nodded. "Jasmine seems nice. We spoke for a bit while I was wandering around out here. But the guy on the other side is rude."

Sina shrugged. "I haven't been over there." She held up a vegetable for me and I took a bite of it, almost snagging a finger. "Hey!"

I chewed with a playful grin.

Gemma spread her hands. "Do you think the reason he was rude was because a young elf was wandering alone in a dangerous area?"

Pi opened her mouth to protest, then closed it. "Oh. Maybe I should use a different shape."

Swallowing my mouth full of food, I regarded Pi curiously. "You say you can turn yourself into different shapes, but I've only ever seen the elf form."

"I can do any shape," said Pi. "But it's easier if I use the same shapes over and over. Kinda like the pictures. The more practice you get with one image, the better you get at it." She turned to Sina. "Can I become you?"

The elf sputtered and choked as she recovered from almost breathing her food. "I'd appreciate it if you didn't. Two Sinas might be a bit confusing."

"It wouldn't be exactly like you," Pi clarified. "By elf standards, they could take us for sisters. Especially if you and big brother get married, it'd be kinda fun."

Sina's face fell. "I have to marry Daric."

"Ew. Gross. Why would you marry him if you don't like him?" Pi shook her head.

"It's complicated."

"What's complicated about telling him no? Bite him on the nose if he won't listen."

Sina gave Pi a sideways grin. "Can you tell your mom, no?"

"Uh," Pi grimaced.

"Thought so."

We caught up for a bit before Sina stood and climbed to the top of the ravine. "No reason Daric should look over here, but just in case he does." The blonde elf whispered to the bushes along the lip of depression. They shivered a little, then grew taller and fuller.

"Well, I'll be dipped in honey and covered in fur. What did you do?" I asked.

She winked at me. "A girl has to have *some* secrets."

Gemma chuckled, "You can speak with plants. Nice."

"A little," Sina admitted, climbing back down to the camp. "Dad's a lot better at it. Talk to him if you want to upgrade your tree, Evan."

"So, you talked to the bushes and asked them to grow, and they did?" That didn't seem possible to me.

"It's a bit more than that, but basically, yes," said Sina.

I wondered what the conversation with a plant would sound like and what you'd offer to convince them to do you a favor. "Speaking of Daric, are the scouts going to tell him you're out here?"

"No. Unless Daric asks them specifically about me, they won't whistle a word about me being here. They respect his status as an elf lord, but don't exactly respect the person holding the lordship."

"What's the plan, Evan?" asked Gemma.

I'd given this a lot of thought as we'd worked with the elves and dwarves to repair the wall. "We'll help with the rebuilding in the morning and check out the giant's homestead in the afternoon. I hope to have a better strategy for getting rid of him after I have a better idea of who he is."

We agreed to set watches, not that we didn't trust the elf scouts, but because of Daric and the nearby giant. Sina and I took the first watch and continued to work on spells. I had the two-dimensional illusion down and spent the time working on three-dimensional illusions and fireball. Sina continued to work on her fireball.

Pi relieved us in the middle of the night. Sina surprised me by inviting me to cuddle up in her bedroll. She didn't have to ask me twice. That weird mind connection we had kicked in and I could tell she enjoyed it just as much as I did.

I had another of those weird dreams. There was a campfire in the middle of the field. I was out of firewood, and the fire was dying. Something about the darkness spooked me and I drew my sword. As the fire sputtered into embers, the darkness itself attacked me. My sword did nothing to keep it at bay, and it swallowed me whole. I couldn't breathe. The inky blackness was suffocating me.

I woke screaming.

"Evan it's me." Gemma was shaking my shoulder. "The giant is back!"

I struggled to clear the cobwebs from my thoughts as Sina yawned next to me. "Giant?" Oh, right. I needed to fight a giant.

"Whack!" The voice echoed across the scrub brush. The cobwebs, their dust bunny neighbors, and any brain lint in the vicinity promptly left Evan-town. I was wide awake and on my feet before you could say buenos dias. I was looking for my leather armor to put it on when I tripped over it.

Gemma, Sina, and I hurriedly put on our gear as Pi climbed to the top of the ravine.

"Wow," Pi stood there with her mouth open. "He's as big as my mom, and he's heading straight for the wall we just fixed."

A deep-throated, "Whack!" echoed across the plain, followed by a sound like smashed pottery.

I clambered up the dirt embankment as I pulled on my remaining boot.

The giant was twice as tall at the stonework he was smashing. Thirty feet if he was an inch. He swung a tree like a club, which shed green leaves with every shuddering impact on the wall. He had a shaggy mane of brown hair, was bare-chested, and wore a dirty pink blanket with yellow cat faces tied around his waist. The soiled makeshift kilt wasn't the best choice for clothing for the giant. Every third or fourth swing it proved to everyone within a quarter-mile that the giant we were dealing with was a male.

"Holy mountain oysters," breathed Gemma. "I really hope the big guy doesn't fart."

CHAPTER 41: FEE FIE PHOBIA

I don't mind admitting I was scared. I was proud of the fact that despite my full morning bladder, I didn't pee myself. That said, I didn't think there was a chance in hellhounds that I, Gemma, or even Pi would have any chance of stopping the rampaging monster.

My companions must have had the same thought, because none of us moved for almost a full minute. Realizing that it was face the giant or never return home, I finally found enough backbone to do what I had to.

"Sina, stay here. We can't risk Daric seeing you. Gemma, Pi, let's see if we can distract the giant."

The blonde elf scowled, but nodded.

"I'm going for the twig and berries." Gemma pulled out a heavy mace. "I don't think I'll miss."

Pi shifted to dragon form and flew into the air. Gemma and I sprinted across the field.

The giant continued to pound the wall, even though he'd already made a hole big enough to step through. Even with the three of us running full speed at him, the giant didn't notice. It wasn't until Pi swooped down and dive-bombed his head that the brute paid attention to anything other than smashing the wall.

The dragon landed on his face, which was hard to ignore. "Hey butt breath, I bet you can't- Aeiiiii-"

The giant grabbed the small dragon and hurled her away. My heart leaped to my throat. I knew Pi was tough, but I'd never seen her tossed aside like that. I resisted the urge to run to her. There was a giant to deal with.

Gemma used her stone skin spell. She reached the giant and roared, bringing the heavy mace down on the giant's foot.

The big brute stopped and gazed down at the troll beating on his ankle. "Stop. Tickles. Bad tiny green thing." I sucked in a breath as he reared back a foot.

Gemma had just enough time to say "Uh, oh," before the foot swung back and kicked her through the wall.

I heard a groan from the other side of the hole. "I... need a minute.... hungry."

The giant glared down at me.

This time, I peed myself. My brain and body froze in terror. What could I even do against this near-invincible monster?

The house-sized monstrosity's gaze moved from me and peered over the wall. "Don't like tiny green thing." To my horror, it raised a foot to step over the wall and stomp on the troll.

"Time to nut up, or shut up, Evan." I did the only thing I could think of and used my fireball spell. Being under the giant, there was only one proper target available, and I aimed for it, right up the kilt.

The melon-sized ball of flame raced away from my hand, narrowly missing the edge of the pink blanket with yellow cat faces.

"Waaaahhhhh! Hoooooot!" It dropped the club and ripped off the blanket, stuffing it into its crotch, smothering the small fire.

My victory was short-lived. The giant howled as he dropped the smoldering blanket and reached for his tree club.

"Stone skin!" I yelled as the hulking monster took a golf swing that would have made Tiger Woods proud. Whether because I'd said the words or maybe because I was desperate, I got myself covered in rock before the tree hit me.

Pain exploded everywhere, combined with a weird trampoline-like feeling. I squeezed one eye open in time to see the ground rushing up to meet me. Today was going to be a very bad day.

***

"Don't move Evan. I've almost stopped all the bleeding."

Sina? She can't come to the outpost. Daric will see her. "Can't stay here..."

"You are *not* moving. Jasmine and I will get you healed up

enough to drink a healing potion."

It was then that I realized I hurt in more parts than I thought I had. I opened an eye. The other eye wouldn't open. Sina and a dark-haired elf I saw yesterday were panting like they'd done wind sprints in PE. I tried unsuccessfully to sit up. "The giant... My friends..." I croaked.

"The giant is gone," Sina said between breaths. "I don't know about Gemma or Pi. I haven't seen them. Evan, please stay still."

I winced as I felt a bone in my arm knit back together.

"Drink this," commanded the dark-haired elf as she shoved a bottle in my mouth.

It was like raspberries but with a strong, bitter aftertaste. I swallowed it and a numbing sensation spread out from the center of my body. I watched in confusion as my hand cycled through every color in the rainbow. My ears rang, my vision grayed from the outside in.

***

When I woke again, the sun was setting. We were in a copse of scrub oak and cottonwood trees. I felt better, somewhat. Instead of everything hurting, it seemed to be focused on my head, stomach, and joints. I tried to speak and coughed.

"Here big brother." Pi in elf girl form handed me a waterskin. I gulped it greedily as she knelt beside me.

"Thanks." My head and stomach felt a little better, and I was super hungry. Speaking of hungry, "Where's Gemma?"

"Hunting."

"Did she..." I didn't want to finish that thought. If Gemma took enough damage, she would lose her mind and attack the nearest living thing to get food. The nearest living thing had been the giant, so that wouldn't have worked out well for her.

Pi finished the thought for me. "Go into a blind rage? Kinda. She latched onto the leg of the giant and started gnawing on him. He flung her in the opposite direction of where he threw me. She found enough rabbits and squirrels to bring her back to her senses."

Elf Pi looked okay, but I knew looks could be deceiving. "What about you?"

She rolled a shoulder. "Broke a wing. I'll need to spend some time in dragon form, so it'll heal right, but I wanted to check on you first." She jerked her head to one side. "Sina and Jasmine are over there, sleeping. They wore themselves out healing you."

My magic bag was lying next to me, so I opened it and took out some dried meat and berries. "Want some?"

"Yes, please."

Pi shifted position to sit beside me. We ate in silence for a while. Every five minutes, I'd use a little healing magic to put some skin, muscles, bones, and such back the way it was supposed to be. I didn't strain myself since I was out of danger. Bramble was sitting on a nearby tree limb, but he didn't say anything.

"I should be fine in a couple of hours," I said to Pi. "Then we can go into the woods and I'll heal up your wing."

"Thanks," was all she said.

I sighed heavily. "That was really stupid."

Pi nodded, but said nothing.

"We can't kill the giant," I continued.

She took another bite of jerky and shrugged.

I shook my head. "I did this totally wrong. I mean, I can use a sword and cast spells, and stuff, but I'm not a rush in throwing fire kinda guy." I snorted. "I need to stick with what I'm good at."

"Magic?" Pi offered.

"No, finding the middle ground." I popped a dried blueberry into my mouth. "I don't like fighting. I like working on problems and finding a better way to do things to make everyone okay. It's why I enjoy cooking. Food makes people happy."

In the distance, I saw Gemma crest a hill. She was carrying a doe on her back.

"You're going to cook for a giant?" asked Pi. "That's *a lot* of food."

"No," I chewed and thought as the troll approached the campsite. "I need to find out what he wants. I don't think he *wants* to destroy the outpost. There's gotta be something else."

The smell of roasting venison woke up the elves. They were dragging their feet, still worn out from healing me. I thanked them repeatedly and worked with Gemma to make sure the deer was done right.

"Jasmine, is everyone in the outpost okay?" I asked as I sliced off some meat for the dark-haired elf.

The three others around the campfire chuckled.

"Mostly, Wizard Evan," she said with a slight bow, accepting her plate. "Everyone that was in the bunker and all the elves on perimeter watch are fine."

I got a sinking feeling in the pit of my stomach. "Oh no. Daric?" Another round of chuckles relieved my nerves a little.

"Daric," said Gemma, "Is trapped in the remains of the barracks. After the giant finished with us, he knocked the building down. Daric hid under the bed."

"But he's okay?" I clarified.

Jasmine sighed. "The prissy noble must have an entire clover patch, and a half dozen rabbit's feet shoved up his butt. He's completely fine, but completely trapped. He's been using every curse known to elven kind to tell us how he feels about that. They can trickle water down to him, but it will be a day or three before we can dig him out. He'll live, but be very hungry."

I drew a circle on the ground and dropped a sugar cube in it. Pushing a little energy into it, the circle glowed, and Bramble popped up next to it.

"Finally! No sugar for a week." The six-inch-tall sprite made a pinching motion. "Peach Fuzz. I was this close to giving up on you."

"Fear not, my annoying yet resourceful friend. I have a job well suited to your many talents," I said, bowing at the waist.

The sprite puffed up his chest. "What can I do for you, oh great dispenser of sweets?"

I loaded up a plate of food. "Take everything on this plate to Daric. He's trapped under what remains of the stone building over there. It'll take you several trips."

Bramble grabbed for the plate of food. And it wobbled as he tried to lift it.

"Wait," I commanded, and Bramble stopped comically in midair. I reached into my pouch and broke off a tiny piece of chocolate. "After you take the food to him, you may eat this one piece of chocolate. Only after every bit of food is delivered. Got it."

The wide-eyed sprite followed the bit of chocolate in my hand, drool dripping from his mouth. "Uh, huh. All of it, then chocolate." I handed him the piece of candy.

Bramble flew to the plate and attempted to lift it. He got one corner an inch off the ground. He made a strangled, frustrated whine as he vibrated in place. Admitting defeat, he took a third of the meat on the platter and disappeared.

"Evan," Sina gasped, "that was Earth chocolate. You know what will happen to poor Bramble?"

"Yep, and he'll be with Daric when it does," I said with an evil grin.

Gemma's shoulders slumped as she frowned. "And I'll miss it."

"Wizard Evan," asked Jasmine, "Was that an actual dragon that attacked the giant, or an illusion you conjured?"

"Uh, an illusion." I managed to not look at Pi as I lied to the elf. "Why do you ask?"

The elvish scout nodded. "It was really convincing. I almost believed it was a real dragon."

CHAPTER 42: I USED TO FEAR GIANTS, NOW I LOOK UP TO THEM

The next morning, Gemma, Sina, and I set out for the giant's hovel. I'd healed Pi's wing, but she said she was still sore from getting tossed about by the big brute. I knew she was scared of him, and I honestly couldn't blame her. For all her size and strength, she was just a kid. I wanted her far away if we came to blows again.

Jasmine rejoined Apna on their scouting patrols and we waved at the elves and dwarves as we passed by the outpost. No one was working on the pile of rubble formerly known as the barracks. It might have been my imagination, but I thought I saw a green mist flowing from between rocks and timbers.

It wasn't hard to find the giant's home. All we had to do was follow the holes from uprooted trees. A couple of miles of rolling plains, and we were there, such as it was. I don't know what I was expecting, but for all its size, the structure didn't qualify as a shack. Logs and branches tied together with hempen rope were set against a rock face. The roof was more tied together trees with branches with leaves on them. It had caked mud on the walls to keep the wind out, but a good rain would probably wash it all away.

There was a garden, with a dozen dying bush beans set in two rough rows. What caught my eye was the scarecrow. It was wrapped in a blue sheet with a strip of blue cloth tied around the head with a piece of yellow ribbon. Two dead and rotting ducks were tied where the feet would be.

"Sina, does that remind you of..." I started.

"Like a four-year-old tried to make a doll of my dad? Yeah, it does."

***

We retreated over the nearest hill, where I sat with my head in my hands. I didn't look up as I spoke with my friends. "Sina, where exactly did your dad encounter that Hill Giant?"

Sina collapsed on the ground and gazed skyward. "Fifty miles north of here and a little west. A small village called Ebongrove."

Gemma sat and started digging ruts in the ground with her heels. "So, a little over a day's travel for someone his size. It's the same giant."

"Geezer couldn't beat him," I said. "I forget. How did he convince him to leave?"

"He fed him baked beans," recalled Sina leaning back on the ground and throwing a rock in the air, "and told him beans are afraid of elves."

I sighed, "Those were some sad-looking beans. Maybe tell him he's too close?"

Sina shook her head. "He might move further away and keep attacking."

Gemma's foot found a rock. She pulled it out of the rut she was digging and threw it. "Why is he attacking the outpost?"

That was it. The real question. Why was he attacking the outpost? "Sina, can I look at your map?"

The blonde elf sat up and dug her map case out of her pack. In two minutes, she had it laid out on the ground as it drew in the surrounding area. I saw nothing nearby to explain the behavior, so I zoomed out, then zoomed out some more.

"What's this?" I pointed to a town on the map.

"Sweetwater," Sina answered. "Felion settlement around an oasis."

"Is it really a desert?" asked Gemma.

Sina shrugged. "A little dryer than it is around here. Semi-arid."

"This has got to be Ebongrove." I followed a rough line north to a mountain pass. "What's this?"

"Galen's Stand, a Shara fort." Sina frowned and pointed across the pass. "On the other side of the pass is Ogre's Rest, a Darower outpost."

"Problems?" I asked.

"It's not called Ogre's Rest without reason," Sina explained. "Ogres stand about two heads taller than the average elf and are as strong as trolls. The fort is pretty good at keeping them out, but a half dozen times a year, they sneak through and raid the farms in that area. Sometimes they carry away sacks of grain and livestock. Sometimes they carry away farmers."

I tapped the map. "That's, what, sixty miles north of here?"

"More like eighty. What are you planning, Evan?" The blonde elf's brow creased with worry.

"I don't know yet," I admitted as I stood and gathered my things.

Gemma started picking her things up as well. "Where are you going?"

"I'm going to ask the giant why he's attacking the fort."

"Uh," the troll stopped in the middle of picking up her pack. "I don't think that's a good idea. I mean, you totally fried his nether eggs just yesterday. I don't think he's forgotten that yet."

"You're right," I said with a grin. "Which is why I'm going to get a friend to ask him for me."

***

With far more confidence than I felt, I marched to the edge of the trees where the giant had his shack. Learning from prior experience, I remembered to relieve myself before facing the thirty-foot-tall redneck on steroids.

Gemma and Sina hid nearby.

Checking my arms to make sure at least they looked right, like Geezer's arms, the disguise spell was working. I cleared my throat and tried to make my voice as scratchy as possible. "Hey, Buddy! Why the heck are ya tearin' up the place?"

The door to the shack flew open and shattered. The wide-eyed giant searched the tree line and found me. "Whack!"

The huge, hulking mountain man crossed the space in three large bounds. He now sported a blue loincloth with ducks. It did nothing to decrease my terror. And I thought nothing more could possibly come out of my bladder.

He skidded to a stop... And sat down cross-legged. A wave of week-old sweat and burnt pubic hair caused my eyes to water.

"Whack." The big man started sniffling. "Whack, beans no grow. You said get away from elves and beans grow, but they not grow, Whack!"

Whack? Geezer's first name is Johannes. Jack. Oh, for the love of dog. A giant with a lisp.

"Now son, what makes you think I can get yer beans growin'."

The giant was on the verge of tears. "Whack and the beans talk. Talk to beans. Make them grow. Please make them grow, Whack."

Dog farts. I didn't know the speak with plants spell. Sina knew it, but asking her to saunter over to enchant the bushes was not a good idea.

"And you thought attacking the elves would get me to come out here?" I asked.

"Boulder break elf houses," the giant reasoned. "Whack show up. No little elf houses here, but Boulder find one big elf house."

Well, that made a certain amount of sense, and now I had a name for the big guy. "I can't just drop everything and come out here and have a cup of tea with the plants every couple of weeks."

"Why not?" Boulder's brow creased.

"Because there are other people that need me, like up north of here," I explained.

"North?"

I pointed, "North. Now you see, son, not everyone knows how good beans are. I'm off to teach the ogres about baked beans, come sun up. Ogres are stubborn. Not as smart as you. I expect it will take me years to convince 'em."

Boulder nodded, seeming to accept my logic.

"Okay," I continued, "Let me take a look at these plants of yours." Walking to the bean rows, I knelt and lifted the wilting leaves. I shivered as I felt his hot breath on my neck.

"Son," I said, "these beans haven't had enough water. Is there a stream nearby where you can get some more?"

"Uh, huh." The giant ran to his hut and grabbed what looked like an old beer barrel. In his huge hand, it looked like a kid's juice cup. "Boulder, get water." He sprinted away.

"Sina," I cleared my throat. It was a little raw from trying to sound like Geezer. "Sina, can you get a couple of these plants to grow?"

She peeked around a tree. "He'll be right back."

"Then hurry."

She trotted down to the garden. "Plants aren't good at hurrying."

"It doesn't need to be much, just do what you can." I gave her a nervous smile. "Please?"

The elf stepped into the middle of a few bushes and started whispering to them. They immediately looked more lively.

"Whack! I have water, Whack."

Sina froze, giving a picture-perfect impression of a deer caught in headlights. I threw up a flat illusion of the bean field. Basically, the bushes minus the elf.

The giant stopped and stared.

I double-checked my illusion. He shouldn't be able to see Sina. Not from that angle. Did his magic resistance extend to illusions?

Boulder set the barrel down and jumped up and down, shaking the ground. "Whack and the beans talk! Whack and the beans talk!"

I breathed a little sigh of relief. More like a lot of sighs, because keeping up the disguise spell and the flat illusion was tiring me out. My joints ached. I needed to end this before I ran out of energy.

Wanting to keep the giant away from my illusion, I walked toward him. The last thing I needed was him getting a glimpse over the top of it. "Yeah, son. The beans were happy to talk with old Jack, and they told me you were taking good care of them. Listen, I'd love to talk more, but I gotta get going. It's a long way to the ogres. If you need me, come get me there."

Boulder scratched his head, and I could almost see the rusty gears in his head grind to a halt. "No," the giant frowned as he crouched down and reached for me. "Whack stay."

CHAPTER 43: TO TALK TO GIANTS, USE BIG WORDS

I swallowed hard and held up my hands. "You know what, big guy, you've convinced me to stay."

He stopped reaching for me, but that was little comfort. My muscles were burning, and I knew I wouldn't be able to keep my spells going much longer. I needed a way out. Could I distract the giant long enough to summon Bramble? The little guy might be able to confuse the giant long enough to...

And then I had it. "Hey son, you know how I said baked beans were the best? I discovered somethin' better."

I dug into my pouch and pulled out a chocolate square. I'd given a small piece to Bramble, so I had most of that piece left. I unwrapped and added two more squares to it. "Try this. It's called chocolate." I hoped Sina could figure out what I was about to do. As soon as the giant ate the candy, we needed to run.

Boulder held out his hand, and I unwrapped the pieces and placed the chocolate in it. It looked comically small in his huge palm.

He sniffed at it. "Sweet?"

"Oh, yeah, son. And it tastes better than it smells, trust me."

The giant licked his hand. "Mmmmm, Chocowate good. Whack give Boulder more chocowate."

"Wait for it," I whispered loudly behind me.

The giant got a curious look on his face. "Fuh. Foh. Fum?" Then a green cloud erupted from under the duckie loincloth. The cloud was fifty feet in diameter, but it was expanding behind

Boulder. Luckily, he turned around to look at the foul-smelling fog. Which is when he let out the second fart.

I was too close and was enveloped in the rank air biscuit. Fighting to keep my breakfast, I dropped my spells and ran. Sina had better reflexes and was already sprinting well ahead of me.

I remembered the caltrops Millow had sold me. Grabbing the pouch, I shook them out of the behind me.

"Ow! Ow! Ow! Ground hurt?"

We shot past Gemma's hiding spot, neither of us bothering to pause. Gemma did a double-take, then took off after us.

"Whack! Whack! Come back, Whack!" the giant wailed.

***

We ran about five hundred yards, then hid behind a rock outcropping. We had a pretty good view of the valley and took turns keeping watch. Boulder wandered about the area calling out for me, well, Jack for several hours. He came our way a few times, but Gemma and I could hide Sina under our Meld with Stone spells until he wandered away.

There were a couple of scary times where the giant went back to the outpost. We used those times to put more distance between us and the hovel. He came back. We didn't hear any crashing sounds, so we hoped he didn't cause more damage.

"How long are we going to wait out here?" asked Gemma. "Not until he stops looking, I hope. That's a giant, remember?"

"We need to make sure he looks in the right place," I said, peering around a large rock.

If Sina had any thoughts, she kept them to herself.

We had a cold camp that night. The giant continued to look for us in the dark, punctuating his search with calls for, "Whack!" at odd intervals. None of us slept for obvious reasons.

Around mid-morning the next day, Sina snapped her fingers at us. Blearily, I joined her, followed shortly by Gemma.

Our new hiding spot was higher up and had a better view of the valley. I could see the hollow where Boulder had his home, but didn't see him.

"What do you see?" I asked.

"He's been moving around his little farm for the last hour, but he's slowed down," said Sina. "I think he's about to do something."

That got me awake. "You can see him? All I see are bushes and oaks."

"Never trust the woods," Gemma recited, "for the trees have ears and the rocks have eyes."

Sina pointed to her face. "Elf. Good eyes and ears are part of the bundle."

She was right. Ten minutes later, the giant appeared, trudging northward.

"What's that on his back?" I asked.

The elf squinted. "Looks like a fishing net with a bunch of junk in it."

"Dancing dogs of Denmark, it worked." I slid behind the rock and improvised a jig.

"What do you mean, it worked?" The troll had her hands on her hips.

"I mean, the giant is going looking for me, er, Geezer, who was me, pretending to be... You know what, never mind." I waved away what I was trying to say and started over. "The hill giant is going north to harass the ogres."

Sina caught on. "Because you told him that's where my dad was going to be."

I pointed to my nose. "Right on the old sniffer."

"But the quest was to kill the giant," Sina pointed out.

"Yes, it was," I waggled my head from side to side, "but I think there's a loophole I can use to make it work."

Gemma arched an eyebrow, "You're going to use a loophole in an elvish contract. With the queen of the elves. This I've got to see."

***

Sina walked with us until we were within sight of the outpost. She drew me into a kiss that made me feel like Thumper from that cartoon about a baby deer. My neck flashed hot, and my toes curled inside my boots.

"See you tonight?"

"If that's the greeting I'm getting," I said. "I'm skipping the outpost and heading straight for the campsite."

I leaned in for another kiss, but she put her hand on my chest.

"Go tell Captain Gabriel the plains are clear."

Huffing dramatically, I watched as she sashayed into the brush. She gave me a wink before disappearing into a thicket.

Gemma elbowed me in the ribs, softly, for her. I shoved her playfully, and we started toward the outpost.

It was a bit better than we'd left it. I had to hand it to the dwarves, they were hard workers. They'd uncovered Daric and had a few feet of wall repaired. The elf lord smiled as we entered the outpost.

He jumped down from a pile of stone and approached. "Evan, Gemma, you made it back. Was your quest successful?"

Pi in elf form ran up and stopped. "I was worried about you, big brother."

"The quest was successful," I said. Daric being friendly? Perhaps being stuck under rubble for a couple of days had done him some good.

He clapped his hands together. "Excellent. Tell me all about it."

I glanced at Gemma, who shrugged.

"Okay, well, we found the hollow the giant had been staying in..." And I gave him a blow by blow of our adventure, minus any reference to Sina. Gemma broke in with a few of the details I missed.

By the end, we had a small crowd of elves and dwarves listening intently to our tale. When we finished, they all cheered. Pi bounced on her toes, grinning from ear to ear.

"So, you sent him to the ogres?" Captain Gabriel shook his head. "Oh, that's evil, and a more deserving group of bandits I can't imagine. Reports from Galen's Stand are that half a dozen farmers have already gone missing this year."

"Very well done," exclaimed Daric, and he clasped me on the shoulder.

I eyed his hand suspiciously, then regarded him skeptically. "What's going on?"

He chuckled. "I insisted on sleeping indoors because I was tired of camping. You tried to warn me, and I didn't listen. Then, trapped as I was, you had a sprite bring me food. I know I can be a harsh taskmaster, but you didn't have to help me. I had given you every reason to dislike me. You showed me a kindness I'm not sure I deserved, and I very much appreciate it. It's possible that I was wrong about you."

"Really." I deadpanned. I didn't buy it for a second, but if he was going to make nice, I would not look a gift horse up the nose.

"I don't blame you for not trusting me," Daric spread his hands, "but elves are all about paying our debts. Allow me to make dinner for you tonight. I know you must be eager to get on the road as soon as possible. You have a quest to complete, a home to return to, and we can be ready to head out in an hour."

Just behind Daric, Gabriel made a shooing motion, followed by a pleading gesture. The message was clear: please take the elf lord away so we can rebuild in relative peace.

"Alright Daric," I shrugged, "tonight you cook."

Pi was bouncing on her toes so fast I thought she might burst.

"I missed you too, Pi," I said with a grin.

She raced up and jumped...

Have I mentioned that while Pi may look like a little elf, she actually isn't? Elf Pi weighs as much as dragon Pi. Ow.

***

We camped at the same campsite we used the night before we arrived at the outpost. As a result, I knew Sina would be at the clearing we'd used where she'd finally gotten the fireball spell down. Gemma found some rabbits, and we still had leftover deer. I gathered firewood while Daric prepared the meal. He took off his armor to cook, and the elf looked more relaxed than I'd ever seen him.

"What are you putting in there?" I was watching Daric prepare dinner for us. Most of the herbs I recognized, others I didn't.

He gave me a wink and grinned. "Special family recipe. Trust me, you'll love the taste."

I watched him and asked lots of questions. Daric patiently answered every one. When he was done, I had to admit, the stew smelled divine. Garlic, onions, mushrooms, thyme, and rosemary created a symphony of scents I couldn't wait to taste.

And the taste, fantastic. I had no idea that Daric could cook, let alone cook well. He even provided extra portions for Gemma and Pi. I ate the whole bowl and asked for seconds. After dinner, I was stuffed and then some.

I felt lighter than air. Like everything my friends said was the funniest thing I'd ever heard. It wasn't until the rocks and trees laughed along with me that I even suspected something was wrong, but by then, I couldn't bring myself to care.

CHAPTER 44: THAT BOY IS POISON

My head exploded. At least that's what it felt like. My vision swam as I tried to focus on something other than my splitting headache.

That's when the truck hit me.

Well, it felt like a truck. My vision swam. I struggled to find said truck, to at least take down the plate number when my eyes found red hair, pointy ears, probably Daric. Better ask.

"Daric?"

"Wake up, you idiot. I want my money back." He stomped on my foot.

Renewed pain brought clarity. I tried to pull my foot back, only to find it tied to my other foot, tied to a stake in the ground. Trying to sit up, I realized my hands were bound behind my back.

Daric's snarling face came into focus. "I. Want. My. Money."

I struggled to make sense of the situation. "Your... money?"

"That stupid Redcap wasn't worth spitting on, much less what I paid him to kill you." The elf lord grabbed my ear and pulled me toward him. I screamed as it felt like he'd yanked it off.

With his other hand, he held my pouch in front of my nose. "Open your magic bag and give me my money."

"You hired the assassin?" I knew Daric didn't like me, but I didn't think he'd have me killed. "Why?"

He released my ear to take hold of my hair and shake. "I don't have to tell you."

He must have pulled some of it out. That or used it to throw me to the ground.

I spit dirt. "No," I said through gritted teeth, "but you'll have to tell the queen. Tell Sina."

He snorted. "I'll tell her you planned to steal Sina away from me. You think I'm blind? You've been flirting with her this entire time. I'm well within my rights to end you several times over."

My mind raced. Had he somehow seen us over the last week? Was he judging by what he'd seen on the first two quests? I tried to cast Stone Skin to protect myself, only to find I couldn't. I couldn't focus my thoughts enough to make my magic work.

Daric rolled his eyes. "You think I'm stupid? You can't use any of your spells. Dream Cactus. It grows all over around here. Addles the brain. It was in your stew."

Must be like peyote or something. I shook my head. "I would have tasted it."

He smiled evilly. "Rosemary covers up the flavor." He shook the pouch. "Money. Now."

Pi and Gemma were slumped over and unconscious. They were breathing. I needed to keep him talking.

"They can't help you," said Daric as if reading my thoughts. "Didn't anyone tell you? I'm five hundred years old. You think I've lived all that time and haven't learned how to poison a dragon and a troll? Reaper root isn't quick, but in the amounts they ate, it will be fatal. They won't live to see the sunrise."

I glared up at him in his fancy clothes. The cocky bastard hadn't bothered to put on his armor, but he had his sword on his hip. "Fine. Tell me why and I'll open the pouch for you."

Daric crossed his arms and paced back and forth for several moments.

I tried to access my magic to heal or unpoison myself. I could feel my magic. It was there. It felt like it was trying to reach me, too.

"You know what?" said Daric, stopping in front of me. "Spilled blood tells no secrets. You want to know why I did it. Power. The queen is a fool for even offering you the world-crossing spell. Fools don't deserve power. They deserve to have it stripped away. You would take that spell and return to San Antonio or wherever it is you really come from. Maybe not today, maybe not next year, but sometime in the future you'll realize the potential of our world and want to exploit it for yourself. You'd gather an army of wizards and return. With the numbers of humans across the veil, you could conquer us easily. That cannot be allowed to happen."

The elf lord kicked dirt in my face. "I was already going to take the throne from that old hag. With only one heir, it'd be easy. I won't bore you with thousands of details in my brilliant plan. It would take all night, and your pea-sized brain couldn't possibly grasp the finer points. The basic gist is this: Marry the princess, kill the princess, kill the queen. Plant evidence to blame the nobles I need out of my way."

Daric dropped the pouch in front of me and dusted off his hands. "I've kept my side of the bargain. Now keep yours. Open it," he growled.

"No."

The elf seemed taken aback. "What?"

"No," I told him, thrusting out my chin. "I. Lied."

He huffed. "Well, I was going to kill you, anyway. As much as I'd like to have my money back, its loss is acceptable to see you dead."

Daric drew his sword and put it against my neck

The razor's edge of cold elven steel parted my skin. I felt my blood trickle down my neck.

"Goodbye Wizard."

CHAPTER 45: ROYALLY SCREWED

A feathered shaft appeared in Daric's shoulder. Stunned, I didn't react fast enough. The elf lord sliced my jaw and cheek as he swung his sword up, catching the second and third arrows swatting them from the air.

I rolled into his legs. That didn't work like I'd intended. I was still attached to a stake.

Daric dodged and received another arrow in the same shoulder. "You!" he screamed and leapt over me.

Sina was at the edge of the campsite. She dropped her bow and drew her sword to meet the elf lord's charge.

I searched the ground. Finding a rock, I finally touched my magic. It was so far away. Like trying to suck water from a lake a mile away through a straw. I used the trickle of power to force myself to throw up. My mind cleared a little, but not much. I focused through the fog in my head. Panting with effort, I softened the rock. Behind me came the clang of metal on metal. As much as I wanted to know how the fight was going, all of my attention was on the rock. I formed an edge, solidified it, and used it to slice my wrists free. It also ripped up my hands, and I almost passed out. Forcing my hands steady, I sawed my feet free.

Finally loose, I stood.

And fell on my face.

Standing was overrated, so I scrambled to my gear and drew my sword. Kneeling, I turned.

Blood was everywhere. Sina and Daric were trading blows. Their blades moved so fast I couldn't figure out where their blades were. They each sported a dozen wounds. Daric had the upper hand, though. His moves were precise, while Sina's were slowing down.

Most of the blood was closer to me. Where had it come from? Something wet dripped on my hand and I realized that most of the blood was mine. No wonder I was lightheaded.

I tried to heal, but the straw was still too long. I dug into my pack and pulled out the healing potion Geezer had given me. Unstopping it, I sucked it down in one swallow. It tasted like bittersweet raspberries. My body tingled all over and I almost panicked as my skin turned purple, then red, then orange.

My head cleared a bit. "Taste the rainbow," I muttered as I felt the cut in my face heal. My vision doubled, then tripled for a scary moment and I thought I might faint.

I tried to stand, but collapsed. In my current state, I didn't have the coordination to fight the haughty elf warrior. Maybe I could distract him so that Sina could finish him.

Screaming in rage, I stumbled to my feet and charged.

For an odd second, I thought he hadn't heard me as I hurtled across the campsite. I should have known better.

As I closed within five feet, Daric shoulder checked Sina, pivoted, and sank his blade into my chest. My flesh tore as I tumbled past. My sword caught nothing but air.

Sina recovered and stabbed at Daric's exposed side.

Daric twisted, turning what would have been a major wound into just a deep gash below his ribs. I screamed as Daric disarmed Sina, sending her sword halfway across the clearing. Then he sank his blade into her thigh. Sina crumpled to the ground beside me.

He backed off then. His offhand, putting pressure on the deep wound in his side. It glowed as he healed himself. I took a moment to do the same and was surprised when I could touch more of my magic. Enough to stop the bleeding and get rid of some poison. I kept my sword pointed at his chest, but I didn't have the strength for a lunge. Daric saw my blade waver and sneered.

Then he let out a grim laugh. "Oh, Sina. It wasn't your time to die. Not yet. Killing you early is going to put such a crimp in my plans."

"The queen will discover your treachery," she spat.

"Maybe," he said with a one-shouldered shrug, "but when I tell everyone about how I desperately tried to save you from a troll, a dragon, and a rogue wizard, I'll be a hero." He gave a breathless chuckle. "She can suspect all she wants. I can spin the truth here in so many convenient ways."

Sina balled her fists. "I hate you!" She spat as she flung a ball of fire at the elf lord's head.

Daric flung his sword arm up to protect his face. Whether by accident or on purpose, Sina's aim was high. The fireball hit the elf lord's red hair, setting it on fire.

He screamed, dropping his sword to put out the flames on his head.

I thrust my sword up, catching him in the chest.

The scream died. Daric stared down in disbelief, then at me. He slumped to the ground.

Panting, Sina stared at his body for a handful of seconds before rolling over and gathering me in her arms.

***

Sina and I spent the rest of the night healing ourselves and our friends. She mostly healed, while I got rid of the poisons Gemma, Pi, and I had unknowingly eaten. It was like running a marathon in spurts. Sina and I would heal as much as we could, then catch our breath, drink mana potions, then do it all again. The potions had the odd side effect of playing strange music. We all heard it but couldn't tell where it was coming from. What exactly is a dancing queen?

By mid-morning, everyone was feeling much better, but exhausted, and had that weird song stuck in our heads. Since we were all spell weary or recovering from being poisoned or both, we stayed at the campsite another night.

Sina and I buried Daric with the rest of the meal he made. We dug a shallow pit a hundred yards from our campsite and put him in. We didn't mark the site. Animals would probably dig him up, but we'd be long gone by the time they did.

Gemma still had leftover deer from a couple of days ago, and she cooked it for us. She asked me for advice on how to prepare it, but I don't remember what I told her. I had my own inner demons to slay, and I couldn't spare the attention away from the war in my soul.

We ate dinner, which I shoveled into my mouth mechanically. Gemma asked how it tasted. I told her it was fine.

Sina stoked the campfire, and I watched it glow and consume all the wood bits we fed to it.

"Want to talk about it?"

I glanced over and found Sina sitting next to me. "Not really," I answered automatically.

"Then I'm going to hold you, okay," she said as she wrapped her arms around me and put her head on my shoulder.

We sat like that for a time. At some point, I began crying. Once it started, I couldn't stop. Tears streamed down my cheeks as all the emotions and trials, and everyone's expectations, and my belief in who I was versus who I was becoming crashed together in a stew of raw emotions. Sadness, heartache, and joy flooded through me, and I was powerless to stop it.

Sometime later, I cried myself out. Sina still held me. Through it all, she hadn't let go. The sideways hug was now a full-on hug.

"I killed him," I sputtered.

"Yes, you did."

"I've never killed anyone before," I croaked. "I mean there was the redcap, but he doesn't count. I knew Daric. He was a jerk, but also a friend, I thought. Kind of. I feel like I should hate myself for what I've done."

"But you don't," said Sina into my shoulder.

I squeezed her harder. "I don't. I feel relieved. Why do I feel like that? A man died. I should feel sad that he's gone. He'd lived five hundred years, and his life ended today, and I ended it."

"If you hadn't killed him, many more people would have died," Sina nuzzled the crook of my neck. "Some of them are our friends. Some he would have killed because they were in his way. My mom and dad would have been on that list. You stopped him."

"I killed him. I'm a monster because I don't feel bad about it."

The blonde elf put her lips right next to my ear and whispered into it. "No. You hurt yourself so that others could live. That you can ask yourself why, and feel sad about the answer, is proof that you aren't a monster." She kissed my ear. "Monsters don't ask why. They hurt and kill because they enjoy it. Monsters come in all shapes and sizes and can live in anyone. Because you're troubled by your relief at living and hurt because of how you feel about Daric's passing proves you aren't a monster. It proves you have a soul. You care."

Sina pulled her head back and looked me in the eye. I held her gaze.

"You took another's life to save those you love and many people you don't know and might never meet." Sina touched her nose to mine. "That's the definition of a warrior. Taking on that pain makes you a hero."

"I don't feel heroic."

Sina gave me a sad smile. "The good ones never do."

***

Sina and I fell asleep holding each other that night. I had nightmares. In them, Daric blamed me for millions of elves dying. He waved at their graves and at piles of elf bodies. He said it was all because I killed him. Several times I woke up screaming. Each time, Pi and Gemma gave me worried looks and Sina rocked me back to sleep.

As we were packing up to leave the next morning, a thought occurred to me. "Hey Pi, you can use your shape change spell to take on any form, right?"

"Yeah, but I have to practice," she said. "I can't just go all sprite, rabbit, or dwarf any time I feel like it."

I rolled up my blanket and bound it to the bottom of my pack. "How would you like to help Gemma travel a little faster?"

Pi eyed the troll, who regarded her and me curiously.

The dragon grimaced. "Er, um, I like her an all, but I'm not sure I like her enough to play horsy. She's heavy."

"What if you could do it as a High-Capacity Tactical Assault Unicorn?" I offered.

"A unicorn?" Pi twisted her head. "That'd be cool. She'd still be too big, though."

I waved a finger in the air. "Not just any unicorn, a High-Capacity Tactical Assault Unicorn."

"Can you show me a picture?"

I held the image of a rhinoceros from the zoo in my head, then created a full image of one in the middle of the campsite.

"Whoa!" Pi breathed as she took in the illusion I'd created. "You have these in your world?"

"Yes, we do," I assured her. "What do you think?"

"Give me a few minutes to study it."

Pi studied the image for twenty minutes. Thankfully, she let me stop before I got too worn out. All during our hike that day, Pi would stop when there weren't any travelers on the road and practice turning into a rhino. Each time I'd offer some suggestions for improvement.

By our third day of travel, Gemma and Pi were whooping and hollering, rampaging through the brush, and scaring the local wildlife.

Our travel speed doubled.

Sina rode up beside me and whispered. "You're not going to tell her, are you?"

"Oh no, not a chance," I said with a chuckle.

***

We arrived back at Lonathas and Pi split off to go to my tree home. I didn't bother disguising Gemma and I, deciding instead to test a theory. Sina and I rode our horses while Gemma led Daric's horse behind us.

We rode through the hard-packed dirt road that led from the edge of the city to the palace. I enjoyed the cool breeze that carried the earthy, spicy scent of the sufra trees the elves used as homes. All along our route, elves stopped and pointed. Unlike before, when I'd felt like a freak, I saw smiles and low bows as we made our way to the castle.

Conversations erupted in our wake. Not having elf ears, I couldn't make out much, but I heard wizard and cursed elf mentioned more than once. It was enough to let me know that my gamble was paying off. The elves of Shara knew who I was. Moreover, they liked me. How much would that change when they found out I'd killed one of their lords?

We arrived at the castle gates and two guards approached us. "Wizard Evan, it is good you've returned. Where is your escort?"

I let the sadness I felt at Daric passing color my voice and my next words. "Our journey was dangerous. Unfortunately, Lord Daricas will never again return to Lonathas."

That seemed to stun the two guards. They looked at each other, then back at me. Silence reigned for several moments before the guard on the left snapped out of it.

"Thank you for returning Thasina to us, great Wizard. Thasina, the queen has ordered you confined to the east tower. If you'll come with me, please." He reached up to take her hand.

Sina slumped in her saddle.

"No." It took me a minute to recognize that the voice that had spoken was mine.

"Wizard?" as the right guard.

"Thasina was present when Lord Daricas was slain. The queen will want her to hear her story from her directly. Why confine her to the tower, when the queen will obviously summon her before she even reaches the tower?" I gave the guards a hard stare, projecting a confidence and superiority I didn't feel.

There were a tense few seconds when I thought they would argue with me. I was pretty sure royal command trumped half-trained wizard. But after a moment, they nodded.

The gate guards summoned a pair of grooms for the horses and an escort to take us into the palace.

The guards took us to the antechamber where Flick was waiting for us.

"Hi, Wizard Evan. Hi Miss Gemma," then he bowed low. "Lady Thasina."

"Hey, Flick. What is the queen's mood?" asked Sina.

"Not very good today," he shrugged. "There was a vote of no confidence. She survived. Her mood should improve with you here."

Sina's brow furrowed. "Is she mad about me?"

Flick shook his head.

Sina stroked her chin. "She's in with the Lords now, isn't she?"

The young elf nodded.

Sina sighed. "Oh, this will be interesting."

After an hour, the door to the throne room opened. A bunch of fancy-dressed elves streamed out. Some were smiling, but most weren't. A guard hurried over to us. He must have been in a rush because he accidentally smacked his helmet with his spear, causing it to ring loudly. The guard winced.

"Saved by the bell," I said, standing up and patting Flick on the shoulder. He led us into the throne room. Servants were busy removing chairs into a side storage room. There were eight guards present, four on a side.

As we approached the throne, I saw that the queen's hair was not perfectly done. There were a few strands out of place and her face was red with anger.

But more interesting than that, was that Geezer was standing just to the right of the throne.

We stopped a few feet from the dais. I looked from the queen to Geezer, then back again.

Geezer was taking deep breaths and held his hands together in a white-knuckled grip. His gray whiskers stuck out even more than normal.

I motioned that Geezer needed to smooth out his beard at the same moment Sina motioned to Lycia that her hair, was frazzled. The pair of them subtly adjusted their appearance.

The queen straightened. "Where is Daric?"

"He didn't make it, Your Majesty," I answered.

"He didn't make it?" The queen's gaze flitted to Sina, then back to me. "What happened to him?"

I let my eyes range over the guards in the room before settling back on Queen Lycia. She got the message.

"Guards, leave us," the queen ordered. "Michael, Rachel, you can stay behind."

The guards filed out, and the servants finished removing the chairs, while Michael and Rachel took positions in front of the queen. Lycia waited until the heavy doors closed before she ran her fingers through her hair and pulled. "What did he do, and more importantly, can you prove it?"

I explained what happened when we got back to the outpost. Gemma and Sina added what they saw.

"You two are looking lively for having ingested deadly poisons," the queen observed.

"I know how to cure poison, Your Majesty," I said simply.

She arched an eyebrow, but otherwise didn't offer further comment. "And the giant?"

We explained how we dealt with Boulder. Afterward, the queen glared at Geezer.

"What?" he said. "I couldn't kill him. Evan couldn't kill him. The kid at least sic'd the oaf on the ogres. That'll tie them up for decades."

"But he didn't get rid of the giant permanently," the queen insisted. "That was the quest."

I had expected the queen to argue that point. "Per our contract, paragraph three, subsection D, equal or lesser value, my solution gave you more value than killing him. It will force your enemies in the Darower to deal with the giant. Heck, they might even kill him."

Queen Lycia redirected her ire at me. "No."

"Mom!" shouted Sina.

"Cici," hissed Geezer.

Lycia rubbed her temples for a couple of moments before directing her gaze at each of us. "Listen, convincing the giant to attack our enemies was *almost* as good as getting rid of him. But killing Daric creates more problems than solutions."

"That's not fair," I interrupted. "I redirect the giant and stopped a coup attempt and that's not as good. Your math is way off," I growled.

The queen took a breath and let it out. "Daric was good at politics. He has friends on the council of lords. If I give you what you want, I'll be seen as rewarding his killer. I'm not sure I can control the lords without Daric's block of votes. Denying you the spell but giving you your freedom will allow me to save face and sway enough votes to stay in power."

"Not. My. Problem," I ground out. "The scales are not balanced. You owe me."

"You're right," the queen admitted, "it isn't your problem. But it is Geezer's and Sina's problem. How long after I fall," Lycia drew her thumb across her throat, "do you think they will live?"

I glanced at my companions. Sina and Geezer wouldn't meet my eyes, and even Gemma looked uncertain.

"I offer you a boon," said the queen. "Any favor you like, except the spell."

My mind raced, pulled in a thousand different directions at once. That was my only way home. My only way to return to San Antonio. I could ask for spell research that would get me close to the spell, but magic was a fickle beast. Even with that, there was no guarantee I'd be able to figure it out. And could I really leave knowing I condemned Sina, Geezer, maybe even Gemma and Pi to deadly elven politics?

I met Queen Lycia's gaze. She looked sad, but I also knew it could all be an act. Manipulating people was what she did. But Sina and Geezer had been living with her for years. They seemed to believe what she was saying was true.

"Fine," I snarled. Turning on my heel, I stomped out of the audience chamber. Gemma and Sina trailed in my wake, but no one tried to stop me. No one, including the queen, tried to stop Sina from following me out.

CHAPTER 46: THE CAT'S OUT OF THE BAG

Guards saluted on my way out of the palace, but I didn't pay any attention to them. I exited the gates, entering the city. I walked toward the edge of the city, toward my home for the foreseeable future. It really was a nice tree. If I had to live in Shara, there were a lot of suckier places to stay.

I had friends, a troll, a dragon, a crazy old wizard. And I had a girlfriend, an honest to dogness elf. I had friends back home too, but somehow my friends here felt more real. Would my friends back home face down a giant with me if I asked them?

I missed my mom. I might not like her most of the time, but she was still my mom. My brother? Well, that was a different story.

My grandma and my dad, if I found a way back, it would be for them. Since my mom had declared my dad a bad influence, I didn't get to see him anymore. I missed him a lot. I bet he felt the same. And Grandma, I could really use her advice right now. She always had the best advice. She always knew exactly what to do.

Somehow my feet had found my sufra tree. I gazed up into its branches. I wanted to yell at it, *Leaf me alone!* The thought of doing that gave me half a chuckle.

Gemma stepped in front of me. "Hey Evan, I know it's not what you want to hear right now, but I'm glad you're staying." She wrapped her arms around me.

Sina held my arm and kissed me on the cheek, "me too."

I hugged Sina back, then Gemma too, briefly patting her back. "Thanks, Guys."

Sina opened the door for me, and we went inside.

Pi was in elf girl form, and her eyes lit up as I entered the living room. "Hey, big bro. How was the castle?"

I sighed.

She beamed up at me. "Tell me about it when you're ready. You look like you could use some rest."

It took my head a few minutes to catch up with what she said, but when it did, the idea felt right. "Yeah," I said in a kind of daze, "that sounds like a good idea." I turned to my friends. "Do y'all mind if I take a nap or something? I... I need to process this. I'm not sure I can, but..."

They each gave me another hug, and I felt their eyes on me as I trudged up the stairs.

Sunlight streamed through the French doors into my bedroom/study at the top of the tree. My bed was still broken, but it didn't matter. It was a reminder of just how much Pi cared about me. The thought was comforting.

I sat on the mattress and stared out into the canopy of the surrounding trees. The leafy branches were eye level from up here. Part of my mind wondered what they called French doors on this world, since there weren't any French.

One door opened and a black cat wandered into from the balcony. It had one green and one yellow eye. "Hello, little one. You look just like my grandmother's cat Fifi. How did you get up here?"

The cat sat and looked up at me. "That's because I am your grandmother's cat, or rather your grandma, Saffron, is my familiar."

Have you ever had your mind stop so fast you could swear you felt and heard a car crash into a brick wall? "F-f-familiar?"

"Yes. Just like wizards like to have an animal companion, we gods often take an ani- er, human companion. It helps to have someone to talk to and bounce ideas off of."

In my head, the wrecked car exploded into flames. "You... you travel between worlds."

Fifi shrugged. "I know you heard the story. I split the worlds to begin with. Of course, I can move between them."

At some point, I'd stopped breathing. I took several rapid breaths to catch up. "You're Fifta? You brought me here?"

The cat waggled her head from side to side. "Yes, and no. I am Fifta, but I didn't bring you here. You see, I taught an elf the spell to travel between worlds a couple of hundred years ago."

Fifi jumped on the bed, and before I could stop myself, I automatically scratched her ears like I had a hundred times back home. I paused, realizing I was actually petting a powerful goddess. I started again as she leaned into my hand.

"Oh, that feels good," the cat said through a purr. "Anyway, as I was saying. This elf, a devoted follower of mine, made the best salmon mousse you ever tasted. He was caught in an orc siege. I already knew everyone in the fort was going to die, but he asked me to get him out of there before the orcs breached the walls. So, I taught him the spell."

I stopped petting, stunned by the revelation.

"Hey! Goddess here. Keep up with the scritches."

"Sorry," I rubbed right behind her ears.

"Oh yeah, there we go. Right," she continued, "so he comes across and sees the human world and naturally freaked. But over time, he came to enjoy it. He saved Geezer from being shot by Confederate troops, met your great grandmother, did the usual thing that humans and elves do, and had a couple of kids with her. One of them is your grandmother, Saffron."

I blinked. "I really am part elf? My whole family is part elf."

"Yes, but it's a recessive thing. Some of your family is more elf than others." The cat yawned. "I rounded your family's ears just like I pointed Sina's more. You and your grandmother got more magic affinity. And it appears your great-grandfather passed the unconscious knowledge of the spell to you."

"Take me back," I said.

"Uh, no. As a goddess, I can go back and forth anytime I like, but even I have rules I have to follow. There are a bunch of gods, and I have to live with them. I take you across and Sume and Ugra will throw a fit. And don't get me started on what Titania will do. But you can do it. You're human. The gods expect you to throw a wrench into the works. Under the right conditions, you can make it work all by yourself. Here." Fifi jumped up, rubbing her face against my cheek.

My mind exploded with information. Like my brain had been plugged directly into the internet and all the information and silly cat videos were downloaded directly into my head. For a brief second, I thought it would drive me insane. Especially the part with the fifty different renditions of the Baby Shark song.

My stomach roiled.

"Whup. None of that. Can't have you throwing up right now. I just got done with my tongue bath." Fifi tapped my lips with a paw and the headache and nausea subsided. All the extra junk fell away, leaving me with a single complete spell.

I had it. Clear as crystal, I understood how it worked and what was needed to make it happen. "Three betweens," I said. "I crossed when it was morning twilight, half sun, half dark, foggy, half air, half water, and jumping between two sides of the ravine. Holy dog hair on a cracker, Queen Lycia was right. I... I brought myself here."

Fifi smiled up at me.

I could get back, I realized. The three betweens were the start, but a lot of other conditions helped the spell be more successful. Star alignments, empowering potions, and a prepared ritual space would all help.

"You can do it, but you better work up to it sport. When do you want to go back?"

And there it was. *The Question.* Fifta had given me for free what the queen had denied me. It was a very difficult spell, with a lot of moving parts. A lot like doing trigonometry in your head while simultaneously baking a soufflé with one hand and trying to catch an over-caffeinated sprite with the other. Doing it quickly was possible, but it carried a high risk of not working, or making the spell caster do an involuntary impression of a cream puff hitting a jet engine.

That elf Fifta had taught must have been desperate. Dog doo, I'd been stupidly lucky at casting the spell by accident. I could cast the spell with much less risk if I had a few months to practice and a week to cast the spell.

Did I want to?

"I, uh..." Sina, Gemma, Pi. Their images and many more passed rapid-fire through my head. "No," I said, realizing it was the truth. I could go back, but what would I be going back to? "I'm going to stay."

Fifi, or Fifta, now that I knew her proper name, jumped down off the mattress and sauntered toward the door. At the balcony, she turned back. "Ah, they grow up so fast. I knew you'd be one of the good ones."

"Fifta. Please tell my grandma I love her. Tell her I'll send her a note soon."

The cat winked. "I will. She'll love to hear from you. You may not know it, but she thinks you're pretty special. I do too."

The End

ABOUT THE AUTHOR

TH Leatherman is a writer and humorist from Firestone, Colorado. He enjoys science fiction, fantasy, puns (lots of puns), winemaking, and the Rocky Mountain lifestyle. When not busy writing his next book, he can be found hiking with his wife and two sons or walking his rescued dogs. He has worked as a stockbroker, street performer, and volunteer wrangler. He graduated Summa Cum Laude from Regis University with a degree in Business Management and a minor in Psychology.

Connect with Mr. Leatherman

Check out his blog and links to other books
https://thleatherman.com/

https://www.facebook.com/TH-Leatherman

@thleatherman on Twitter

https://www.instagram.com/th.leatherman/

Reviews!

Authors (especially me) love reviews. Good, bad, or indifferent tell me what you think. You can do it easily on Amazon and Goodreads, but anywhere book lovers congregate is appreciated.

www.ingramcontent.com/pod-product-compliance
Lightning Source LLC
Chambersburg PA
CBHW071110250626
47159CB00002B/679